WHEN YOU STAYED

GENERATIONS OF ROSE RIDGE
BOOK 1

ASHLEY MUÑOZ

Cover Design: Qambar Designs
Photographer: Regina Wamba
Editor: Kimberly Hunt
Developmental Edits: Memo's in the Margins
Proofread: All Encompassing Books

❀ Formatted with Vellum

CONTENT WARNING & NOTE

This is a Motorcycle Club Romance, however, because it is within the brand of Ashley Muñoz it will focus primarily on the romance vs. the dynamics of the club itself. This is not considered a dark romance. With that said, there are a few things to watch for while reading—there are references to SA and a scene of assault to the fmc none by the MC. Sexually explicit scenes intended for ages eighteen and above. Foul language throughout, and an attempted abduction of the fmc, with the use of gun violence. References to the loss of a pet.

This series is the second generation of the Stone Riders. While you can read this book without reading the first series, you will have a better understanding of this world if you do. Additionally, there are references that aren't explained in detail in this book that took place in the Christmas novella: *A Rose Ridge Christmas*. So if you do want to read anything, I would highly recommend the novella.

MOTORCYCLE CLUB TERMS AND SAYING'S

Cut: Usually a leather or denim vest with the club insignia referenced as patches, or colors. It identifies which club you ride with, and show loyalty to.

Sweetbutt/ Bunk Bunnies: A term used for girls who aren't in a committed relationship of any kind but have been given permission to be in the club and spend time with its members.

Old Lady: A female inside the club that is either married to or in a committed relationship with one of its members, age is not a factor when referencing this term.

Property Patch: An honor amongst clubs as it's a way for women to show which member they're committed to, this is an elevated status that shows you belong with someone from the club, however, this does not mean someone wearing a property patch is a member of the club.

Church: a meeting place for the highest-ranking club members where decisions are made and private club matters are discussed.

One Percent Patch: 99% of all motorcycle clubs are law-abiding clubs that gather for more of a brotherhood, hobby, or sense of community. However, one percent of these clubs wear this patch indicating they do not abide by the laws outside of the ones set by their clubs.

This may include violent actions for protection, illegal means of earning money, and more.

President: In terms of the motorcycle club this person is the highest-ranking member, making all final calls and decisions.

'Going Non-Legitimate in business vs Legitimate': This refers to illegal business deals, under the table vs legal dealings with a paper trail.

'Going to War.': This is a term used between clubs that would result in extreme violence between rival clubs. This is often to claim territory or due to feud or vengeance.

STONE RIDER
FAMILY TREES

when
you
stayed

PROLOGUE

Connor
Age 19

IF I WEREN'T MARCHING TOWARD THE END OF SOMETHING I'D WANTED MY entire life, I might actually enjoy this little walk. I might even take a second to tip my head and bask in the beauty of the stars, and how this really was the perfect place to pop the biggest question I'd ever ask anyone. Ironically, if I had a choice in any of this, it would have been right here that I laid down the blanket, propped the pillows, and made sure her favorite song was playing.

I'd been in love with Royce Quinn as long as I could remember. She was supposed to be who I ended up with, so asking her to marry me shouldn't be a big deal. But every time I pictured it, my stomach tensed, and I had the strangest urge to throw up.

I wasn't ready, and I knew she sure as hell wasn't. Which was exactly what I told her father when he'd approached me three days ago with a velvet box and a ring.

I'm counting on you, Connor. She needs to get out of Rose Ridge, and the only way she'll go is if you put a ring on her finger and explain how serious you are. Don't give her the option to do long distance. She needs to move with you.

We were all leaving. Or trying to.

Silas and Natty had fled to Italy, taking Rook and Ryle with them. My best friend Ford was headed to some fancy school to become a mechanical engineer, and his little sister Ellie was going to an art school for dance. My sister was on her way to an academy up north, which meant the only two kids left were the Quinn sisters.

Royce and Taryn.

Killian was the president of the Stone Riders, the motorcycle club that our lives all revolved around. He couldn't leave, and I assumed his heart would just stop beating if his wife, Laura, took his daughters and left him behind, so this was his big plan. At least for his eldest daughter, who had recently graduated from high school and had no plans at all to leave town.

None of this was mine to fix, and yet I was walking toward the abandoned cabin as slowly as if I were headed to my final meal on death row. Not only had Royce and I been arguing more than we ever had in the past, but I found out something rather major I had yet to share with anyone.

Not even my parents.

It was the sort of life-altering information that had me changing my plans from attending college to packing a bag tonight and leaving while everyone was asleep.

Beyond any of that, I knew Royce well enough to know she'd turn me down. Royce had her own dreams, and while she loved me, I would never compare to them. I'd hung around for a year past graduation to appease my family and to see Royce graduate, but it was my turn to leave.

It was my chance to figure out which pieces of the past fit into my future.

The light from inside the small, one-bedroom cabin came into view, making my heart race. The tiny structure sat on over ten acres of land, sandwiched between the massive motorcycle club that was well over four thousand square feet, and on the opposite end of the property was

Royce's two-story house. Originally it was divided into two separate properties, but the club had purchased the house years ago, which was where Killian had raised his kids. The entire acreage was protected with fences, security cameras, and guards.

Royce was already waiting inside, which I knew was going to piss her off. Royce hated this cabin. I wasn't sure if it was because of what happened when we were kids, or if it was something else, but she hadn't set foot inside it after that Christmas we were attacked. The same holiday that seemed to shape this very moment.

We were warned years ago that the man responsible for the attack would return. That he was coming for the club, and for anyone still loyal to the Stone Riders. It was why our parents were so desperate to get us out of here. It all happened nine years ago, when I was ten, and now it seemed like an invisible clock seemed to hang over our heads for when he'd be back.

Max was his name. He was my friend Rook and Ryle's uncle apparently. He was also a crazed man with a vendetta against the original leader of the club, Simon Stone. It extended to Simon's offspring, and whoever was still a part of the club whenever Max decided to enact his revenge.

My unwavering loyalty seemed to tighten around my chest like a cable wire as I drew closer. I would do this because Killian asked me to. I would do this because I'd do anything to keep Royce safe, even if it meant sacrificing our futures.

With a deep breath, I pushed the door open and found Royce sitting at the small table, her arms crossed and an angry scowl on her pretty face.

"Connor King, you better tell me what the hell I'm doing here right now!"

I was going to miss her. Many people underestimated Royce because she walked around with her head in a cloud and wore pink to every single event in her life, even funerals. What they didn't see was her quiet resilience, or her ability to adapt to things out of her control. My heart warmed as I watched her anger flush against her chest, and it took me back to when I'd realized how badly I wanted to marry her.

"Sorry, Roy."

She scowled, and I felt bad because she'd asked me to stop calling her that, but old habits were hard to stop. "Sorry."

With a shake of her golden hair, she shot to her feet. "I want to know why you texted me to meet you here. If you're breaking up with me, you could have just texted that like a normal person."

I stepped closer. "I'm not breaking up with you."

Her blue eyes were dim under the single light fixture over the table, but they were frenzied too.

Words seemed to die on my tongue. If I opened my mouth, I'd explain all of it to her, and she'd hate her father, and Royce loved her dad. She thought he hung the damn sky, moon and stars...all of it. There was no way I could turn her against her favorite person.

"I have a question for you." I smiled. It was wobbly, but I tried to fix it before she caught on.

Her gaze snapped to how I began lowering to one knee. Those eyes I fell in love with at the ripe age of five blew wide and her nose flared.

"Connor."

It was a warning I couldn't heed. This would break us once and for all. She'd be lost to me, but I was going to lose her regardless once she realized I wasn't headed to college. I deceived her, and I didn't have any plans to explain myself...not now at least. Maybe in a few years, once I figured a few things out.

I knew it even as I gave her the best smile I could and held out the velvet box.

"Royce Hannah Quinn, will you do me the great honor of—"

Royce flew to her knees in front of me and shut the box, with a tear sliding down her face. "What are you doing, Connor?"

I couldn't seem to swallow as I saw the same fear in her eyes that mirrored what was in mine.

"Trying to propose."

She searched my face; her hand still wrapped around the box that was clasped in mine.

"You can't."

I whispered between us, "I have to, Royce."

Her golden brows furrowed. "Why...I don't understand."

This wasn't worth my energy to go in circles. Royce would figure it out eventually, and I was leaving. Not in two months, like I had told everyone. I was leaving tonight, and I wouldn't be looking back. Even if Royce said yes, she'd be packing her bags and coming with me.

"Your dad...he wants you to be safe. It's been nine years since Max made his threat...he's scared if you stay behind, you'll get hurt."

She clamored to her feet, panic stamped across her features. "But I already told him I want to intern at the Hollow. He said he was fine with it."

I shook my head because she'd figure out the rest of it.

"He..." she trailed off, still pacing.

"He loves you, Royce."

Her sharp gaze sliced back to me, and I realized I should probably stand up.

"You knew I'd say no, Connor. I just graduated two months ago. You took a year. I haven't even had that."

I ducked my head, nodding.

"And where would we live, in your dorm room?"

I had to lie because I wouldn't tell her where I was really headed or that if she had said yes, she might be in even more danger than she would be here. "I'm assuming your dad would make arrangements for us."

"So, you would get to chase your dream while going to school, but my dad wanted me to be your wife, at home all day and allow my own hopes to wilt away?"

She was angry, and I didn't blame her. I was hurt, but I was also loyal.

Too fucking loyal.

"Connor, we've been struggling for months...we both knew we were likely about to break up."

That was also true. I wanted to poke around my past, and I had no intentions of including her. Or anyone, for that matter. It had created a divide between us.

"I'm trying to protect you, Royce. Even if we weren't together, you know I'd always want you safe. No matter what. You're my family."

She seemed to soften with that, and with a heavy sigh she walked into my arms where I hugged her close. She smelled like roses and some kind of fruit—it was divine, and distinctly her. Always had been, but I was curious now if there was any other smell that I might enjoy more. Maybe someone else out there might fit me more perfectly. There was nothing wrong with Royce, but she had felt more like a friend than my girlfriend this past year.

"I love that you asked, it's sweet of you. You're so loyal and I'm going to miss that." She sniffed, then pulled back. "I wish you all the best with college, and everything you're looking for." She finished by pressing a kiss to my cheek.

I wasn't sure what to say, but her hand stroking the side of my face got my attention.

"You walked here, right?"

I nodded right as she got a familiar determined look on her face…it was the one that meant she was about to do something reckless.

"Don't, Royce…You—" she ran past me and slipped outside.

I darted after her, but she was already inside of her Jeep, tearing away from the cabin and driving toward the clubhouse.

"Royce!"

She drove past me without so much as looking back. I was going to get my ass chewed for messing this up, but what was I supposed to do? I couldn't force her.

As I was about to break into a run to chase her, I realized this wasn't my problem anymore.

I had done what Killian asked of me, and it didn't work. This was his burden now.

My best friend arrived at my door nearly an hour later.

I immediately asked, "How bad was it?"

Ford stepped inside my room and let out a sigh. He looked a lot like his dad, with the same chestnut-colored hair, similar hazel eyes, and fair skin that still looked red from our lake day. Poor fucker took way too long to tan.

"Killian was pissed. Royce threw a tantrum."

I grabbed my duffel bag and plopped it on the edge of my bed, packing it. "I did my best."

"Did you have to tell her it was her dad's idea?"

I shrugged. "You know Royce. She knew me asking wasn't normal."

Ford's brows caved as he picked up a framed picture out of the brown box on the desk. "How so? You two were going to get married at some point, why wouldn't she think you'd ask before you headed off to college?"

Had he really not picked up on all our arguments, or how Royce hadn't been around nearly as much this summer?

"We were likely going to break up right before I left. There hasn't been much to talk about lately. We're growing apart. She also hates that cabin and knew I'd never propose there."

His gaze flicked over to me before settling on a different picture inside the box. "Why not tell Killian that?"

"I don't know, I was already in shock that he demanded that I ask her to marry me to begin with."

Ford let out a small laugh. "Still shocked you managed to keep it from your parents. I bet they would have gone toe-to-toe with him about it."

"Dad falls in line pretty quick because of the club order."

"Not your mom, though." Ford laughed again while pulling out a pink sweater.

I gestured toward it. "Can you take that box back to Royce for me?"

His shocked expression dug a little too deep into my sternum. Royce and I were supposed to be end game material. We had talked about our future all four years of high school. For years we were inseparable, annoyingly so. We took each other's firsts and always vowed to be together for all our lasts. I was madly in love with her, to the point that I nearly lost my friendship with Ford. He was sick of it at one point, got tired of me choosing her to hang out with over him...so yeah, this news was probably surprising to him.

"You're serious, then. You two are finished?"

I turned away and continued pulling items out of my dresser.

"What was the final decision Killian made regarding her choice to stay behind?"

Ford let one of the framed photos clink against another in the box. "She has to agree to live under his roof, have escorts from the club everywhere she goes. She won't have any freedom from the club, she'll be watched and guarded at all times, and she can't date anyone from the club."

Guilt pricked at my chest. "I can't even process the idea of her dating someone else, much less a member."

"Knowing you two, you'll be back together before you leave for college, so you won't have to worry about her falling for some Stone Rider."

More guilt seemed to assault me as I watched my friend from across the room. He had no idea that I'd be gone tomorrow morning and where I was headed, he couldn't follow.

"I don't think there's anything that's going to happen after this for us. Just take the box to her for me. I need to close this chapter once and for all."

Ford hesitated before clearing his throat, staring at the box. He seemed like he wanted to say something.

"You okay?"

He blinked, and whatever was there instantly left. "Consider it done."

SIX YEARS LATER

ONE
ROYCE
PRESENT DAY

When I was a little kid, I had fostered a dream birthed in the basement of a simple house shrouded in ivy. Renovated as a coffee house, the top floor was used by avid book lovers in search of a hidden gem or discounted paperback. At the end of the wide hall to the back of the house, and through the purple door, was a set of stairs. Thousands of stickers lined the walls from over the years. State's, sayings, Post-it notes, taped messages, and pictures littered the walls as you descended into the base of the home. There, in the bottom, you'd find magic...or in simple terms, a wooden stage, built up to be tall enough for the crowd to see who would walk across it, braving a moment under the bright lights to perform.

This was the Hollow.

A sacred space where artists came to sing, to perform and create art. A place where music liberated the soul and healed the heart. I had sat in the sound booth with my mother, as young as four, watching as artists took the stage, and while my sister would draw or watch movies, I couldn't tear my eyes away from the way their music made me feel.

That dream had tenderly tugged at the packaging of my heart and found a way inside, prepared to remain until I was old enough to tend to it. I wanted to own and run the Hollow. I wanted to be the person to welcome the artists and give them a place to belong. At eighteen, my father tried to rip me out of Rose Ridge to keep me safe, but all it did was thrust me into realizing that wish.

It was in the way they gripped the microphone, and their eyes took in the audience. The way the house lights dimmed and burst to life around each new note they sang. The way the crowd swayed and moved to the pitch of their voice.

That twinkle in their eye when they finally found their stride, and they remembered exactly what had driven them to step onto that stage to begin with. Some people wanted to be under the lights, and I was the person obsessed with turning them on, providing a spotlight for those who deserved it.

I'd protect this place with a fierceness my mother had taught me, which would ultimately redirect my entire future. In retrospect… maybe I should have let it go and walked away, maybe then my heart might still be in one piece.

"She's incredible," I whispered.

The small booth was barely big enough for Nick, Rodney, and me to huddle around a sound board. Nick adjusted a few buttons while we all watched the stage, but it was our boss Rodney who let out a heavy sigh followed by, "She's got potential."

"She has more than that. Look at how she's affecting them." I gestured to the crowd, spellbound by each lyric. Rodney had already pulled out his phone to disconnect from the conversation. My fists curled against my sides as I watched him completely ignore me. He did this often, where he'd downplay talented artists, acting as though there was nothing spectacular about them. Then those artists would become memorable, and our little dot on the map, not so much.

"Well, thankfully it's not our job to decide either way," Rodney quipped. Nick gave me a sympathetic head shake but didn't say anything. I understood what Rodney was saying about it not being our decision, and while that was true, it angered me that he didn't seem to care about these artists. Whereas I probably cared too much.

I inspected him, watching as he checked out and scrolled on his phone. I hated his dark goatee that was in the shape of a triangle, plastered to his chin like a shape on a felt board. The rest of him was all limbs and torso, with no muscle or fat, just skin and bones, and that damn goatee.

The Hollow might only be a stage for performers, and our venue a space for a few high-profile producers to come and check them out, but it was also an essential part of boosting tourism in Rose Ridge. I had started as an intern, grabbing coffee and helping with whatever I could until Rodney felt guilty enough that he actually hired me. I was the person who found the talent, communicated with them, and ensured they had a memorable experience at the Hollow. I made barely above minimum wage, but I had a plan to fix that.

The song faded as the woman closed out her set. She was the last person to sing tonight, which meant Rodney would leave directly after. I'd been putting off this conversation for exactly five days, trying to give him ample time to approach me, but I'd finally reached my limit. I eyed him as he packed up his things and did the same, so we'd have a reason to walk out at the same time.

"Night, Nick." I waved while pulling my leather bag up my shoulder and grabbing my helmet. Rodney had already made his way down the steep steps leading from the sound booth. He'd hauled his jacket on, along with a scarf, and after waving at the bartender, he veered off toward the exit.

I was hot on his tail even as a few people waved me down, trying to get my attention. I had to get to Rodney before he left.

Shoving the heavy door open, I jogged toward the parking lot, catching him at his car. My dad was going to be pissed that I hadn't texted his guard dog that I was leaving. Ever since I was eighteen, he'd forced one of his members to tail me, but there wasn't time.

"Did you ever get a chance to look at my proposal?" I asked Rodney slightly breathless.

The night sky was lit by obnoxiously bright streetlights, breaking up the darkness. I could make out the lines of his face and the way his mouth refused to lift into a smile.

"Royce, you know I have a soft spot for you. Mostly because of your mom, but also because I know how much all this means to you. I mean, heck you've been running around the stage and club since you were, what? Seven?"

Courage expanded in my chest. He was right, I had been running around the stage and even pretending to run things since I was old enough to hold a clipboard. By all rights, I should have this in the bag, but Rodney had a strange way of rewarding loyalty. My mother was one of the regulars that used to sing at the Hollow. She would bring in a crowd like no other whenever she took the stage. Through the years, she had turned toward writing music instead of singing it.

"But you're only twenty-four years old—" Rodney's tone brought me back to the moment. "You barely scraped by with community college, and you don't have enough experience to run a place like this."

I had to take a second to breathe because my first inclination was to argue with him. I didn't barely get by in community college. It took me longer to complete because I was also interning in DC at a record label a few days out of the week. Dad hated that period of time because three of his men were sent with me each time I went. Rodney had no idea how qualified I actually was.

I knew Rodney was leaving and was about to put up a job listing for his position. I didn't want to just run the club and manage the music. My eventual goal was to own the entire building, including the bookstore and coffee shop located upstairs.

My mouth parted with a well-calculated response when his eyes drifted to the side, and he let out a sigh. "Then, there's that."

The sound told me what Rodney was referring to, but I looked anyway. Five or six bikers rode together in a cluster toward the side street where the parking lot exited. They were there for me, waiting to follow me home. Rodney didn't need to know that though.

"What about them?" My heart paced rapidly, but I played stupid. This couldn't be about my father. I refused to believe it, not when Rodney loved my family so much. My mother was a staple here, practically a part of the Hollow history. At this point, by all rights, I shouldn't even have to ask Rodney for his blessing to take over for him, but Mom told me we had to play it by the book.

"I heard some gossip last week that the Stone Riders have a new leader."

A laugh spilled from my chest because that was the dumbest shit I had ever heard. "Don't you think I'd know if my father stepped down from being president of the club?"

Rodney sneered at me, lifting his too-thin lip. "No, actually. I don't."

Shit, he had a point there. But by that standard, he shouldn't know anything either.

"Okay, I'll humor you. What difference would it make if he stepped down?" I asked, confused at his concern.

Rodney rubbed at his small goatee patch. "Well, if there is a new president, then shit will get stirred and the town will pay for it."

This was so stupid, which I conveyed with a slow blink. "I'm not a part of my father's club, but I can tell you that he isn't looking for a replacement any time soon." Dad was healthy for being in his fifties, and despite what Rodey said, I would know if he were stepping down. Dad didn't tell me a lot, but him not being the leader would certainly be a topic we discussed as a family.

Rodney glanced around and let his eyes linger on the motorcycle parked a few spaces over. "You aren't part of his club, and yet you ride?"

Of course I did. My father had taught me to ride a motorcycle before I learned to drive a car.

"What does any of this have to do with me running the Hollow?"

He ran a hand over his balding head. "Taking that risk isn't an option for me, Royce. I owe the town that much, and I'll be retiring. I plan to enjoy the peace."

Red crept into my neck as anger stirred in my veins. "What drama have I brought to your doorstep within the past six years, Rodney?"

"There's been no drama because I'm the one in charge. If I hand things over to someone from that world, then it's giving them access to even more of our town. Right now, there's a boundary of how far they can go and what they can do. I'm the one holding that line. I shouldn't have even given you a job to be honest, but I owed Nick a favor."

Owed Nick a favor? That meant he didn't care that I had been volunteering my time, or that I had improved things for him? What did Nick care if I worked there? Rodney laughed as he must have read my expression.

"He always hoped to have a shot with you, assumed if you worked there, eventually you'd fall for him or some shit like that."

My stance shifted the smallest bit as I crossed my arms. "So, it didn't matter that I had been a stellar intern or willing to stay after hours to clean up. That I drove all the way to DC and back in one day just to get you a band when you needed a bump in numbers? It didn't matter that I helped…" I realized I was wasting my breath.

I was bitter and annoyed, but I had to push it down and try to get Rodney to see this from my perspective.

"Rodney, I love this job. I only want things to improve over time and for this to be a place people can continue to come for generations. My goal is to create somewhere talent gets discovered. I want it to be a place that helps artists emerge into the industry. Please let me do that. Let's pretend my dad's motorcycle club isn't a part of it. I'm qualified for this job. I'm *good* at this job. You've had triple the sign-ups for performances, and you've had more foot traffic and more people buying drinks. I'm good for business. I help do your books, so I know that's not a lie."

His head dipped with a laugh while he toyed with his car keys.

"Tell you what, kid," he smirked. "I'll give you a trial period of three months. If in that time it's confirmed that there's no new leadership or no drama stirred up for the town, then I'll give you a shot."

Trial period? What the hell did that mean?

I imagined sticking something incredibly sharp inside Rodney's eye socket, which helped me plaster on a fake smile.

"Really?"

He yanked his car door open and slid inside. He shouted one last thing at me before closing his door. "I'd check in with your dad and those rumors circling before you get your hopes up because something tells me you're not getting this job."

Asshole.

TWO
ROYCE

Spring had arrived, which meant all the fields I loved walking in were about to go from brown to green. The wildflowers were on the verge of returning, and best of all, the air was going to carry that sweet honeysuckle scent. I plucked a pink wildflower out of the ground and carried it back home with me so I'd have proof that winter was finally over. This last one felt extraordinarily long, probably because I kept assuming Rodney would promote me.

The land we shared with the club was beautiful especially in the spring. Our home had the best access to the lush fields and walking paths bordering a steady stream. As a kid, I snuck out of bed early in the morning to go sit in those fields so I could watch the sun rise.

I barely slept after facing off with Rodney about my botched job interview. Hell, I couldn't even call it that. I had practically thrown myself at him and begged him to let me manage the place. My pride still stung over how poorly that all went, but I knew it was only a matter of setting a few facts straight. Dad wasn't leaving the club, and I'd confirm that as soon as he was up and ready to talk. I had gotten home near one in the morning after that last set finished, and Dad stopped staying up that late years ago.

The sun rose, pushing out the periwinkle blue that clung to the horizon, which meant Dad should be up soon. I began the trek back, taking in the view of the fields and the way the valley looked against a fresh spring sunrise. My smile spread as I lifted my face, taking in the warmth and the hope of a new day. Anything could happen, even Rodney changing his mind.

The house came into view, and worried that I might one day forget, so I tried to memorize every detail. The forest green siding, the red chimney popping from the top, the flower baskets that Mom had Dad hang outside of each of our windows, the deep inset porch with a comfy swing. This was home, and because I was nearly in my midtwenties, I knew one day I'd leave and this memory might fade. My heart twisted as frail as the wildflower in my palm when a rough wind swept through the valley.

"Did you wear my boots?" A yell pierced the air from the top floor, forcing my mind off the idea of growing up and leaving.

I glanced up, seeing my sister staring at me from her bedroom window. Her blond hair was shorter than when I saw it three days ago.

"No!" I called back with total false confidence. She'd have to beat me to the front door to prove that I did in fact wear her boots.

"I'm coming down. If I see any mud on those boots, I'm going to wear them in your room and ruin your favorite pink rug!"

She slammed her window closed, and I rushed inside to slip off the boots so she couldn't prove that I had worn them. We always shared clothes, but every now and then she got irritated over something in particular, especially if she'd gotten it in a brand deal.

Taryn met me at the base of the stairs right as I began kicking off her boots.

"I knew those were mine." She folded her arms, glaring down at my feet.

I shook out my hair, ignoring her ire. "Thought they were mine," I lied. To get her mind off that fact, I asked, "Where have you been?"

"In Tennessee for a brand thing." Her shoulder lifted like it didn't matter, but really it did. My sister had worked her ass off to become an influencer who helped younger girls eat well while learning to shop in affordable places. Her entire brand was based around being the new normal girl. She lived at home like I did, but she left all the time. Dad didn't force any bikers to follow her because she moved around so often. I heard he was thinking of hiring private security, but Taryn would lose her mind if he did.

"Do you know if Dad is up?" I walked through the foyer toward the kitchen. It was still early, so I had no doubts he and Mom were still sleeping, but I was hoping for a miracle this morning.

Taryn followed me, hopping up onto the counter, letting her feet dangle. She was wearing my oversized T-shirt that dropped to mid-thigh. I'd gotten it at a concert a few summers back, and somehow it had ended up in her closet. With her cell in her hands, and her blond hair slipping over her shoulder, she replied distractedly. "He never came home last night. Mom slept over at the club too, I guess he got in late and had a meeting all night or something."

"So, he's at the club?" I popped a blueberry into my mouth.

Taryn nodded distractedly. "I think they're all up and moving over there. Mom texted me that she wanted me to start breakfast."

"How come she didn't ask me?"

My sister lifted her head, narrowing her blue eyes at me. People said we looked like twins, but that wasn't true. Taryn had an edge to her that I didn't. Her eyes were a darker blue than mine, her nose was more like Mom's, and she had more curves than I did, making her the magnet for men whenever we went out.

"Mom knew you got in super late; she was being considerate."

Oh. Sometimes it was hard to put the big sister thing on the back burner especially when I felt like my little sister's life eclipsed mine.

Taryn jumped down from the counter and grabbed a handful of blueberries. "What's so important that you have to talk to him anyway?"

"Rodney's being a dick." I eyed the blueberry container again, wondering if she was going to eat them all.

Taryn moved to the fridge and pulled out a carton of eggs. "And you're what, going to have Dad beat him up or something?"

She knew me better than that. I scoffed, "No, of course not. I just need to ask if he's stepping down from being president."

My sister froze, mid egg crack. "I think you need to tell me what's going on."

I let out a sigh. Taryn was the kind of person who would drive over to Rodney's house at seven in the morning and demand he explain himself. She reacted first before getting the full story or thinking through the repercussions. So, I did a little damage control.

"Rodney heard a rumor about new leadership in the club, and I want to know if it's true."

She laughed, like it was a ridiculous thought. Which was exactly my reaction to his outrageous claim. "You already know the answer to that, Royce."

"I know, but I need to let Dad know Rodney is talking."

She dipped her face, stirring the eggs. "Well, when you go, don't wear my boots. I need them for my next batch of content."

"Are you leaving again?" My stomach dipped in worry. I missed my baby sister, and while I knew we were getting older, she was still only twenty-two.

"Just to Pyle."

I scrunched my nose, thinking of our neighboring town that was even smaller than Rose Ridge. Pyle, Virginia, was a factory town, and home to the Death Raiders, a club led by a good man named Lance, but his club was technically a rival to our dad's. There was enough bad blood between Dad and Lance that we were always warned not to go into Pyle for any reason. Although, I knew deep down Lance had a soft spot for all of us kids, he was my Uncle Silas's best friend, and while he didn't like my dad, he wasn't a bad man.

"Why?"

She took the pan off the burner and set it to the side. "An old mill that is extremely cinematic and seems like it could be trendy."

"Do you want me to tag along?" I loved going with her to film her content, but sometimes she preferred to be alone.

"That's okay, but don't tell Dad. He'll send a bunch of Stone Riders with me." She rolled her eyes, but I tilted my head, inspecting her for idiocy.

"You know how he feels about rival territory, T. Don't be stupid."

She winked at me, which made me furious. "I promise I'm not being stupid, big sis."

"You literally are going to force me to tell Dad."

Right as my sister's eyes rounded and she was about to open her mouth, the front door opened and our mom walked in.

"Morning, girls." Mom's gold-white hair fell to the middle of her back, her peachy skin was red from the early morning, which meant she likely walked home, and over her long-sleeved shirt, she wore a faded black leather property patch. It was a symbol, like what the men in the clubs wore, except hers told the world that she belonged to my father, which meant no other member would ever dare try to flirt or touch her. We were at a fun cookout once when some drunk idiot from a different club decided to ignore that symbol, and it wasn't just my father who reminded him what it meant. Taryn and I were young, but it was Connor's mom who had walked us to the truck, turned on some cartoons and made sure we had juice boxes. I was old enough to know that the club surrounding one man, with my father at the center wasn't good.

Mom knew better than anyone what it was like to feel like our world was small due to rival clubs and danger. Dad, being the president, made nearly everything off-limits. She'd understand, but she would also ensure our father knew about where we intended to go. Taryn had more freedom than I did, but I wasn't about to let her abuse it.

With a sigh, my sister softly spoke so our mom wouldn't hear, "I won't go. I promise, okay?"

I raised my brow at her. "You better not, T. I'm serious."

She lifted her hands as if to surrender and walked upstairs.

I rode along the dusty path to the club that connected the two properties. My bike wasn't a typical make or model that rode within biker clubs. Mine was a sports model, a Kawasaki Ninja 500 that had pink fenders. I really didn't care what anyone thought of it. My sister had the exact replica of mine, but the fenders were purple. We were both extreme clean freaks about our bikes though, so the dust from the uneven terrain wreaked havoc on my beautiful bike.

My speed slowed as I approached the posterior of the club. The Stone Riders didn't reside in a dump by any means—the club was a massive, multi-level house with wide windows, manicured lawns, and a private apartment reserved for the president. That was where our parents stayed whenever they slept over at the club, or we stayed there as a family, which hadn't been the case for years. Taryn and I didn't go near the club often, and if we did it was when the members were all at work, during the day.

I made my way around the side of the house and parked near the garage. A few guys huddled around an open hood, fixing an old car. I sat up on my seat, lifted my pink helmet and released my long hair from its confines. It blew behind me in a shock of cold wind that moved in from the hills. Early spring was typically warm in Virginia, but we occasionally had our surprises. While my helmet was pink, my leather jacket was black and fit like a glove. On the inside I had sewn a Stone Riders club patch. I stroked my finger over it out of solidarity and habit. When I was younger, I begged my father to let me join the club. At one point, I had even asked if I could lead it one day. He entertained me back then, but the truth was there was still only one female member of this club, and that was my Aunt Natty.

Loose gravel crunched under my boots as I walked toward the bursts of laughter spilling from the garage. I felt a weighty pair of eyes on me, almost judgy, like I didn't belong here. I had no idea why Ford Ryan chose not to leave for college, but him sticking around and pledging to the Stone Riders didn't make him any better than me.

"Hey, Dad." I called while sliding in next to him and his best friend, Wes Ryan. They cracked a joke about a busted radiator, which had my eyes searching their still handsome, but weathered faces. Tan lines, wrinkles, gray hair, and white scruff. Their eyes still had a spark of adventure, and a fury that would only be tamed on the back of a bike.

Dad's arm came around me loosely. "Royce, hey, honey. What are you doing here?"

He let me go for two seconds, and Wes slid his arm over my shoulders, pulling me into his side. "We miss seeing you up at the house. We see Taryn tons, but we never see you."

My eyes flicked across the garage, landing on the primary reason that I had stopped going to family events at the Ryan house. Ford, the eldest and only son of the Ryan family, never left, and because he didn't, our dads assumed we'd stick together. Perhaps we would have if Ford hadn't been a colossal dick while growing up. Even once all our friends had left, he continued to regard me coldly and always with a glare.

Ford didn't even live with his parents anymore, not now that he was twenty-five. Which meant there really wasn't a reason to stay away from family dinners up at the Ryan house. Jealousy wormed through me at the idea of Ford living on his own, in that little cottage style house my mother had driven me past once. He probably had a girlfriend or a roommate too. Even if I wanted a cute apartment or house of my own, I couldn't live in it alone. I had once asked Dad if both Taryn and I could live together as roommates in Rose Ridge. His answer was the same as it was six years ago when I had asked: If I chose to stay in Rose Ridge, I would live under his roof and accept his protection. The only exception to this would be if I wanted to move into the old cabin, which would never happen in a million years. I hated that creepy place.

"I miss you guys too. I'll have to swing by for dinner or something," I said into Wes's side. Once he released me, I moved to the edge of the hood, getting my dad's attention again.

"Can I talk to you?"

He glanced over his shoulder, then dipped his head. "Of course."

I followed him as we moved toward the back of the garage where a few old couches were set up. Dad wore his leather cut over a long-sleeved shirt, jeans that had been worn so much, they were barely hanging on, and a pair of brown boots. His hair was mostly gray now, but it was longer and he kept it slicked back nicely. Dad's nickname in the club was *the Wolf,* and while I didn't fully understand when that started, I knew everyone referred to him as that. Even all these years later.

"What's wrong, honey?" His gaze tapered as he stared at me. I sometimes wished I had inherited his green eyes, but it was only his nose and jawline that I'd seemed to get. Taryn looked more like Mom with the shape of her face and mouth. We both got Mom's blue eyes, and her golden hair, but Taryn's was a closer match than mine. I had Dad's smile though, and it was something I always loved being reminded of.

"This is going to seem like a weird question, but did you by chance step down as president?"

He let out a small laugh. "What?"

I focused on the howling wolf sewn into the patch on his shoulder and the one that designated him as president of this club. My gut seemed to flutter with nerves as I wet my lips and tried again. "Did you?"

"Even if I did, Royce…you know I couldn't tell you. Club business is—"

I shook my head, interrupting him. "I know, but for something as big as this, I know you would have told me."

He shrugged as if that were the end of it. "See, there's your answer. Why are you asking, anyway?" The Wolf of Rose Ridge glared back at me, calculating and assessing if I were a threat. I'd be annoyed if I weren't completely used to it. Dad had to inspect every angle, check every box even if it came from within his own house.

I tugged at a loose piece of fabric from the couch, unsure how to explain this part. It felt pathetic, but very few people understood my obsession with the Hollow, thankfully my dad happened to be one of the few who cared.

"Rodney is retiring, so I applied for the manager position. He'd consider giving me a shot, but only if I could prove that you hadn't handed things over. He told me if there wasn't any town drama started because of our club, he'd give me the promotion."

Dad tilted his head. "Did he give you a gap of time to avoid said drama?"

"Three months."

Another flick of his gaze to the back wall where I knew Ford sat. My stomach tightened with worry. Why did he keep looking back at him?

Leaning forward, I placed my elbows on my knees and continued, "Rodney said that the club controls too much in town. That he was one of the few people stopping you guys from having control of one more place in town."

"That's a whole lotta shit to spew to the daughter of one of the most dangerous motorcycle clubs in the state." Dad's jaw tightened.

Rodney and I had worked closely for years, so it didn't seem strange for him to speak freely in front of me, but maybe Dad was right.

"Yeah, I suppose. But you're not stepping down or anything, so there'd be no issues to even worry about, right?"

My father's gaze fell to the floor. "I'm getting older, Royce. If we do have trouble that comes knocking, then I'm not sure I'm in the best position to protect everyone."

"Yes, you are," I replied automatically, without thinking, because my dad was the foundation my entire life rested on. He was a rock, completely unmovable.

His smile was warm and encouraging, but his eyes did that dance where they moved to the one person I didn't want to inherit this club from him.

"We've been talking about handing things down...Wes is ready too."

No.

His gaze returned to the far wall where a leather cut hung. It was Ford's grandpa's, Simon Stone—the original leader of the Stone Riders. "It hasn't happened yet, and I don't know how Rodney knows anything about it, but it will happen eventually."

"You and Wes have been a part of this club for like thirty years or something crazy like that. Please, you can't seriously be considering this."

"With the right person, it'll work. You need to trust me. I know what I'm doing."

I felt that weighty inspection from across the room. Ford was watching me, but I refused to look. My teeth were practically glued together with how angry I was. New leadership meant things were about to get turbulent and if things got messy, that meant my shot at being the new manager of the Hollow was as good as gone.

Dad began talking about my sister, and how worried he was about how frequently she left without telling him where she was going, but I couldn't focus. My gaze finally lifted, landing on the boy across the garage, who wore his own leather cut, similar to my dad's. I hadn't been surprised when I heard Ford was pledging, but I was shocked that his parents didn't seem to care. Especially his mother. As far as I knew, Callie had always been against it, but perhaps she'd changed her mind.

This was all his fault. If there wasn't a legacy to hand leadership to, then Dad wouldn't even consider stepping down. My mind went back to when we were kids and how we'd once argued about me inheriting the club over him. Ford was so upset at the idea that I might get what had been my dad's because he felt like it was rightly his based on his grandfather.

How stupid of him to ever assume any man would give me a shot like that.

It gave me an idea, though. If Rodney was so worried about things getting dangerous for the town, I'd have to stick around and make sure they didn't.

THREE
FORD

My cat hated my house.

It honestly made me consider whether it might be haunted because whenever I took him from my parents' and let him out of his carrier in my living room, he'd huddle in a corner. Which wasn't like him at all, and it wasn't like I had other pets in the house to scare him.

"Is he sick?" Johnson asked while biting into a candy bar.

With my hand stretched toward my cat, I glared at my friend. "He's not sick."

"Seems sick."

Gus wasn't coming out of the corner no matter what I did. "Fuck."

Johnson finished his candy and wadded up the wrapper while huffing out a laugh. "Ever think it might just be your house?"

"What's wrong with it?" I had a roof over my head, fuckin' walls and plumbing. Sure, it wasn't as nice as my parents' house, but between their place and the club, I was hardly home anyway.

Johnson's hair was white by choice, he liked dying it that color and using a shit ton of product to style it. Which was unfortunate because his helmet completely ruined it. "You have a wicker couch for starters."

I stood, deciding Gus would come out on his own. "It was on sale."

"Normal couches also go on sale, Ford." Johnson waved at my dining room in a wild gesture. "And real tables, what is this?"

I shrugged because how should I know? It held my food, what more did I need?

"Did you pick up all the reports?" I asked while biting into a chip. I scanned my kitchen, trying to see if there was something wrong with it too. It was ugly, but it was functional.

Johnson reached for the backpack near my wicker couch. "I got all but Dead Roses."

I resisted the urge to yell at him. While I was more subdued than angry most of the time, the longer I was around the Stone Riders, and especially now with this new role, the more frequently the urge to scream surfaced.

"Did you even try?"

Johnson's eyes bulged. "Did I try?"

"Did I fuckin' stutter?" Seriously, why did I pick him to be my second? He was always eating something with sugar, always singing along to some song in his head, and laughed way too loud. And apparently, he lacked a set of balls that had dropped.

He turned the wrapper of his candy down so he could take another bite. "Your dad scares the ever-loving shit out of me. Being there alone with your mom and having him show up is a risk I don't want to take. I'm not touching that with a ten-foot pole. I've heard rumors about your dad reacting poorly to guys being near your mom."

Fuck. This really was my dad's fault; the rumors were all true.

With a heavy sigh, I held out my hand. "Give me the bag. I'll go do it."

"You sure?" Johnson asked as if I had any choice now that he had chosen not to do it. I scanned his five-foot-three stature, his stocky build, and his glacial eyes, and remembered he was one of the most loyal men I had ever met.

"I'm sure. But do me a favor and see if you can get Gus to acclimate to my house."

"Aw, come on. Anything but that."

I held up the bag as if to dare him to go to Dead Roses and get the reports from my mom.

He swallowed again while hesitantly glancing at the bag, then at my cat. "Does he have any treats?"

Gesturing toward the cupboard, I took the bag and my chips and left the house.

The sun was bright with spring emerging, which the people of Rose Ridge took advantage of by jogging, shopping, and in some cases, swimming. Some idiot was down at the docks with a paddleboard. The river wasn't gentle enough for paddle boarding or swimming, and hopefully someone would tell the moron that before he got himself killed.

I parked my bike in front of Dead Roses, the only tattoo shop in Rose Ridge. I had a theory about why Mom and Dad's shop was the only one in town, but no one really knew for sure. My hunch was that no one wanted to compete with the Stone Riders. Glancing down the block, I saw a flash of blond in front of the Drip and paused.

There were no open parking spots in front of the popular café, but that never stopped Royce. There, next to the door on the sidewalk, was her sports bike with pink fenders. I could offer more theories on why I believed she did this, and sure it could have revolved around the fact that the coffee shop also belonged to the Stone Riders.

However, Royce would pave a path for herself anywhere, but in Rose Ridge, she walked around as if she were royalty. Fuck, I guess maybe she was, being Killian's daughter. Those who knew how much of the town our club had bought up would treat her exactly the way she acted, but what bothered me was how everyone who didn't know seemed to treat her the exact same way regardless.

With irritation itching under my skin, I turned my back and pushed inside my parents' shop.

My mother lifted her head at the sound of the bell ringing over the door.

"Ford!" Her smile was warm and genuine. Even as she aged, there were things about her that would never fade, like her hazel eyes, and the expression she got on her face when my father entered a room. Or the way her emotions became too strong when she watched my sister dance. She hated the silver strands that had invaded her chestnut hair, but she was beautiful.

She had stopped tattooing clients, but still oversaw the day-to-day operations. It kept her busy with me out of the house and my sister Ellie a few dance recitals away from landing a spot in some prestigious school.

"What brings you in, honey?" My mother wrapped her arms around me, her forehead coming to my chin.

"Reports." I sighed. This shit was already getting old, and I'd just started doing it. Which was why I had tasked Johnson with it. My mom chuckled under her breath with a slight smile. "I thought Johanson, or Johnston, came and got them."

"Johnson, and he would, but he's scared of Dad."

That made her toss her head back with a full-bellied laugh.

Shaking my head in disappointment, I tried to guilt her. "You guys are mean, you know he's not totally wrong for being nervous."

"I suppose not." She moved around the small reception desk and let out her own sigh. "Speaking of. Do you know where your father is?"

"He's talking to Killian about routes."

My mother began stacking a few papers before pursing her lips. "I know you're busy with your new role, Ford, but please tell me you're being careful. The club went legitimate after Killian took over and now—"

"Now, you have to trust that we know what we're doing." I gently took the stack of papers from her and slid them into my bag.

Mom's smile was feeble as she glanced at the patch over my left breast. "When will that be changing?"

Currently, it said my name, but soon enough it would have a different title sewn there. My mother wasn't happy about that change either, and she was one of the few people who knew about that development.

"Soon, but things are still under wraps."

She dipped her chin, making her lighter brown hair shift over her shoulder.

"Mom, you can't tell Laura or anyone. It's important that you don't let it slip."

Her eyes were red when she looked at me again. "I know. I also know that Laura is going to murder Killian when she realizes how he kept this from her. You're all being so reckless."

"We're doing everything within our power to keep people safe. I know you can see that, deep down, under all of this. You know we have no other choice."

She stalked past me toward the back office. No one was in yet because the shop didn't open for another hour. "We've been fine all these years. I don't see why that would change. Max was toying with us, that was all."

Mom didn't know everything, so I tried not to get frustrated with her. Still, hearing her dismiss this one thing that had defined my life in such a major way was surreal. When I was ten years old, a rival motorcycle club attacked us, during Christmas. They shot at Connor's family in broad daylight. I watched Uncle Silas's mouth turn blue as we all worried he'd lose his life right there in the club office. I remembered my mother's panic attack after my father rode out with the rest of the Stone Riders when they needed to get a doctor. The madman behind it was named Max, his club was the Destroyers. He was technically Rook and Ryle's uncle, and when he met Rook, instead of killing him, he gave him a warning and left a threat for my family.

"Mom, you know I love you, but the only reason we've kept you updated on as much as we have is because of that threat. But we aren't leaving this to chance or risking the town. Max said he'd be back once we're older, and he has a debt to settle with you, especially because you're a Stone."

"I'm a *Ryan,* have been for well over twenty-five years." She quipped while tugging open a filing cabinet.

The urge to roll my eyes was strong. My mother was nothing if not stubborn.

"Born a Stone, Mom. Raised by a Stone."

She waved me off, but she knew I was right. Max held back from finishing all of us off that night all those years ago because he wanted his nephews to join him when they grew up. And while Mom didn't know this, he had been back…and he had left us with enough fear that we made drastic changes within the club.

"I don't want you getting in over your head…the cops we have on payroll can't help with this new venture the club has made with the local shops and your construction business."

While I didn't like being reminded of it, I knew she was right. If the FBI came sniffing, we'd be ruined.

"I'm being careful, I promise."

My mom returned to the spot in front of me and clasped my face between her palms. "You're so young to be carrying such a heavy burden, my love. I want you to find some joy in this life, because the club will never be enough. Not the women, or the loyalty…you need substance, roots to keep you grounded."

"That's why I have Gus, Mom." I joked while pressing a kiss to the top of her head. I already knew the club would never fill that gaping hole in my chest. It had been a long time since I'd touched a woman, and if I were to go for one, she wouldn't be from the club. I wanted roots. I wanted what my parents had, but I wasn't sure that was in the cards for me.

Mom patted my chest as she moved back to the filing cabinet. "Speaking of that moody cat, you need to go see him. He's been more ornery than normal. Honestly, I wish you'd take him home with you."

I needed to get back to the club before it got too much later. Sliding the straps of my backpack on, I gave my mother one last smile. "I already picked him up. He's at my house right now."

"Good, maybe keep him there," Mom suggested jokingly.

"I could never take him from such opulence, Mom. His standards are far too high." With a quick kiss to her cheek, I walked out of Dead Roses, aiming for my bike. I was about to straddle it when I caught sight of a flash of gold.

Royce was outside, sipping her iced coffee while talking to some guy with dark, cropped hair. I remembered seeing her with him at the movies one time. She was there, holding popcorn while he held her hip, and the two walked toward some cartoon movie. Another thing about Royce was she hated anything that required her to grow up.

She was like the female version of Peter Pan.

Still living at home, still wearing pink like it would go out of style if she stopped. I was even present to see her apply fake tattoos once, with water and a washrag because, according to her sister, Royce could never decide on something as permanent as a tattoo. She still ate Lunchables and even used a kid's lunch pail for work. She still sucked on lollipops, way too fucking frequently for my sanity. But that was Royce, a pink bubble floating around Rose Ridge without any cares or responsibilities. She was annoyingly unaware of her charm too.

She had a very grown-up set of tits that pushed against almost every shirt she wore, and a high, round ass that practically begged for me to stare at it, but I never did. No matter how tight the leather she wore, or the leggings on the rare chance that she didn't dress for a ride. I kept my eyes on my feet, to remind myself that they should never be headed in the same direction as Royce Quinn.

Sometimes living in a small town was pure shit, and running into Royce had always been one of the most consistent reasons for that. Which reminded me of what Killian had told me regarding Rodney and the Hollow. If she got her dream job, she'd be here to stay.

If she didn't…well, then maybe she'd finally leave.

FOUR
ROYCE

THREE DAYS HAD PASSED SINCE RODNEY GAVE HIS THREE-MONTH ultimatum. Each day felt like I was walking on eggshells. Dad's comments about handing things over didn't sit right with me. The way he kept looking at Ford had me staring up at my ceiling two nights in a row, my gut warning me there was something I wasn't seeing.

That, or they weren't telling me.

Which meant I had to find an alternative way to get answers.

My plan was set. Eggs were scrambled, toast had been buttered and coffee brewed. Now, I just waited for my mother to come down for breakfast. She only indulged in a savory breakfast during the weekends. Otherwise, she stuck to lighter fare, mostly because she was typically on the run, heading out to the senior center to volunteer. I'd help her whenever I had free time, but lately that wasn't very often. Which reminded me I had an unread message on the Hollow social media account from a band in Wisconsin. The band was hoping to go on tour, and trying to find local venues along their route to play at. This always sent a thrill through me, checking the calendar and seeing if we could help make their dreams come true. I was scrolling through the month of June for open dates when my mother entered the kitchen.

"Morning."

"Good morning!" I slid my phone onto the counter.

Mom's blond hair was frizzed and tangled, which had me frowning at her. "Did you try the sleepy scrunchie?"

Taryn and I were in our influencer era, mostly because Taryn was one. I tried everything that promised to make my life easier, or my skin softer. The overnight phenomena that made your blowout remain intact, was one my sister and I tried immediately.

"That thing does not work. I tried it, but I can't get my hair to stay." Mom slid onto the leatherback chair that sat nestled under the lip of our kitchen island.

I nudged her mug of coffee in front of her and let out a disappointed sigh. "Did you watch the video tutorial?"

Taking a generous sip, she nodded. "Three times, Royce."

She was obviously a lost cause. I'd have to text Taryn and let her know because once again, she wasn't in her bed when I woke up this morning and I went searching for my lip gloss that I knew she'd stolen.

"What's with the breakfast?" Mom asked, sipping from her mug once more. The sun cut through the large windows in our kitchen, highlighting her dark lashes and blue eyes. Dad had replaced most of the wall with glass, except for a few spaces where he'd placed floating shelves. Otherwise, the kitchen was all-natural light, broken up by trim and a few long curtains.

Wiping down a spot on the counter where I'd spilled coffee, I tried to keep my tone light.

"Just thought you deserved it."

Her knowing smile had me panicking. She always seemed to know more than she should and see more than what was there.

"Tell me what's going on, honey."

I sagged into the seat next to her and vented about Rodney and the unfair ultimatum he'd issued me regarding my father's club. I watched as Mom's golden brows dipped with worry and then raised as shock settled in. Her lips pursed and her fingers tightened around her mug as I moved through the story and then explained what Dad had said about the shifting leadership.

Then she stared off into space.

"So?" I asked.

Her hair slid over her shoulder as she shifted toward me. "Honey, your dad has been considering handing things over, but I'm sure he could hold off for three months. There'd be no reason at all that he wouldn't be able to. We aren't going anywhere. He just has this simmering worry that there might be something coming, and he can't keep everyone safe."

With a scoff, I shook my head. "He's being ridiculous."

My mom's eyes softened, and if I hadn't been paying attention, I might not have caught her lip tremble. "He'll always be strong, always be my Killian, but he's also feeling old. His body aches more, he's got a few health concerns."

Worry caught my heart in a vise as I asked, "He's okay though, right?"

"Yes, baby. He's fine, I promise you."

My mom set her mug down and gently pulled my hand into hers, as whatever revelation sparked in her mind. "Callie texted last night about all of us going over for dinner tonight. Why don't you come with us so you can chat with her, and we'll try and sabotage your dad and Wes's plans on stepping down. Surely, they can give you three months before stirring the waters with new leadership."

My mind was curious about how the members would even respond to new leadership. If it was Ford who would take over, would they like him, or would it be an issue that he was in charge? There were a lot of original members who were part of my father's crowd, and those men, I couldn't picture following a young twenty-five-year-old.

"Count me in."

Me: Where are you?

I slid my phone back onto the bathroom counter as I wrapped my hair around the curling wand. Taryn hadn't been home in days, which wasn't like her. Most of the time, I could keep tabs on her, but she was twenty-two years old. It wasn't like she was a child, but she typically told me where she was going. I'd already checked her socials, and she hadn't posted anything in over twenty-four hours, which was also odd for her.

Taryn: My friend's place.

I was going to kick her ass, I thought as I rolled my eyes.

Me: Which friend, Taryn. Stop being annoying.

Taryn: But it's my favorite thing to do. I'm with Mya, she's leaving her deadbeat boyfriend and wanted some backup while she moves out.

Mya was a hot fucking mess to put it mildly. Ironically, it wasn't even that she exclusively dated men in biker clubs, but she had a pretty bad drug problem. I didn't love that my sister was there with her or said deadbeat boyfriend. Because chances were said boyfriend was in a motorcycle club.

Me: Isn't Mya in Richland?

I was going to be late at this point if I didn't get a few curls in my hair and swipes of mascara in. I wasn't typically late to events if I could help it, but I'd taken the entire day to schedule out the whole summer line up for the Hollow. I hated that even if Rodney didn't give me the promotion, I still wouldn't walk away. I loved it too much.

Taryn: Yeah…

Connor's dad had a cousin who led a motorcycle club in Richland, we grew up knowing him as a pseudo uncle to all of us kids. He was the one who saved Connor's parents back when they were shot at during that Christmas we were attacked. Gripping my cell, I typed out a quick reply before sliding my phone into my back pocket.

> Me: Can you please give Uncle Giles a heads-up that you're there, that way if there's any issues, he'll be aware of it? Also, I opened your new mascara. Next time don't leave it on the counter. 🤍

I didn't check to see what she said in reply because my parents were leaving any second and if I wanted a ride, I had to get my ass downstairs.

At least that's what Dad had called up to me five minutes ago.

Slapping my hand against the light switch, I made my way downstairs. Dad was checking his phone while the car outside warmed up and Mom slid into her coat.

"We almost left you."

I walked up and pressed a kiss to my dad's cheek. "You would never."

Cold, brisk air expanded over my face and down to my exposed neck as I walked outside. I had on a small leather jacket, but it didn't cover any exposed skin from the cut of my shirt. Sliding into the back seat of my father's truck, I relished the warmth coming from the air vents.

Wes and Callie Ryan's home was roughly fifteen minutes from where we lived, positioned up along the hills of Rose Ridge. The location allowed them a breathtaking view of the valley. Which was part of why I loved visiting so often while growing up. The Ryans had significantly more money than I was used to. While my grandmother was wealthy, and my parents seemed to make ends meet just fine, we didn't have a luxurious home or luxury cars.

The Ryans had both, and more to spare.

This was mostly attributed to Wes Ryan's television show that he'd had for, in my humble opinion, way too many seasons. Once he finally stopped filming, he began producing and funding other media ventures, which resulted in making him an ungodly amount of money.

This was all gossip, of course, via the youngest member of the Ryan family: Ellie.

"When was the last time you came up, Royce?" Mom asked from the front, interrupting my thoughts.

I hadn't even recognized we'd already reached the Ryans' drive-way. I watched as their solar lights lit up the asphalt to their rather large, four-car garage bay. Off to the side was the house, massive and gorgeous like I always remembered. I loved coming out here as a kid, especially at Christmas when their entire house would glow from the inside out.

"It's been a while," I replied nervously.

The reality was I hadn't been back since I was a teenager. I was fifteen, it was a Christmas Eve party, where our families had all gath-ered. I would never forget that event because it was the first time I gained the upper hand with the eldest Ryan child. He'd held a card out for me to take, and I'd snubbed him. The look on his face made some-thing in my chest shrink, but I remember burrowing into Connor's side, pushing the feeling away.

Mom continued talking. "Well, Callie was excited when I mentioned you'd be coming with us."

That was good. I had no idea if Ellie was still living here, or if she had moved out like her brother. Ellie was twenty-two just like Taryn, so it was possible that she had. What a waste of such a big house. If I lived here, I'd never leave.

Ambient lighting shone overhead as we exited the car and made our way to the front door. Callie really had a thing for solar lights based on her walkway and yard. There was a rather large patch of grass in front, protected by a tall, white fence, which had even more lights attached to the top of each post. With how remote their house was, I guess it made sense to have the added light to help see .

Callie opened the door and immediately stepped out, wearing a soft cotton dress. It swooshed around her ankles, making her look elegant and classy. She pulled my mother into a hug and asked. "Did you bring the salad?"

Mom wrapped her arm around Callie's middle and sighed her answer. "Of course I did, it's the walnut one too." We followed the two inside, watching as they quickly fell into their own language where they laughed and snarked back and forth, faster than any of us could keep up. Sometimes I forgot that the two had been best friends since before I was born. I'd heard the story several times, but over time I got a few of the details mixed up.

Something about how Mom visited Rose Ridge with Callie. According to Mom, Callie had been left the land the club sits on in her deceased father's will. Mom was the one who encouraged her to stay here and push the local bikers around until they conceded and gave her what she was owed. I guess things didn't go according to plan because Wes was the president at the time, and he'd never moved on from Callie.

Their love story was honestly so sweet, but crazy when you really thought of it.

The man didn't kiss or screw anyone for nearly a decade. Pure insanity.

Even I wasn't that dedicated to my first love. It took me about a year to date again after my breakup with Connor. I guess that meant what we had wasn't fated, or true love, not like Wes and Callie.

"Royce!" Callie noticed me as we paused in her foyer. She pulled me into a quick hug, which made me feel like a kid again, poking around her house when I had no business being there. She seemed to know what I was up to and never called me out on it.

"Thanks for having me."

Sheer, ridiculous opulence expanded before me as we pulled apart, and I slid out of my coat. Floor to ceiling windows that covered the front of their home, and went up, all three stories. Light carpet that hadn't ever seemed to dull or stain for as long as I could remember, and then throughout the kitchen and dining area was hardwood.

"Hey, Royce!" Ellie suddenly called as she took the last few steps leading to the second floor. She looked like her mother with dark hair and hazel eyes, fair skin and the same exact smile. "I love that band, and the way that's cropped is so cute!"

I glanced down at my T-shirt that I had modified myself. The band was an all-female group that sang moving songs to powerful rock music. It was like mixing poetry and the best electric guitar sets you've ever heard in your life. "Thank you. It's good to see you, Ell." I pulled her petite frame into a hug. She was dancing last I heard. Ballet, or something. Maybe she taught it? I had no doubt that I'd find out during dinner.

Ellie pulled back and then flicked her eyes to a spot behind me. "Lucky for you, we're all here tonight, which almost never happens."

I felt his heavy gaze before I turned. Ford stood there, wearing an easy smile, but it wasn't aimed at me, it was for my parents. Unfortunately, it was breathtaking. His eyes lit up when he smiled. His teeth were white and straight, which was no surprise, as I recalled how he'd been in braces for two years in high school.

A rock crashed inside my belly as his lips seemed to flatline the moment he saw me watching. Why did he hate me so much? He was there that night of the proposal, when I'd rushed over to the club to yell at my father. When I had barged into the office, Ford was there, sitting with his sketchpad out. He was drawing a neighborhood from the looks of it, or a house. His eyes had lifted when I entered the room, and instead of disdain, surprise had brightened his hazel eyes. I remember because it made my feet falter, and I nearly fell because Ford not frowning at me had made my belly swoop, which wasn't something I should have felt so soon after breaking up with Connor. My dad never asked him to leave, even as the most private of details from my life were hashed out in front of him. Ford said nothing to me about my fake proposal or the fact that Connor had disappeared the next day. Maybe he blamed me.

Perhaps all this time, he assumed I had broken his best friend's heart, and I was the reason Connor left without saying goodbye.

"Royce, honey, you remember Ford?" My mother sidled up next to me, with her hand tugging mine. She was acting as though we were children and not both in our midtwenties.

I tried to play it off like it didn't bother me, but Ford wasn't speaking up.

"Of course I remember him. We've known each other since birth."

Mom added, "I know, but you two haven't really been around one another in a few years. Since graduation, right?"

Since he'd witnessed my father give away my future only for it to land back in his lap as a burden.

"It's been a few years," Ford finally said, as if he weren't the one to always draw back, pull away and never be in the same room as me. His eyes shimmered the smallest bit while he seemed to fight another one of his smiles. If I didn't know any better, which I didn't—I'd say he enjoyed smiling as long as it wasn't me it was directed at.

"Dinner is ready!" Callie called from the kitchen.

Mom turned away first, leaving me standing there with Ford towering over me. When had he gotten so tall? I raised my brow at him, encouraging him to speak, but he pushed past me toward the table. I watched the leather on his back, feeling an odd sense of familiarity settle into my core. That patch was like a beacon, directing me home. It only reminded me he shouldn't be here.

Callie had made a delicious meal of chicken marsala that had me reaching for seconds. Ford sat across from me, which was horrible because I had a front-row seat to watching his jaw move, creating an awareness that I didn't like. His brown hair was trimmed nicely, so it was off his neck but looked tousled on top, his brows were thick, matching the color of his hair but pairing almost artistically with his hazel eyes. My gaze trailed down to his nose, straight, almost model-like, and then that jaw that I'd memorized as a preteen from how many glances I'd snuck of him. After I'd turned fifteen, I'd stopped and couldn't care less about him, but now…

Now, it felt like I couldn't stop looking.

Ford Ryan was fucking hot.

"The dance is really intricate." I caught the tail end of Ellie's sentence while she wiped at her mouth demurely.

"She's already been offered a showcase," Callie proudly explained while Wes flicked his eyes affectionately toward his daughter. This felt mildly uncomfortable as it seemed the Ryans had decided to brag about their children's accomplishments, and unfortunately my parents had absolutely nothing to be proud of when it came to me aside from my being able to book incredible bands. Perhaps I should mention my volleyball skills from high school were still pretty decent, and my team would be the one to be on at the next club cookout. I was also really fucking good at sudoku.

Taryn had gone to college for some sort of marketing degree, but she wasn't using it in the traditional sense. However, her millions of followers and the paycheck she cleared from her views certainly should be bragged about, although I knew she'd never want that.

"That's awesome, Ellie." I smiled while biting into my chicken.

Ford took the opportunity to ruin the evening. "What about you, Royce? What have you been up to?"

Why was he speaking to me? He never spoke to me, and now, this…a blatant offense. "Well, I've been busy down at the Hollow."

"As an intern, right?" Ford followed up, and I hated how the dark green hue of his shirt made his eyes practically glow under the lights.

I smiled. "Nope. I get a paycheck now."

"She's up for a promotion. Rodney is stepping down." My dad added unhelpfully.

"Is that so?" Wes declared as if Dad hadn't already told the entire club what Rodney had told me. I knew he had because that was how the club worked. Nothing was private, and no one had any secrets. Which meant Ford was also aware of Rodney's ultimatum…I didn't like that he was privy to my private business, while I knew nothing about his.

Dad and Wes suddenly burst into conversation around the other various shops in Rose Ridge that were either closing or opening something new. I was grateful the focus was off me and finished my second helping by scraping my plate.

"Ford, what about you? What have you been up to?" I confidently tossed back at the man across the table from me.

Dad and Wes stopped their conversation while Mom and Callie exchanged a glance, and Ellie checked her phone.

"Not much."

I couldn't help flicking my brow up again, silently egging him on to say more than four words. When he didn't, I set my fork down.

"So, you're unemployed?"

Callie spat some of her drink out while Mom quickly jumped in to correct my blunder. "Sorry, she means—"

"It's fine. I essentially asked her the same thing," Ford interjected.

He did, but I was surprised he was admitting to it.

He kept his shrewd gaze on me while he replied, "Construction, mostly."

I caught how Wes watched our interaction, and when Ford said construction, his brows reached his hairline.

"So, you work for that jerk who's ruining our small town with all those homes that are going up on the west end?" I asked, leaning on my palm. His stare was a challenge, and I absolutely accepted.

"Royce," my mother warned, but I kept smiling.

Ford sipped his water before clearing his throat. "Do you know how many families in Rose Ridge would kill to have a newer home?"

No, I did not.

Ford continued, "People who have shown up at town meetings and zoning committees. People who are desperate to stay but need more family-friendly neighborhoods."

With a sigh, I grabbed my drink. He was acting like he was single handedly solving homelessness in Rose Ridge, which he wasn't, so I cut him off.

"And how many of those families will be able to afford those homes? I'm not naive enough to believe that those houses are going to go to residents first. Some out-of-state billionaire will buy them and rent them to Rose Ridge residents for triple the market rental rate. They're not going to get those houses."

His glare was glacial as he tightly gripped his fork. "That's not my call."

"Of course it's not. You'll build and build like a good little worker and make sure our town is ruined."

"That's enough, Royce." My dad interjected with a tone that had me snapping my mouth shut.

The table was quiet for a long, awkward minute where the redness in my face seemed to grow. I didn't regret what I had said, but I felt ashamed that I had said it all at the table full of his family and the people who were protective of him.

"Sorry, I was out of line. I apologize." I softly spoke to the table, glancing briefly at Ford for a second before returning my gaze to my plate.

If Taryn were here, she would have backed me up. His question about the Hollow dripped with underhanded mirth, and yet not one person called him on it. Which was fine, I meant what I had said about his job. I hated all the homes being built because I knew for a fact the residents in Rose Ridge couldn't afford to buy them. It would ruin our town if we continued to allow out-of-town wealth to swoop in and seize up all the property.

Callie spoke up about dessert, breaking the silence, and then Mom joined her, and the subject was changed. Once we finally finished eating, Dad went off with Wes while Mom and Laura continued talking. I had no clue where Ellie or Ford went, so I was left to wander around the house alone. It wasn't like I hadn't wandered the Ryan's house a billion times before, but it felt drastically different to do as an adult. I meandered down the hallway that led to the mudroom. There was an entire section of framed photos dedicated to the Ryans' old Great Dane, Maxwell, which had me smiling. I loved that dog. His regal pose in each picture made me smile as I remembered how often I would go to him when our family came over.

Maxwell was always present in my time playing at the Ryan house. I heard they'd had to put him down when we were in high school. I hadn't wanted to come by because of what happened at Christmas with Ford. Things between us after that only worsened to the point where we could barely sit in the same room at the same time.

I had allowed my anger towards Ford to prevent me from supporting the rest of the Ryan family through such a difficult time. Regret pricked my chest, making my nose burn.

Suddenly, something warm and soft rubbed against my leg.

A stout, gray cat wound in and out of my legs while purring.

I bent down to pet him and found his name tag.

"Hi, Gus. How are you?" I scratched under his neck, loving how he kept purring. Taryn and I didn't have pets growing up, but perhaps now that I was an adult, I should consider it.

"You're so handsome." I scratched behind his ears while picking him up. He was heavy, making my arms sag a bit, but I slowly made my way back into the living room where Ellie was on the couch, scrolling through her phone.

She glanced up at me as soon as I entered, "Oh, you found Ford's cat."

Disappointment settled in my gut as soon as she confirmed who he belonged to.

"How could such a magnificent creature belong to someone so horrible?" I said in a sweet tone, as if I were baby-talking to the cat. Ellie laughed along with me before holding her arms out for the feline.

"Ford had to leave him behind when he moved out. I think he probably misses him, even if he takes him home from time to time. And Gus misses the affection. I'm never home and my parents aren't either, so the poor guy gets lonely."

What a crying shame. Gus was awesome. How could Ford leave him behind, he had a house in town, why couldn't his cat go with him?

"Royce?" my mom called from the kitchen. I smiled at Ellie and waved before padding over to where Mom stood with Callie.

"Honey, tell Callie what you told me."

It felt a little forced and awkward, but it was a chance, and I had to take it. So, I slid onto a stool and explained my predicament with Rodney. I waved my hands too many times, and I think I even shed a tear at one point, but through it all, Callie looked earnest. The truth was, regardless of the ultimatum, my frustration stemmed from losing my independence. If Rodney didn't want to hand things over to me, a new manager would be hired, and they might not want to keep me on. They may change everything around, and the idea of losing the only thing I'd ever dreamed of owning made me angry and emotional, which all came out in my explanation.

"Oh, Royce." Callie moved to hold my hand, while Mom held the other. Suddenly, I felt thirteen again, coming over to the Ford house to clean, hang out, and spend time with Ellie when she wasn't even my friend, she was Taryn's. Callie had always taken me under her wing, guiding me with a gentle hand when she knew I had a crush that couldn't be managed. A crush that wasn't reciprocated.

"Well, I know Wes is planning to step down, but I really don't think it'll be as tumultuous as you think. Ford is going to step in, and he's—"

I knew it. Why did it anger me so much to know that Ford would take over? I couldn't wrap my head around the fact that he was going to be the one to inherit the club after my father. Maybe it was because I knew if he did, then the club would officially be lost to me. I bristled, snapping a little too harshly, "Since when are you okay with Ford being a part of the club?"

Callie's eyes shuttered the smallest bit as she searched my face. "Sweetheart, it's difficult to explain how we got here. Perhaps someday I'll be able to tell you, but I had to accept things in pieces, small pieces. With time—" She shook her head, but I had already stopped listening.

It was pointless to argue with her. She wouldn't be talking to Wes.

I slid my hand out from under Callie's and gave her a quick smile. "Well, thanks."

Her gaze slid over to my mother, and the two silently shared a moment before I stood up.

"Mom, I'm going to wait outside. No rush. Callie, thank you so much for dinner."

I left the women behind and stopped near the foyer to get my coat. The cool night air felt like heaven against my flushed skin. Deep down, it was more than just the too-warm temperature of seventy-two degrees the Ryans had their thermostat set to.

I was mortified that I had asked Callie to talk to Wes about his choice in stepping down. Of course she rejected me, her son would take things over. She doubted there'd be any turbulence, but I knew better.

"You gonna quit the Hollow now that Rodney is acting like a little prick?" Ford suddenly appeared near my parents' truck. He wore his leather jacket that had his club patches in place. My eyes wandered to the way his name looked, sewn in red against the black leather. The majority of leather cuts had the member's name sewn in white, but legacy members had theirs sewn in red.

I considered whether I should be relieved he knew about my situation. Maybe he'd take pity on me, and he'd hold off on taking the reins for a few months. I discovered a while back, as an intern for the Hollow that accepting pity didn't bother me. In fact, I often relied on it.

"I plan on proving him wrong, actually." I lifted my chin.

Ford's arms were crossed, but I couldn't make out his expression in the dark, even with all the solar lights around.

"How do you think you're going to do that?"

I stepped closer. "By making sure there are no hiccups with the club or any big changes."

Ford's jaw tensed before he dipped his head. "So, your response to this is to try and control a club with over two hundred members, instead of just moving on?"

"Why would I move on?" That was completely crazy to even consider.

"What else did he say?" Ford ignored my question, now toe-to-toe with me. When had he moved so close?

I shrugged, choosing to embellish a little. "He said Dad stepped down and that him stepping down was not desired and the new president was hated by everyone."

"Well, he's misinformed. My leadership will be met with excitement." Ford grinned.

"I doubt that very much." I smiled sweetly in return. "How about you take a road trip for three months, Ford. Get out of Rose Ridge for a bit and stretch your legs. You never did leave for college or go find a pretty wife. You're almost thirty, better get going."

His scoff seemed to rake down my spine. "I'm one year older than you."

"Really? Weird, you look much older."

"You know, Rose...the world doesn't revolve around you. If you're worried about not getting a promotion, then perhaps you should be the one who leaves."

Moving with him away from the house, I snapped harshly, "First, don't call me Rose, my name is Royce and you know that. Second, I never suggested that it did. If you're so positive that there's not going to be any problems, then I guess you won't mind if I stick around the club to ensure that."

"Knock yourself out, sweetheart. Although, I wouldn't want to offend your delicate sensibilities. Things have changed since you were around it last, not even your pops or mine like to stay late because those pretty Sweetbutts like to earn their titles."

My face flushed a horrible crimson at the picture he'd painted me. I wasn't a prude, nor a virgin, but picturing Ford with women who entertained him the way Sweetbutts did, or bunk bunnies…it was making an odd feeling stir in my chest.

Ford walked past me, but his shoulder nudged mine on the way. I couldn't help but glare as he moved toward his bike and mounted it. Before he left, I wanted to say something else. I needed to know that I had gotten under his skin as much as he'd gotten under mine.

Out of nowhere, I yelled, "You don't deserve Gus!"

His smirk was like a firecracker going off in my chest. Why did he infuriate me so much?

"And you don't deserve your dream job, and yet you're going to make sure you get it, won't you?" His bike started, making it impossible to reply so I flipped him the bird while he gave me another one of those smiles.

He rode off seconds later, and I realized way too late that I had just stood there watching until he was completely out of sight.

FIVE
FORD

I pulled up to the construction site with my coffee in hand and a death grip on my cell.

Apparently, our outposts had been hit overnight, and all of them had been done after our cameras were destroyed, so we had no idea who was responsible. My mood was shit, and Johnson was aware of this, which was why he was the one communicating with our crew this morning.

I eyed the name on the side of the truck and thought back to what I had said to Royce when she asked where I was working. What a fucking joke that she didn't even know. That was typical Royce. Self-absorbed and unaware of literally anyone else around her. I didn't just work in construction; I owned the company and employed over eighty people. She sat on her high horse about this town not changing, unaware that the club had shaped all the major changes within it.

For years she hadn't taken up any space in my head, so it was an odd sensation to go through my workday still pondering our conversation from three days ago. She said she'd be hanging around the club from now on to ensure nothing would happen, and I'd yet to see her. I was on edge with the worry and stress that she'd randomly pop up. As much as I tried to deter her with rumors of the Sweetbutts being too wild, or the chaos of the members, the truth was I didn't want her in the club. She was a distraction, and I didn't know how I would respond to seeing other members around her.

I was grateful to my men who didn't need me much as I took call after call, trying to sort through who it was that had hit our outposts. I texted Killian and Wes and informed them we needed to have a church meeting tonight to make a plan. Finally, after pissing away almost the entire workday dealing with this shit, I moved to the mobile trailer that I had set up my office in and took off my hard hat. I just needed to bury myself in actual work that wasn't related to the club, get some new plans made up for the next phase of construction that I had in mind. I owned the company, which made cutting corners easier than they should be.

I didn't skimp on any construction process, because I truly did plan on having the residents of Rose Ridge getting these homes. However, I buried evidence in the basements and hid bags of money inside the drywall of a few garages. I knew where it was all hidden, each and every house in about three dozen different neighborhoods. None of it was hidden at the clubhouse, so if the feds came looking, even with a warrant, they'd find shit.

My phone buzzed with a phone call, which wasn't exactly normal especially when I saw who the caller was. I pressed my thumb to the green button and lifted the phone to my ear.

"Rook?"

He waited for a second before replying, "Ford."

Smartass. "What's wrong?"

"Me calling you out of the blue has to mean something's wrong?" Rook laughed, and it made me miss my friend. He was living in London last I heard, but he moved so frequently, it was hard to keep up. It hurt when his family left, and even if they came back once a year for a big vacation, it wasn't the same as having him here. I heard his younger brother, Ryle, was still with his mom and dad over in Italy, but my intel wasn't always up to date.

"Yeah, sorta."

He let out a sigh. "Unfortunately, you're correct. Listen, I have as much info on this as I'm going to share, so don't ask a bunch of follow-up questions, okay?"

That was cryptic. "Okay."

"You know I work in tech, which means I'm always watching out for anything that could lead us to Max or whatever might hurt the club."

"That's so kind of you, Rook. You know you could just come home and stop being a chickenshit."

He laughed again, and but someone yelled out a coffee order in the back, making him muffle his phone. "Do you want this tip or not?"

After the day I had, I'd take any tip that might help make sense of how we'd been hit.

"Yes."

"Royce is in a video that's trending on social media."

This had nothing to do with the fucking outposts. I let out an annoyed sigh while I rubbed my forehead. "What the fuck does that mean, Rook?"

"It means this video is landing on the FYP of anyone who has ever looked up anything motorcycle or biker-related."

I still wasn't connecting what he was trying to break down for me. "I don't understand...why is she trending?"

"Because she's in underwear, and as far as the bikers' for you page...I think that's because of her tattoo."

"What tattoo?" Fuck, did my voice just crack?

Rook waited to reply, but I heard him typing, then distractedly answered. "The one that links her to the Stone Riders. I'll look to see where this video originated, but you might get further talking directly to her. It seems as though it's an ad for the underwear she's wearing."

An ad? That didn't make any sense. "Are you sure it's Royce and not Taryn? They look alike occasionally, when Taryn lets her hair grow out and wears high heels."

Rook laughed. "I grew up with them, Ford. I know which sister is which. Honestly, it doesn't really matter which one it is, the link to the Stone Riders, and it being connected to either of Killian's daughter's is the fucking problem."

My chest felt a little too warm as I closed my eyes and tried to make sense of this. Rook joked, "Or you could pull it up on your laptop and verify it for yourself."

"Fuck off, you know I'm just trying to confirm who it is before I take this to Killian."

His laugh pissed me off enough that I pulled the phone away from my ear.

"Can you find out if this was planned, or if someone leaked it on purpose," I snapped.

"Yeah. I'll be in touch." Rook continued laughing as I hung up.

In another version of my life, I'd open the app, swipe over to this video ,and stare at whatever mess Royce got herself into this time. In this reality, I had to worry about how this clusterfuck was going to affect the club.

I ran my hand through my hair, trying to decide how I was going to break this to Killian when Johnson ran into the trailer. He was breathless and panicked.

"Killian called, he said he needs that meeting now. Something happened with Royce."

Fuck.

My boots echoed against each step as I made my way down into the cellar, lit with only a few overhead hanging lights. Shelves still lined most of the walls with a shit ton of food and weapons, but in the center of the room was a large table with twelve chairs tucked underneath. This was where we held church, and the room upstairs was merely to throw others off the scent of the true nature of what the Stone Riders had become. We couldn't trust anyone at the moment, including our allies. With the changes in our ranks, we were not only vulnerable, but at the moment, we were weak.

"Prez." Killian dipped his head in respect as his hand came down on my back in passing.

A strange swarm of feelings hit my stomach, but I pushed them down. My mouth parted in reply, trying to figure out what to say in response because things had been fucking weird since I took this role over six months ago.

There were only a few people who knew that I was currently the president of the Stone Riders motorcycle club, and for the time being, we had to keep it that way.

Dad came in next, slapping me on the back and then the rest of my closest men made their way over—Logan, and Rev, followed by Johnson with a Twinkie sticking out of his mouth. Kody, Slade, Norman, Dane, Orson, and last, Connor's dad, Jameson, filled the remaining chairs at the table.

They each greeted me with a respectful nod, while relaxing into their spots. I knew we had to keep this brief because there were men upstairs who didn't need to get curious about where the core leadership of this club went.

"We have the outposts to go over, but Johnson said something happened to one of your kids, Killian?" I lifted my chin toward where he sat at the other end of the table and then tapped my finger against the surface. I was trying to ensure no one thought I cared that this had to do with Royce being in a video in her underwear. Although I still hadn't pulled it up, and I wasn't sure I would, I wouldn't show her father that I cared one way or another.

His angry scowl deepened as he leaned on his elbows over the table. "I've been made aware of a video circulating of Royce..." His jaw clenched, and I didn't envy him having to talk about his daughter in a compromising shot, in front of us. "She uh..."

Fuck, this was painful to watch. I stood up, so everyone's focus went to me.

"Rook called and told me the video links her to the club."

Johnson was in the only rolling chair at the table, which meant he moved around like a toddler. He slid forward and glanced down the length of the table. "How did it link her to us?"

Killian locked eyes with me, silently asking me to be cautious.

"Her tattoo—it's of our patch." There were a few murmured comments around the able, but I didn't want to give them much time to discuss Royce.

"Did this report come from Silas?" I asked Killian.

Killian's head tilted to the side. "No. It came from the Chaos Kings."

That meant this video really was everywhere.

"So why is the video trending, is she in a fight or something?" Johnson asked while casting a nervous glance in my direction.

Killian's jaw tensed.

My fingers wrapped tightly around the edge of the table to get some semblance of control. "Royce is modeling in the video."

Johnson still seemed confused while pulling out another Twinkie. "What could she possibly be modeling that would show our patch? I've never seen any tattoo, and she wears tank tops and shorts around us all the time."

"Fuck, kid. You don't stop, do you?" Killian grumbled, running his hand over his head. It was one thing hearing it alone, but now in front of everyone was testing my resolve.

"Underwear, okay?" Killian snapped. "She's modeling fucking underwear according to what I heard. If you look up that video yourself, I'll cut your fucking fingers off, Johnson."

My second man in charge lifted his hands in defense. "I'm not. Jeez. I would never look at your daughter like that."

"Well, the issue is, half the internet is…so what are we going to do about it?" My dad asked, leaning back in his chair.

Killian continued, "According to my wife, Royce shot this ad nearly a year ago, so the timing of this popping up now is questionable."

Dad glanced up at me, then back at Killian. "With the outposts being taken out, now this…it's not coincidental."

Killian let out a heavy sigh. "This situation with Rodney giving her this bullshit ultimatum of keeping things quiet here for three months, the outposts, and now this. Maybe I'm wrong, and the company is pushing the ad themselves, but my gut tells me it's someone trying to start shit up."

I had to agree. Regardless of why it was out there, if it had been shot over a year ago, it didn't make sense that it was suddenly going viral. But I hadn't seen the video myself, so I wasn't sure if there was some ulterior reason that could be happening.

Voicing a few thoughts, I asked, "Have you asked Taryn about it, maybe see if she knows of some trend that could have pulled that video out?"

Killian shook his head. "She's giving me a whole different set of issues we'll need to address at some point."

Why would that require the club's involvement? It was something I would have to push aside for now.

"What needs to be done?" Rev directed his question to me, which I knew he did on purpose. The men were supposed to show me the same respect they once did Killian.

"I'll talk to Royce to see what she knows about the ad."

Killian's eyes blazed with anger as he lifted his head and focused on me. "Why the fuck would you be the one to talk to her?"

"Because I'm the president of the club, Killian, and I need to deal with this. Aside from that, I'm her age and she doesn't care what I think of her." I acted like I didn't give a shit about this one way or another, but I didn't like the way his implication dug at me.

Right as Killian opened his mouth to argue, Rev spoke again, "We have hackers we will reach out to, get it removed from the internet, maybe they can help us trace the source too."

I gave him a nod of approval. "Take Johnson and Logan to help."

"Regarding the outposts. I want to hear what each of you found, but we also need to talk about Rodney." My tone was sharp, getting everyone's focus.

"The Hollow is currently owned by Bernie Hatfield, who is going to sell it. I plan to buy it for the club, but I need Rodney out of the way. Put a few details on him. I want to know who he's talking to and why he gave Royce that three-month ultimatum. He wanted her worked up enough that she'd reach out to us about the change in leadership. It was calculated. He's likely hoping to use her like a game piece to shove us into position. We know he's working with a rival club. We just need confirmation on which one that is."

Killian cleared his throat. "Let's skip the detail and bring him in then."

Scaring him was a balancing act. Too much fear and he'd skip town or even hurt Royce. Not enough fear, and he might walk all over Royce by dragging this three-month bullshit out. Of the two outcomes, I was more comfortable with the latter, but like hell was I about to admit that to Royce's father.

"I think meeting him where he's at will be more insightful with who he gives up. Coming into the club under duress will make him say shit that likely isn't even true."

Jameson's gaze slid over to Killian who had his brows drawn in. Did he know that I was using his daughter as a pawn? Even if he did, I didn't care. There was a reason I was now sitting in this chair and he wasn't.

Johnson somehow found another sweet treat to chew on while asking. "What do we do if we see him meeting with someone while we're out and about?"

"Be discreet." I explained by spreading my hands on the table. "Take pictures if you can and report it as soon as possible. We know he's talking to someone; we just want to know who benefits from us not changing leadership for three months, and why."

A text lit up my phone. I recognized that it was Yeti, one of the older members that had been a part of Killian's regime.

> Yeti: I gotta wolf cub up here.

My stomach tensed as I texted back quickly.

> Me: Which one?

> Yeti: Oldest. She's drawing quite a few eyes.

> Me: Why is she here?

> Yeti: You know I don't know that. I already tried talking to her, she handed me a basket of cookies and hugged me. I couldn't kick her out after that.

Fuck.

"Everything okay?" Killian asked, taking a sip from his beer.

I glared at my phone, unsure how to reply. It was one thing to pull Royce aside and chat with her about the video, to which Killian seemed to barely agree. But it was something else entirely to have his daughter be seen in the club after the rumors about her video began circulating. I'd need to get her out before her father caught wind of it, or else he'd take that shit out on the prospects who likely had no fucking clue she was his daughter and completely off-limits.

"Yeti has a situation upstairs that I need to go address. I'll be back." I slid out from my chair and glanced over at Johnson. He already knew that meant he needed to step in and keep things going. I didn't have an official vice-president yet, but some of the men around the table were still hoping Killian would take up that role so he stayed as a connection to the new members and old. It would be smart, and while I respected and trusted him, I also wanted to begin my own legacy.

Johnson began talking about the outposts as I jogged up the stairs and pushed through the door leading from the cellar. The music blasting in the club hit me first. It was a low, melodic beat that was familiar but not. Like a remix or something. I liked that it was different from the classic rock or other modern shit the guys always picked.

Men wearing leather cuts were huddled around the two pool tables in the main room. A few were sitting on the couches, Sweetbutts were in men's laps. Bunk bunnies that I'd seen around were tucked under the arms of a few members. I bypassed people, and the ease in which I did was a relief. My balloon of anonymity was about to pop as soon as it became public that I was the one leading this club instead of Killian.

The second he stepped on the floor, he drew people to him. The women were smart enough to stay away. After he'd been married for well over twenty years, no one even tried to approach him in that way. Killian was a faithful man, like my father and Jameson were. They didn't touch any woman who walked through those doors, never had.

Someone shouting had my head swiveling. I needed to locate Killian's oldest daughter. I should have known she'd be over by the Alexa touchscreen. She was leaning against the counter with her heart-shaped ass swaying in a pair of jeans that drew my gaze. I forced my eyes up, like I always did. No matter how badly it burned that the men next to her hadn't stopped staring, or that one of them looked like he was two seconds from touching her.

The two members hanging near her tried to talk to her, but she seemed focused on finding a song to play, like it was a jukebox.

"Royce."

She ignored me, swiping her finger over the screen. Jay, one of the members drooling over her, flicked a quick look at me before stepping closer so I could hear him.

"We got her. We'll make sure she's out of sight as soon as her pops comes up."

Jay was going to get his ass beat after I got Royce out of here.

"No need, she's leaving with me." My tone was sharp, and my patience was practically gone. She still wasn't turning around. "Royce."

"I'm looking for a song, Ford," she yelled over the music while focusing on the screen. Jay laughed into his beer while the other member, Zane, seemed to also think it was funny.

It wasn't so much that they were standing too close to her, it was that I didn't have the time to sit here and play whatever game this was. Which was the reason my hand shot out and why my fingers curled inside the back pocket of her jeans and yanked her away from the counter.

Her back was against my chest within seconds, her hair against my nose.

I unfortunately inhaled, and a memory I was sure had been buried, resurfaced.

We were kids in elementary school. Maybe eight or nine…*"We're stuck as gym partners, Ford. I know you're not my biggest fan, but I'll stay out of your hair if you stay out of mine."*

"Your hair is always in the way," I said snidely, uncomfortable with how happy I was that she was my partner.

She turned around in front of me, forcing her curls to bounce near my chin.

"Then help me put it in a ponytail. I'm not good at it yet, and Mom didn't have time to do it for me this morning."

I had no reason not to help her. If I didn't, then her hair would be in my way and distract me the entire class period. So, I gathered the thick strands into my fist, and when she held out her purple hair tie to me, I wrapped it around her hair and made sure it held. But even as I tried to hold my breath, the smell hit me when she ran her hand down her hair.

Roses.

Royce Quinn smelled like roses in the strangest, sweetest, most infuriating sort of way.

"What the fuck, Ford?" Royce seethed, lifting her chin so it was angled over her shoulder. My chin was at the crown of her head, but my fingers were still tucked inside her pocket, against her ass. For some reason I hadn't pulled them out yet.

I rasped against her hair. "You can't be here."

She tried to step away, but I kept her in place. "Yes, I can. My dad is the president of this club, and I can be anywhere I want. I told you I was going to show up, and you responded by telling me to basically go for it."

That's right, she had warned me she'd be around more, but I didn't think she was being serious.

"Unfortunately, due to yet another one of your fucking messes, you can't be here. It's actually imperative that you're not."

She yanked out of my hold and spun around. Her eyes were wide, cheeks flushed, and her hands...those landed on my chest. Accidently, by the way she glanced down and removed them.

"What the hell does that mean—" she started, but my hand shot out, grabbing hers so that I was pulling her away. The fewer people who saw her here, the better, and if I could get her out of the club before her father noticed, then I might avoid a huge scene.

"Ford, what the fuck?" she snapped as she stumbled behind me. We were outside, in the back, under a full moon and a clear night sky. There were lights strung up from the back patio to the fire pit, illuminating the grass and paved path. Beyond the yard were parked motorcycles, and past that was the abandoned cabin. I continued walking toward the old apartment yard. The fence was in rough shape, but it was still functional.

Once we were behind the gate, I released her and immediately wanted to go back in and get her a jacket. Her shirt dipped enough that most of her chest was exposed to the cold air.

"If your dad came out and saw you in there, you know exactly what would happen."

She tucked her arms over her chest. "That was a long time ago. I'm an adult now, he wouldn't react that way."

"Really? I'm so tempted to let you test that theory, but unlike you, I do actually care about this club and if people get needlessly hurt because of it."

I wasn't present for it, because I would have done something if I was, but I heard about it. She was seventeen, hanging out in the club, and one of the prospects who was hoping to become a member didn't realize who she was. They groped her, became aggressive, and Killian practically killed him. My dad had stopped him barely in time…a few more punches to the face and the man would have died. It could have had disastrous repercussions that even our paid police couldn't save him from. Royce was scared enough that I assumed she wouldn't return, but here she fucking was.

Did she even see how they looked at her?

Did she even care that she might be putting herself in harm's way again?

"It's been a while, but—" Her voice was soft, her lips pouty and too plump. I watched her mouth move and pulled myself together.

"You nearly got someone killed the last time you were here."

Her hand shot out as if to hold an invisible reason for her presence. "I told you I was coming around, you said I could—"

"I didn't honestly think you'd be stupid enough to show up!"

"I'm not stupid, Ford. I'm desperate." Her eyes shuttered as anger seemed to steal her tone and features. A small part of me felt guilty.

That part of me was tucked back behind my heart, buried in a proverbial drawer that I had sealed shut.

"Not my problem, Royce. I honestly don't give a fuck if you get your dream job. People get passed over for their dreams every single day. You'll survive. Maybe it's time you joined the real world and started acting like a grown-up. While we're at it, let's have a little chat about that viral video of you that's making the club members get all up in a frenzy about the Wolf's daughter."

Her face paled, then her brows furrowed as if she were trying to work something out. "What are you talking about?"

Her hesitation nearly gave me pause, but I ignored it. "Did you happen to engage in a video ad for an underwear company?"

"What…yeah, like a year ago, why?"

"Any reason it would suddenly be popping up on club members' algorithms?"

She yanked her cell from her back pocket, a confused expression stamped on her face. "Seriously… What the hell are you talking about?"

She must have been truly confused because she didn't even snap at me when I moved next to her shoulder to see what she was pulling up. In the search bar of her app, she typed a few ideas, which included terms for the underwear ad, and "girl in underwear" but she never came up. She tried again using the brand she'd done the ad for, and again, she was nowhere to be found.

I gently took the phone from her and typed in the search bar "biker babe underwear."

And the first video was her.

Fuck me, this video would be ingrained in my head forever. In the video Royce looked sun-kissed, which complemented her bright eyes and blond hair so nicely that she practically glowed. Her makeup was a bit heavy, but they'd made her lips this pinkish color that I would unfortunately imagine smeared all over my cock when I gripped it at night.

"I don't get it," Royce mused, clicking on the video and watching it play.

I most certainly got it. I wished so badly I didn't, but my God, I did.

She wore a pink thong that stretched high up on her hips, with a low-cut cropped shirt. It was more of a bra with ample cleavage, and it was see-through, showing peaked, rosy nipples. Below her breasts, the pink fabric went to just above her belly button, showcasing her ribs and abs. She did a little jump in the video which made her tits bob and then the video transitioned so she was standing in front of the camera with her ass bouncing.

Her manicured nails, which were painted the same color as her thong, lightly pulled up on the fabric that slid up through her crack and spread into a T across her lower back. Her hair bounced in soft, glossy curls against her tan skin, but my eyes fell to her ass. Her perfectly smooth, round—

"What the fuck is that?" My voice was practically gravel as I stared at the black tattoo on her right cheek. Even though I'd heard them mention it, it was different actually seeing the skull with roses budding from the eyes that made up our patch.

Royce probably rolled her eyes based on how blasé her tone was when she replied, "It's a tattoo."

"Royce, it's not just a tattoo, it's the Stone Rider patch. You didn't think that might be a bad idea when shooting this ad? Since when do you get real tattoos? I thought you only did the temporary ones."

She lowered her phone to glare at me. "First of all, this was never supposed to go anywhere but their website. I never agreed to them sharing on their socials. Second, the team loved that I had it along with a few other tattoos. They thought it would make my modeling stand out. Third…what the hell are you talking about? It sort of sounds like you don't really know me very well, Ford. Which tracks since you've barely said two words to me over the past ten years."

Something sharp stabbed at my chest, nearly making me inspect the truth in what she'd just said. Instead of giving into it, I brushed past it. "Well, you certainly stand out, Royce, but that's never been a problem for you, has it?"

Her brows tugged in closer as she tucked her phone back into her jeans. "What is that supposed to mean?"

I wasn't even really angry with her. I was angry at the fact that she'd always been this person so elusive and out of reach to me, and yet the whole damn world seemed to access her so easily. "Weren't you all worried about me causing drama for the club by stepping into the president's role? Yet, you're out here, literally showing your ass for the whole fucking world to see, and on it you have a neon sign pointing to our goddamn club. Jesus, Royce, do you ever think through a single situation?"

Her lip wobbled the smallest amount, but she lowered her chin almost as if she didn't want me to see it.

"Again, you don't fucking know me, Ford. You're referencing things that happened when I was a teenager. You're assuming I don't get tattoos and talking about how I don't want to grow up. Get a grip, Ford. I am grown, you just weren't invited to be a part of it any of it, so you made up all these assumptions about me."

Humiliation was that thing poking at my chest, I could see that now. She was right, but her comment about how I'd not been invited to be apart of her growing up was too painful for me to humble myself. "You expect me to believe that? You do float around life in a bubble, Royce. No real consequences. Daddy will clean up every mess you make. That's how it's always been, and that's how it will always be. You don't deserve that promotion but I'm sure you'll get it because you're Royce Quinn and you get whatever the fuck you want."

Despite feeling I had gone too far, I couldn't seem to stop. I knew it for certain though when her hand came up swift and firm as it flew across my face. I'd missed that she'd started crying, and fuck, that actually hurt to see.

"Fuck you, Ford."

Her head shook back and forth, but she said nothing else.

That hidden, jagged chunk in my heart tugged and tugged, trying to pull out that guilt and the concern I'd once had for her. They were feelings I had battled with my entire life—ones she so carelessly toyed with. I'd care that I hurt her now if she cared how badly she hurt me back then.

What mattered now was keeping her safe, and at this juncture there was only one way to do that. "I need you to stay away from the club."

Her chin wobbled the smallest amount before her face finally fell and her hair slid in front of her. She remained like that for a few seconds before she lifted it again, as if she'd become determined.

"Maybe I'll become a bunk bunny or a Sweetbutt." Her shoulder lifted. "I like them. They've always been nice to me. I'll stick with them. I can be here, and I don't care if they talk about my video, those women will protect me. They watch out for their own."

The image of her waking up in Johnson's or Kody's bed, with tousled hair, smudged eyeliner from being fucked all night...it practically ripped that buried chest out of its proverbial grave, and whatever I'd been so careful to conceal was now exploding inside my chest.

"You'll just start sleeping with random members?" My eyes narrowed, hoping to intimidate her, but she smiled in return like what I had said was a great idea.

"Maybe. I haven't decided yet, but the point is, you can't tell me what to do. Neither can my dad or anyone else. I don't think I should have to stay away simply because men can't control themselves. What happened when I was seventeen wasn't my fault. That man was at fault. I should be allowed to exist in these spaces without fearing that I'll be abused or harmed. Sorry if that creates work for all of you, but I'm going to do what I want to do because I don't cater to men or their needs. I cater to my own."

Goddammit.

"If you so much as step—"

"Royce?" Killian pulled the gate open, poking his head into the space. Worry tugged his features down as he stepped further inside.

I realized too late that this probably didn't look great, that I was over here, hidden away with his daughter who was now crying.

"Hey, Dad." Royce gave him a feeble smile while swiping at her face.

His eyes flashed as he looked between us. "What's going on?"

"He talked to me about the video. I'm really sorry for making things harder on all of you."

Killian stepped forward and wrapped her in a tight hug. "Oh, sweetheart. You didn't. We just want to be sure you're safe. I'm sorry if Ford didn't convey that properly." His eyes shot up to me in an angry scowl.

"Why don't you head on home, and I'll be there in a few."

She nodded, then turned to leave without glancing back. Killian followed behind her, likely wanting to ensure she got on her bike safely. I was close behind him as we made our way back toward the club. Once she was out of earshot, had started her bike, and moved down the trail toward her house, Killian swung his head in my direction.

"Is there something I need to be aware of regarding you two?"

I stared at her taillights, still curious how she pulled that thing I had buried out and made a mess of my chest with it. I also absolutely detested how sexy she looked on that bike.

"Ford, I'm only going to tell you this once," Killian warned. "She hides a lot from the public. There's a deep place in her heart where she stores away all the hurt from people. The rejection, the anger. She puts on a mask for everyone else, smiles and acts like nothing fazes her, then breaks for weeks alone, behind closed doors. She needs someone who understands how to be tender with her."

"Can you please get to the point?" I droned, sounding bored when, really, my heart hammered a painful rhythm.

His eyes flashed, and I worried that The Wolf of Rose Ridge was about to tear the fuck into me.

"Sure. You're too fucking harsh for someone like her. Leave her alone."

I wanted to defend that I wasn't trying to be with her, nor did I care that he assumed I liked her when I didn't. I was trying to protect the club.

But instead, a very odd thing came out of my mouth.

"I'm not always harsh. I could try to be tender."

Killian's eyes blazed again, searching mine. "You can try all you want to, Ford. Just not with her."

With that, he moved from the steps and took off toward his bike, where he'd follow his daughter home.

I was left standing there, trying to figure out why his disapproval hurt so much.

SIX

ROYCE

The glow of my phone was the only light in my room.

Which was good because I looked like a fucking mess at the moment. Kleenex was scattered around me, I had a bag of Flaming-Hot Cheetos tucked against my chest, and my hydro flask against my face.

I swiped to the next video, hoping the void in my chest would feel less invasive if I found enough funny videos to fill it. I'd been at it for three hours to no avail.

"What the hell am I looking at?" Taryn's sharp voice suddenly interrupted my doomscrolling. The light from the hall filtered into my bedroom, making me wince.

"Shut the door!"

She complied with a heavy sigh. "Royce. What the hell?"

I sniffed as she made her way closer. She turned on my side lamp, which had a pink sheer sheet over it, casting my bedroom into low-lit ambience.

"Who did this to you?" She stroked over my head, where my hair was tucked inside of a hoodie. She knew when I wore the heated onesie with a hood that I was battling insecurity and heartbreak.

My sister looked like an angel as I stared up into her blue eyes.

"You're going to laugh as soon as I say it," I confessed with a swipe at my nose.

Her dark brows crumpled as she began rubbing my back. "Ford Ryan is the only other boy besides your boyfriend who ever made you cry. Did he do this?"

Was that true? Had Ford been like this our entire lives?

"I was trying to piss him off by going down to the club. I didn't tell you everything the other day about Rodney. He told me that as long as things with the club didn't change for three months, I could become manager, but if they do change, then I can't have the promotion. So, I went down to the club, trying to ensure that there was no change in leadership."

Taryn's face soured. "That fucking asshole."

"I tried to talk Mom and Callie into dissuading Dad and Wes from—"

My sister interrupted me with a groan. "Royce, you didn't."

Defensiveness clouded my chest like a storm. "What else was I supposed to do?"

Taryn let out a heavy sigh, then pushed my hair back again. Sometimes it felt like she was the older sister, not me. She was so sure of herself and independent. She wasn't afraid to chase her dreams even if it meant she might not catch them. I couldn't fathom the idea of not having something I worked for. But Ford was right…every single day people didn't have the luxury of living out the life they wanted to live. Every day people got passed over for jobs they were more than qualified for. It being a dream of theirs didn't really make a difference one way or another.

"You were supposed to tell me the whole story. I would have thought of a new plan with you."

I frowned up at my sister. "Where have you been, T? It's been almost five days. I've been a pathetic mess for a week."

Taryn plucked my bag of Cheetos from my chest and began shoving the wadded Kleenex into my trash bin. "I'm sorry, Royce. I did a branding shoot up near DC. I thought I texted you."

Shaking my head, I sniffed again. "It's okay. Tell me about this plan that you have."

"Well, I would have found a way to blackmail Rodney, so he had no choice but to give you that promotion. He's essentially doing the same thing to you, Royce. Ever wonder why three months was significant to him?"

No, I hadn't.

Sitting up and adjusting my hood so it fell back, I asked, "So you think Rodney knows something, or might be working with someone?"

"Yes, I do. Think about it." She adjusted herself onto my bed, so she was sitting hip to hip with me. "He's had the oldest daughter of *the Wolf* working right under him all this time. The Stone Riders are still a big deal all these years later, and Dad has certainly made a name for himself. It's leverage he could have used in a number of different ways, but if he needs there to be no change in leadership for three months, then perhaps there's someone else who's asking for that."

I stared ahead, completely baffled by her thought process. "Ever consider taking over for Dad down at the club?"

She laughed, but it was a sad laugh, and I wasn't sure why. I wanted to ask her, but she moved on too quickly.

"Tell me what Ford said."

I didn't want to jump back into it. The pricks that had landed in my chest from his words were still so painful, but my sister needed to know. She knew everything about me, including the tiny crush I had on him when I was younger.

"Do you remember that modeling shoot I did for that underwear brand, CozyCo?"

She tipped her head back remembering, then let out a chuckle. "Yeah, they gave you a bunch of free underwear as payment or something, right?"

A flush of embarrassment hit me. "Hey, nice underwear is expensive. They paid me in over four thousand dollars' worth of clothing. I know because I price-checked each item on their website. I got lingerie, swimsuits, and pajamas. It was a great deal."

My sister tugged a Cheeto out and popped it into her mouth. "You know what, you're right. That was actually a good deal. I bought a bra the other day, and it was like eighty dollars. Which is insane, right?"

That brought me back to what Ford had said. "Well, that small video clip of me showing that pink piece…it somehow got posted like everywhere."

"They're probably trying to push the line again or something," Taryn muttered, picking out another long, orange piece.

"No, well, I thought I had a contract that stated it wasn't to be used for social media use. It was only going on their website. I requested that because of the tattoo on my ass, but after I dug the contract out, I realized it wasn't agreed upon on their end, it was only listed as a preference."

My sister's eyes suddenly grew. "Oh, shit."

I nodded. "I guess the algo has me under biker chick in underwear or something. The video landed on a ton of club members FYP, and they're all talking about me. Ford tore into me about how reckless and stupid I am." My throat became tight again, making me trail off.

My sister sat up and let out a sharp exhale. "That motherfucking asshole."

"I mean, he's not entirely wrong…I didn't realize that video would ever be shown anywhere but their website, and the demographic for their customers is like eighty percent women. I just didn't think—"

Which is exactly what Ford had accused me of.

Taryn moved off the bed. "Who hasn't blundered something that accidently made its way to the internet? He's being a dick."

My shoulder lifted in a shrug. "Maybe it *is* time for me to grow up. Maybe me chasing this dream of the Hollow is selfish, and I should move out." Which would mean I had to leave Rose Ridge. There was no way to have both in Dad's world—that's what he'd always told me. Ford was telling me to give up my dream, but what he meant was that I needed to grow up and leave Rose Ridge altogether.

"Royce, you've wanted to run the Hollow since you could walk. If you give up on that, I will knock your kneecaps out."

"Violent, T."

She walked over to my closet and began pulling out various items of clothing. "Sorry, sometimes the club stuff rubs off on me. I have all sorts of violent thoughts throughout the day. Especially toward men, they really are the worst."

I got off my bed and began sorting the different things she was tossing on the floor. Black dress. A corset and heels. A long dress that had a high slit.

"They are…well, except Dad. What are you looking for?"

She glanced over at me and smiled. "An outfit for you to wear. You need a girls' night."

"Who is even around to do that?"

"Nova, Ellie, and me." She held out a dress and inspected it. "I know you're older than us, but not by much. Go get changed. We're taking you out dancing."

"Nova is back in town?" Connor's little sister had left Rose Ridge, and as far as I knew she was in college up near New York, but that was all from what Taryn had told me.

"Wait, where did this dress come from?" The dress she'd picked was gorgeous. It was a deep purple, almost black, with a low bust. The skirt was short and would be enough to cover my ass, but I'd pair it with netted stockings.

My little sister clicked her tongue. "It might have been sent to me from one of the brand deals I got. It's way too long for me."

No, it wasn't.

"T…" My throat clogged up. My sister knew I didn't make the kind of money that she did, and I rarely bought myself anything new unless I'd thrifted it. Taryn snuck surprises into my wardrobe all the time, and I never failed to catch her.

"Do you think Dad will get pissed if we go to the strip club in Pyle?" Taryn asked, ignoring my attention to her generous gift.

She didn't like fessing up to always taking care of me.

"Dad will literally have a heart attack," I assured her. There was no way I was getting into even more of a mess than the one I'd unintentionally created. Besides, I had made a deal with him all those years ago, and I didn't want to break my end of things.

Taryn rolled her eyes. "Fine. Then let's go to the Hollow."

My voice came out too high as I tossed my hand out. "Where I work?"

My sister came out of my closet with her own dress. "Oh, come on. When is the last time you actually got to enjoy one of those bands and dance?"

My mouth parted, then shut. It had been years.

"Fine, but if Rodney is there, we don't make a scene. It's one of my rare nights off, and I don't want to draw attention to the fact that I'm there."

"I fear that might not be possible due to the dress, my love, but we'll hide you."

With that, I followed my sister into the bathroom.

Ellie Ryan was a fantastic dancer.

We all knew this, but we assumed her abilities were limited to ballet. But no, the girl could draw a crowd, and somehow even make the rest of us look good while doing it. I could dance, but mostly that meant I moved around or jumped in place. The band playing was incredible, with a rockier, folk vibe.

We'd been dancing for well over an hour and finally taken refuge at the bar, ordering some drinks. Charlie slid my favorite mocktail in front of me, and I was grateful because adding alcohol to my already fucked-up scenario wasn't a good idea.

"Royce, it wasn't even the company who posted the original." Nova turned her phone around to show me. She'd had her eyes on her phone ever since I had spilled the drama around Ford's freak-out, and my accidental popularity. The video now had well over a million views, and while most of the comments were disgusting, there were quite a few in defense of me, saying this was obviously leaked from the company's page, which I didn't think was true until Nova just proved it.

"So who posted it?"

Nova's hair was lighter growing up, but now it was dark, long, and sleek, which made her look almost exactly like her mother, Penelope. She turned her phone back around. "Probably some unknown user or something."

Connor's little sister had always been like an extra sister to me, and while I didn't harbor any anger toward her brother, it worried me that she harbored it toward me. Throughout the years, while Taryn would hang out with her, and they'd invite me, I would hang back. But now, it had been well over six years, there was no reason to keep worrying. As far as I knew, Connor had moved on as well and was happy with his life wherever he ended up. It wasn't like I hadn't asked about Connor, or tried contacting him but the answer was always the same. Which was that he was doing great, but moved around a lot and work kept him busy.

Ellie sipped her Lemon Drop and then leaned in. "I know Ford is super stressed about work. By the way, he's the one in charge. I didn't want to say anything at that dinner, but it's like *his* company. But I bet he is being a dick because he's stressed." Her focus was on her glass as she added, "That or he has a crush on you."

I nearly choked on my drink. "I can promise you, he does not."

Finding out that he owned the company made my little outburst at dinner even more embarrassing.

Nova tipped her head back, taking a generous sip, and then blurted, "Connor once told me that he hated that Ford called you Rose. Said it seemed flirty to him."

"He still has the Christmas card he tried to give you all those years ago. You left it on the side table and didn't even open it." Ellie added with a lick of her tongue over the rim of her glass.

My mind was a blurred mess when I attempted to remember that night.

"I'm sure I took it with me." I tried to argue and defend myself against something that made me sound so unkind. Perhaps it ended up with all my other personal items that were still at Connor's house. I'd never gotten my box of things from him, and it was still bothering me that he hadn't even had the decency to give me my stuff back. So much time had passed that I was now way too embarrassed to bug Penelope or Nova about going over there to look around. Surely, they'd just tossed it all.

My sister reached over and grabbed my wrist, likely to get my attention over the loud music. "Whatever happened to that guy you were sort of seeing?"

"Julian?"

Her blue eyes sparkled under the lights. "Yeah, him. Are you guys still casual or what's going on there?"

Ellie and Nova both watched me from over the rim of their drinks. I felt strange about explaining my dating life in front of them. Not that I owed them anything, but I used to date Nova's older brother, and now with Ellie's older brother I was…what? Fighting? My mind threw me back to being pulled flush against his chest, and how his hand wrapped inside my back pocket. In the moment I was seething angry, but there was no denying that I'd tugged that moment out and replayed it more times than I cared to admit.

Dipping my chin, I tried to brush past the subject of Julian. "Still just casual."

The truth was Julian was fun when he wanted to be, and I enjoyed that side of him. He had too many opinions for my liking, at least where motorcycle clubs were concerned. I argued with him once about why I didn't think biker clubs were bad, and he'd spent an hour outlining why they were a danger to society. He didn't agree with what my father did, and he'd slighted half of everyone I knew in his monologue. It wasn't going anywhere, but when I got lonely and he wanted to go out, I'd accept.

Taryn gave Ellie a look, and something silent passed between the two of them. "Well, either way, I think Ford needs to be taken down a notch."

Ellie smiled. "He absolutely does. He's been in a funk forever."

"What did you have in mind?" I asked, while glancing up the stairs leading past the bar. Rodney would typically be scaling those to check on things, but I hadn't seen him all night. Nick waved at me from his spot above though, and I gave him a small wave in return.

Ellie grabbed her small clutch. "Someone else drive, but we're headed to my house. I have the best idea ever."

SEVEN
FORD

THIS WAS SUCH A BAD IDEA.

I knew it was, but fuck, I needed to do something to punish myself for what I had said last week when Killian told me to stay away from Royce. The small, single fuck I let him see I had regarding his daughter was not just humiliating, it was dangerous. I had been down this path before, the one where I stared at her for too long. Or I drew her face from sheer memory in my sketchpads, which were later discovered by my own parents.

If anyone knew how deep my past obsession really went, they'd knock me over the head and toss me into the bay. I was a sick fuck who had gripped my cock three different times throughout the week to the video of Royce in that outfit.

Thick ropes of cum had coated my shower wall, my comforter, and a goddamn sock. Like I was fifteen years old again, getting hard after seeing her in her first bikini.

I had to do this.

"Hi, Fordy. My gawwwwd I was so excited when you texted me." Jasmine popped her gum while sliding into the chair across from me.

Shit, was I supposed to pull it out for her?

I didn't want to date women, I wanted to fuck them, but I hadn't been successful in even doing that in years. Even after seeing Royce at the movies with the cropped-hair guy, I tried to fuck someone, but I ended up kicking her out of my room at the club. I needed to stop this fucking obsession and the only way to do it was to kill it.

Jasmine was someone who had come by the club a few times and had dry humped my leg while we sat on the couch. I had let her, and she thought it would turn into more because I wasn't telling her no. It ended the second Killian came into the room. No fucking clue why, but the man had a way of killing any desire to be seen with women romantically.

"I had the dirtiest dream last night, Fordy, do you want to hear it?" Jasmine touched her toe to my calf under the table. I glanced around the room to see if our waiter was on his way, but he was still a few tables over.

"Sure."

Jasmine had chocolate tresses that hung down in fake extensions, past her tits. Her eyes were wide and rimmed with fake lashes that were a little too long, and she was incessantly chewing gum. We were about to eat lunch, for fuck's sake, and she was chewing gum.

"Then you were there and you went down on me and I'm telling you it was the best orgasm I ever had."

"In the dream?" I clarified because what the fuck was she talking about? We'd never fucked or even come close to it.

She continued chatting, but my phone chimed with a text.

> Mom: Do you have Gus at your place?

I shot back a reply quickly.

> Me: No, why?

> Mom: I can't find him anywhere. Ellie says she saw him last night, but that was when she accidently...never mind.

My brows furrowed as Jasmine mentioned what my tongue did to her clit in her dream.

Me: Ellie accidently what?

Mom: …It seems Ellie and the girls played a prank on you.

Confusion muddled my mind as I tried to work out what that meant.

"Are you listening, Ford?" Jasmine asked, finally dropping the goddamn *y* at the end of my name.

The waiter arrived next to us, but I was still trying to understand what happened.

Ellie: For the record, you deserved it.

"Good afternoon, can I start you out with some drinks or appetizers?"

Jasmine spoke up, "Yes, I want a mimosa and we'll take the cheese platter."

Me: Deserved what?

"And for you, sir?" the waiter asked but my focus was still on my phone.

Ellie: Me helping Royce kidnap your cat.

I slid out of the seat, which made the waiter step to the side in surprise. I tossed down a fifty-dollar bill on the table. "Sorry about this, but I have to go."

"Are you joking me?" Jasmine shrieked while I walked out of the restaurant.

Me: I need Royce Quinn's cell phone number.

I was currently pacing my living room. I couldn't just drive to her house because Killian was already pissed about how I treated her last week. He was also under the delusion that I liked her or wanted to date her. Which, now I could prove to him wasn't true because I had gone on a date.

Well, fuck, I bailed on a date but still.

Rook: You haven't talked to her about the video yet?

Me: I did, days ago. She apparently stole my cat as a way of responding.

To draw her out, my initial impulse was to torch the Hollow, but even I knew that was a little too unhinged.

Rook: I'm laughing my ass off. Wish you could see it.

Me: Very fucking funny. Now, her number, please.

Rook: Jesus, Ford. Get a grip, it's just Gus, it's not like Royce did him any harm. Here you go- 804-557-9090

Me: Thanks, I owe you one.

Rook: Oh, I know, and I fully plan on collecting.

I saved her number in my phone and ignored Rook's text about cashing in on me owing him, before punching out a message.

Me: Where is my cat?

I could force her to meet me at the club, or I could tell her to come here to my house. I glanced around and heard Johnson's voice in my head about how ugly my house was. No, that wouldn't work.

Pain in My Fucking Ass: Who is this?

Me: Very funny. Where is he?

Pain in My Fucking Ass: No idea

What if she had gone into town and wanted to buy Gus treats at the pet store? For all I knew, she planned on keeping my cat. Maybe I should go there and check.

Me: Do you think I'm playing? Because if so, then perhaps I need to encourage our club to visit the Hollow tonight, full force. Rodney wouldn't mind, would he?

The dots on the screen jumped around a few times before she finally replied.

Pain in My Fucking Ass: Fine. I'll drive him back to your parents' house and hand him off to Ellie.

Me: Considering she proved last night that she can't be trusted, I don't think so.

More dots appeared and disappeared, but I smiled knowing I had her. I could let her drive to my parents and call it good, but I wasn't about to let her out of this without having to face me first.

Pain in My Fucking Ass: Dad and Mom are headed over to Uncle Jameson and Aunt Penny's. Should lessen the chance of your death if you want to come over and pick up your son.

Such a fucking brat, and yet I had a smile on my face I couldn't seem to shake.

Me: I'll be there in twenty minutes.

Pain in My Fucking Ass: Wait...

Me: What?

Pain in My Fucking Ass: Will you please bring me a vanilla latte from the Drip?

Me: After you literally stole my cat? No, Royce, I'm not bringing you a latte.

True to her word, Killian's truck was gone when I arrived, which would mean he and Laura were gone. I didn't see Taryn's bike either, so it seemed it was just Royce who was home. I had driven my truck, with Gus's carrier sitting next to me in the passenger seat. Right as I made it to her front door, I got a new text from her.

Pain in My Fucking Ass: Just come up, the code is 6943. I can't move, otherwise I'd come downstairs.

Did that mean she was hurt? I didn't like the idea of her being hurt any more than I liked her stealing my cat, but I pushed down the feeling so I could remain unfazed.

I tried the code, entering the house cautiously. The house I remembered from being a kid and teen had remained the same. The entryway had a small alcove for shoes and coats, beyond it was the spacious living room and kitchen, separated by an intricate arch. An open dining space connected to the living room, which then wound back to the kitchen.

I edged toward the stairs which would lead to the second floor.

Once my feet hit the landing, I winced the smallest bit because I hadn't slipped out of my boots. I wasn't sure if that would matter and couldn't remember the Quinn's policy on shoes in the house, so I kept walking. Killian and Laura's room was on the opposite side of the house from Taryn and Royce's. While the girls didn't share a room, they shared a bathroom which connected their bedrooms.

Nervous to reveal that I knew exactly which room belonged to Royce because I had it burned into memory, I lightly knocked on her white door.

"Come in!"

Wrapping my hand around the gold knob, I pushed inside and then came to an abrupt stop. Royce was wearing a set of thin pajamas while lounging on her bed. The top of her pajama set dipped enough that her cleavage was outlined by the tiny lace of the neckline. Her shorts were practically underwear for how high on her thighs they went. She had so much skin showing, my mouth might have dropped open.

"He's been sleeping for a while. I couldn't bring myself to move him." She stroked the top of Gus's head, who was curled in her lap. How the fuck had I stooped low enough in life that I'd become jealous of my own cat?

Her eyes sparkled as she took in what was in my left hand. "You brought me a latte!"

Yes, and I was ashamed that I had. She didn't deserve it, and I was only rewarding bad behavior.

I stepped closer, handing off the latte, ignoring when our fingers brushed. The heat curling in my stomach made me feel like a fucking teenager. I stretched my hand while taking a few steps back. "Well, you wouldn't be stuck there if you hadn't stolen an animal that doesn't belong to you."

Her pink mouth covered the small hole in the plastic latte lid while she took a generous sip.

"I wish my parents had let us have one growing up."

To avoid staring down her thin shirt, I sat down on the edge of her bed. I watched as she continued to run her fingers over my cat's fur, and that's when I realized he was purring, as if this was the happiest he'd been in a long time. I liked that he was purring, and I liked even more that she had made him so content.

"You never had a pet?" Why was I indulging this?

"No. We had talked about it a bunch of times, but it never happened. We would always go to your house, Connor's, or Rook's if we got an itch to play with animals. It always seemed to make Taryn and me happy enough that when we got home, we didn't bring it up again. But this is nice. You must have loved having pets as a kid."

I had loved it. We had Maxwell, until he passed, but even while he was alive, Ellie had her dachshund, Millie, and a hamster. I had Gus, along with a turtle and a guinea pig.

"Well, you're an adult now."

Royce finally lifted her head, so I had those navy eyes to stare into. "You think I should get one? I need to find a place to live first, and make sure they allow pets."

"Didn't realize you had plans to move out." If I remembered correctly, she had to live at home unless she agreed to leave the city. Did that mean she was finally going? That's what I wanted, right? Why did my chest feel so tight then?

She lifted her shoulder, which made the strap keeping her top up seem incredibly thin. Shit, her tits were too big for that measly amount of fabric to be considered a pajama top. It only made me think of the video she'd done for that underwear ad, and all the bullshit I had said to her a few days prior.

"I've been contacted by a few modeling agencies since that video went viral. I could look into that, see if I can make some real money with it."

My throat swelled with the need to apologize, but now I was frustrated too.

"Thought you wanted your dream at the Hollow?"

Gus stretched his front paws out, as if he were waking up. Part of me didn't want him to, because this seemed to be the longest conversation I'd ever had with Royce Quinn that didn't involve arguing or fighting.

She drug her fingers over Gus's head again. "The Hollow will always be my dream, but I have a gut feeling it's not going to work out. Rodney has too much power, and I feel like he's planning something. But, let's say I got it, I'm not sure it'll pay for my own place outside of Rose Ridge. Taryn makes a real living off what she does, and if she can do it, then maybe I can too. If they give me a script and tell me what they want me to wear...I don't see the harm."

The fucking harm was that people would see her body, but aside from my own issues, both she and Taryn were linked to Killian, which meant they were linked to the club. While it wouldn't be easy to connect Taryn to the club, because of Royce's tattoo, there was no undoing her connection to it. If I brought that up, we'd just argue again, so I kept my mouth shut.

"Do you have any idea how much of a salary Rodney makes from the Hollow?"

Her brows dipped, which drew my attention to her freckles. Which unfortunately took me back to a memory of one summer when we were at camp.

"Count how many freckles I have on my back, Ford. I told Connor, if I have more than him, then he owes me his dessert after dinner." She wore a pink swimsuit that had strings tied in the back, showing most of her back, which I had already been staring at. Which was why I didn't need to count, I already knew exactly how many she had.

She had five more than last summer.

"When my mom was there, she barely made ends meet."

My fingers itched to pet my cat, but only because I missed Gus. At least that's what I was telling myself. My eyes were on her face, but my fingers were idly stroking through soft fur, edging closer to where hers were. They were also itching dangerously close to the apex of her thighs where her shorts had ridden up indecently high. She was bare from the video I'd seen and how narrow the underwear she wore was, but even now, I could see the outline of her pussy that pressed against the thin fabric of her shorts.

"She was donating almost all of her paycheck to a nonprofit that helped the elderly. If I remember from reading over the reports, she also gave a chunk to the bartender. She didn't need the job, so your dad was fine with her only taking a portion home. It had something to do with her roots and how she started with the Hollow. Rodney clears over seventy-five thousand a year."

Royce froze with her fingers nearly touching mine, her mouth gaping. "What did you just say?"

I was about to repeat myself, but she straightened, which made her tank top dip lower, and my cock swell inside my jeans.

"I do the books, I don't see his salary, but I see how much the club makes…it doesn't make enough a year for him to make that."

I contemplated telling her all of it, that we'd been watching Rodney for a while now. That Bernie had been concerned that his manager was stealing from him, and reported him to the police. Our contacts in the department told us the report was buried, so the club approached Bernie and offered to handle Rodney for him, and in turn he agreed to sell to us when he was ready. Royce wasn't doing the real books. She was likely seeing whatever Rodney wanted her to, the rest he was stealing from Bernie. If I trusted her at all, I'd tell her.

No, she'd tell Taryn. Possibly Nova and Ellie. "Rose, I hate to say this, but Rodney shows you only what he wants you to see, and I have a feeling he's been doing that for a while."

"But…how—" she trailed off, but her fingers had sunk back into Gus's fur, grazing mine. My breath hitched, which made me instinctually pull back out of fear that she'd pull away first.

It was self-preservation.

I could see her mind was still reeling, her eyes were unfocused off to the side as if she could do all the math in her head, finding where that extra money might have gone.

I needed to apologize for the other night. The words burned my tongue, but right as my mouth parted, someone slammed the door shut below us.

Feet hit the stairs right as someone yelled, "Why is Ford's truck here?"

Royce stared at the open door like it might grow fangs and detach, then she glanced at me as panic surged her forward. "It was supposed to be a joke because you hurt my feelings."

My brows fell inward as I tried to work it out, but right as I did,

Killian filled the doorway. He was wearing shorts, running shoes, and a hoodie with his chest heaving.

"Ford, what the fuck are you doing in my daughter's room while she's in her underwear?"

I swiftly got up from the bed, my mind racing as to what the fuck had just happened. But the next person to barrel through the front door helped clear it up.

"Dad is on his way back, this was genius, Royce—Dad's going to kill him, I came back as soon as I could, so I didn't miss the show!" Taryn yelled while quickly scaling the steps and sliding to a stop outside Royce's door.

"Oh wow, he's…death stare. Okay, this is actually kinda awkward." Taryn's voice trailed off as her gaze bounced around from her dad to me, then to her sister.

My jaw hurt from how hard I was gritting my teeth, but if I opened my mouth, I'd yell at the woman in front of me who had somehow pulled out that drawer in my heart…

Royce set her coffee on the side table before getting to her feet. "Dad, I can explain this."

Killian moved, and there was no way I was going to fight him in his own home in front of his daughters, so whatever he needed to do to me, I'd allow it. Even being president of the club wasn't enough to combat a father's need to protect his daughter. I knew this, and with Killian that need was amplified by about a thousand percent.

His fist landed against my jaw, making my head snap to the side and blood well up in my mouth.

"No! *OhmyGodwhatIhavedone?*" Royce stammered all in one sentence before shifting around the room, trying to get between her father and me. "Dad, I stole his cat. I told him to come over!"

She'd set me up knowing this would be the outcome.

Why was it that instead of hating her, I had a pride swelling in my chest?

Killian punched me again and then gripped me by the back of the cut and drug me out into the hall. Taryn was quick to move to the side as I tried to get my feet under me.

"You're in your fucking underwear, Royce. I told you that men from the club were completely off-limits. These were the conditions you agreed to when you refused to leave Rose Ridge. I told you this place wasn't safe anymore. I told you it didn't have to be college, but it had to be something. Anything to get away from here, and you agreed. You agreed to all of my terms."

This view I had where I was essentially dragged behind Killian allowed me the perfect view of Royce running down the stairs after us, clutching Gus to her chest. Her tits bounced like in the video, and for once I didn't look away, and I didn't try to hide it. I watched, and I smiled.

"I'm in my pajamas!"

Killian laughed sardonically. "Royce, you've created enough of an issue for me, if you could put on some fucking clothes and keep them on, that would be helpful."

"You don't get to treat me like I'm a child. I may have agreed to your terms after you forced my boyfriend to propose to me, by the way!" Royce shrieked at Killian who had finally released me.

"I get to treat you how I see fit. I'm your father, and this is not a normal family or a normal situation. You can't simply rebel and come out unscathed. You're going to get yourself killed."

"What is going on here?" Laura walked in through the kitchen, holding a paper bag of groceries.

Taryn pointed. "Ford devastated Royce, she was a wreck when I found her."

Laura let out a small gasp while cutting her gaze to Royce.

"It wasn't that serious, T."

Her younger sister made some sort of sound. "You were in the onesie with the heated battery pack, Royce. You weren't even searching for bands on Tik Tok, you were watching funny pet videos."

"I got him back by stealing Gus…and not telling him that Dad would be home within minutes," Royce clarified quickly as if she wanted to move on from what her sister had revealed, with a slight flush to her neck and face. Apparently, her sobbing with a blanket onesie was a big deal.

Gus was still purring as I finally gathered myself enough to swipe at the blood on my lip.

Laura set her bag on the counter and moved to the sink, coming back with a wet rag. "And who did this to you, Ford?"

I didn't respond, so Taryn decided to. "Dad punched him twice then drug him down here by the back of the cut."

Laura's blue eyes scanned my face, her brow puckered the smallest bit, and then she released another sigh as she dabbed at my lip. "Need I remind you, Killian, that you are Ford's godfather?"

"Daisy, don't start. He was in Royce's room while she was in her—"

"Pajamas?" Laura cut him off with a raised brow. The two stood staring at one another in a silent battle. I took that as my cue to leave.

"Can I take him?" I held my hands out for my cat, and Royce handed him over with a guilty expression.

"Ford, we'll talk about this later." Killian said softly, still staring at his wife.

I shook my head, my jaw was bruised as shit, and I didn't want to look at him. "You said everything that needed to be said, Killian. I heard you loud and clear." With Gus in my arms, I didn't look back as I exited the house and descended the porch steps.

I was nearly to my truck when the door opened, and someone's feet moved behind me. Taryn caught up to me with her arms crossed over her chest.

"My sister feels guilty about this, but you should know it was my idea."

Once I secured Gus into his carrier, I shut the passenger side door and made my way around the front.

She wanted a reply, and I knew she was nervous about how this would impact poor Royce who had a heart of gold and a conscience that couldn't bear the thought of injustice. I used to love that about her, but now it was a bit insufferable. "Understood."

"You going to keep being a dick to her?"

My eyes slid up, taking in what she was wearing for the first time, and then I smirked while closing the distance between us. "You going to explain to her why you're wearing that?" I flicked my hand toward the thick, black sweatshirt she wore.

Her face flushed pink as she took a step back.

"Don't go to war with me, wolf cub, and I won't bring war to you."

Her mouth twisted to the side before she tucked her arms in close. "You made her cry. I took that seriously. I can't see her like that over you anymore."

"What do you mean anymore? Royce and I haven't interacted in years."

Taryn glanced to the side, "Royce has always..." She trailed off. "Never mind, I'm just protective of her."

I was getting distracted, and I didn't need to know anything more intimate about the Quinn family while my jaw still ached and my pride seemed completely eviscerated. With my hand on the door handle, I met her gaze. "Your sister declared war with me a long time ago. You want me to be nicer, then she's the one who needs to wave the white flag."

EIGHT
ROYCE

Age Fifteen

The Christmas party was beautiful.

The Ryans always knew how to dress up their tree and decorate their home in such a way that it made me feel like we were in a storybook. Covered in gold and white ribbons, bulbs, and twinkle lights, the tree had to be fifteen to twenty feet tall. With it set against the huge window, we could watch as the snow fell.

It would have been perfect if Ford Ryan weren't attending. He'd told me I should try letting Connor breathe once in a while at the start of Christmas break. Then, when I saw him again, he had touched my hair, and when I asked him why, he told me because it looked fake.

I'd harbored a small crush on him since we were nine years old, after the one Christmas where he'd kissed me on the cheek. I kept thinking I could convince him to do it again. So, year after year, I'd make a total fool of myself trying to get his attention. I'd do just about anything to have him look at me. Which included sleepovers with Ellie, even though she was Taryn's friend. I had also asked his mom if she'd let me come over and clean the house for a few bucks. I never needed the money; I just wanted to see Ford.

By the time I was thirteen, I finally got over the crush and let him go then fell headfirst in love with Connor. Which was infuriating because as soon as I released my crush on Ford, he started paying attention to me. He was always watching me, always trying to sit next to me in the car if we were going somewhere, but never talked to me. He always snuck up to see what Ellie and I were doing, and when I hung around Connor, he acted like I had the plague.

Now at fifteen, I just wanted him to disappear because he was so cruel to me.

He walked into the living room wearing a black turtleneck and tan pants. It was the nicest I had ever seen him dressed. He held a card to his chest while he nervously watched the group. Connor had made a joke that I laughed at, then Rook said something funny. Ryle was off playing with Nova or Ellie, and Taryn was trying to prank Connor as usual. Ford held the card so tightly we all made fun of him, saying it had to be his letter to Santa.

Then he extended his arm to me. The card said "Rose" across the front.

Rook and Connor watched us, even going as far as to make kissing sounds. Ford's face was pink, and I realized that was my moment of vindication. I didn't take the letter from his hand.

I let it hang there until Connor barked out a laugh and Ford dropped it to the table next to me. Turning my back on him, I flicked my hair over my shoulder and began laughing with Rook and Connor once more. When I finally glanced back at Ford, the card was gone, and so was he.

The memory of when I was fifteen played in my mind while I wrapped the basket in cellophane. A painful jolt rattled my heart as I combed back through the memory. The heartbroken look on Ford's face, the way his hand had extended, but shook. I couldn't bring that version of things and line it up next to the pain he'd caused me back then. I had felt so justified in how I snubbed him.

Perhaps he didn't care, but maybe he did. Maybe he'd clung to how I treated him that Christmas all these years and used it as a way to punish me. I let out a heavy sigh, breathing through my nose as I added a dark green bow to tie off the crinkly plastic.

Once I finished, I stepped back to inspect it. Ford was probably going to hate it, and not even open it, but I had to do something to apologize for what happened. It had been two days, and I hadn't seen or heard from Ford. Which was fairly normal, since we barely ran in the same circles, but for some reason ever since this thing with Rodney happened, it felt like I was seeing Ford all the time.

Not seeing him suddenly felt unsettling.

Butterflies swarmed my stomach as I paced my bedroom. What if he didn't want to see me, or he laughed in my face? What if he tossed it in the garbage?

Worrying my lip while staring longingly at the gifts secured inside the gift wrap would not magically solve this. I had to try.

My phone pinged with a text, drawing my attention.

> Dad: Can I talk to you, honey? I'm in the garage if you have a second.

We also hadn't really talked in two days. He was at the club, and when he wasn't, he was on a ride or off somewhere. I was mad at how he'd handled everything, even though I was the one to set it up…he didn't have to punch Ford. I never thought he'd hurt him. Then there were things he'd said to me that had dug a hole and planted a seed of bitterness in my heart.

But I loved my dad, and I didn't want this wedge between us.

After pulling on a hoodie and jeans, I ventured toward the garage.

When I opened the side door, I heard a basketball game playing on his television while Dad was half inside the hood of the older Chevy that he'd been restoring. My gaze flicked up to the wall, where several framed photos hung. Shaded images with outlined drawings, made up of erased material. It was like reverse art, and I loved it. I couldn't draw, so I tried doing what my dad did with shading paper only to erase designs into them, mine never turned out like his did. His were beautiful. The one he did of my mother was my favorite.

Running my finger along the gold paint of the car, I dropped to my elbows. "How's it coming?"

Dad lifted his head, his green eyes so severe and sad as he took me in.

"About as well as it was the last time you popped in."

So not super far. "How come you aren't over at the club?"

All my life, Dad had been busy with the club.

He set the socket wrench next to him and then placed his palms on the edge of the frame of the car.

"Just decided to hang here today and work on this."

I watched him work while my brain wrangled that response into something coherent. But I couldn't make it make sense. "But it's Friday. You always have church on Friday."

I knew this because the last Friday I had been at the club, I'd had my ass chewed by Ford for innocently showing up in a viral video. Something that was still on the internet, and I could not figure out why. I'd reported it and asked others to, but it was still up.

My father wouldn't look up from the engine as he continued to work. Eventually, he cleared his throat and changed the subject. "Look, honey. I wanted to say I'm sorry for what I said to you. It was wrong and fucked-up. You aren't causing me problems. I was just caught off guard by him being in your room. I know Ford isn't a bad guy, but I can't stand the idea of you being with a guy from the club."

I shook my head, feeling my throat swell with emotion. "You were right. I wore that pajama set on purpose. I wanted to get under Ford's skin, but we're not dating or anything like that, so you don't have to worry."

My dad let out a small laugh while shaking his head. "Think you've been under Ford's skin for a while, honey."

I didn't know what he meant by that, but I kept going. "I know what I agreed to when I was eighteen, Dad. But Max never came…isn't there some way we can negotiate some freedoms? Besides, I'm older now. Most of your fear was over the fact that I was just eighteen."

My father tilted his head back, searching the ceiling. "Your mother told me the same thing. However, the video you showed up in has changed the situation."

"Changed it how? I know it's never okay to draw attention to the club…I get that, and I know I'm your daughter, and you don't want anyone to be able to target me—"

"No, honey…it's this Max thing. That video is essentially a map for him to follow, and a red flag being waved in front of a bull. Whoever released it to the public platforms knew that. I have my suspicions that they're working with Max and making a play for us. So, I want you here now more than ever."

We sank into the chairs in front of the sixty-inch flat-screen, while Dad let out another heavy sigh. Meanwhile, I let out a shuddery breath that felt more like a sob which was lodged in my throat. Just when I thought my cage had broadened enough to slip outside of, the door slammed shut.

"I can't risk anything happening to you, Royce."

"So, if I leave and run around like Taryn, then I can move out and lose the detail of Stone Riders who follow me everywhere, but if I want to live anywhere within Rose Ridge alone, I can't?"

Dad reached over and pulled my hand into his. "Max can't find you out there, baby. It's like finding a needle in a haystack. Here, you're a pin on a billboard, he can simply yank out whenever he wants."

"But what if he never comes? I'm stuck in this limbo?"

He paused, considering my words until he pulled back and slapped his thighs. "Okay, how about a compromise?"

"I'm listening."

Dad's green gaze locked on mine, "You find someone who can keep you as safe as I would, then you're free to leave."

I was chronically single, so this seemed like a losing opportunity for me. "I mean, there's Julian, but we're really not dating, it's casual."

My father's nose scrunched in disgust. "Julian won't keep you safe, honey. He's absolutely not an option."

Okay. I withheld the urge to roll my eyes. "Then who would meet your standards, Dad?"

He stared off to the side for a long time until he sighed. "I'll figure this out. Just give me some time."

Great. That didn't sound cryptic at all.

Dad stood and pressed a kiss to the top of my head. "Love you, honey. Thank you for being willing to listen, it makes me feel better knowing you're safe."

My heart melted like it did when I was a little girl and he'd pick me up and place me on the back of his bike. We used to ride all over the property, and he'd give me and Taryn turns, returning only to leave again because we begged him to. He built us Barbie houses, sewed our ripped stuffed animals, painted our nails as little girls, and best of all, he treated our mom like she was a queen. Taryn and I both grew up seeing true love in real life, and now that I was older, I realized how rare of a gift that was. My dad was the best, so really, this request he had wasn't that big. I'd do this for him, and I would find a way to withstand whatever he came up with for this compromise.

"Can we do karaoke tonight?"

My Dad hung his head, but I didn't miss the smile that lit up his face. "Guess it has been a while since we've done that."

Hope and excitement lit me up. "Mom would love it. She's still sort of mad at you for hitting Ford."

"She's mad at me for more than that."

I knew that but didn't want to say anything about it. She was pissed at Dad for coming down so hard on me about what I was wearing.

"So you'll do it?" I brought my hands together excitedly.

Dad pulled me into his side. "Yeah, I'll do it."

Growing up, our mom would throw the best karaoke nights. We'd have a themed dinner and ambiance. A few times we were able to even go to the Hollow for our fun, using the stage. That was ages ago though. Now I was more than happy with gathering in our living room with the lights dimmed, fresh margaritas made up, and cozy pajamas.

"Okay, which decade are we singing tonight?" I asked.

Taryn was wearing an oversized tshirt with sweats and thick socks. "I vote for early 90's pop. Like Brittany Spears and Christina."

"Oooh, that's a great era." Mom yelled from the kitchen.

Dad was drinking a beer while reclining on the couch, wearing his sweats.

"When was the last time we were all together like this?" I asked, sifting through songs on the karaoke machine.

Taryn glanced up at me briefly before lowering her gaze back to the song choices. "Well, we're growing up, Royce. It's natural for us to be apart sometimes."

I didn't like that. It made me realize how lonely I truly was. I missed my sister, but aside from that, I missed my family. Our unit had always been tight growing up. Dad and Mom created this epic childhood for us, and even with Dad leading the Stone Riders, it only enhanced our connection. My family was everything to me, and feeling them grow distant was the worst.

"I know, I just miss everyone."

Dad watched us intently before saying, "We'll always be here, you know that. I honestly hope neither of you ever move out, but when you do, we'll be here."

Mom walked in holding two frozen margaritas.

"I remember when you girls were little and you asked to wear those matching dresses. Royce you'd always pick pink, and Taryn you always wanted purple."

Dad joined in with a smile. "And those shoes, you both always had to have those shoes with the little heels."

Taryn laughed. "Mine always had to have gems on them. I liked having rings too for when I held the microphone."

"Until mom bedazzled our microphone's." I added with my own laugh.

Abandoning the machine, I curled into the couch. Mom handed me a glass which I accepted and sipped from. Taryn remained by the mantel, where we'd placed the karaoke machine on top of a side table. She flipped through a few songs while holding her microphone.

"How about we promise to do a family karaoke night once a month no matter where we go, or move to?" My little sister suggested.

Mom and Dad searched the space between us. "What if one of you moves out of state?"

"Right now I don't think that's going to happen, at least not for me." Taryn said then looked at me.

I shook my head. "Not me either." Not that I had any prospects at all of moving anywhere, which again brought on a deep sense of sorrow. I just wanted to stay in Rose Ridge with my family, and never lose this feeling.

"Well, then let's plan on it. Once a month, karaoke." Mom promised.

I looked over at my Dad who had pulled my Mom under his arm. "Only if dad promises to sing every time."

He groaned, but Taryn pointed at him. "Yes, he has to promise!"

We all laughed before the first song was queued up and my little sister broke into a ballad.

My face hurt from smiling, and after all the laughter, I couldn't remember the last time I had so much fun with my family, and it made me completely forget all about Rodney, the Hollow and best of all, my guilt over Ford.

NINE
ROYCE

ATTACHED IMAGE

Nerves attacked my stomach as I bit my thumbnail. Her not replying was a reply within itself.

My fingers flew over the screen as I replied.

Taryn: ....

Me: WHAT MESSAGE?

Taryn: Just that you care, sis.

Me: What's wrong with caring?

Taryn: Nothing…it's just, you used to care a lot about him, and I'm worried what it could lead to if he doesn't respond the way you want him to.

Me: I was a kid, T…I'm not still into him or anything.

Taryn: Good. Then, yeah, give him the basket. I think that's a good idea. You have a big heart, sis, I just want to be sure it's never taken advantage of.

Me: 🩶

It was the day following our karaoke night, and the guilt over Dad hitting Ford had eaten me up. I rode my bike toward the new part of town and slowed once I got to the flashy sign revealing the up-and-coming neighborhood. I wasn't sure where Ford was exactly, but I planned to ride around until I found him. A myriad of vehicles lined the narrow street, while a massive industrial garbage bin sat against the curb, totally in the way. Further down was a flatbed truck loaded with heavy machinery.

The new neighborhood had three homes already complete with FOR SALE signs out front, and the rest of the lots were either dirt or concrete with framing set up. Men milled about like little ants, all over the lots, each doing something different.

I had no idea how to find Ford in the mix, but I had a general idea of where to head.

The only open spot I could find to park where dirt wouldn't land all over my bike seat was near one of the completed houses, which was rather far from where all the movement was. A little walk wouldn't hurt. Sliding my helmet up, I set it on the seat and then began unwinding the bungee cables I'd wrapped around the basket to keep it on the back of my bike. I was sure I looked ridiculous riding around Rose Ridge, but I didn't really care.

Gathering the basket in my arms, I began walking down the paved road toward the largest mix of people. There was someone pointing, yelling, and seemingly directing people where to go. That had to be Ford.

Dirt floated in the air in a cloud, drifting in my direction, which made me rethink my outfit. I wore a pink cropped shirt that showed my midriff and my leather riding pants. My hair bounced against my back as I picked up my gait, trying to cover more ground. I was nearly to the center of all the commotion when someone whistled. I knew better than to turn my head, but I hoped it was a one-off. Another whistle joined in, and a person catcalled, then another. Suddenly there were machines cutting off, and men shouting salaciously as I walked.

I faltered, remembering there was a video of me on the internet, wearing almost nothing that men had been staring at for the past few days. Could these specific men have seen it? A lot of them were members of Dad's club. I had done my best to push the thoughts of that video away, ignoring it as if it were something I could pretend didn't happen. It wasn't just that making me want to curl into a tiny ball right there on the dirty asphalt, the red tainting my cheeks had to do with growing up around the club and dealing with the assholes there.

Ford was quick to assume that I didn't care if someone got hurt on my behalf, what he didn't know was how many times I hadn't reported being touched. There were at least ten different instances that I'd been touched, groped, or crowded into a corner at the club. I knew that if I had told my dad, he'd have killed them. The weight of their lives literally hung around my neck like a stone, and I felt completely silenced and forced into complacency because of it.

I walked around in a bubble because to others it was a faux confidence that they couldn't touch. It was my own version of armor, but it took time to erect that bubble around myself. In town, it was easier, but in a place like this…with all these men, I could hardly breathe, much less pretend.

My palms began to sweat, and nerves began snaking up my body, tightening around me like vines. The whistles grew louder, and there were a few of them that began walking toward me.

"Royce?" a gravelly voice pulled me from my thoughts, forcing my eyes up.

I let out a breath of relief as I took in the familiar stature thundering toward me.

Ford wore an expression that I assumed would be reserved for someone he wanted to kill. I thought perhaps it was because he was still mad at me, but the closer he got, the more his eyes softened and his brows relaxed.

"What are you doing here?"

A ball of emotion swelled in my throat as he gently held my elbow, guiding me away from the prying eyes.

"I…"

The whistling stopped, but one guy yelled over the rest, "Show me those pretty pink panties, baby."

I was going to throw up.

Ford shifted so that I was mostly blocked, and people could no longer see me. Which made me feel instantly better.

He yelled toward the man on the roof, "Jake, go pack your shit up. You're done."

The man groaned and yelled back, "For the whole fuckin' day?"

Ford's tattooed arm tensed as he shifted. "Permanently. Get the fuck off my jobsite."

Inhaling a quick breath, I started to argue, but we were suddenly walking faster. Tears gathered in the corners of my eyes as he gently tugged my elbow and led me to a small trailer that seemed to be his remote office. The sign next to it read, *Wild Rose Construction.*

Once inside with the door shut, I spun on him, one of the damn tears fell from my lash. "Don't fire him just because he catcalled me. I didn't mean to get anyone in trouble."

Ford ran one hand through his hair as he set down his phone on the desk with the other.

"You didn't get anyone in trouble, Royce."

"I literally just got that guy fired."

Ford eyed the basket in my arms before gritting his teeth. "He got himself fired."

"Ford…" I droned, annoyed that he wasn't saying what I knew he was thinking. Regardless of what he said, he blamed me for this.

He gestured toward the basket with his chin and leaned his butt against his desk.

"What's that?"

Lifting my arms, I made it so he could see more of the items inside the cellophane. "Uh…this is a gift basket."

"For me?" he asked, all gravel in his tone.

I caught something pass over his face that I hadn't expected. Excitement or curiosity, something other than disdain, which gave me courage to step closer.

"I was wondering if you'd like to make a truce. I was really hurt by what you said at the club that one night, which is why I—"

"Got my ass kicked by your pops," Ford filled in the rest of the sentence for me.

"I thought maybe he'd grumble and scare you off. I never assumed he'd actually hit you."

Ford lowered his face with a bit of a laugh. "Well, you weren't there for his lecture after I made you cry that night outside of the club. He basically told me to leave you alone and stop talking to you."

"Oh…"

The air grew warmer and silent as he watched me with a small smile gracing his handsome face. He really was striking. He was like one of those male models, posing in a dramatic scene that felt vulnerable and dreamy. The kind you didn't want to look away from for fear you'd forget how their jaw was carved or how the shape of their nose seemed to fit their face, or how that one piece of hair fell across their brow just so.

His question pulled me out of my thoughts. "So, can I have it?"

Jolting forward, I nearly tripped as I came back to the moment. "Right. Yes."

His hands came underneath the basket, covering mine, which reminded me of when they'd grazed each other while we had pet Gus. Our eyes met, and while I had expected him to pull away again, he remained in place. His gaze hooded in a way that made me wonder what was going through his mind.

I had to snap out of it. Ford was a brute and had only proven as much the last few interactions. "This is mostly for Gus, but I added in a few cinnamon rolls from the Drip and some organic beef sticks to maybe munch on while you're at work."

As I said it out loud, I felt silly for thinking he'd like it.

But he took the basket from me and began inspecting it under the clear plastic.

"You didn't have to do all this."

"I know." Glancing to the side, I nodded. "I like creating gift baskets, though. I do it for the bands that come to play, so it's sort of second nature for me."

Ford tilted the container to the side and smiled. "You put in a few bags of peanut butter M&M's."

"That was always your favorite, right?"

His small nod made something flutter in my stomach. I brought my arms in over my chest, as if I could protect my heart from him finding a way inside of it.

"I didn't think you noticed me enough to know my favorite candy."

That was stupid. "I noticed everything about you, Ford."

His head snapped up, and those eyes branded me so severely I wondered if when I got home I'd have shades of amber and green highlighting my skin. To prove my point, I began listing a few facts I knew about him.

"You like turkey sandwiches but hate mayonnaise. So, you use

Dijon mustard and fake cheese so it's not super dry. You prefer purple-flavored Gatorade. You're insanely good at fixing things, and you have a humble confidence. You dress modestly because you don't place any pride in materialistic things. Your favorite Christmas movie is Gremlins. You hum to soothe your anxiety…or at least you used to. You turned down a full-ride scholarship to one of the top tech schools in the country to stay home and be near your family."

Was that too much? I probably freaked him out. His jaw was still bruised from when my dad hit him, which I noticed because a muscle inside it fluttered while he twisted to set the basket next to him.

"You think I stayed to be near my family?" His question was made up of mostly curiosity, like he was shocked that I had chosen that lie to believe of all things. What good would come from him explaining some other reason, like a girl or a relationship I didn't know about.

"So, about that truce?"

"Consider the white flag waved, Royce Quinn."

My nose crinkled as I worked through that. "A white flag means surrender."

"Same thing in this situation," he smiled at me, and it was the kind of smile I had witnessed him give my parents that one night. The kind he reserved for everyone else.

"Should we hug or shake hands or something?" I asked nervously.

Ford's smile remained in place, but his head shook back and forth.

Rude. "Why not?"

He remained where he was, staring at me, even letting his gaze linger on my lips, and then he rendered me speechless.

"Because if I touch you, even once…I won't stop."

My face flushed, his eyes seemed to sparkle with something that fizzled inside my chest, and right as I opened my mouth, his trailer door burst open.

"Boss, Banner just about cut his whole goddamn finger off!" Johnson yelled in a panic.

His gaze flew to me with a bit of a wince before returning to Ford.

The moment seemed to snap back into place like a tight rubber band.

"Course he did," Ford drawled before pushing off the metal desk. He gestured at Johnson with a tilt of his chin.

"Walk her back to her bike and fire anyone who talks to her."

"Ford that's not—" I started, but his stern glare told me he would not budge on this.

I closed my mouth and followed Johnson out. Right as I was about to walk past Ford, he glanced over his shoulder with a smirk.

"Thanks for the basket, Rose."

I flushed pink all the way from my head to my toes.

TEN
ROYCE

The bell chiming over the door of the Drip was incessant. So much so that I drafted a text to my Aunt Natty. Her coffee shop was too popular for her to have something as obnoxious as a bell chiming every time someone walked in.

> Me: Aunt Natty, you have to remove the bell over the door. I've been sitting here for over ten minutes, and the bell hasn't stopped chiming.

Typically, when I texted her, Rook, or Ryle, they'd respond the next day. Uncle Silas wasn't the texting type. If I saw him in person, he'd side-hug me, but that and letting us play in his lemon orchard was about as much affection as he'd ever shown. Which was why I was surprised when my phone pinged with a new text.

> Aunty Natty: Royce! Oh my gosh, I've missed you, sweetheart. You know what, I'm going to ask Ford if he'll remove the bell because we can't have incessant chiming.

Me: You're the best. Also, when are you coming back this time?

Rook and Ryle had been enrolled in academies abroad, but Rook had graduated well over four years ago and Ryle was on track to finish this year. So really, there was nothing keeping them away anymore unless they were worried about Max like Dad was.

Aunt Natty: Hopefully soon. Actually, how would you feel about going to the cottage and sprucing up the place? Just dust, and air everything out, maybe put on some fresh sheets? I'd pay you, sweetie.

Me: Of course I will, no need to pay me. I'll head over right before I go into work tomorrow.

Aunt Natty: You're the best. Love you, see you soon!

"Hey, you're here." Julian slid into the chair across from me, drawing my attention.

I set my phone down, watching him check his own. "I've been here for nearly twenty minutes."

We agreed to meet at one, and it was almost half past the hour.

His handsome face twisted in a wince. "Sorry, babe."

I hated when he called me that, and I'd told him as such several times.

"You wanted to chat?" I sipped from the coffee I had to buy myself since he'd arrived so late.

He glanced over my shoulder briefly, toward the chiming door at my back. "Yeah, I wanted to ask if you'd consider getting me a spot at the Hollow for a friend of mine?"

"Uh..." Wow, he was asking me to do him a favor while also helping someone else...this felt weird. "Can you give me some more information?"

He touched his cell again, making my eye twitch. "So, it's someone I grew up with. She's traveling through Virginia on these small tours, playing coffee shops and smaller venues. I mentioned the Hollow, and she was wondering if there was any way to fit her in this upcoming weekend."

Irritation bristled under my skin as I smashed my lips together. Not once had he even come down to the Hollow to see me, much less take actual notice of how incredible of a venue it was. I didn't blame him for trying to help his friend out, but how he assumed I'd drop everything annoyed me. "I already have a band slotted for this weekend."

Julian's gaze trailed someone over my shoulder, and I realized a second later that Ford had walked up to the counter. He was in his club cut and white T-shirt that revealed all the ink spread out along his arms. The man across from me shifted in his seat, seemingly uncomfortable, which reminded me of his utter dislike for the Stone Riders.

"Is everything okay?" I asked, flicking my eyes to Ford and back to Julian.

He leaned closer, furrowing his dark brows. "No, I just…why wear the leather vests inside places? I don't get it."

From anywhere in the shop, it would look like we were cozy or flirting. Which was probably what Ford saw when he turned with his black coffee in his hand. His glower was typical Ford, but after the moment we had in his work trailer, it felt different. I instantly sat back, holding his gaze, but he flicked a curious glance to Julian then back to me.

I nearly shook my head, as if to tell him that I wasn't on a date, but what difference would that make to him? I probably imagined the moment we had, even if he did say that he could never touch me because he wouldn't stop. He hadn't made any sort of move after that.

Ford took a sip of his coffee, locking his focus with me for two long seconds before turning and walking away. Right as he got to the front door, he ripped down the bell that hung above the frame.

I tried to fight a smile, but lost.

"So, what do you think, babe?"

Still watching the door, I rolled my eyes before turning back to Julian. "I already have a band booked, but I'm happy to keep your friend on the callback list."

"There's no way to push her up?" he all but begged.

"No, Julian. There's not. These bands applied for their slot months ago. I'm not going to bump them for your friend who is randomly stopping through town."

He began attempting to convince me, but I pushed his voice out and thought back to what my dad said about how Julian couldn't keep me safe. He'd never been more right.

All I needed to do was officially cut him loose.

~~Rodney works for the mob.~~
~~Rodney works for Max.~~
~~What if Rodney worked for the devil?~~
~~Rodney serial killer?~~

My chin was propped against my palm as I wrote out my thoughts and crossed them off as I considered the likelihood of each idea. I had a pink planner in front of me with stickers, Post-its and markers. I didn't care where I was, I brought them with me everywhere.

"This seat taken?" Someone slid onto the stool next to me, breaking my concentration. I fought the goose bumps erupting along my arms as I turned toward the hazel eyes already watching me. His voice sounded as rough as gravel and yet it grazed my ear as smooth as glass.

"It *was* holding my jacket, laptop bag, and purse," I couldn't help but smile at how Ford looked perched there, among my things. He hadn't moved a single item.

"So, no, then?"

"What are you doing here?" Why did my voice sound so flirtatious, like I was one of the girls from the club, simpering in his presence.

Charlie gazed at me briefly, and I held up two fingers. With a nod, my favorite bartender turned his back to us and prepared our drinks.

"Did you just order for me?"

The music blared, so I had to dip my face closer to say, "Charlie makes the best drinks. Trust me, you'll like this one."

"So whatever he gives me, that one is your favorite?"

"I guess you could say that." I tilted my head in curiosity. "Why?"

He shifted slightly. "I think you might have been right about how I don't exactly know you anymore."

I didn't know what to say, but his knee shifted to where it touched mine.

"So tell me what else. You like getting tattoos?"

My face felt warm. "I do but I collect them like secrets. Placing them in places no one can see."

His mouth twitched, right as the drinks were slid in front of us. He eyed the planner in front of me and lifted his chin. "You like to be organized?"

Lifting my shoulder, I explained. "I do for the Hollow. For my own life, I don't mind being chaotic. I like pink, that hasn't changed. I like riding, and baking if I get to eat whatever I'm making."

"Do you still like those fields out by your house?" The way his eyes seemed to brighten at the mention of those fields, I was nearly robbed of speech. How did he know about those? I loved walking in those fields as a kid. I used to do that for hours if Mom and Dad let me. I'd dance out there, I'd sit in thunderstorms out there, and write out ideas for the Hollow. I kissed Connor for the first time out in those fields because he knew they were my favorite place. Maybe he'd told Ford.

I opened my mouth to reply, but the band finished their set, which meant I had to run to greet them. "Shoot, hang on. I'll be right back."

I wasn't sure if Ford would still be there when I returned, but I had to focus on my job. The band thanked our venue for hosting them, and I slipped through the back curtain onto the stage seconds later. The mic waited for me as I took position in front of it.

"Let's give it up for Hankered." The room exploded with applause. My face hurt from smiling as I stared out at the hundred or so people gathered along the floor. When I was a kid, there were couches and tables set up, but once Rodney took over, he'd cleared it all out for the dance floor. Now, there was just seating near the bar and along the walls, in some places. Otherwise, you'd have to go upstairs.

"We have another incredible set prepared for you, but while we wait, go give Charlie a visit and order my favorite drink from him. It's a lavender sunset; you won't be sorry!"

I caught Ford's smile as he sipped the drink that I had ordered for him. There was an odd spark in my chest at seeing him sitting there, in my spot, and watching me work. The smile cresting his handsome face made my knees feel weak, and the words he'd spoken earlier became like an anthem in my head.

I wondered if I could test the no touching waters with him, see how serious he was about it.

I turned the mic off and turned back toward the band.

"Royce, you're the best." The band members began hugging me, which was normal, but when I got to the bassist, it got weird. His arms twisted around me in a tight vise, his lips landed near my ear, and with the way we were positioned near the curtain, I didn't think anyone could see us.

"I saw that video of you. I haven't stopped fucking my hand to that image, and I knew playing here tonight that I'd see you. Baby, your short skirt is doing things for me."

My heart squeezed and thudded against my chest as panic swarmed me. My throat swelled, and my eyes burned as I pushed him away, but his hold on me was rock-solid.

"Let me go." I rasped angrily, but all we did was back up, where I'd be hidden from sight within seconds. Tears gathered as I tried to breathe. His bandmate saw me struggle with him, but didn't do anything to help.

"It's a celebration, Royce. We just finished a set, let's relax with a little fun."

"Get off me!" My nails raked down the only skin I could reach, which was his arms.

The bass player was suddenly ripped away from me and pushed down. I followed Ford as he shoved the man further into the back, knocking over a table that held water and snacks. I held my breath as I watched the entire situation unfold. I knew there was no way I could stop this, nor did I really want to. The man was a fucking prick who deserved every moment of Ford's wrath.

A few of his bandmates wandered close, and I wasn't sure if they were going to intervene or not, but they just stood aside and watched. It seemed their apathy wasn't just for defenseless women.

"Motherfucker." Ford landed a heavy hit into the bass player's face. "Don't deserve to fucking breathe." Another hit.

The pathetic mess could barely stand as he tried to get up. I wasn't sure if Ford was going to stop. I'd never seen him fight before. Dad had hit him twice, and Ford hadn't fought back a single time. I knew he was only being a good friend, but there was an edge to his hits, and a rage that seemed determined.

The bass player hadn't moved in a good while, while Ford continued to slam his fist. "He's going to kill him." Someone shrieked.

Oh shit. I stared at his patch, and something kicked into gear in my head. This was bad. For my dad, the club, for Ford...I had to get his attention.

"Ford!" I yelled, running closer. He didn't stop.

Mom once told me that whenever Dad got into a mode where his protective instincts took over, there was only one way to make him stop before he killed someone. Remembering what she said, I pushed my fingers through Ford's thick hair, grabbed a fistful, and yanked as hard as I could. His head reared back with a wince. "Ow, fuck."

Holding his hair, I made sure he met my glare. "You are going to kill him."

I could tell Ford considered continuing, so I squeezed harder. "Let him go."

"Rose, he should have known he'd die the second he chose to touch you." Ford's voice was pure venom, all midnight murder. It made my heart twist around in an unfamiliar, alarming way. His words regarding touching me and not being able to stop made a little more sense. Whether this was a protective nature bursting from knowing me my whole life, I wasn't sure, but regardless, heat swarmed my chest.

Releasing his hair, I kneeled next to him and cupped his face between my hands, ensuring he was still looking directly at me. "And you stopped him. You broke his entire face, Ford. He probably pissed himself. I'm still shaken up, and I'd really appreciate it if you came and talked to me."

He released the bass player, who was coughing and groaning. Still alive, so that was good. Ford got to his feet, and instinctually I wrapped my hand around his and began pulling him toward the back where an employee break room the size of a hall closet was located.

Once we were inside and the door was shut, I spun on him.

"What the hell was that?"

Ford held his hand out, tilting it to see how puffy and red his knuckles were. "What the hell was what?"

"Ford, you literally almost killed someone because they were a little—"

Twisting his neck and emanating a hiss, he cut me off. "Don't you dare try and downplay what he did to you. I had to sit there and watch while your face distorted in fear and you know what, Rose?"

He stepped closer, breathing hard. I backed up, knowing his question was rhetorical.

"That look on your face wasn't shock, it was knowing."

"Knowing? What are you talking about?" I let my chin fall, but he caught it.

Searching my face, he continued. "You knew what was about to happen next, and you knew that because it's happened before. So, you're going to tell me who else has touched you the way that fucker touched you, and how frequently it has happened."

Oh my God. He was going to go on a murder spree.

I pushed past him, crossing my arms. "That's kind of you to care, Ford, but it's really none of your business."

"You are my business, Rose. You have *always* been my business."

I scoffed, rubbing my forehead. Was he honestly serious with this routine? "You have barely glanced in my direction in years, Ford. Fuck, before that. Since we were kids. I honestly thought you forgot who I was at one point."

"Ever wonder why?" he asked with a bit of gravel caught in his throat. I'd almost consider it emotion, but I wouldn't dare assume that Ford Ryan had a heart.

"Of course I wondered why. You kissed my cheek when I was nine, and then you ignored me for years, until..." I recalled the dashed pieces of hope in his expression when he'd held that Christmas card out to me.

"Until you made fun of me and my attempt at peace."

That was rich. Fucking gold, coming from him. "Your attempt at peace, Ford?"

He didn't move, just stood there, barely a foot away, the scent of his cologne and the leather from his cut filled my lungs. I secretly loved that his smell was so familiar and felt like home.

"You had been cruel to me earlier that week. Why would I suddenly assume you wanted peace?"

His poker face seemed to slip as sorrow etched away the hard edges along his eyes and jaw. "Because I caught every single stare you sent my way, Rose. Every time you came over to see Ellie but slept in the hall near my door. The times you waited in my treehouse and lingered in all my spaces."

"You were a childhood friend." My arms came up again, folding over my chest.

With a smile, he added, "You had a crush on me."

Mortification thrummed through me. "So what?"

A small flutter of his lashes revealed a flash of panic. "So, I expected you to know that I had the same feelings for you."

My mouth parted, but Ford suddenly stepped back and ran his hand through his hair.

"Don't worry, Rose. It's long passed."

Why did hearing that create such a painful ache in my stomach? It rolled along a wave of rage that had suddenly burst inside of me and came sputtering out in a horrific accusation.

"You're lying."

His derision grated along my soul, making it flip and erode. "If I still had a crush on you, Royce, trust me, you would know about it."

My anger was a violent thing in my veins. It burned and pinched in a way that I hadn't ever experienced. Which was why I goaded him further. "Really, how?"

His lips curved maliciously, but his gaze was still soft, too soft for how cruel he was being. I knew his next words would be a proverbial fist, crushing my heart into ash. Yet I stood there, listening anyway.

"Because I would do something about it, Royce."

The rejection seemed to cleave me open, forcing me away from the wall. I pushed his chest and seethed.

"Just like you wouldn't be able to stop touching me if you started?"

He fell back a step, his eyes were ablaze, but I didn't let him get a word in.

"Why pretend you care who touches me, Ford?"

A muscle in his jaw feathered. "You're my responsibility. Killian has everyone watching over you. No one gets to touch you, Royce, not when your father is The Wolf of Rose Ridge. Not when he has the kind of enemies that would love to use you as bait."

"So that's it? This was all about my dad?"

His throat bobbed, but he hesitated.

"Was this all about my dad, and the club, Ford?!" I repeated on a yell.

His mouth parted right as Rodney ran in, cutting off our conversation.

"Royce, what the hell happened? An ambulance just arrived out front, and the police are on their way." His shrewd gaze cut over to Ford. "No drama...right." He scoffed before exiting through the same door he'd come in.

I flicked a quick look at Ford, daring him to stop me before turning around and returning to the only dream that ever mattered. Ford was telling me exactly how he felt about me. I just needed to believe him.

ELEVEN
FORD

We had no real idea who had destroyed our outposts.

We thought we did, but after everyone brought forth their discoveries, we realized there were too many gaps and things that didn't add up. Johnson had a map on the table in front of us, pointing with his finger. "Tire tracks led west, which would mean—"

"Fucking Death Raiders." Rev cut in, which warranted a few murmurs and curses around the room.

I glanced up at Killian to catch his expression, but his brows were folded in, like he was trying to piece it together. I knew this wasn't Lance, or his club, the Death Raiders. While the leader refused to ally with us due to the bad blood with Killian, he was willing to work with me. We'd already set up a meeting where I gave him two cases of unregistered weapons as a sign of good faith.

"I'll reach out to Lance and ask if they have anyone who saw which clubs were out near his club, or in Pyle." I sat forward, pulling my cell free.

My eyes snagged on the screen.

No new messages.

I wasn't sure what I had expected, but Royce not texting or calling wasn't really it.

Although that wasn't entirely true. She usually reacted when I got under her skin, and after last night, I knew she was pissed at me again. I assumed I'd have at least a middle finger emoji or something from her. The bass player I nearly killed didn't want to press charges. Perhaps he was warned off by discovering that I was part of a club, or it was because Royce would make her own report. Either way, he would not be a problem.

"I say we attack 'em—send a message." Kody, one of the men at my table suggested. Killian and my dad both watched him, likely waiting to explain to all of us why it wouldn't be a good idea to start a war with another club without solid proof, but he just stared at the map.

It was Jameson who made a sound of exasperation. I couldn't believe they were becoming the old-timers, and that I was stuck with these other idiots.

"No need to start unnecessary shit," I replied cooly.

Kody's blue eyes snapped up. "But it's obvious it's them."

Johnson flicked a brow up, aimed at Kody. "Just tire tracks, nothing concrete."

I added, "I'll reach out to Lance myself, but no one moves on their own. That's final."

Kody's jaw tensed, but he gave me a nod. Killian didn't reply or offer his own thoughts, which on one hand was nice that he wasn't trying to undercut my authority. On the other hand, his agreement could have gone far with the men. He knew what it was like to step into this role after someone else had held it. Having the support of the previous president meant a smoother transition, which left me wondering if he had done it on purpose.

"I'll reach out once we have news from them." I finalized the meeting with a slam of my hand on the table. The men dispersed and began moving around the cellar. Killian headed toward the stairs, and I followed him to the top of the club.

Once we were near the office, I tilted my head. "Killian, a word?"

I could see it in his face that he was still pissed at me, his jaw was so tight it looked like he was chewing on a shit ton of gravel. I ignored my father's curious glance as Killian trailed me into the room and shut the door, preventing anyone else from following.

"You need to say anything else to me that you haven't already said with your fists?"

I took a seat at the desk, which would soon have my photos and my shit on it. Not his.

Laura would eventually clean out her side of the office too, making way for Johnson. Even though her role technically shouldn't change with the club, out of loyalty to Killian she would remove all her items from the desk across the room. She would take her plants out, making the room look stark and empty. It would hurt, but then again, this was the way of things. The order was changing, and it was either a clean cut or it was a bloody mess.

Killian's arms folded across his chest, covering the lingering president patch on his cut.

"Said all I needed to say. But can I ask what happened to your fist?"

"Then why the fuck are you freezing me out down there? And no, you can't."

His nose flared, and I knew I had him.

"Fine, I'm still pissed."

I knew it. "Well, that isn't going to work for us, Killian. The men will pick up on it."

"Well, you being near my daughter doesn't really work for me, Ford. So what the fuck do you want to do?"

I slowly stood from my chair and pushed it back. "Near her in what capacity? I haven't—"

He stepped closer, slamming his hand down on the desk. "You were at her work last night, pulled her off stage and behind an employee door. You think the men are loyal to you now that you're going to wear that patch? They were *my* men first."

My face likely conveyed how angry I was getting because all I seemed to do was pull myself back from Royce, and it was still not enough.

"Your men lied to you. So fuck off with that loyalty bullshit. A bass player was feeling up Royce and pulling her behind the curtain even as she tried to break free of his hold. I ran on stage and pulled him away from *her*."

"Bullshit," he seethed, leaning over the desk.

The door to the office opened, and my dad and Jameson walked inside.

"The fuck is going on here?" Jameson asked, but my dad was the one who replied flatly.

"Royce."

Jameson lifted his chin like he understood exactly what he meant by that.

I searched the three men standing in front of me, confused.

"What does that mean?"

Jameson flicked his eyes to my dad who let out a heavy sigh. "Think if you approached this whole thing with her differently, it would go a bit smoother, son."

"Approached what?"

Jameson patted Killian's shoulder, which made the Wolf finally collect himself with a shaky breath. "He can't even admit it, so he has no place chasing her *or* confusing her."

"Admit what?" I snapped, feeling irritated by their inside joke shit.

My dad was the one who sat on the edge of the desk and softened his tone. "You had a full-ride scholarship to Virginia Tech."

My neck felt a little warm, so I rubbed it then searched each of their faces. "So what?"

His steady gaze remained on me as he continued, "You had your dorm room assigned. You had a roommate, and classes picked."

What was he getting at?

Jameson spoke up next. "Yet you stayed."

"My family is here, I—"

"We're Connor's family too, and Royce was *his*. He still left," Jameson added, cutting me off.

I internally bristled at his comment, carefully ensuring it didn't show on my face.

"Connor had his own plans," I defended, but I knew it would fall flat because fuck, I had mine too.

Killian finally spoke again, anger still lacing his words. "Tell me the honest reason why you pissed away your entire future, and I'll shake your hand right now and give you my blessing."

My heart dropped to my stomach, but I wasn't ready to have this conversation.

"I don't need your blessing, Killian. I need your loyalty. Either give it to me or fuck off and leave. I'm not tolerating this shit."

There was a beat of silence before my dad spoke up again.

"He's right, Killian. You need to table this or come to a decision. He needs your support."

Blazing green eyes would strip the skin directly from my bones if they could, but Killian dipped his face. "Fine."

Right as I was about to leave, Johnson popped his head into the office.

"The men wanna know why the Wi-Fi is off?"

My gaze flicked quickly to the three men in the room before I cleared my throat. I couldn't pretend this was Killian's order, although I knew he'd back it.

"Stays off until we can get the video down."

My second in command seemed to realize what I was referring to, and with a quick nod of his head, he exited the room as quickly as he'd entered.

My dad let out the first laugh, then Jameson. Killian didn't join. He blew out a breath and ran his hand through his hair before muttering something that sounded a lot like, "You better not break her fucking heart."

I left the three of them in the office and slammed the door behind me.

I was a glutton for punishment as I sat exactly where I had the previous night. Right where Royce had tossed her laptop bag, her purse, and her jacket. If anything, she should thank me for keeping her shit safe. I was also keeping her safe though, which was a large part of why I was here again.

Royce had yet to emerge from the back curtain where she was

helping a band set up. This one was all women, which made me feel less stressed. Charlie, the bartender, set two drinks in front of me. I didn't particularly like the sugary lavender drink that Royce ordered the night before, but I would drink it because it made her smile, and tonight that was all I was aiming for.

Finally, she slid out from behind the curtain and darted down the side stairs as the lights in the room began lowering. Purple replaced the overhead house lights, casting the room into a dark, moody vibe. Once the first string of the electric guitar was plucked, a deep red instantly invaded and replaced the violet tones. The heavy bass filled the air next, and a smooth, soulful voice began singing.

The band was incredible, but my gaze was fixed on the woman cutting through a thick crowd, making her way toward me. She was wearing fishnet stockings and a tight minidress paired with combat boots. My breathing hitched as Royce drew closer, and I saw she hadn't spotted me yet, which was why those pink lips were slung up into that gorgeous smile. The second she faltered in place, white-tipped nails clutching the iPad to her chest, I knew she'd realized I had returned.

She needed a second before she seemed to blow out a huff of air that tossed the strands around her face away. Advancing, she set the tablet down and aptly ignored me.

The band was loud, so I placed my boot on the floor so that I was elevated. "Hi."

Her gaze remained on the screen. No response.

I slowly slid her drink in front of her. "I ordered this for you."

Still no response other than her teeth sinking into her bottom lip. This would not work for me.

Abandoning the stool, I moved until I was behind Royce and caged her in with both arms against the bar.

"What's it going to take for you to talk to me?"

Spinning around, Royce's eyes narrowed as she lifted her chin. She didn't seem to notice or care that she was still caged between my arms.

"How about an apology?"

"An apology?" I searched her face.

A nod. "Yes, to start."

I laughed, glancing to the side before returning my attention on her. "If I thought you'd accept a real one from me, then I'd take you out of here right now."

She pushed at my chest, making me falter back. "See, that right there. Stop confusing me. You're here because of the club, right?"

Arms folded in tight, Royce glared at me, but it wasn't her usual petulant stare. This one had something different in how her brows flattened and her nose flared. She was hurt.

Closing the distance, I leaned in so she could hear me and apologized. "I'm sorry, Royce. I was a dick last night. What can I do to make up for it?"

The band transitioned songs, which meant the lights in the room shifted as well. This time, pink burst everywhere, highlighting her high cheekbones and golden hair. My gut tightened with how desperate it made me to touch her.

"I want partial custody of Gus," she demanded, tilting her chin.

Genuine laughter curled inside my chest, forcing a smile to pop on my face. It seemed to make one appear on hers as well as she finally lowered her arms.

"Partial custody? You can't be serious."

"I am. You can share."

Pointing at my chest, I tried to explain. "He's *my* cat."

"And you hurt *my* feelings, so I'd like to have him tonight, please." She seemed so confident, and, fuck, it was cute.

"The only way you'll have him is if you stay at *my* house." Why was I offering that? Gus was currently at my parents', and if she said yes, that meant I'd have to go all the way there to get him. Which I didn't want to do because it would wake my mother up, and she'd want to talk to me. Probably about what happened earlier that my father no doubt told her.

Royce looked shocked that I'd even suggest that. "I'm not staying with you."

"You can't have Gus any other way." I really didn't know why I was making this a standard when it really wasn't that big of a deal to me. When I'd forced Johnson to take Gus one time, he had texted me the whole night telling me how much he hated me for it. I should just tell her yes and let it be an olive branch. Yet...the idea of her in my house was too appealing.

She stared at me for a long moment before she lifted her shoulder. "I'll just steal him again."

Another smile slipped, and my chest felt...light. I was about to argue with her when suddenly someone walked up to her from the side.

"Royce, babe. I got off early."

We both turned to see the guy with cropped hair who had taken her to the movies and who had been with her inside of the Drip, on what looked like a cozy date. He wore a button-down shirt that was open at the collar. Even his jeans looked crisp and new.

"Julian..." She stepped away from me and faced him. He pulled her into a hug, and while she seemed a bit wooden, she didn't stop him. I watched as his hands moved to her waist, and then in agony as his mouth descended and he kissed her.

Old insecurities ripped through my chest, replacing the light that I had felt with a frenzied darkness. This was the role that Royce Quinn would always play in my life. I'd fall for her charm, her wit, and her fucking petulant, bratty attitude. Then she'd end up in someone else's arms.

I was only ever falling for her.

And I was fucking tired of it.

Instead of yanking her back to my chest or pushing him away and explaining he didn't get to taste her, I took a step away. Then another.

Her back was still to me as she began explaining something about how they'd talked about the weekend lineup, but she let Julian lay another kiss against her forehead while he seemed to try to appease her.

I left through the exit and didn't look back until I parked in front of the club, and light poured over the darkened rocks by my feet. Johnson knew I was coming, and once I had arrived, he spilled out of the front doors with two girls attached to his side.

"Boss, look who popped in tonight."

Jasmine gave me a little wave from her spot near my second in command.

While it was true that I had stayed in Rose Ridge for the slightest possibility that Royce might one day see me, I knew it was beyond pathetic that I continued to wait on her. It had been six years since Connor left, and since she'd been single and available.

If nothing had happened yet, it never would.

With a smile up at the women, I left my helmet on my seat and walked toward the porch where Jasmine fit under my arm and I ignored the buzzing coming from my pocket where my phone was tucked.

Even once I pulled it free and saw the texts waiting there, and her new contact name, I turned it off and tossed it in the office. I didn't need to reply because it wouldn't make a difference if I did.

> Wild Rose: Where did you go?

> Wild Rose: Ford, are you still here? I'm looking all over the place, did you leave?

> Wild Rose: Guess I'll catch you later...

TWELVE
ROYCE

This wasn't the best idea I'd ever had; I could admit that. What I couldn't confess, however, was the real reason I was about to travel across the back of the club property at midnight.

Dad and Mom were both already fast asleep and likely had been for a while. I typically got home around twelve, or later depending on the band that was playing. Tonight, I parked my bike closer to the garage than the house and pulled out my phone.

> Me: You close to coming home by chance?

It would be nice to have my sister with me, so I had more confidence about this decision. That or I could ask her to talk me out of it.

> Taryn:...No, I won't be home until morning.
> Sorry, big sis.

I wanted to ask where she was and why she'd turned off her location sharing, but I was too focused on this terrible idea that Ford had placed inside my head earlier. Julian had ruined the vibe we had going, where Ford had flirted with me in a way that might have led to an overnight situation. Maybe a hookup. I wasn't sure, but I was interested.

Clutching my phone, I ran upstairs to change into a pair of tight jeans and an even tighter tank top that dipped low enough that my cleavage looked incredible. Over it, I pulled on my leather jacket and then yanked my combat boots back on. I was out the door, quietly shutting it behind me seconds later. I walked my bike toward the edge of the fence line before turning the key over and riding to the clubhouse.

There was no guarantee that Ford would even be there, but it was the weekend and the odds were high that he would be. I was curious about Ford's departure earlier. I was mad at him, but I liked flirting with him…even if he made it feel like learning another language just to decode if he was, in fact, flirting. He confused me so much. Why suggest having me stay overnight, and then disappear the next second and ghost me?

It only made me that much more confused by his actions. One second he seemed to hate me, the next he acted like he wanted nothing more than to hear my next thought and see how close he could get before actually touching me.

I parked alongside a few other bikes, near the backyard, and dismounted, leaving my helmet on the seat.

Music blared from inside, welcoming me like an old friend. Someone stumbled out the back door, and I shifted to avoid him before taking his spot in the back hall. A few people were making out, backs against the stretch of wall, but I kept my gaze forward. Even when I heard heavy moaning and saw a girl drop to her knees. This felt mildly thrilling, walking through these halls, knowing my father wouldn't pop up and there wasn't anyone who would pull me out like a toddler.

Whoever had picked the music tonight had done a decent job. I liked the emotion and angst behind the lyrics. I bobbed my head to the song as I ducked into the kitchen and sidestepped another member who barely gave me any notice. Most of the members were either high or drunk. Which was good, that meant a lot of them were likely sleepy and headed to bed soon.

The pantry was open, and I knew where the snacks were stored, so

I dug in the white box for a treat. Once I had peeled away the wrapper and taken a generous bite, I glanced across the hall into my dad's office and froze. The door was open, which wasn't normal if Dad wasn't in the club. I knew Wes wasn't here either, so who was in the office?

Creeping forward the slightest bit, I tilted my body enough that the wall hid me as I peered inside. I heard a giggle first, and then a deep, familiar laugh.

One that had recently given me confusing goose bumps.

Realization dawned, and I stopped caring about being seen. I walked into the office, pressing my hand to the door so that it swung wider. A light on one of the desks illuminated enough of the room that I had no trouble seeing what was inside.

With his legs wide, Ford reclined against the cushioned seat with a woman who had long dark hair, straddling his lap. They were both fully clothed, but she was giggling and playing with his hair, while she nuzzled his neck. She couldn't see me, but Ford's hazel gaze locked onto mine instantly. There was something that hinted at a challenge in them, but I didn't know what that meant.

Seeing her in his lap stung my heart like a venomous barb. It throbbed inside my breast, making my nose flare and my air feel constricted. Tears burned at the edges of my eyes and begged to fall, which felt like part of the unspoken challenge. It almost seemed as though Ford wanted to see me break. As if he needed some reassurance that his departure earlier and now finding him like this wounded me.

I could laugh and make a joke about this, but I wouldn't. Our friendly flirtation was over.

Ford waited to see what I would do even as the woman I now recognized as Jasmine Hersh's long hair swayed against her back as she pressed another kiss against his neck. He wouldn't push her away, and if I didn't leave, then would he fuck her right in front of me?

How had I gotten to this place where I cared who Ford Ryan touched?

Because if I touch you, even once…I won't stop.

I wanted his hands on me. I wanted his gruff voice against my ear. His hair between my fingers. Jasmine seemed to finally realize Ford wasn't moving. She pulled back and then glared over her shoulder at me.

"What the hell are you doing in here?"

My petty smile made her glare worsen.

"I was waiting to talk to Ford about when he'd like me to come over tonight." I abused the conversation we'd had about Gus, making it seem so much more than me playing with his cat, but I was too petty to care.

Jasmine narrowed her eyes, then swung her pretty, stupid face back at Ford. "Are you hooking up with her after me? I mean, I get that you're in a motorcycle club, but that's pretty messed up, especially after we—"

"Sorry, I assumed our plans were canceled when you started making out with the fucker with cropped hair," Ford cut her off.

"Julian?" How had he not seen how unhappy I was to see him?

I hid a delighted smile that he'd revealed his own jealousy. Jasmine was just a pawn, a tool to wound me.

"If you'd stuck around for more than the two seconds our kiss lasted, you'd know that I told him to leave. He was trying to use me to help his friend. It's why we met at the Drip the other day. He wanted me to bump a band, and when I told him no, he assumed he could win me over with affection. Unfortunately, I don't have any for him, so that didn't go well."

"Julian Thomspon?" Jasmine asked with a raised brow.

I blinked at her.

She let out a small sigh and then removed herself from Ford's spread legs. "Julian brushed me off two days ago because he said he was into someone else. That was probably you. Now, based on how Ford only paid attention to me after he caught you kissing another guy tells me he's also into you…So, I'm gonna go."

"I'm not into her," Ford argued.

That stinging venom curled inside my lungs this time.

Jasmine moved to her purse, where she dug through it until she produced a small tube and began reapplying her lip gloss. "You left me during our date the other day after ignoring me the entire time. I can tell when a guy is into someone else, so save it."

They'd gone on a date? That meant she wasn't a pawn at all…she was someone real in his life. Suddenly, I felt like complete and total shit.

"Jasmine, there's nothing going on with me and Ford. I was trying to piss him off for being a dick earlier. We're childhood friends. Please stay." I took a step back toward the door.

Ford's nose flared as he finally got to his feet.

Jasmine flicked her gaze between us. "I don't exactly believe you."

My heart felt like it had been untethered from my chest, in the oddest way. Even after Connor and I broke up, I'd never experienced this before. I'd never felt as if I couldn't catch a breath, or like my heart was so bruised, it wouldn't beat properly anymore. I hated how deep Ford had already dug under my skin.

"Ford has never cared about who I date, or what I do. I told you… we're childhood friends. We were just joking with each other. I'm sorry that I interrupted. You guys have fun, I'm going to go home."

I turned away from them and began walking down the hall. There was a loud, chaotic shout that came from near the front of the club. It had several members hollering and excited, but I used it as an opportunity to escape. Two steps away from the hallway that would lead out back, I froze when I heard my name called.

It flung me back six years to the last time I had heard it spoken in that tone. That cadence.

Connor.

Turning slowly, I found my high school boyfriend standing there with that same familiar smile. Same dark hair, blazing blue eyes, and wide jaw. I walked toward him and flung my arms around his neck, hoping the feel of his arms around me would somehow stitch up the damage Ford had created.

My eyes landed over Connor's shoulder, on Ford who lingered in the hall from which I had just fled. Jasmine shoved her shoulder into his arm as she rushed past him, her jacket on and purse swung over her chest.

My eyes closed as Connor hugged me back, then he pulled away and inspected me.

"Been a long fucking time, Roy."

"Yeah, it has. Where the hell have you been?" I tugged at the familiar hoodie he wore, and alarm bells sounded in my head when I realized why it seemed familiar. *Taryn.*

"I have a lot to tell you, but first—" he swung his head around and located Ford—"I need to talk to Ford. Will you stick around, or do you need to head back home?"

It was late, and I didn't want to overstay an already awkward situation. One that had me nearly weeping on my way out. "I should probably go."

Ford walked closer and snagged me with that intense glare. "We aren't done talking, Rose."

"Oh, I'm done, Ford. Completely finished, in fact." I angrily explained, while my voice shook.

Connor looked between us, a dip between his brows forming. "Come on, Roy. Come hang out for a while. Please?"

Ford held my gaze, unwavering and determined. I wanted to go lick my wounds in private.

"I just want to go home, Connor. I'll catch up with you later."

"Not until you hear me out, and you understand what happened here tonight," Ford snapped.

Pointing at my chest defensively, I said, "I know exactly what happened. I cockblocked you. I'm so sorry, Ford, but I left in plenty of time for you to salvage that."

"Goddammit, I was never going to fuck her. I was never going to kiss her. Fuck, you're going to hate me for this too—" he suddenly dipped, aiming for my waist. Before I could even sputter another word, he'd pulled me up and tossed me over his shoulder.

"Okay, guess we're doing things the hard way. Nice to know you two haven't changed at all," Connor droned while Ford began walking toward the kitchen.

"The cellar?" Connor asked, following Ford.

"Ford, I'm going to kill you." I seethed while I hung over his shoulder, getting the perfect view of his ass. I lifted my head in time to see Connor smile down at me, but it was more of a smirk.

It had been years since I had gone down in the cellar, and I knew the same was true for Connor. Which was probably why he looked amazed as Ford carried me down the stairs like I was a sack of potatoes. The drafty air wrapped around me instantly. Everything was upside down for me, but I saw the shelves that had always been lined up since I was a kid, and I thought I saw a long table with chairs around it, but I wasn't sure.

"You guys have church down here?" Connor asked after passing the table.

I tried to swing my head back to see, but Ford continued walking past the shelves until we were drawing closer to the back.

"Come on, there's a heater in the back by some couches and chairs," Ford replied.

Why didn't he answer the question?

Finally, Ford flipped me over his shoulder and gently set me down on my feet, but I was so lightheaded, I fell back onto something soft. Underneath me was a two-seater couch, across from me was a recliner which Connor took, and between the furniture was a space heater. Ford laid a blanket down over me before taking a seat next to me, spreading his legs wide.

Which only made me think of Jasmine sitting atop him.

"You two seem...the same, but different," Connor smiled as his eyes bounced between Ford and me.

Ford spoke first, replying with a bit of an incredulous scoff. "It's been six years since you've seen us, Connor...so maybe you don't exactly have a good frame of reference for it."

"I'm sorry for that, I really am. I have my reasons, but I'm not talking about how you look. There's like an animosity between you two...what's going on?"

Before Ford could say there was always animosity between us, I slid my leg over my knee and bounced it. "Well, right before you got here, I nearly walked in on him fucking Jasmine Hersh."

Connor's brows raised like he was surprised. "The cheerleader from high school?"

"Yes, that one!" I said, right as Ford groaned.

"We were never going to fuck because I would never—I didn't even touch her," Ford cut off, trying to defend his actions.

I gaped at him, swinging my gaze. "She was straddling you, Ford. She was kissing—"

Connor's laugh was so loud that it had me snapping my mouth shut and leaning into the couch.

"Wait, are you two together?"

Ford was the first to act outraged. "Nothing is going on between us. Just because I didn't want to fuck Jasmine doesn't mean I care about her."

"Then why did you drag me down here?" I snidely shot back to which Ford glared.

Connor continued to look between us before smiling. "I've missed you guys."

"Why don't you tell us where the hell you've been and why you left without so much as saying goodbye." I snarked, irritated with them both.

Connor winced and then drug his hand through his hair. "It's a long fucking story."

"We knew you were alive, Connor. We just didn't know where you went. It obviously wasn't college," I softly explained, keeping my old hurt out of my tone. I didn't want to marry Connor back then, but when he'd disappeared the next day without saying good-bye, it hurt. What was worse was when I had asked if I could visit him at his college during a season when I missed him, he'd ghosted me.

When he didn't reply, I was dead set on making the trip until his mother finally explained that he wasn't there. That he was keeping it a secret as to where he was, and they weren't allowed to share until he gave them the okay to do so.

Six years later, we still never knew where he'd been all this time.

"You guys know that Jameson isn't my biological dad, right?"

Both Ford and I nodded, and I felt the man next to me shift so that he was somehow taking up even more space. I had my legs pulled up, covered by the blanket. My toes nearly touched Ford's hip and would if he kept moving. I wouldn't leave first; he would have to.

"Well, I did some research about who my bio dad was...Mom was willing to tell me a few things, but I could tell it was sort of hard for her. So, I looked into it on my own, and it led me back to the Chaos Kings."

"In Richland…" I stated, trailing off as more alarm bells rang in my head. I needed to talk to my sister.

Connor nodded before launching into his story.

While I was listening, my mind kept going over odd details from Taryn and a few strange ones from Ford. I sensed I was being lied to. I could understand that coming from Ford, but if I were being lied to about his place in the club, that meant my dad was in on it, and everyone else.

But if Taryn was lying to me…

There was no way that I would be able to process that. My brain seemed to agree because before I knew it, my eyes were drooping and I was nodding off. I heard bits and pieces of the conversation, and at one point Ford laughed, but I couldn't keep up. Not even when his hands trailed over my feet, lightly rubbing the soles. I think I tried to kick him, which resulted in both my feet being pulled into his lap.

I remembered lying odd on the arm of the couch, and I heard Connor warning me that my neck was going to get a crick in it. Ford hadn't stopped rubbing my feet, so my eyes fluttered closed and I fell asleep.

Something poked my cheek enough that my eyes cracked open. Where the hell was I? Connor telling me he was moving me because I looked uncomfortable as fuck came back to mind.

Where had he put me?

Lifting my head, I glanced around and came face-to-face with a firm, hard stomach.

Blue denim was under my face and on my arm was a limb, covered in black cotton.

Ford.

Why was I lying in Ford's lap?

I pulled my arm out from under his, and his hips jutted up the smallest bit. That's when I realized what had been poking my cheek.

OhmyGod.

Ford was hard as a rock, thickening even more by the second. I lifted my face again, then placed my hands down on his thighs to try to push up, but the second I began moving, so did he. His hand came to my head, where his fingers ran through my hair, but the pressure on my skull had me pinned against his thigh, which meant I felt every inch of him harden inside of his jeans.

With another thrust of his hips, I wondered if he were doing this on purpose.

He groaned and muttered something that sounded like my name, which had me trying to leave his grip so I could see his eyes. His head was tilted back, resting against the back of the couch, but he seemed like he was asleep.

Was he dreaming about holding my head like this, while he thrust his hips and…

Nope, I could not even fathom him wanting me like that because I'd be right where we left off yesterday if I did. So, instead, I slid out from under his hold and scrambled to my feet.

His eyes shot open, but he seemed disoriented, like he wasn't sure why he was in the cellar, and more importantly, why I was in his lap.

"Why was I sleeping on you?" I asked, pushing pieces of my hair back into place.

Ford stretched, and as his hips lifted, I could see the imprint of his hard-on even more than before. "Relax, Rose. Connor moved you before he left, said you were going to tweak your neck."

"So he moved me so that my head was in your lap?" Why did my voice sound so panicked? Nothing happened, it was fine. Even if something did, I was an adult, and Ford was…well, if something were to happen, I wouldn't be upset about it on a physical level. My outrage was confined to the pesky emotional level. He had only ever broken my heart, which made me reluctant to stare at how thick that outline was in his jeans or how good he looked just waking up from sleep, while his eyes still held that droopy, sleepy quality.

Ford smiled up at me. "After I told him to, yes."

My brows curved as I tried to process that. Since we were in the cellar, it was impossible to see how early it was, but my phone revealed it was just after seven in the morning. I'd slept here overnight. I'd slept in Ford Ryan's lap overnight.

"Do you know where this couch is sitting?" His sleep-roughened voice scraped against some place tender and extremely aware inside of me.

I hid it by turning my back to him. "In the cellar."

He slowly got to his feet, and I refused to see if that pipe was still thick against his thigh. "No, this is sitting directly over the door that used to lead down into the tunnels. Which means, this is exactly where—"

"You kissed me," I whispered.

I wanted to press into the moment and ask all of my questions, but I was so scared that he'd ruin it by being his typical dickish self. Before I had a chance to say anything, he walked closer. "We didn't finish our conversation last night, Rose."

"We weren't in a conversation last night, Ford."

His smirk was devastating. "You were explaining how last night, while we were talking about our custody agreement of Gus, your boyfriend—"

"He's not, and never was, my boyfriend."

Ford stared at me. "You kissed him."

"He kissed *me*," I argued.

"You kissed him back, Rose. While I was standing right fucking there."

Why was he being so stubborn about this? "You kissed Jas—"

He was in my face within seconds, seething. "I never kissed her. I haven't kissed any—"

Trailing off, he shifted on his feet, releasing a curse.

"You haven't kissed what?" I asked on a breathy whisper.

The door leading down to the cellar opened, and footsteps echoed around the space, breaking the moment. Ford stepped back and glanced to the side, likely trying to see who had come downstairs.

"Ford!" That was my father's voice.

The man in front of me cursed before hanging his head. "This is going to be pretty bad. You might want to head upstairs."

"But he'll see me," I whispered, inching closer to him. The cellar wasn't huge, but we were currently hidden from anyone who walked down.

Ford's smile was small, but it was genuine.

"That's why it's gonna be bad, Rose. He's going to know that you slept down here with me, and it's going to lead to another round of him hitting me."

I flinched, remembering the last time they'd been in a fight. "He hurt you last time."

"That's because I didn't fight back."

Dad roared for Ford again, and I chose to fold the blanket that I had slept under last night so it looked less like we'd slept together and more like we were down here talking. My hands were in my hair, adjusting and fixing it when I felt Ford's fingers raking through the ends.

I froze and stared at him.

"This time, if you're not here, I can fight back. So maybe slide past him quickly, and then run up there."

My dad's voice rose again. "I need to talk to you about Connor's visit. He reached out to me as a courtesy, but we need to chat about what the fuck he meant by you being down here with Royce."

"He sold us out!" I mouthed quietly.

Ford didn't seem surprised, but when he moved to step away from our little furniture circle, I gripped his hand.

"We can run, I bet there's still a door that leads outside somewhere in here." I had heard stories about it from Penelope when I dated Connor. He was a baby when she'd slipped through one during an attack from a rival club or something.

Ford shook his head and leaned closer. His mouth was right at my ear and his hand landed on my waist as he said. "All that was sealed off years ago. Tunnels, doors, all of it. There's no way in or out."

That didn't seem safe, but I'd save my breath on that.

It was time to face my father. I glanced around for my jacket so it would hide my shirt and how low the neckline dipped, so there would be one less reason to murder Ford. Once I found it, I pulled it on and zipped it all the way up to my chin. Right as I finished, my dad rounded the shelf that had been concealing us.

His green eyes blazed while his jaw locked. "Royce."

"Dad." My hands moved to the back of my jeans where I tucked them.

His leather cut hung over his white T-shirt. The short length drew my gaze to his wrist where he had a tattoo of three flowers, one of which represented me.

"Want to explain why you slept down here?"

I wasn't a child, so I didn't have to explain myself, but for the sake of him not hitting Ford, I did.

"Connor said he wanted to see us, hang out like old times. We came down here, and I fell asleep on the couch."

His gaze swung over to Ford. "And where did you sleep?"

Internally I screamed for him to say the recliner and lie. It would be so much easier if he didn't explain what really happened, but that wasn't Ford.

He was an idiot.

"Also on the couch."

Dad's lips peeled back right as he stepped forward as if he was about to punch Ford again. I took that as my opportunity to leave. I knew Ford wanted to defend himself, and if this was how they settled things, then I'd let them. Besides, I had a list to get back to and items that needed to be checked off, and an ex-boyfriend to corner and demand answers from.

THIRTEEN
ROYCE

MOM WASN'T HOME WHEN I GOT BACK, BUT THERE WAS A NOTE TELLING ME she'd left me some French toast in the microwave. Plucking a cut strawberry from a bowl on the counter, I ran upstairs to check Taryn's room.

Empty.

I pulled out my phone and saw that she hadn't texted me yet.

With the arrival of Connor, it still felt as though she would randomly pop up as well. Probably wasn't even the same hoodie that she'd worn, and the smell, that was…it was Connor, and Taryn would never go there.

"Stupid," I whispered while exiting her room.

While I showered, I brushed off the nagging feeling that I was being lied to. There were things my sister wasn't telling me, and we told each other everything. She was never gone this much, and if she was, then she'd leave me endless voice notes as to how miserable she was.

The more I thought about it, the more frustrated I became. I needed to talk to my ex-boyfriend.

I didn't have Connor's cell phone number anymore, so I was on my way to his parents' house on my bike. Stopped at a red light, my foot on the asphalt, I watched as the cross traffic moved through the intersection. Rodney's white Tesla flew down the road, heading toward the docks. I made a split-second decision to follow him.

Part of my anger revolved around him and the discovery that he'd been lying about his salary. I should have known when he bought a brand-new fucking Tesla. I'd assumed he had savings or something, but no, he was skimming off the top. Now I was determined to discover what he was up to. I twisted the throttle, going faster so I could catch up with him. There were two other cars in front of me, but I still had my eyes on him. He cut over toward the bridge until he was nearing the waterfront, which is where the other cars left us. I had no idea if he'd noticed me following, but my stomach flipped. I knew I was too close for him not to pick up on the fact that I was there, but I had nowhere else to turn off.

Finally, Rodney veered toward an abandoned lot, where two bikers were already parked and waiting for him. I continued to drive, so I couldn't make out which club they were from. I would need to make a U-turn. I crested a hill and found a spot to turn off, but the moment I pulled into the gravel lot a bike came rumbling from behind me. I twisted to see who was approaching and immediately groaned. Ford pulled his motorcycle in front of me, blocking me from going anywhere.

I let a curse fly, dropping my feet and pulling on the brake.

Ford wore a smug grin, a backward-facing hat, and a pair of dark sunglasses. His boots came down, planting in the gravel while he steadied his bike. I wore my pink helmet, visor down so he couldn't see my face. I remained prepared to ride away until he lightly tapped on the dark film over my eyes.

"What do you want?"

I was in no mood with how confused Ford kept making me. He'd flirt, hurt, then reveal something that threatened to tug my heart from my chest. I had too many questions running through my head: Like why he said he wasn't into me but told Connor that he wanted him to lay my head in his lap. Why did he push my face against his erection this morning, and why did he seem to care if I kissed Julian, and what was he about to say when he'd mentioned not kissing.

Instead of tapping again, he reached over and slid my visor up with his finger. I knew my eyes blazed with ferocity, and I wished I could see his so I knew if he was affected at all by me the way I was by him. "What exactly are you doing out here, Rose?"

His raspy voice wrapped around me in such a way that all I could think about was how that must have felt against Jasmine's ear when she was in his lap last night.

"Why do you keep calling me Rose?"

I couldn't see his eyes, but I caught his dark brows caving inward. He quipped, "Do you not know what your name means?"

How did he know what it meant? People didn't typically walk around with that knowledge running through their head.

"Back to my question…why are you following Rodney?"

"How do you know I was following him?" I asked with a bit of a sneer.

Ford didn't smile this time. His head swiveled over to the abandoned lot that now lay below the hill we were on.

"I don't want you near this, Royce."

"Well, you don't really get to make that decision, Ford." I winked and then went to pull my visor back down when he reached out to stop me.

"I'm serious. Rodney is into some dangerous shit." He pulled his shades off, revealing a bruised eye. That's when I registered the cut on his upper lip, and a small bruise on his neck.

I smiled. "Dad got ya pretty good, huh?"

"Not as good as I got him. I think we might understand one another now though, so there's that."

Glancing back toward the lot, I reminded Ford, "I work with Rodney nearly every single night. What exactly do you think is going to happen?"

Something dangerous moved behind Ford's eyes. I saw it that night I had cupped his face when he nearly killed that guy. "Just don't follow him anymore. The last thing I need is them assuming you know more than you should and deciding to kill you because of it."

I hadn't considered that, but like hell was I going to tell him that.

I decided to change the subject. "Did you ever figure out why Connor was in town?"

Ford held my gaze as he nodded. "Your dad wanted to see if he'd accept a job from him."

"What sort of job?"

Amusement lit up Ford's features as he glanced to the side. "You'll have to ask him about that, but Connor won't be taking it."

"Why not?" I asked, confused.

Ford pushed his sunglasses back into place on his face. "Told you. Your pops and I finally understand one another."

With that cryptic response, Ford twisted his fist and took off. Leaving me sitting there, confused and unsettled.

I decided not to hunt down Connor and instead used my rage to tick off the request Natty left me with. Some time alone, up near my favorite place on Earth was probably a good idea anyway. The Silva cottage was surrounded by a grove of trees, and a patch of grass that was big enough for a trampoline and clubhouse. Not that either of those things had been in the yard any time recently, but I remembered playing on both as a kid.

White brick that was once red encased the home, with black shuttered windows and a beautiful, screened porch that I used to love sitting in as a kid when it would rain. Their home always felt like a fairy tale to me, with streaks of sunlight parting the trees and the scent of lemon on the air from the nearby orchard. It was magical.

Using the key kept inside of a hidden fake rock, I unlocked the door and made my way inside. Longing and nostalgia tugged at my emotions, making my eyes water. I missed how full Rook and Ryle used to make this space feel. The cottage was smaller, much tinier than the house I grew up in, but it was cozy too. Leather armchairs, over-filled bookshelves, thick rugs that accented dark wood floors.

The cottage was quiet as I moved to the windows and unlocked each one to push open. I paused when I got to the boys' room, seeing that their window was unlatched. It was an odd thing, considering Uncle Silas would never leave their home open. He would have double- and triple-checked all the doors and windows.

Glancing down at the hardwood floor, I saw the smallest hint of a boot print. Anxiety twisted inside me as I stood and turned in a circle. No other prints could be seen, and nothing else seemed out of place.

Two twin beds sat on either side of the room, matching bookshelves with way too many books. Rook's side had a few framed photos, along with a ceramic bowl for loose change. I checked their closet, slightly worried an intruder might be hiding inside, and came up empty, then hesitantly inspected the rest of the house. No other window or door was unlocked, nor were there any more boot prints of any kind.

It was probably something from a while back, but to be on the safe side, I returned to their room and snapped a quick picture, which didn't turn out at all. Heaving a small sigh, I got to my knees and angled the camera a bit better to see if I could make it turn out. That's when something else caught my eye. It was a piece of lined paper, half under Rook's bed. I would have never invaded his privacy, except I saw my name written on the paper.

But it was still under his bed, and it belonged to him.

Shaking my head, I stood and exited the room before I was tempted to do something like dig through all of Rook's belongings. Before I talked myself out of it, I shot the picture off to my dad, letting him know the boot print seemed off but that no one was here and the door was locked. After that, I stowed my phone and wiped down Natty and Silas's bathroom, which was easy as it was just dust from how long they'd been gone. I refreshed their bedsheets and shook out all the rugs.

Music played from one of the speakers in the kitchen while I made my way from one room to another. It took longer than I assumed it would, but I had a feeling that had a lot to do with the shit sleep I got the night prior. I'd yawned more than a few times. I had even broken down and dug out an energy drink that I knew the boys kept in the shed, tucked inside of a small fridge.

While I was still outside, I inspected the space under the boys' window to see if there were any more boot prints. I couldn't find any, so I wandered back inside. The sky transitioned from a bright blue to a heavy purple, which meant I was going to be late for work if I didn't hustle.

I was just about finished with the house when I bit down on my thumb, passing by the boys' room once more. I had swept and mopped inside, but there was still that bundle of papers slipping out from under Rook's bed. I would be doing him a favor if I tidied it up and stacked it so that the edges didn't stick out.

That felt right. I quickly made my way back to his bed and got to my knees where I gently pulled a few pages free. My name caught my eye again, and my gaze trailed over the text on the page.

Just tell Connor you don't want her to go.

In pencil and different handwriting was a response.

No, Connor always invites her, and if we say anything, then he'll bail to hang out with her.

This is a dumb way to communicate, by the way. I feel like I'm in third grade, passing notes.

Connor will be suspicious if he sees us texting. This is better because he thinks we're doing the fantasy football draft.

That had to be Rook's comment…which meant the person he was communicating with had to be Ford. I remembered the afternoon at Connor's house when both Rook and Ford kept scribbling on a paper back and forth, saying they were filling in their fantasy draft picks. Connor never thought anything about it, neither had I. A burning began behind my chest as I processed the memory and now laid this one over the top of it, trying to compare the two. They were gossiping about me, right in front of me, and I never knew.

Why do you hate Royce so much?

My heart rammed against my chest as I moved down the page, reading Ford's response.

She's spoiled and acts like the whole world revolves around her.

Rook replied with: **Connor acts more spoiled than she does, but yeah, I see that whole world revolving around her thing. That and she's always with Connor. We never get a break from her.**

Fuck you, Rook. I glared at his text and my eyes burned as I continued reading what Ford wrote back.

That's why we both have to approach him about her. He'll accept it if it's from both of us.

At the end of their exchange, I dropped the letter and swiped at an angry stray tear that had made its way down my cheek. I knew Ford and I weren't the best of friends growing up, and we argued more often than not, but I didn't assume he hated me.

I never thought his ire toward me was real. Subconsciously and stupidly, I had thought he harbored secret feelings for me, but I was wrong.

Dead fucking wrong.

Out of curiosity, I snagged another page that was tucked nearly exactly where the last one was. This was similar in how they chatted back and forth, but it was bit more one-sided.

I don't want to go if she's going to be there.

Dude, you're being lame as hell. It's a birthday party...I'm turning sixteen. Royce has been invited to every party since we were in diapers. I can't just say I don't want the Quinn family to come.

This was like a car wreck I couldn't seem to look away from. I knew reading any further would hurt my feelings, and yet I couldn't seem to stop.

Not the entire family, just tell your dad that you don't want Royce to come. Let's not have any girls, that way my dumb sister doesn't get to go either.

I don't mind Ellie being at my party.

Ford wrote back, but it was clipped and short.

Whatever, I just won't go if she's there.

I remembered that birthday of Rook's. There was tension when I arrived, and while I had smiled brightly at Rook, I felt Ford's angry gaze land on me. Shortly after, he left, and Rook told everyone he wasn't feeling well.

It was me. I was the reason Ford would leave events, parties, and any sort of gathering that brought all of our families together. The delusion that I had regarding my friendship with Ford was more than embarrassing, it was devastating. How had I gone so long not realizing that he hated me this much?

The humiliation spread through me, forcing angry tears to slip down my face.

I swiped to no avail as new ones fell.

Realizing that someone disliked me wasn't the end of the world, I could handle rejection. I didn't like it, but I could manage it. This wound hurt because it was Ford. In light of what happened last night with Jasmine, and even before that…this clarified things.

Ford hated me, and any kindness that he'd shown me was just his way of pretending. He was playing me. Likely telling everyone bull-shit about me behind my back. My life felt like a poorly woven sweater that seemed to come undone with the lightest touch. Trapped inside a prison of my own design because of my desire to stay in a town that I should have left long ago.

I had to get up. While there was no band arriving tonight, there were accounts to balance and a variety of emails I needed to get to. Maybe in the past, Rodney wouldn't have cared if I took the night off, but after the situation with the bass player and Ford, he'd been snappy and snarky. I informed him that I was assaulted, and that Ford came to my rescue, but he argued that what Ford did was outrageous. It made everything worse. He then lectured me on having any Stone Riders in the club and how that was a bad idea. I listened, unsure with what I should do. He was holding my dream position hostage, and all I wanted was for him to walk away so I could have it, but I felt like I had no choice but to do what he wanted.

The sky was nearly dark outside when I finally tucked the two pages into my jacket pocket and began closing up the house. I was supposed to start my shift around four, and now as I glanced at my watch, I saw it was close to seven.

I'd ignored the few alerts that came through on my watch, noti-fying me of someone attempting to reach me. Once I pulled my phone out, I sifted through the notifications. A throbbing sensation continued behind my eyes, but I blinked past it.

> Rodney: You coming in tonight?

> Rodney: A little warning would have been nice.

> Rodney: Are you on your way, I have a rep from Ion Records here, asking if he can talk to you about the upcoming set for next week.

> Rodney: Where the hell do you keep the set list?!

> Rodney: Shit, Royce. I thought you wanted this promotion. This little stunt does not bode well for you.

Fear gripped me for a second before I remembered what Ford had said about Rodney faking the accounts and hiding things from me. He was using me. I wasn't sure how yet, but I was going to figure it out.

Just as I moved to my bike, I glanced over my shoulder, checking the darkened trees. There was a branch that snapped in the other direction, making my head turn. Something twisted in my stomach, forcing me to straddle the leather seat and pull my helmet on. I started my bike and then quickly shot off into the evening dusk.

As I drove back into town, I couldn't help but remember the boot print I'd found in the boys' room. Someone aside from me had been visiting the orchard.

The way my insides were shaking when I got into town had me turning into a neighborhood that I shouldn't have been in. I was feeling reckless, and I wasn't sure what to do with all of the emotions at war in my chest, but going to work wasn't an option. Someone could have been watching me. They could have taken me.

Fuck.

I parked a few houses down from the place I knew I shouldn't be and pulled my phone out, dialing a number.

"Royce?"

Anger exploded from me as I yelled, "Where the hell have you been? You left me, Taryn. I've needed you, and now, I could have been abducted tonight, and you wouldn't have even known."

"Whoa, slow down. What are you talking about?"

I paused, rubbing the stress out of my forehead. "Where are you, T?"

"I'm home. Geez, Royce. I know we need to talk, but you don't typically hit this sort of level of upset out there in the wild. You need to come have your crashout at home."

A sob got caught in my throat. "Fuck you."

She paused, and while she typically would curse me in return, this time she didn't. Her voice was gentle as she said, "Tell me where you are so I can come get you."

More anger surged as I swiped at my eyes. "You'd know where I was if you hadn't turned off location sharing."

A long pause on her end followed by a deep sigh skittered down my spine, warning me that she might just confirm everything I was afraid of.

"Where are you, Royce?"

"I'm parked on Ford Ryan's street."

My sister made a sound, and then I heard the door shut on her end. "What do you want to do in Ford's house, Royce?"

I knew exactly what I wanted to do, but I had no idea if it would work. "I want to steal Gus back. If he's not there, then I want to steal something else. I want to mess with him the way he's messed with me."

Keys jingled and knew my sister was on her way to me. Something in my chest eased, like releasing a pressure valve.

"I'll be there in eight minutes."

A smile slipped along my mouth, reluctantly. It took fifteen minutes to get into town from our house, but I loved that my sister would drop everything and come for me when I needed her. I was still pissed at her, but now I was marginally less pissed. I hung up and watched the house, hoping like hell that a cute gray cat was currently sleeping inside.

We cut through a side yard and rounded a quaint house. It was surrounded by a waist-high white picket fence, bordering an overgrown yard. The home was white brick with black trim and a red, chipped door.

"The man needs to update the house," Taryn said quietly.

I ran my hand over the top of his worn picket fence while we made our way to the entry gate.

"He also needs a good landscaper or to buy a mower. Are we going in through the front door or—"

Taryn kept walking until we passed his house and moved to the neighbors'. "Just follow me and keep your head down like I told you."

"Should I be worried that you're so good at this?" I asked, pulling my baseball hat lower on my head. Taryn had brought me a black shirt, and a hat. My sister wore similar clothing to help conceal us.

Once we were near the neighbors', Taryn slipped into the shadows between the two houses. I quickly followed her as she jumped over Ford's side fence and jogged toward the siding where a few basement windows were visible.

"Taryn," I hissed, ducking low to try to keep up.

She pulled open one of the windows while glancing back at me. "Stop saying my name."

Dammit, we hadn't discussed code names. Instead of asking my question that I had for her, I blindly shadowed her. She jumped down into the basement, completely unafraid that there might be snakes or spiders...or dead bodies. Who the hell knew what Ford Ryan had in his basement.

Regardless, I'd never let my baby sister jump into the dark alone.

Crouching low, I got onto my hands and knees and slipped my feet in through the window. Sliding on my belly, I moved backward until my legs and waist were inside.

"There's a table under you." Taryn guided my legs until I was dropping down to the desk. Once my feet were solid, I crouched down again and jumped to the floor.

"Now what?" I whispered.

The room in front of us was dark, but the lights from the street filtered in from the windows. Cement ran under my feet, with a few worn rugs tossed down, a worktable sat on the far side of the room, a few shelves, and an old vacuum, nothing out of the ordinary.

Taryn didn't waste any time moving to the stairs. My stomach rolled nervously as she climbed each step. "Maybe we shouldn't do this. What if Ford thinks we're breaking in and shoots us?"

I knew he had a firearm, I'd seen it holstered at his hip a few times and tucked into the back part of his jeans.

"We're going to be careful, don't worry." Taryn promised while turning the knob. "Also, he's not even home right now."

She pushed through the door, and I followed as closely as possible.

"How do you know?" I asked as anxiety hummed through my chest.

Ford had a few lights on, illuminating the laminate flooring. White, rustic cabinets hung in his kitchen, with Formica counters that looked almost purple. Horrible.

Taryn softly replied, "Ellie has a big recital tonight, which means their whole family is there."

I watched my feet, seeing the laminate on the floor was brown. There once was a time that all our families would be there for Ellie's recitals. Back when our chosen family was all still here, and Dad didn't force everyone to leave out of fear.

"My God, this is awful." Taryn shook her head, making her way to the dining room.

I gasped. "Is that an outdoor patio table?"

The circular shape took up most of his dining room, and there in the center where an outdoor umbrella would slide into, he had a baton of some kind. Curiosity got the best of me as I leaned over the table and pulled it out. With my fingers around the base, I quickly snapped it down toward the floor, seeing several inches of thick rubber extend.

"He has a baton as the centerpiece on his table."

Taryn made some sort of humming sound before taking it from me.

"I guess you never know when you're going to have to beat someone to death." If she only knew how close Ford had already come to that, and with no assistance from a rubber baton. His fists did the job just fine.

With a small shake of my head, I moved my gaze to the rest of the furniture. Taryn did as well, which had her groaning. "Oh my God, the lawn chairs… Have Callie and Wes even seen their son's house?"

I ran my hand over the metal bar of one of the chairs. "There's no way."

Taryn suddenly stopped in her tracks as she made some sort of pained sound.

"It's…wicker, Royce. He has a wicker couch," Taryn said, like the couch was a mystical creature.

I came shoulder to shoulder with her and saw what she was seeing. Sure enough, the two-seater couch looked like something from the seventies. "Wicker and *denim*…how is that possible?"

She turned toward me with huge eyes as a smile spread over her face.

"I know you want the cat, but can we please do my idea?"

Shit, I was there for Gus, and I hadn't even tried to find him. Searching corners of his house and around the floor, I aimlessly asked, "What's your idea?"

"I'd need to see his bedroom first in order to tell you."

My poor stomach rolled again. "I don't think we should, let's just steal some stuff and go. Gus? Here kitty kitty."

Regardless of my protests, my sister continued through the house until we made it to a small hallway with two closed doors in front of us.

"You take that one—" she gestured to the side.

I shook my head. "Absolutely not, we go together into each one."

With a sigh, Taryn grabbed the knob for the first door and pushed it open. The room was dark, but the curtains were open, so the street-lights helped illuminate the room.

My hand shot to the wall where I flicked on the light. "Gus?"

A basic queen-size bed sat in the center of the room, with a sheet and a singular, thin, scratchy-looking blanket. One pillow. No headboard. Gus would hate it here. There was no chance he was in the house anywhere. Surely, he'd run away if Ford ever tried to keep him here.

Across the room was a dresser with a flat-screen TV perched on top.

"How does he live like this?" Taryn sighed. "There's not even a nightstand for his phone charger. It just sits on the floor, plugged into the wall like a little sad, pathetic wire."

I stepped over the threshold and moved closer to the dresser, seeing a few framed pictures. One was of him and Connor when they were kids. Another was of his family. I traced his smile with my eyes, feeling a strange warmth in my stomach at the sight. His grin was beautiful and full of life, like he had a whole secret identity inside that smile where he went to a bank job, came home to a loving wife and kids, with a dog.

He looked so complete…so unlike each time he looked at me. My mind suddenly served a memory of each time Ford had looked at me like that but I didn't know what to make of it.

"Oh my freaking gawwwwwd." Taryn practically shrieked behind me.

I turned around and found her looking inside of Ford's top dresser drawer.

"Taryn," I snapped, "that's such an invasion of privacy."

Her fingers plucked up a tiny bundle of photos while a huge smile stretched over her face. Her eyes were huge like she'd discovered the juiciest secret. I moved closer, now curious.

"What is it?"

In her hand were wallet-size pictures with blue backdrops.

"Wait." I slid the top picture off the pile. My blond hair was curled to perfection, my lips were a glossy pink and my eyes had blue shadow, too intense for my skin tone, but I hadn't listened to Taryn when she told me.

"That's me, junior year of high school."

Taryn made a victorious humming sound as she slid the next picture off the pile in front of me. "And here's you, sophomore year."

My hair was shorter and straight. I had braces on, but I hadn't smiled with them showing, it was one of the few times I didn't show my teeth when smiling.

She slid the next one in front of me. "And freshman year."

There was only one person I had given every single school picture to, and that wasn't Ford. I snatched them out of her hand and sifted through each one.

Eighth grade year. Seventh. Sixth. Fifth. Fourth. Third.

My fingers moved, seeing all the various years of my life flash literally before my eyes. Each and every one was of me.

Why did he have these?

"He must have others in here," I said, shifting in front of where Taryn had been standing. She had an infuriating smirk stamped across her face.

He had a gun in the drawer, a roll of cash, a bag of weed, a tea bag for a sore throat, a video game, and more pictures. Then my fingers froze when I came across three flimsy thongs, all pink…and…*mine.*

My brows curved as I pulled them free. "I left these at Connor's house. I know because—"

My sister was watching me like she was watching a murder documentary. My curiosity regarding her and Connor was officially piqued, so I did something reckless. I didn't want to hurt her; I just wanted to see if she'd have a reaction to what I was about to say.

"Connor would pocket my panties whenever he'd slide them down my legs, and we'd…"

Taryn quickly spun around and moved to the closet before I could catch her reaction. I had no clue if she cared or not, but I decided not to push it.

Dropping the panties and the pictures, I migrated to the closet with her and inspected inside. There, on the top shelf of his closet was a simple, brown box.

Standing on my tiptoes, I yanked it down, and my confusion only worsened. A long-sleeved shirt, a few swimsuits, more framed photos. Chapstick, nail polish, and a few hats.

"This is my stuff. Everything I had at Connor's. I had assumed it was tossed when he left."

Taryn gently tugged at the sleeve of the shirt inside the box. "Why does Ford have it all?"

Searching the contents of the box, that anger swirled and amplified as I tried to come up with a reply. My sister seemed to understand my struggle and took over for me by shutting the box.

"Well, if this is all yours, then let's take it back, I brought your old Jeep because I thought we were stealing Gus."

I nodded, battling the burning in my nose.

He had no right to have these in his possession, especially after being so cruel to me. I scooped up every single picture he had of me and shut the drawer.

"I don't care about Gus anymore, I just want these."

Taryn moved with me as I exited the room. "But I was going to stage his house with nice things! I wanted to pull a Sweet Home Alabama on his ass."

"No. Just this." I said, storming toward the front door. I wasn't using the damn basement window again.

"Wait, you can't go through the front!" She tried to keep up with me.

I held the box close to my chest and yanked the door open. "Watch me."

FOURTEEN
FORD

I felt ridiculous holding the massive bouquet of roses.

There were several eyes on me as I used my free hand to loosen the top button of my dress shirt. My dad glanced over at me, and I knew he was trying to tell me to stop fidgeting. We weren't in our cuts, and it made me feel naked without it.

"One more hour, Ford." My dad warned, leaning in close.

I gave him a hasty nod. This wasn't anything new for me, but now that I had stepped into the role of president of the Stone Riders, it seemed difficult to leave my house without my cut.

There was also the fact that Royce Quinn had once again found a way to slide beneath my skin. I'd ignore the worry that she'd never left and that she might actually be in my very veins. For two glorious seconds, I thought we'd have peace, and I had daydreamed what that might look like. I should have known, like always, it would look like a fight, her pretty pink lips pursed tight as she fought against the slew of curses, she likely wanted to throw at me.

Her sapphire eyes glimmered with anger, and that rosy flush that crept up her neck and even tinged the tops of her breasts. When Connor had suggested moving her, I didn't even give him the chance to suggest anything other than placing her head in my lap. I knew she was pissed at me, and fuck if I hadn't been pissed at her, but something visceral cracked open my chest at the idea of her being anywhere else.

Once Connor left, I had traced Royce's face and gently pushed pieces of hair away from her brow. The drawer I hadn't allowed myself to open in such a long time was exposed and spread everywhere in my chest. It was a mess of things I hadn't gathered back together yet, and for the time being, I was letting it all sit there. Until I was strong enough to build all that shit back up once more.

She made one crucial mistake with me, and that was revealing that she didn't like Jasmine sitting in my lap, or me spending any time with someone other than her.

Royce was possessive of me…jealous even.

Fuck, that thrilled me.

It was a rope in a sea of stars that I would tug on, yank and mangle into submission if I had to, because while I had been angry with her all this time, I finally realized I didn't need to be.

My dad's elbow jamming my side had my head lifting.

The lights were still low in the auditorium, and my sister took the stage again as the star performer of the night. There was a name for her role, but fuck if I remembered it. She'd been dancing since she was a little girl, and I knew her having her own showcase, and even earning a spot in some prestigious dance academy was worthy of all the accolades she constantly received.

Tonight was one of those showcases where Mom, Dad, and I showed up for the full two hours and then went to dinner together to celebrate her. Ellie flitted across the stage like a leaf blowing in the wind.

She was graceful and nailed every single turn, leap, and whatever else the fuck she did.

As a big brother, I was proud, but I was also distracted.

Killian: Wanted to pass this along- Royce found it today while she was up at the cottage.

Attached image

Why the hell was Royce up at the cottage? Had she been there alone? Son of a bitch.

The audience clapped right as another text came across my phone.

> Rev: Two wolf cubs were just spotted leaving your house.

My eyes narrowed on the screen, making sure I read that right.

> Me: As in Royce and Taryn?

> Rev:...

Motherfucking shit. I glanced up and saw the next set being transitioned onto the stage.

> Rev:...

> Me: TYPE FUCKING FASTER

Dad elbowed me in the arm right as another text came through.

> Rev: Yes.

Fuck.

"Ford," my dad whispered angrily.

I handed him the roses. "Sorry, I have an emergency. Give these to Ellie, please."

His eyes were harsh as he watched me stand up and walk out. I felt guilty as hell for causing a disturbance as they were right in the middle of an intensely dramatic scene. The violins were in a loud crescendo as some man dipped Ellie. I was about to push through the exit doors when I caught sight of a familiar face.

I did a quick double take, but when I looked back, he was gone.

My eyes had to be playing tricks on me, but to be sure, I quickly sent out a text.

Me: Did I just see you in Rose Ridge at a ballet
concert?

I tucked my phone back into my pocket as I made my way outside. My bike was parked next to the building. Once I reached the leather saddlebag, I pulled my cut out and slipped it over my shoulders. That's when my phone buzzed again.

Rook: What the fuck sort of question is that?

I smirked down at my phone while I quickly typed out another message.

Me: I swear I saw you in the Rose Ridge
theater of arts.

Rook: Well, I'm not. Besides, why would I show
up to watch your sister dance?

He was right, of course, and I laughed off the notion that I saw him until I realized…

Me: Never mentioned Ellie was dancing.

Rook's dots danced a few times, then stopped. He was difficult enough to reach, so I decided not to push it and changed the subject.

Me: How about this…you tell me if you've
been in the cottage recently, so I don't go tear
your house apart board by board to make sure
there isn't some person leaving behind boot
prints in your bedroom.

Rook: …

I glanced around me while I straddled my bike and punched out a reply.

Me: Just answer please.

Rook: Don't tell anyone, I don't want it known that I'm back. Yes, it was my boot print, and me outside when Royce was finished cleaning. She looked really upset by the way, and then I think I scared her.

I tipped my head back in frustration, but also relief. The tightness in my chest was unbearable, thinking Royce might have been in the cottage while someone else was there.

Me: I won't say anything…but you were at the recital?

Rook: What difference does it make if I'm at the recital, maybe I'm dating one of the dancers.

I laughed as I punched out a quick reply.

Me: Whatever you say, but if you are in town would it kill you to find a way to come see me?

The dots danced for a minute or so before the screen transitioned to an incoming call.

"Connor?"

Yelling echoed from the background before he shut a door. "Wanna tell me why the fuck Royce and her sister just pulled up to my house with a box of her old stuff, asking why I gave it to you?"

Oh, fuck.

Running my hand over my jaw, I blew out a breath. "I'm on my way."

Another female shout echoed from his side of the phone. "You better fucking hurry, Ford. I should not be dealing with this."

I ended the call, about to pocket my phone when Rook's text appeared on my screen.

Rook: I'll try, but there's some shit that's a bit complicated...I don't know how long I'll be here.

I shot back a quick reply before sliding the device into my front jacket pocket.

Me: Okay, stay safe.

I arrived in less than ten minutes because Connor's parents lived in an older neighborhood near the river. I didn't see Royce's bike anywhere, or Taryn's. Instead, there was a familiar Jeep that I remembered the Quinn sisters sharing in high school, parked in front of Connor's garage. I parked on the opposite side, in case she had the inkling to hit it or something.

Connor had told me last night that his parents were in New York visiting his little sister, so they weren't home and no one was there to protect Connor from the Quinn sisters murdering him. I jogged up the front steps and pushed through the front door, already hearing Royce yelling from somewhere near the kitchen.

It was a straight shot from the small circular foyer to the long hall that would connect to the kitchen and open-concept living room. The hardwood gleamed as I kept my gaze low, still trying to figure out what the hell I was going to say, and then Connor's dark head of hair came into view. It looked mussed from sleep, skewed and sticking up everywhere, but my focus was on the familiar black hoodie he was wearing.

On instinct, I swung my gaze over to Taryn who was watching me with furrowed brows and panic stamped across her features. She was worried I'd say something about it. I raised my brow at her, as a way of silently reminding her what I had said about going to war with me.

If she tossed me some help in this situation, then I wouldn't bring any attention at all to what her big sister's ex-boyfriend was wearing.

"Ford, fucking finally!" Connor sighed. His arm swept wide as if to hand the entire conversation over to me. Royce's scowl was so intense I took a step back.

"You called him?"

Connor sounded exasperated. "Of course I called him. He's the one you have the issue with, not me."

"That's my stuff, Connor. You had no right to give it to Ford."

Connor was about to defend himself when I finally spoke up. "He didn't."

Blue eyes rimmed in white glared back at me as Royce crossed her arms and waited for me to expand. Except I didn't want an audience for this.

"Can we talk somewhere private?"

Taryn's nose flared as she swung her gaze to her sister and back to me. I knew she had something to say, but she was fighting it. Royce seemed to think so too as she glanced over at her sister expectantly.

"We can talk here."

I shook my head. "It's private, and if you broke in to my house, then there's shit you missed. At least let me give you all of it."

"I'm not going to your house, you'll probably mur—"

"Aww fuck. He isn't going to hurt you, Royce. Just go talk to him. You've been badgering me for almost half an hour about this shit, and he'll answer all your questions, go with him."

Indecision flickered in her expression as she checked back with Taryn silently.

"You should go, Royce."

Royce still didn't seem convinced and blew out an angry breath as a way of showing it. "I don't want to go anywhere with you, Ford. I hate you and want nothing to do with you."

That hurt, but I'd been dealing with her apathy toward me my entire life. So it was nothing new.

"Noted. Now, can you please come out here and get on the back of my bike? I promise to give you what's yours and then get the fuck out of your life."

She blinked too fast for me to catch the welling of tears I'd hoped would coat those thick lashes.

"Go, Royce. It'll help you get the closure you need and talk about the letters you found at the cottage."

"What letters?"

Taryn's brows raised as if she were surprised I didn't know what she was talking about. Then, with an imperceptible nod, I realized she was throwing me a bone and trying to help me with her sister. Royce likely wouldn't tell me about them, and now she'd have no choice but to.

"I can't believe you talked me into going home first to drop my bike, Taryn. Let's get this over with." Royce finally stormed past Connor and down the hall that I had just walked out of. She threw the door open and briskly jogged down the steps. I gave a small nod to Taryn and then to Connor before following her.

She sat atop my bike with her arms crossed, and I hated that even wearing a tattered sweater and jeans, she was still the most gorgeous thing I had ever seen. Even knowing she hated me, I still swung my leg over and then waited for her legs to cradle my hips. She was resistant, but the second I started the bike and slipped my helmet on, she moved closer until her hands hung loosely at my sides.

Once I began moving, she was pressed against me, with her arms wrapped tight around me. I decided I'd take the long way back to my house, because having her this close to me was the best feeling I'd ever fucking had in my whole life.

"We're here. Where's my stuff?"

I set my keys down on the small side table and locked the door. Royce flicked a brow up, and I laughed.

"Don't pretend you didn't grow up in a house where everything remained locked, and your dad was always on high alert."

Royce released her arms from being fastened over her chest and moved toward the living room, staring at the framed photos on the wall.

"Your house is ugly."

I slipped out of my boots and withheld the urge to remind her that at least I had my own place.

"Noted."

"Stop saying that. It drives me crazy," Royce snapped. Her head shook as she moved into the dining room and removed the baton I had in the center of the table. After jutting her hand down, the weapon slid to its full length.

"You have a lot of weapons hidden around here."

I didn't say anything.

"Like more than my dad has hidden around our house," she continued.

Heading toward my bedroom, I called over my shoulder, "I don't have to worry about kids running around, so might seem that way."

She scoffed. "*Yet.* Just call Jasmine back up, I'm sure she'll spread her legs and let you fuck her bareback. Probably beg you to finish inside."

Dammit. My anger stirred, and all the shit I had built to withstand her and all this fucking toxic shit that always brewed between us seemed to dissipate, and there was no protection from how raw I felt. Reaching for the shoebox I had tucked away in the top part of my closet, I pulled it down and turned toward where she leaned in the doorframe of my room.

"I didn't call her, Royce. She was at the club when I got there."

"Because you went on a date with her. I can't believe you flirted with me after taking her out."

I slammed the small shoebox down on my dresser, which made her eyes snap to it and her nose flare.

"What is that?"

Seething, I said, "Hopefully the fucking end to all of this."

I wanted her to open it in front of me, but I also didn't. This felt like handing her a blade to slice through our past, and an opportunity to create new wounds.

She stepped forward and tentatively wrapped her hands around the box. She didn't open it. I watched as she hugged it to her chest as if it were precious.

"Is this it?"

Other than what she'd left inside of my chest? "Yeah, that's it."

Lifting her chin, she said, "Then I'd like to go home."

Nodding, I remembered what she'd said back at Connor's house. "Show me the letters."

"What?" she faltered back a step.

I took one closer. "This morning you didn't hate me. You wouldn't be this angry that I stole your box of shit from Connor. You're mad about the letters. Show me."

Her dark brow flicked up. "You stole it from Connor?"

"Connor asked me to take the box to you that night he proposed. I took it, just didn't give it back to you like he asked."

"Why?" Her back was against the wall, and having her in my bedroom was way too fucking enticing.

"Show me the letters."

Her head moved from side to side. "You can't bargain for them while also threatening to keep me here."

I smirked. "You can walk home."

She bit down on her bottom lip like she was deciding what to do. "I'll hand them to you, but don't read them. Just like I won't look in this box. We'll trade, and then you take me home."

The urge to kiss that smart mouth was intense. I had to lower my gaze to the floor while I thought over what I was about to do.

"Deal."

Royce still seemed to war with indecision, but eventually let one hand fall from the box and twist behind her. She pulled a few pieces of folded paper from her back pocket.

"Where did you get these?" My brow furrowed as I stared at her outstretched hand.

"I was cleaning up at the cottage. These were falling out of a book under Rook's bed. I would have left them, but I saw my name."

My stomach flipped with unease as I began tracing my memories for what I had written to Rook about. I had never given him a letter of any kind or sent him anything. Whatever was on the note had her angry enough that she wanted nothing to do with me and wouldn't even look inside the box.

"Okay, you have them, now take me home." Royce demanded, clutching the shoebox to her chest once more.

I dipped my head in agreement. "Lead the way."

The moment she cleared the door, I shut and locked her out.

"Hey!" her fist landed against the wood in a thud. "Ford, you promised."

Ignoring her, I unfolded the pages and began scanning the text.

"Ford! Take me home or I'll start ruining your house."

She could have fun with that; it was already a complete piece of shit.

"Fine, I'm looking in the box."

Didn't care, I wanted her to anyway. I read through the conversation I had with Rook when we were sixteen. I had been jealous of Connor, and of the fact that she'd ignored my card at Christmas. Why would seeing this hurt her so much, though? We were little assholes, but so was she back then.

Swinging open the door, I found Royce standing by the television stand with the top of the shoebox lid open, but she'd yet to pull anything out.

"You're pissed at me for something I did when I was sixteen?"

She gently plucked the first item out of the box and held it up, fanning herself with it. *The Christmas card she'd rejected.*

"Seems you're still pissed at me for something I did when I was fifteen, so why not?"

Raking a hand through my hair, I pulled the ends in frustration.

"You didn't even read it."

Determined, she set it down and faced me. "You were so mean to me over winter break, why would I ever read a card from you when I knew it probably said that you hated me or something."

"Well, now you'll never know." I moved to snatch the card from her, but she pulled her hand behind her back.

"No, it's mine now."

I stared at her, breathing hard. "It's always been yours, Royce. You just didn't fucking want it." Did she realize I was talking about my heart and not the stupid card? Did she have any idea at all that I was completely and achingly in love with her?

"What if I want it now?" Her breathy whisper scraped against the edges of my heart, burning something in my chest. I didn't want to get hurt again.

All she'd ever done was hurt me, and she either didn't know or she didn't care.

"Maybe there was a chance to have it, and that time has passed."

Her lip wobbled the smallest bit, which prompted my hand to come up to her jaw and cup it.

"Because there's someone else?" She searched my face.

The pathetic laugh that scraped up my throat hurt because of how thick it felt. "How could there be anyone else when you're still the only girl I've ever kissed?"

Her frantic gaze searched mine, and I could see the small pieces beginning to click for her.

"But…you've had girls. I've seen you with them."

Lifting my finger to tuck a stray strand of hair behind her ear, I explained. "Did it all without kissing, Rose. The thing that drives me mad is that I still have no idea what you taste like, or what it would be like to—"

"That's why you drew an alarming number of sketches of my lips, right?" She tilted her head, as if examining me in a completely new light. "I found them in the shoebox…there were so many sketches of me. Some of my mouth, my face, my hair…"

A flush wound up through my neck and face as I tried to laugh, but it came out choked. "Keep looking and you'll even find a few of your tits and ass."

Her slow blink told me she hadn't quite processed what it all meant yet.

"So you sketched me, wrote me this card…stole my box from Connor then talked shit about me to Rook. I don't get it…"

"Why did you care about Jasmine, Royce?" My question took her off guard from the way her mouth went slack, and she dropped the card back into the box.

"Well, I—"

"Only honesty here," I whispered.

Those blue eyes burned as she stared back at me, then with a defiant chin lift, she admitted everything. "Because I was jealous. I already told you that I once had a crush on you, and you told me that if you still had one on me, you would have done something about it."

Hope inflated my chest dangerously, perilously. "What do you think I'm doing right now?"

Her eyes slammed closed as she shook her head. "Confusing me. Can you just be fucking honest about whether you like me or not?"

I pulled her face between my hands and forced her to look at me. "Like you?"

She nodded slowly, but the pull in my belly had me moving my mouth to catch whatever words she planned to say next.

Her lips were made of silk, her jaw felt like glass as I cradled her close and slowly moved my mouth against hers. She let out a tiny groan as she kissed me back and placed her hands against my chest, curling her fingers against the fabric of my shirt.

I carefully licked at the seam of her lips, requesting deeper access, and she obliged on another moan. Hot and wet, her tongue slid against mine as I moved my palm from her jaw down to her hip, where I held her steadily against me. This was everything I'd ever wanted. Bliss.

Perfection.

Royce pulled back first, staring up at me as if I had tricked her. Something pinched tight in my chest as I realized that's probably how she'd view this entire thing.

"I stole that box, Royce, because you'd given so much of yourself to him…it wasn't fair that he'd hand it all back as if it hadn't ever mattered. I had lived vicariously through him for so long that I felt like they were my memories too. Those times you smiled, kissed him, gave him a picture of yourself, but you never gave one to anyone else. The times you would kiss him but stare at me. The times you didn't think I saw you slide your panties down your legs when you'd wear dresses, so he could touch you. Did you know that Connor used me as a way to get away with it? His parents would always say yes to those late-night movies you'd tag along to, as long as I was down there with you guys. Did you really think I was unaware that he was fingering you under those blankets? I knew, Royce. I always knew, and I wanted the tiny gasps you let out. I wanted to see what your face looked like when he made you come undone. I was so obsessed with you, I was willing to steal every single scrap of whatever was left of you."

Her eyes fixated on my throat, but I caught her lip wobble. "Ford."

"My wild rose," I whispered in reply before pressing my mouth to hers again. It was tentative, like a whisper of a kiss asking if she wanted this again. Her reply was to open her mouth and slide her tongue against mine.

Gripping her ribs, I pulled her against me right as a loud pounding on my front door broke the moment, forcing Royce to pull away.

"It's Taryn."

"If you two have killed each other, I'm gonna be so pissed!" A muffled yell came through the door.

I released her and then forced myself to take a step back. When she remained where she was, and then lifted her chin, a tiny piece of hope fluttered in my chest.

"I have to go." She sounded like she wanted to stay.

I didn't argue, just stood there staring. I finally kissed Royce Quinn, and now she was about to go home and put up walls, creating reasons why she shouldn't have done it.

"Ford, I need to put eyes on my sister!" Taryn yelled again, which made Royce smile.

I liked seeing it, so I smiled back.

She glanced at the door before swiveling her head back to where I stood.

"Good night, Ford."

My lip twitched. "Night, Rose."

FIFTEEN
ROYCE

THE RIDE HOME WAS SPENT WITH TARYN TALKING A MILLION MILES A minute about how annoying Connor was. I stared out the window, absently running my finger over my lips.

I kissed Ford Ryan.

Ford kissed me. He cradled my jaw, pulled me close, and slid his mouth against mine.

"Are you listening to me?" Taryn snapped.

"No."

She made an irritated sound. "Why was Connor even in town, has he told you?"

I shook my head. "Nope."

"What's with you? You're acting weird."

We were nearly home, which meant I could push Taryn off a little longer. I needed some time to be alone with my thoughts.

"Ford kissed me." I picked at the shoebox in my lap.

Taryn swung her head over. "I had a feeling things were headed in that direction. Was it good?"

"Huh?"

My sister laughed. "Oh my God, are you okay? You're out of it."

My lips still felt numb, my skin pebbled from where he touched me. The way he whispered something against my ear.

"Royce, I swear if you let this asshole break your heart again, I'm going to kill him. No joking this time. I have some ideas on where I could bury the body."

Taryn parked, and I slid out of the Jeep, tucking the box to my chest.

"Are you going to be okay?" Taryn came around and held my elbow.

I nodded. "I just need to shower, after cleaning up at the cottage."

We turned and went inside the house. Mom was curled under Dad's arm while they watched some TV show, in the living room. Seeing them still enjoying one another all these years later made my heart ping around in my chest. All I had ever wanted was the kind of love that they shared. Twenty-five years together and they still stared at one another as if no one else existed. Dad still called her "Daisy," which Mom shared with us a long time ago that it was the most precious thing he could ever call her. It made me wonder what someone might call me if they loved me with that sort of abandon.

My wild rose.

"Hey, girls!" Dad called, snapping my mind away from what Ford had said. Mom lifted her hand in a wave.

Taryn and I both mumbled-out hellos while we made our way upstairs. Once I was in my bedroom, I set the shoebox down on my desk. Despite wanting to read the card, I wasn't lying about feeling gross after the cottage. I hadn't had a chance to go through my regular routine after falling asleep in Ford's lap the night prior. I needed to feel like myself before I read a letter that was addressed to fifteen-year-old me.

Once I was under the hot spray, I tried to replay the things Ford said. I tried to think past his words and go deeper to the way his voice shook and pitched in various ways. There were pain points that surfaced through those cracks inside the cadence of his confessions. It was as if he'd pulled open a drawer and I was dropped inside, forced to sort through the jumbled mess until it made sense.

I knew I needed to process all of this logically. That Ford and I had a physical attraction that was calling all the shots regarding that kiss… but the irrational part of me wanted to call this something more meaningful. Finally, back in my room, I settled into my bed with the box in between my legs.

The top lifted easily, and I carefully plucked the Christmas card out. Gold outlined a green tree on the front, and when I opened it, the printed text wished me a Merry Christmas. The uneven, black scrawl was where my gaze dropped and began to read.

Dear Royce,

I know you probably don't want to read this, and I don't blame you.

I haven't been nice to you, but in my defense…you've been just as cruel to me. Which is a stupid excuse, I know that. But I'm tired of fighting with you, Royce. I'm tired of holding a grudge against you for not choosing me.

I know you want Connor.

I know you probably won't ever want me, and I can live with that. But there's a few things I need you to know first before you make your choice.

First, I've loved you my entire life. I know you might not believe that, but you were too young to remember when Connor used to walk around, telling everyone you were going to marry him one day. Your mom and his thought it was so cute, and by that point, I knew it would be too late to tell my side, that I wanted you too.

I used to watch you when you were young, and I'd tried not to care about you. You became this test to me, that I had to pass. I wanted to prove that I didn't care that Connor wanted you for himself, or that you seemed to like him better than me. When we were ten, I finally caved and kissed you. Sometimes I wonder if you ever think about that day, and if you ever want to try again, but this time on the lips. I wonder what your lips taste like all the time, and I know that makes me sound like a freak, but I'm just being honest.

You need to know that if you were to ever forgive me, and you thought you could stand me for two seconds, then I wouldn't make you regret it. I wouldn't waste the chance to love you.

That's all I'm asking for, Royce. One chance to show you that I could make you smile too. We're in high school now, and I hate that you keep looking at me like you hate me. I'd give anything for you to look at me with a smile, or with that expression you give him.

Please, just give me a chance.

Love, Ford

My fingers trembled from holding the piece of cardstock. My face was wet from allowing tears of frustration and regret to stain it. He'd tried to tell me exactly how he felt, and now here we were, adults and being horrible to each other, all because I chose to reject his offered card.

Did Connor know that Ford felt this way? I wanted to go back to Ford's and ask him to explain it all and tell me everything. I wanted to fight with him. I wanted to kiss him again.

I slid the box off my lap and quickly got up. How come he didn't try again?

If that was really love, then wouldn't he have tried again when we were older? Connor and I were broken up for six years, and Ford hadn't tried to bring it up. He hadn't attempted to do anything…there were no signs or anything at all that he still had those feelings. Which made a seed of doubt take root.

"Don't worry, Rose. It's long passed."

His comment from when we were in that room resurfaced, making me rethink this entire thing. What if this was just young, teenage love, but he'd outgrown it?

A gentle knock sounded at my door, and my first thought was that Ford had found a way to come back. When I opened it, my brows flicked up in surprise.

"Connor?"

His frame wasn't quite as broad or as tall as Ford, and it was an odd realization that as my ex stepped past me, inside the room, I had begun comparing the two. "Can we talk for a second?"

"Sure." I turned with him as he settled on the edge of my bed. I shut the door and moved to the desk chair.

His dark hair was mussed from what seemed like his fingers running through it. His blue eyes were red and watery, tired. I found myself grateful for a warm brown gaze that made me feel like warm honey on a summer day. Connor's face was more narrow, still handsome, but he didn't have the scruff along his jaw that Ford did. The one I had fantasized feeling against my inner thighs.

"Did you and Ford get everything figured out?" He raised his head, his tired eyes earnest.

I nodded. "I think so…although I still have a lot of questions."

"That sounds about right for him."

That was true. Ford was notorious for being secretive.

"Did you know he had feelings for me?" I needed to know, so I asked.

Connor's dark brows lifted to his hairline. "Ford?"

"Yeah…he had feelings for me about as long as you did. Tried to confess it when he was sixteen."

Connor's shock was genuine. "No shit?"

"So you didn't know?"

He shook his head. "No. He argued with me all the time about not liking you or wanting you to be at gatherings. I assumed he really had an issue with you."

I used my thumb to pick at a smudge of nail polish on my desk. "Yeah, me too."

"Well, as much as I want you to be happy, Roy, I actually came here with a bit of a warning."

"A warning?" The pink, dried gel polish wasn't coming up, but it really helped to keep my mind off things.

Connor's hands came together as he flicked his gaze to my door. "I came back here to give this same warning to your dad and the club, but you know how things go with passing down info."

A laugh bubbled out of me. "Yeah, as in none of it gets passed down."

"I heard what happened with you and your boss. You should know that Rodney is working with a rival club. A dangerous one from what I gathered. They're called Murdoch Devil Riders, and as far as I know, they have territory south of Virginia breaking into North Carolina."

My stomach flipped around as the first sign of that lurking danger seemed to finally draw near. "Any connection to the club that attacked us when we were kids?"

Connor shook his head. "Not that I know of yet."

"How exactly do you know about any of this?" I stopped picking at the gel paint. My thoughts began tangling and tugging like warm dough. He'd mentioned going to find more out about his bio dad, with the Chaos Kings. Did that mean he'd pledged with them? He was always supposed to be a Stone Rider. Jameson, his *real* dad was one, how could he not pledge with us?

Connor dipped his chin. "I've been helping Giles."

"So, you're a Chaos King then?" I challenged.

He smiled, but I bristled. How fucking dare he. My voice rose as I began berating him, "You were raised by Stone Riders. You were always going to be one of us. How could you pledge with them?"

"Because it's part of my history, Royce."

I stood, feeling infuriated by his disloyalty. "Rose Ridge is your history. The Stone Riders *are* your history. Your mom and dad's story started here!"

He stood with me, gaining his own ire. "No, their story finished here. It started in Richland. Dad was the president of the Chaos Kings, and I found out my bio dad was the VP. Get off your high horse, Royce. You and Taryn act like your dad's club is the only one that matters."

"It is the only one that matters, Connor," I snapped harshly.

He shook his head. "Look, like I told Ford, I don't owe you my loyalty nor do I owe you an explanation. I'm merely trying to warn you about your boss, and another thing." He blew out a breath. "Your dad asked me if I'd be interested in being your private security."

"WHAT?!"

He glanced at the door with a wince. "I didn't accept the job."

"He was going to pay you?!"

"He's worried about you, and he knows you want to move out. I think he's trying to find a middle ground that he can live with."

What the hell was wrong with my father? "So some other psycho is going to eventually accept that offer and I'll have a private security detail?"

"Well, I'm not a psycho for starters, but I heard someone talked your dad out of it..."

"Not a chance. Dad couldn't be talked out of protecting me or Taryn, unless..." I tried to piece together who might be brave enough to stand toe-to-toe with him. Not even Connor stood up to my dad when he'd told him to propose to me…but Ford had. Ford stood up to my father more than once. The memory of what he'd said on the road that day… *I think your father and I understand one another now.*

Connor continued talking, cutting into my thoughts. "Taryn isn't escaping so easily. Her constant trips to Richland are causing problems."

So she was slipping off to Richland, just like I thought. "So, what does that mean?"

Connor's cheeks flushed the smallest bit, and deep down I realized what was happening.

"She's been going to the club in Richland, hasn't she?"

His hands slid into the front pockets of his jeans, which made my gaze drop to his arms. He'd gotten so much ink since we'd broken up. Fuck, the Chaos Kings patch was right there on his forearm. How had I missed that?

"She's there for a friend as far as I know, but Giles and your dad are worried about it. She's been staying in the club."

I tried to gather my thoughts. My chest was tight. "Oh fuck. In the club? That would mean she's…"

"Seeing someone," Connor supplied, but his voice went a little too high as he said it. I quickly turned to catch his expression. He didn't like this.

I wanted to ask him why he didn't like this, but he also looked… lost, and I knew how he reacted when he felt cornered or lost. He'd lock up and leave.

"I'll look into it." I waved him off.

"Look, I just wanted to touch base. Tell you I'm sorry if I messed anything up for you. I'm glad you didn't tell me yes all those years ago, Roy. I'm proud of you for chasing your dreams, and for never being forced out of the one place you've always wanted to be."

Emotion clogged my throat as Connor drew closer, and then his arms came out. I walked into him and wrapped my arms around his waist.

My mind flipped back to when we were dating and how different this felt. This felt like hugging a long-lost friend or brother. Someone I cared deeply for, that I would fight for but would never have romantic feelings for again.

"Roy, there's another warning I'll leave you with. Ford isn't being entirely honest about everything…you're not in any danger with him. He'd probably kill someone for you, Royce. No doubt about that, but protect your heart."

With that, he pulled back. He gave me a sad smile before turning for my door and leaving.

SIXTEEN
FORD

It was just after lunch when I arrived on the jobsite. I'd gone to visit Lance Hess, the president of the Death Raiders to see if they had any leads on the photographs regarding the tire tracks near our outposts. Other than confirming they had nothing to do with it and sharing that I was the new president it was a waste of time. Once I got home and traded my bike for my work truck, I slid out of my cut. I had a few things I had to review and sign off before my guys could move on to the next phase of construction. The completion of the concrete pour was most important because I needed Stone Riders to oversee it. I had exactly seven men in my crew who were also members, all of whom could manage it. There was something we'd agreed to bury for a rather large player in the mob syndicate.

Someone I didn't even want to acknowledge knowing, much less say out loud for fear they'd come sniffing. I wanted to work with them about as much as I wanted to shoot my own foot off, but they paid well and offered a sense of ease when out looking for allies. I wouldn't exactly say that working with Juan Hernandez was safe, but my father knew him through Archer Green, who was the president of another club in New York. Mayhem Riot had also helped us out ten years ago, so any thread I could pull on, I all but yanked.

Johnson had already arrived, and so had the other men who had gone with me to the meeting with Lance. We'd filtered back in at different times, always aware of how it appeared when we left and arrived places as a unit. If anyone was ever asked about our activities, they wouldn't be able to pin us.

I slammed my truck door shut, then began jogging toward my work trailer before coming to a quick stop. Parked directly next to the small set of stairs leading into my trailer was a Yamaha sports bike with pink fenders.

Royce.

I hadn't heard anything from her since she left my house the night prior. Since I'd kissed her and handed her the most vulnerable confession that I had ever written down on paper. I wouldn't be admitting that I had stayed up way too late, waiting to see if she'd text me. Well, that was until Connor messaged me and told me that he'd been with her.

Old jealousies had poured into my chest cavity like acid when he told me he'd gone to see her and warned her about me. Connor was a good guy, wanted me to know what he told her, which apparently wasn't much, other than to be careful with me because I wasn't being honest with her. Which, he wasn't wrong, but I didn't have any choice in that matter.

Heaving in a huge breath, I jogged up the steps and yanked on the door.

There, sitting in my chair was Royce. Her feet were on my desk, her motorcycle boots had pink laces woven through the loops, and the tops gaped, being loosely tied. She had on leather riding pants and a pink tank top that was snug under a leather jacket. For two seconds I thought of my name stretching across the back of that leather, telling anyone who saw that she belonged to me.

"What are you doing here?" I asked, setting my phone and water down. I acted like I wasn't watching her every move, but I examined her glossy lips slide into a smirk. She lifted her feet and let them swing down to the floor. She moved around the desk and then perched on the edge of it, right in front of me.

"I read the card."

Well, fuck. We were jumping right into it. My heart didn't seem to understand the difference between the way her voice tilted while saying that and someone holding a gun to my head. It was hammering dangerously fast against my ribs while I slid a stick of gum into my mouth.

Lifting my brow, I turned toward her. "'Bout time."

Her eyes shone with anger. "That's all you have to say?"

"What the fuck do you want me to say, Royce?"

She shoved off the desk and was now toe-to-toe with me. Her forehead came to my chin, so I was able to smell that hint of roses that lingered against her skin and in the strands of her hair. "How about that you're sorry."

A scoff worked up my throat. "For what?"

Her brows hit her hairline as she began her incredulous tirade. "For writing that, for feeling that way, and never doing anything about it. For letting me be with Connor when all that time it could have been you. Six years, Ford. It's been six years since Connor and I broke up, and you haven't done a damn thing about it. You haven't tried to talk to me or come to me. You said you loved me, and I call bullshit."

Her hair was in loose curls, bouncing against her chest as she waved her hands, and her face grew pink. I knew I should apologize and tell her how I'd fucked up, but all I could think about was how badly I wanted to kiss her.

"Royce"—I let out a sigh—"you broke my heart. I loved you when I was a kid and a teenager, but it transitioned into this toxic thing. I wouldn't call it hate, but I resented you. I got really good at shoving my feelings for you inside of a box."

Her head tilted, gaze narrowing. "Well, I stole that box back. So, you can use those masculine balls I'm sure you have and tell me how you feel now because I'm not going to start falling for you again if you secretly hate me and want nothing to do with me."

I checked my watch. I had exactly zero minutes available for the conversation, but, fuck.

Grabbing one of my hardhats, I placed it in her hands.

"What are you—" She sounded perplexed.

I lifted my arms wide, feeling a slip of all the crazy obsession in my chest that was leaking out. "I named my fucking construction business after you, Royce."

She seemed confused as she checked the hat then the wall behind me. "You call me Rose."

My arms dropped. "To your face. In my head, you're Wild Rose. You're one of the most beautiful things that can be found in the wild. You can survive in the most unbearable of environments, something that shouldn't grow but does. It's the rose that was here long before the dolled-up version sold in stores, the one limited to bushes and thorns. A wild rose isn't held back by any of those things. That's you, Royce."

Her mouth parted on a silent gasp while her eyes grew moist. On a shuddered gasp, she said, "Fuck you, Ford."

"What?" I growled.

She slammed the hardhat down on the desk beside her then her hand shot out and she slapped me in the chest. "Fuck you and your beautiful words. Fuck you and your Christmas card." She slapped me again as tears slid down her face. "Fuck you and that box you hid inside. Fuck you and—"

I slid my hand into her hair and pulled her against me. Our mouths met in a heated rush while her fingers wound tightly into my hair. She kissed me back while her tongue slid against mine, and it was the best fucking thing that had ever happened to me. I didn't even know if I was doing it right, I hadn't lied when I said I hadn't kissed anyone else aside from her. I'd drunkenly fucked before, but never kissed. No one but her, that one day when I was ten, and it was on the side of her face.

I cradled her jaw, trying to savor the taste of her when she tilted her head in a different direction, which somehow managed to deepen the kiss. Shit, it felt good. She was petal-soft and tasted as good as she smelled. I wanted to drown in her, every single sensation and every single breath against my mouth.

"More, I need more—" She broke away on a gasp. I didn't allow her to stay gone for long as I pulled her back, a rumble vibrating in my chest. I lifted her hips and set her down on the edge of my desk then notched myself between her parted thighs. My hand slid up her back, holding her tight to my chest. Her hair was so silky, and her skin so soft, but I wanted to touch more of it. My senses were overloaded as I held her jaw and tilted her face up.

I thought back to all the times when I'd seen her kiss Connor, and I'd imagine what it would feel like if she were kissing me. I'd see the way she moved, and I'd wonder if she'd ever be that reactive to me. From the sounds she was making, I could confidently say she was. She couldn't stop touching me, my biceps, my forearms, and my hair.

She was everywhere, as if she'd been wondering all the same things I was.

Someone opened my trailer door, but I didn't stop kissing Royce. The moan that crawled up her chest indicated she had no intention of stopping me either. The intruder cleared their throat, and still I slowly pulled her lips between mine, savoring every second of having her in my arms.

"Boss, the city planner is here, he needs to talk to you." Johnson's voice finally broke through the air, and Royce slowly slid back. I watched how her hooded eyes remained on my mouth, as we both seemed frozen with me still between her parted legs, and her hands still gripping my forearms.

Johnson was stationary in the room, but I didn't care, and the way Royce smirked told me she didn't either.

"Boss, he's right outside and on a deadline," Johnson piped up again.

I curled a piece of her hair around my finger. "Are you working tonight?"

She breathed out a reply, "Yeah, until midnight. It's an earlier night."

"Okay, I'll pick you up."

She tilted her head, dragging her finger up and down my arm. "How exactly am I going to get there then, because I'm not leaving my bike."

"I'd never ask you to leave your bike, baby." I pressed a kiss to her jaw, right as Johnson cleared his throat again.

I finally turned around and addressed him. "I'll be there in a fucking second."

His jaw flexed, then he slid outside. Leaving us alone again.

"So this is how it's going to be? You're taking me to work and picking me up?" she asked with a smile.

I loved that fucking smile.

"Yeah, Rose. This is how it's going to be."

Her hair slid over her shoulder, making me want to shove her jacket off. "And if I say no?"

"You wouldn't be here, sitting on my desk, wet between those silky thighs if you were going to say no, Rose. We're doing this, and we're not wasting any more time. You're mine." Pinning my forehead to hers, I whispered on a shaky breath, "Fucking finally."

"I hope you're sure, Ford, because once I'm yours, you'll have a hell of a time getting me to leave."

That made me laugh. "Never been surer, Wild Rose. I'll see you tonight."

I kissed her one last time before grabbing my hard hat.

SEVENTEEN
ROYCE

The band playing wasn't holding my attention.

I felt really shitty saying that, but it was true. My distraction was warranted, considering the development with the man who'd kissed me senseless earlier. Ford had pulled up in front of my house to pick me up for work, slowly lowered his sunglasses, and smiled at me. It had frozen me in place, feet glued to my steps as I took a mental picture. It was one dipped in rose-colored glass. I refused to see any red flags that might accompany this new thing that had finally burst between us.

When he dropped me off, he'd held my chin and kissed me breath-less. I had walked into work feeling as though I floated in on a cloud, and now I was sitting at the bar, drawing a heart around my name and Ford Ryan's like I was fourteen again.

"Hey, Royce?" Nick suddenly appeared in front of me, hesitant as if he was nervous about interrupting me. He had messy blond hair that was too shaggy, but otherwise, he wasn't a bad-looking guy.

"What's up?" I shut the notebook, heat expanding in my chest that he might have seen it.

Nick glanced over his shoulder toward the hall behind the stage. "Rodney isn't coming in tonight, and I really need to get something from his office. I know you do the books for him and wondered if you could unlock it for me?"

My brows curved. "Rodney isn't coming in tonight?"

His hands slipped into his jeans as he shook his head. "No."

Rodney never took time off work, and more so, he never really left the office unprotected. I did the books, but he was always hanging around outside the office. Not that I'd ever felt the need to snoop before, but I did now. After that ominous warning Ford delivered about not following him, then Connor. I wanted to know what he was up to.

Sliding off the stool, I waved Nick to follow me. I had the keys to access his office, but there were still a ton of cameras that would track our movements. It looked way better for me to enter his office with Nick, then it did for me to go in all alone. We walked around the stage, toward the back where Ford had taken me that day, he'd nearly killed that bass player.

After pulling my keys out, I slid the silver metal into the handle and twisted. The darkened office awaited us, but I quickly found the lamp. Nick walked around me and veered straight for a drawer that held extra cords.

"Thanks, Royce."

"No problem, I needed to do a quick bookkeeping check anyway." I waved him off as he slid back out and rushed back to his sound booth.

I glanced around and shut the door to ensure no cameras were watching inside the office.

Then I began snooping. I checked the cabinet for anything out of the ordinary, looking through receipts and files. There didn't seem to be anything that I could find. Feeling exasperated, I pulled my cell out and called my sister.

"Hello?" Taryn answered.

I pinned the phone to my shoulder and began searching through another large drawer. "I'm snooping in Rodney's office. What should I be looking for?"

She paused for a second before matching my energy. "Where have you checked so far?"

I began listing everything, and then she hummed in reply. "Okay, check under the desk."

I eyed the open leg space for where the chair fit. "There's noth—"

"No, like taped under the desk, Royce."

"Oh." I would have eventually figured that out. My hand went to the metal frame, feeling around and then stopping when I got to a lump that was contained by Velcro.

"He has a gun underneath the desk."

"Not exactly out of the norm," Taryn mused. I had to agree.

Pulling open the small slot for pens and pencils, I found a matchbook. "There's something here with an address written onto it."

"Send me the picture of it and then be sure you put it back," she urged, and I moved my phone, doing exactly as she said.

Once I texted her, I could hear her further away from the phone, probably on speaker.

"I'm looking it up now."

I sifted through a few more drawers to see if there was anything else I could find while Taryn looked up the address.

"By the way"—I picked up a notepad and flipped through it—"I kissed Ford Ryan again. I think I'm going to spend the night with him tonight."

There was a sudden choking sound in the background, then a loud, "What the fuck!"

My eyes bulged as I stared down at the phone. "Taryn, please tell me you're not in the same room as Dad right now."

"Uh…I'm sorry! I didn't know you were going to randomly tell me about hooking up with Ford!"

"I am going to kill him!" Dad yelled in the background. I rubbed my eyebrow. "Are we sure he's talking about Ford and not some other random completely unrelated thing?"

Taryn whisper yelled, "He was fine two seconds ago, this is definitely about Ford."

"Dad, stop it!" I yelled, hoping to get his attention.

Taryn's voice was still a bit of a whisper, "I took you off speakerphone, dork. I'm outside now. Dad is being calmed down by Mom who called Callie."

"Oh, great. So, this is like a whole thing now. Callie and Wes are going to know that I kissed their son, and may be spending the night with him?"

My sister made a sound that could only be construed as shrieking. "Wait, so you're together?"

I smiled, slumping into the rolling chair. I'd make a terrible spy if this was all it took for me to give up my search. "Yeah, I think we are. I showed up at his office today and tried to pick a fight with him, but it ended with him kissing me."

"That's why he picked you up for work." Taryn sighed dreamily. "Okay, this is so cute. You've had a crush on him for so long. I'm happy for you, Royce."

"I'm happy for me too." Although I was also apprehensive about what Connor had warned me about. I needed to figure out what he meant by that. I wanted to tell her about it, but Taryn was intense enough that she'd kidnap him or hold him hostage until he confessed to whatever Connor was talking about.

"How bad is Dad freaking out?" I asked, tugging at another random folder.

The sound of a door opening and closing sounded on her end before she answered. "He's yelling on the phone at someone. It sounds like it might be Ford because he's using a lot of cuss words. Something about warning him several times."

Yeah, that sounded about right.

"Also, I looked up the address. It's a bar near Murdoch, Virginia… which is super close to the border of North Carolina."

"Are there any pictures of the bar?" I sat up and checked through the glass window into the hall to ensure no one was coming.

Taryn replied with a sigh. "I pulled it up on my laptop. No, there's not much here. Are we going on a road trip?"

I bit my lip thinking back to what Connor had mentioned about the club that Rodney was working with. "Not on our own. As much as I hate the idea of it, I need to talk to Ford and then Dad. It might take a day or so for them to calm down and not want to kill each other. Dad's the president though, so it's not like Ford has much power there. Hopefully Dad can't bully him into breaking up with me."

"He better not," Taryn yelled from somewhere away from the phone. "I will lose my shit on him if he does. But so will Mom, so I think we're okay."

My cell lit up with a text against my face.

> Nick: Where did you go? The set is nearly finished.

"I gotta go. I brought a change of clothes with me, so I probably won't go home unless something goes wrong with Ford."

"I'm so happy for you. Ignore any calls from Dad, love you byyy-ee." Taryn called excitedly.

I hung up and rushed out of the office, locking it on my way.

Ford waited at the bar as soon as midnight rolled around. Nick would lock everything up, so I didn't have to do anything other than say goodbye to the band. Once I was finished, I saw Ford standing near the stool I typically perched on, with my bag slung over his chest and my pink helmet in his hand.

He'd brought my helmet for me to use while riding on the back of his bike. I expected his face to be solemn or stern like it always was anytime I saw him, but that famous Ford Ryan smile that other people were lucky enough to receive was now aimed directly at me.

That cloud I had floated in on was seemingly back under my feet, forcing a dopey grin to spread across my face.

"Hey."

Ford didn't reply, he just tipped my chin up and kissed me. Right here, in front of everyone. I suppose he wouldn't care since he'd kissed me senseless while Johnson watched on. I gave in to the feel of his mouth on mine, the warmth against my chest as he pressed closer, and the strange feeling of shelter that I'd never experienced before. He was like one of those weighted blankets Taryn was so obsessed with.

"Ready?" he asked, his voice all gravel.

"Yeah."

His mouth moved to my ear, and I felt the smile in his voice as he said, "You packed overnight clothes."

Not a question, but an observation, probably from peeking what was inside my bag. I didn't feel embarrassed, but a slice of heat slid through my chest.

"I did."

He wrapped a loose curl around his finger. "See, look at that. We're already in sync and shit."

I laughed, pushing at his chest as he walked me out. The ride over to his house was quick. Honestly, I probably could have walked with how close it was, but I already knew Ford would never allow that. Instead of parking in front of the house, or behind his construction truck, he pulled something from his pocket and after pushing a button, the garage opened.

With his feet down on the ground, he moved us forward inside the small space and turned off the engine.

The garage door slid shut behind us, and I hopped off first, pushing my helmet up.

"Can I take a shower?"

Ford released a rumble, which sounded like a laugh. "Yeah, baby, you can shower."

I liked when he called me baby, almost as much as when he called me Rose. This version of Ford was unsettling, but in a good way. Like discovering a new language, or a new color.

Ford led the way in through the house, and flipped on lights as he went. His house was as ugly as the last time I saw it, but seeing it with him inside of it, without being angry and hurt over items he stole or the card I rejected, made it seem a little less horrible.

"I know, it's bad." He joked, but I caught the way his cheeks turned the slightest shade of red. I considered how ridiculous it was that this giant of a man would be embarrassed by something as simple as the interior of a house. One he owned, which far surpassed anything I had done.

Reaching for his hand, I held it there and smiled. "It's not. I like it."

Ford grabbed a bottle of water from the fridge, and then handed one to me. "You want to help me make it less ugly?"

"When you're ready, I'd be happy to, but you should be proud of this place."

He sipped the water and I watched the way his throat moved, and somehow found it extremely erotic. Once he was finished, he slipped out of his cut, laying it over the back of one of the chairs in his dining room. Although calling it that was a stretch.

"I'm not sure I can tell you all the things I'm ready for, Rose."

My stomach flipped around at his confession, and instead of replying I slid my jacket off and laid it across the back of another chair. My boots went next, until I was in my white socks, wiggling my toes. Ford stared down at my feet with an expression that nearly broke me. It was gentle and cautious, as if he were nervous.

"Are you…" I wanted to ask if he was anxious, but that might reveal that I was.

He stepped closer and placed a firm hand at my hip. "Scared to have you in my house, where you're comfortable enough to walk around in your socks? Am I nervous that you're about to be naked in my shower?"

"Yeah," I breathed in reply.

His forehead pressed against mine. "Fucking terrified."

"Oh, good, then we really are in sync and shit." I pressed my hand against his chest.

We stayed like that while we let the severity of this decision between us settle in.

"Go shower. I'm going to make you some food."

He pressed a kiss to my forehead, then I grabbed my bag and headed for the hall. Ford's bathroom wasn't as horrible as I imagined it would be. It was a little dated, but clean. I found fluffy towels folded and snugly kept on the small shelf. Inside my bag held all my products, so I pulled them out while the water warmed. The pressure and temperature were perfect, and I relaxed immediately under the spray. There was something so therapeutic about not being at home. As much as I loved my family, and the protection they provided, it was a cage.

A protective shell designed from the fear of a desperate father. Ford had given me wings, while allowing me to preserve my roots. Wild rose indeed.

The realization that I was spending the night at a guy's house without having members of the club outside the door was suddenly a thrill inside my chest, like a match being struck. Emotion clogged my throat with a sharp burning sensation that manifested as a giggle.

Then a full-bellied laugh.

I'd finally left the shelter of the Wolf, only to be found by a man who owned a cat. Speaking of…where was Gus? I shut off the shower, and wrapped up in the fluffy towel, drying off.

Once I brushed out my hair and moisturized, I pulled on a cropped T-shirt and pair of cotton underwear. In my bag, I had shorts I could slip on, but I hesitated. Ford didn't seem shy with me, but I really didn't want to risk him not fucking me tonight. The kiss earlier in the day had left me aching in a way that I hadn't ever experienced before. Sure, I hadn't had sex in a long time, but the way Ford touched me was like a slow burn heat that coiled tightly within me, ready to burst into a wild inferno.

I hated to compare the two, but secretly, where I'd never tell anyone alive, even Connor had never made me feel the way Ford had with just a simple kiss. Inhaling a deep, steadying breath, I closed my bag and left the bathroom.

A soft glow across the hall caught my attention. It was Ford's bedroom, with the door wide open, shades drawn shut, and a simple lamp clicked on next to his bed. He'd gotten two small nightstands on either side of his bed, and a gray feather duvet covered the mattress. I walked in with a warm buzzing in my belly, radiating against my skin as I set my bag down on his floor. I was going to sleep in Ford Ryan's bed tonight.

Venturing back toward the kitchen, I found Ford standing with his hips facing the counter while he diced up cheese and strawberries. He'd stripped out of his white T-shirt, jeans, and even his socks.

He stood there in a pair of dark green boxer briefs. The sinewy lines of muscle that ran up his tatted arms were so mouthwatering that I couldn't break my gaze. I tried to see as much of him as I possibly could, and yet it still felt like it wasn't enough. He had so many tattoos

I'd yet to even see or begin exploring. His abs had baby abs that I had the strangest urge to trace.

It seemed he was making us a charcuterie board, which honestly would be divine. Stepping closer, I was about to ask about it when I saw the bundle of gray curling around his ankles.

"Gus!" I gasped, briskly lowering to my knees against the ugly linoleum.

His fur was soft against my face as I pulled him into my arms and got to my feet. "I've missed you so much, handsome."

I was smiling from ear to ear when I finally glanced up at Ford. He was completely frozen. Jaw locked, eyes blazing and searching my face, my chest, and down my body. He swallowed, which made his Adam's apple bob.

My happy grin fell the longer Ford just stood there, holding a knife, while our snack board went untouched. "Ford?"

He made a disgruntled sound that could rival a wild animal. The knife went to the counter in a clatter and his gaze shuttered. "Fuck me, I can't do this."

My heart wilted, worried that all his hate for me would outweigh whatever semblance of affection he found. His comment regarding how he used to care for me once tangled like a bramble in my mind as a pathetic question tumbled out. "Why—"

I didn't get a chance to finish before he placed his thumb against my bottom lip.

"Need you to put him down, because I can't wait any longer to fuck you."

His thumb barely released my bottom lip in time for me to gently drop Gus so he landed on all four of his paws and ran toward the living room. Ford pulled me into his arms, his hands going under my ass to lift me, then his mouth pressed against mine.

My legs wrapped around his waist as our mouths moved sideways, our tongues warred, and my fingers ran through his hair. His muscled abdomen flexed under my aching core. Ford walked us into his bedroom and gently set me down on his mattress.

I gripped his biceps as he hovered over me and fit his hips between my parted thighs. I could feel how thick and fucking long he was as his erection pressed against my core, separated only by our underwear.

"There is one thing I have always wondered about." His voice was raspy and deep as he spoke close to my ear, his mouth nearly touching me there.

"What?" I gasped.

His fingers tugged at my underwear, and he smiled. "Does your pussy feel like silk? Because I always imagined it would."

I didn't have a chance to form a coherent reply as Ford moved down my body. He stared at my center, where the gray fabric covered my pussy.

With a groan, he stroked a finger over the obvious wet spot there. "I can see how wet I'm making you."

Lifting on my elbows, I watched with rapt attention as he carefully placed his hand under my thigh, lifting it the smallest amount. "I could get used to seeing this. In fact, I plan on having some fun with this. I hope you don't mind."

Then his eyes were up on mine. "I'm going to slide into you with my tongue, Rose. Which means, you will spread your legs for me. You will fuck my face. You will not hold back anything from me, including an orgasm. Do you understand?"

"Yes," I breathed, focusing on how handsome he looked between my legs, prepped to bring me pleasure.

"Now let's start with this thong, I'm fucking gone for how you look in it. Need to see it soaked by your needy cunt."

He curled his fingers around the fabric and stretched it against my core, yanking it down my crack so the majority of fabric was soaked by sinking between my pussy lips.

"Look at that." He said in awe.

The friction felt divine, so I rocked my hips as he continued to pull at the garment.

"Mmm," he lowered his face with the fabric still stretched against me, but his tongue began tracing over it and where my sensitive lips pushed out past the thin fabric.

Ford muttered between licks, "I want to keep these."

My hands were in his hair while he played with me, licking and tracing a path with his hot mouth. My clit poked against the soaked fabric of my thong, being pulled tight, and Ford seemed to notice as he gently lapped at it and pulled with his teeth.

"Ford, please. Move the underwear." I needed to feel him. I needed his tongue on me, his fingers…something.

His hazel eyes flicked up as he continued to play. This time he used his finger to slide along the outside of my bare lips and then carefully dip below the fabric, into my pussy.

It was torture, but it felt incredible.

"More, please. Ford, give me more." I begged.

It seemed he was done playing as he adjusted his position until he was between my legs, and then with a swift tug his mouth was on me.

His tongue slid through my center and deep groans of approval echoed through his chest. My fingers slid into his hair as I did exactly as he instructed and began to fuck his face.

The sounds in the room were sloppy and wet as he sucked and licked me without abandon. He had fully let go of something as he pushed my thighs back and dove into my center with eagerness. His ministrations began a fury of need and desire building within me. I was a reckless creature, dying for more.

I clawed at his hair, drug him closer, and rocked my hips against his face.

Even my begging was filthy. "Are you as wet as me, Ford? Can I taste you like you're tasting me?"

He groaned in reply but hadn't let up from sucking my clit into his mouth.

I ground against his face even harder. "Wanna feel you, have you stuff me with your cock. Please, Ford. *OhmyGod.* I'm going to come."

I was crying. Actual tears were about to flow from my eyes as his mouth refused to let up.

Until it was too much, and my thighs clenched around his face, trapping him with his mouth attached to my cunt and my orgasm spilling on his tongue. The stars dancing behind my eyes, the way he held me, the sounds he made. I loved how desperate he was for me. It added to how badly I had come against him.

He gently gave a few more swipes of his tongue before sucking, and then he was moving.

No one had ever tasted me and then kissed me. It was more than that though, Ford's hand came to my jaw while he stared down at me in reverence.

"Open your mouth, Royce."

Staring up at him, I did as he said. Then I watched in shock as he spat directly into my mouth.

No, he spat my *release* into my mouth.

"Swallow." His hand moved to my throat, where he could feel my compliance.

His heaving chest nearly brushed mine as he explained, "That's your punishment for talking like that while I was eating you out. You made me cum inside my boxers, so you get to swallow your release. Next time you talk to me in such a filthy fashion and I'm not in a position to—what is it you said?" He tilted his head like he was remembering. "Stuff you with my cock? You're going to taste your punishment."

Heat shot through my core. My hips bucked, and I suddenly wanted to feel how messy he'd become. I wanted to taste him.

"Why not have me clean you up?" I asked demurely.

His eyes went wide for two seconds before he acted like I hadn't taken him by surprise.

"That what you want?"

"You made a mess of me. It's only fair I see the mess I made of you."

His small laugh made his stomach dip. I could see it by the way his muscles contracted.

"Fuck, what am I going to do with you?"

I shifted, so that I was leaving the bed. I slid my thong down my legs and left it on the floor, and then I did the same with my shirt.

I stood naked in front of him.

"I'll sleep in one of your shirts."

He smiled. "Yes."

I began crawling back onto the bed on my hands and knees. "I want you. All of you. I'm on birth control, and I'm clean. No need to be careful with me. I don't want to wait."

He gripped my chin and held it firm. "We fuck once, and it's as good as havin' a fucking ring on your finger, Rose. You're mine for always. I won't ever share you with another."

Sometimes his words landed like warm rocks in the bottom of my stomach. Soothing but dangerous, and terrifying. Staring up at him, I gently brushed the few dark pieces of hair away from his brow, and saw something gentle and tender. Something that made my heart pinch tight as if it'd been caught in a snare, and I couldn't get free.

"I think I've been yours, Ford, for a lot longer than you realize." I searched his face before pushing on his chest. He followed my direction, lying down on his back so I could straddle him. His boxers were slid down low enough to free his cock, and with my eyes on his, he helped me sink down onto him.

Our palms met right as I slid my hips forward, and then our fingers interlaced.

"Who knew all this time, Rose, you'd fit my cock perfectly." His voice was rough as our pace quickened and his erection filled me so intensely that my spread legs quaked with every leisurely shift forward.

My breathing came out ragged as I replied, "Don't remind me how much time you wasted on that grudge, Ford. I'm still trying to forgive you."

His humming reply was interrupted when he curled forward and wrapped his mouth around my nipple. The feel of his hot mouth against me sent a shockwave of heat through me. My hips canted briskly as my orgasm built once more, my breathing was short and my hands flew from Ford's to the back of his head where I held him in place. His eyes slid up, latching on to mine while a cunning smile crested his lips as he slid his tongue over my pebbled nipple.

"Forgive me, Rose. Fuck, please forgive me because I can't ever walk away from this."

"No." I pulled his face up and slammed my mouth against his. "No walking away."

Our movements became frantic, tense, and desperate. My cries grew as his cock hit home harder and harder with each passing roll of the hips. Our mouths connected in a frenzy as his groans echoed, and my cry shredded my lungs. My head tipped back as my orgasm shook my limbs, wringing me tight only to let me freefall. Ford licked up the column of my neck right as his arms circled my waist in a viselike grip.

He froze for a second while he held me to him, and then after a few slow pumps, his face rested against my bare chest, and his breathing came out in small bursts. "Holy shit."

Holy shit, indeed. "That was incredible," I rasped, still feeling boneless and light. Ford helped me slide off him, and I instantly snuggled into one of his pillows. He rolled and pressed a kiss to my shoulder. "Maybe no shirt tonight, I want you exactly like this."

I was starting to drift, but I remembered him coming into the room with a warm rag to clean me up, then he pulled the blankets up over my shoulders before sliding in next to me.

"Is this weird for you?" I whispered into the dark, feeling sleep begin to drag me under.

He waited a second or two, but eventually Ford replied, "No, Rose, it's not weird. It's everything."

EIGHTEEN
ROYCE

FORD SLEPT ON HIS STOMACH, WITH HIS DARK LASHES FANNING HIS peaceful face. It took me back to when we were kids, camping or at a random sleepover, and I'd see him asleep. I never cared if his lashes looked sooty and thick, or how his back looked, and certainly there was never any ink to obsess over.

I'd been awake for what seemed like hours, but I was too comfortable to move. More so, I was too enthralled with memorizing each and every piece of ink I could find on Ford's body. It was like a little treasure hunt. Along his ribs, he had a few poems from various periods of history. There was a space reserved for his last name, and the club patch. He had a familiar-looking field tattooed onto his arm, it looked like the one outside my house.

Then there was the one of two blue eyes, encased in lashes, seemingly staring. Somehow, I knew they were mine. A random piece of golden hair, with a poem tumbling down the strands.

My favorite addiction. You break me, and I still crave.

Another that rounded a pair of pink lips: *You dare me to taste, I dare you to confess.*

Intricate pieces of heartache and pain that painted his torso, and seemingly grew fingers, reaching for my heart. I wanted so badly to go back in time and read that stupid Christmas card. I wanted back the time that was stolen from us.

A burning sensation began in my nose as I let my fingers trace over one last design. It was a flower, one that looked so much like a wild-flower, but there was something distinctly different about it. I used the browser on my phone to scan the image to tell me what it was.

Wild rose.

My chest nearly caved at how faded the lines were, and how he must have had this ink staining his skin for a long time. This confession permanently stamped into his future, regardless of who he ended up with. He'd tainted his entire body with traces of *me*.

I was in nearly every design that outlined his form. The muscles that shifted under his skin would have to do so with the reminder that I was branded on his heart. Ford lied about his crush, and the love he had for me. He'd never stopped.

"Why are you crying?" His raspy voice broke into the quiet, while his warm hand gripped my hip. I was barely clinging to the sob that was stuck in my throat.

"I'm not."

His head lifted, his assessing gaze searching my face for the lie. "You are. Are you regretting last night?"

My hand shot out to his jaw, holding it and caressing the soft beard that was growing there. "Not even close. I hate that we could have been here sooner. I hate that I didn't read that card, Ford. I hate that I hurt you. I was so…" I was unsure how to even explain it. "I used to come over to your house just for a chance that you'd notice me. I would actually ask if I could clean for your mom, do you remember that?"

His rumble of laughter made the tension in my chest feel lighter. He resumed his spot in bed, lying down then pulling me against his chest. "She had a housekeeper who helped with the deep cleaning who came once a week. But I think she knew what you were doing because Ellie mentioned it. Said she thought you had a crush on me."

A tear slid down the side of my face as I laughed. "Such a big crush, Ford. When you kissed me in the cellar when we were kids…it was like this dam burst. I was obsessed with you, and you didn't seem to care, or to notice me. The rejection stung."

His nose slid across my jaw before his mouth found a way there. "I was insecure because Connor followed you like a puppy. I assumed you wanted him."

"So you pushed me away." It wasn't a question anymore, I knew it was what he'd done.

His warm breath fanned my neck. "He talked about you incessantly. Wanted to marry you and have babies with you. Told anyone and everyone who would listen. I got angry, and I took it out on you."

I pulled his hand up to my chest and laid it over my heart. "What sort of things did you imagine for the future? If I hadn't rejected your card, and you hadn't pushed me away. If Connor wasn't in the picture…what would our future have looked like?"

"I don't know…back then I wanted to go to college, and one day build things…I guess I pictured you in a wedding dress at one point. Getting married in those fields you love so much."

The one he'd permanently drawn onto his skin. "Go on…"

"I never pictured a cat…I pictured a dog, and a house. The one in my mind back then looked more like my parents' house, and less like a rundown piece of shit, but it was also where our kids grew up."

"We had kids?" My voice was rough with emotion. I followed along with his words, seeing myself in a beautiful white dress, and a house that didn't exactly look like this one, and a boy and a girl who looked like a blend of each of us.

Ford drew a design into my skin before agreeing. "I want them eventually."

"Me too."

"Good, then when you're ready to hop off the birth control, let me know, we'll start practicing."

I smiled, even as I swatted his chest. He caught my hand and kissed my palm.

"I'm dead fucking serious, Rose." Rolling over the top of me, he caged me in with his arms.

Tracing a line up his chest and along his throat, I asked, "Does that mean I'm getting a property patch?"

I'd always wanted one when I was little. My mother had one that she wore when there were big club events, and anytime we went somewhere that would have bikers. It was a leather jacket that had her name on the front, and on the back had my father's wolf insignia along with the club patch, and in big white letters, said: Property of the Wolf.

Hers also said President's Wife along each shoulder, because he was the leader, and she was his woman. It was a way of telling everyone in the motorcycle club community that she wasn't patched to a random member. She belonged to the president of the whole goddamn club. Ford's mom had one as well, but hers had the club patch, not the wolf.

I assumed Ford would tell me, "hell yeah," since he'd been so open and engaging about our relationship, but he immediately rolled off me and sat on the edge of the bed.

"Shit, I forgot I had church this morning."

I wrapped my hands around his waist, placing my head against his back. "Surely dating the president's daughter gives you a pass, right?"

His head turned, allowing our gazes to meet. Mine was playful, silently begging him to come back to bed. His was something else… there was that warning that Connor had left me with, and it shone through Ford's eyes. He wasn't telling me something, and while I was typically pretty good at conjuring up fake scenarios and ideas of what it could be, I simply refused to.

I knew he wanted this. He wanted me, I believed that to my very marrow. So why was he holding something back?

Right as he opened his mouth to respond, someone banged on his front door. Gus ran into the bedroom, darting under the bed as the pounding stopped, only to start again.

"Who the hell is that?" It was like eight in the morning.

Ford's determined gaze swung to the bedroom door as he heaved in a sigh. "I'll give you one guess." He stood from the bed and moved to the dresser where he yanked out a pair of sweats. "Honestly, I'm shocked he gave us the night."

That had me scrambling out of bed. "You think it's my dad?"

"I know it's your dad."

Sure enough, seconds later my father's voice came muffled through the door. "Ford, open the fucking door."

I was naked, and my father was about to burst into Ford's house. *Ohmyfreakinggosh.*

Did my mother know about this? I needed to call Taryn.

Priorities, though, I needed clothes. My bag was on the floor where I left it, so I ran over to it and tossed it on the bed, yanking out the underwear, bra, and leggings.

"Just shut the door, we'll be a second anyway." Ford kissed my forehead before leaving his room, shutting the door behind him.

I quickly pulled on clothes while I heard my father enter the house. "Do you have your phone off, or what's going on?" I heard him say.

Ford rumbled a reply, but it was too low for me to catch.

"Where's my daughter?"

Oh no. I shimmied into my leggings, trying to pull them up before the two of them started fighting. Ford was yelling over him, but Dad kept cutting him off, so it was hard to make out. As soon as I was dressed, I yanked the door open.

"Dad!" He was standing too close to Ford, the two glaring at one another. Ford's jaw was tense, and his eyes were hard. He was shirtless, in just his sweats, barefoot too. I was going to commit the image to my memories, merely for the fact that his hair was mussed from when I'd run my hands through it.

My father's sharp green gaze swung over to me, his mouth twisting angrily. "Royce, go get in my truck."

Ford shifted his stance so he was closer to me. "Killian, if she's going anywhere, then I'll be the one to take her."

My dad didn't laugh. He didn't scoff or groan. He stayed completely quiet, which made my hands shake. "Dad, I'm with Ford."

"You don't know him!" Dad screamed in reply, his face a deeper shade of red. "You don't know this world, Royce. I've kept you close enough to keep safe, but far enough so you aren't aware of what we do. This is a different world we live in now. Different from when I led things..." he trailed off.

Ford reached my side, pulling my hand into his. "She knows me better than anyone, Killian. She's known me since we were fucking toddlers, for fuck's sake. Don't try and act like she's some outsider who doesn't know shit. Give her the credit she's due as the daughter of the fucking Wolf."

"So what, Ford? You going to patch her, keep her concealed in that club, or maybe have her be here, in the middle of town where you have three rival members watching you?"

Why would they be watching Ford? Unless they had eyes out on everyone.

"Yes, I plan to patch her." Ford replied, his voice tight.

My dad scowled deeply. "And does she know what will happen to her dreams as soon as you do?"

That had me freezing in place. My blood went cold. Was my dad going to make me leave again?

"How about you both tell me what the hell is going on?" I argued.

Dad and Ford stared at one another for a loaded moment before Johnson appeared at the door, swinging it open.

"There's movement on the perimeter of the city. We should get to the club."

Dad dipped his head. "Royce, get your things. You're coming home."

"She'll be riding with me." Ford said forcefully.

I stared between the two of them until my dad's jaw clenched tightly. "Consider how it will look to have her on the back of your bike, Ford. I once had to make the same decision, and I'm warning you that you're not protecting her by painting a target on her back."

Dad always made it seem like dating a club member would be disastrous, but it really felt like he was going too far with Ford. There were plenty of girls who dated members, and they were fine. Maybe because he was related to a Stone, and the threat delivered was specifically toward the Stone family. Callie would be all that was left of that, but Simon Stone raised my father as if he were his own, so the man threatening us would have to know that.

"Killian, she stays with me. End of story." Ford held my hand, pulling me behind him as we entered his room and he shut the door.

He began sifting through his drawer for a shirt, then a pair of jeans. His movements were jerky and quick.

I walked over and slid my hand up his back, then wrapped my arms around his waist.

He froze and then placed his hands over mine.

"My dad means well."

He laughed, but it came up more like an angry scoff. "I know he does, but he's really starting to piss me off."

Stroking his abdomen, I didn't reply. I kissed the wild rose inked into his back, and hoped we'd all be okay. It wasn't until we were riding away, my chest glued to his back, that I processed how Ford declined a direct order from my father. Did that mean he'd get in trouble or kicked out?

Or was the warning in my gut right, and my father wasn't the one calling the shots at all anymore.

Despite what Ford argued with my dad, he pulled up in front of my house and parked behind Dad's bike. My mother was already near the front door, pushing her fingers into my father's hair, while the two of them talked.

She looked worried.

"Are we going into lockdown?" I glanced back at the gate near the entrance to our drive, and saw a few Stone Riders parking there as sentries.

Ford glanced up at the sky, but his sunglasses were on, so I couldn't see the way the sun hit the hazel. "Yeah, Rose, we are."

My stomach dropped as my mind went back to a time when I was nine, and my father was kneeling in front of me telling me I had to pack a bag, that we were headed into the clubhouse and we'd have to stay there until it was safe again.

Ford's hand gently cupped my face as he turned it away from the direction of the club, "You're with me. No matter what, you're with me, which means you're safe."

I tried to let that take root in my heart even as my hand wound around his. He slid off his bike, helping me get off as well. My legs felt shaky as I stood in front of my childhood home. I already knew my father wouldn't allow Ford to come in, and that's what made me feel nervous.

Squeezing his hand, I walked toward the house and Ford paused at our front porch. "I need to tell you something."

"Royce!" Taryn burst through the door, ignoring Ford and our parents. She looked different. Her blue eyes were wide, her mouth was tense. She was panicked and frenzied.

I released Ford's hand and went to her. "What's wrong?"

"I need to talk to you." Her anxious gaze bounced between Ford and me.

"What about?" I asked, confused at her insistence.

"Uh, just something, but it's really important." She shifted, and that's when Nova made her way outside. Her dark hair was braided to the side, her blue eyes striking as always.

"Hey, Nova." I waved. She glanced at Ford, then back at me.

"Can we talk in private, Royce?"

Ford dipped his chin, but I caught his smile. "Don't think I can do private during a lockdown, Rose."

Nova folded her arms over her chest. "Are you suddenly Royce's keeper?"

His laugh slid against my neck as he stepped closer, then pressed a kiss to my hairline. "I've always been her keeper, Nova. Now, it's just not as frowned upon because she's aware of it."

Heat swarmed my chest as I processed that he'd been keeping tabs on me far longer than I ever realized. The memory of skimming my fingers over each of his tattoos seared my mind as I smiled at him.

"So that's super cute, but this is girl talk, and it's private." Taryn's eyes flicked over to Nova then quickly back to me, and I knew she was trying to tell me something. I knew my sister well enough to know when something was important, and whatever this was needed to be kept private.

I squeezed Ford's hand and faced him. "Come find me later?"

He considered me, then glanced at Nova and Taryn. He seemed to be struggling with his decision, but he leaned in close and rasped, "Keep your phone on you. Keep a weapon on you. Don't go with anyone, anywhere for any reason. The second you're done, text me. Understand?"

I nodded, but it was cut off by his kiss. "I'll be back."

He turned back to his bike, and while it started, I followed my sister inside.

Mom was packing one of her cloth grocery bags with food, which meant she was planning on staying over at the club. I wanted to resist the idea with everything inside me. Not because I hated the club, but I hated this feeling of fear that gripped my heart and swelled in my stomach. I hated the memory of being stuck in that club, and pretending the sky wasn't about to fall. The memory of watching my father ride off into the dead of night, unsure if we'd ever see him again snapped back like a painful flash.

I ignored how tight my chest felt, and followed Nova and Taryn upstairs.

Once we entered Taryn's room, she secured the door. I perched against Taryn's desk while my sister took the chair that was off to the side, and Nova sank onto my sister's mattress.

"So you and Ford?" Nova raised her eyebrow at me.

I nodded.

Nova smiled brightly. "I always thought you two made more sense than you and Connor. No offense."

"None taken. Connor was a great boyfriend, but I had a crush on Ford long before your brother ever asked me out."

Taryn was busy staring at her phone, completely disengaged from the conversation.

"Anyway, so I started asking around about the video thing. I know a guy who has connections, and while everyone was busy hacking and looking at where this originated from, I looked at which club was responsible."

Holy shit. No wonder they wanted to talk to me in private, she'd just dropped a bomb.

Taryn crossed one leg over another, leaning back. "How do you know it's a club?"

"Because she's Killian Quinn's daughter." Nova deadpanned like it was obvious.

She had a point. "Okay, so which club was responsible?"

Nova tucked her hair behind her ear. She seemed nervous, even more so when she wet her lips and cleared her throat. "So this is the part where I really can't have this information leave this room because you're going to be upset, and rightly so, but my contact is a good friend of mine. Even if they're part of a shit for brains club."

"Just tell us, Nova," Taryn snapped.

"It was the Murdoch Devil Riders."

My ears perked up, which had me shoving away from the desk. "Murdoch?"

Taryn turned her head toward me, but neither of us spoke.

"You guys can trust me. Tell me why you're looking at each other like that, what's wrong?" Nova asked.

"You have a friend in this club, the Murdoch Devil Riders?" Taryn asked.

Nova's face flushed. "We're dating. It's new…and complicated."

Taryn scoffed. "Fuck, Nov. Do your parents know?"

"No, and neither does Connor. I'd like to keep it that way."

My voice was cold as I shot off my own reply. "I would hope so. You dating anyone outside of the Stone Riders is bad enough, but someone who leaked a video of me?"

"Dad is going to freak." Taryn shook her head while releasing a sigh.

If my gut was right, then it wasn't my father who was going to be upset, it was Ford. Hell, he'd probably start a war over this.

"You can't say anything." Nova shot to her feet, bringing her hands together. "I'm begging you guys. I wanted you to know so you could put it to rest. I was able to convince them to take the video down, so it's not up anymore."

I rubbed my forehead, feeling frustrated. "Should we thank you, Nov? Fuck, they took an extremely vulnerable video of me and blasted it on the internet. I was harassed, nearly assaulted because of that video."

"I know, it's unforgivable. I know." Nova held her hands up. "But it wasn't Matt who did it. He just knows someone in the club who did."

"Nova, we love you, but you cannot be serious about dating someone from a rival club. Especially after Dad forced everyone to leave Rose Ridge. The threat from Max is still hanging over our heads. I mean, shit, we're in lockdown as we speak." Taryn argued, tossing her hand out every so often.

Nova waved her off. "That's Matt and a few of his friends. They rode to make sure I was okay. I'll tell Uncle Killian once I'm no longer within range of being held hostage by my mom and dad."

"So you're telling them then?" I asked, trying to catch up.

Nova pulled her fingers tightly together. "I'll tell them I'm dating Matt, but it can't ever get out that they were the ones behind the video…"

My sister slowly stood from her chair and let out a sigh. "The men who came here with you are a danger to us, Nova. Surely you can see that, otherwise what motive did they have to release that video of Royce?"

Nova seemed shocked by Taryn's statement with how her brows curved in, and her lips thinned. "Matt isn't like that…"

"But you can't speak for his club." Taryn laughed, but not in a way that would be considered funny. "You don't even know if they're somehow connected to the Destroyers do you? That asshole who came here and threatened us as kids, the one who's related to your best friend…which, by the way, what does Ryle think of all this?"

Nova's grimace was answer enough.

"He doesn't know?"

"We're not as close as we used to be, mostly because he fucking disappeared. Have you two tried talking to Rook lately? It's impossible to get either Silva brother to respond to texts, DMs, phone calls, or anything."

I hadn't really thought about the Silva brothers in a while, outside of what I read about when I was cleaning their house. I had a bit of a bone to pick with Rook.

"So we're supposed to let you leave and ignore the danger this club poses to ours and lie about it all so your boyfriend stays protected?" I asked bluntly.

She was going to pretend like we didn't need to be in lockdown, and downplay who was here, but really, they were extremely dangerous.

"Can you just trust me? They don't want a war," Nova begged.

I argued right back just as vehemently. "But a war is exactly what they're going to get, Nova. You're being stupid and reckless. You know exactly who they'll use as bait when the time comes."

Her eyes slammed shut as she turned her head to the side. "Matt isn't like that. He would get me out if it ever came to that."

There was no use in arguing with her, she had her mind set. Taryn must have figured that too because she tipped her head back, catching my gaze.

"Thank you for telling me, and for getting the video taken down, Nov. I truly appreciate that, I hope you know that. I just love you like a little sister and want you to be okay."

"I know, but honestly, Royce, I don't think a war will start over this." Nova joked.

My resolve was starting to wane, and something like a rabid animal began burrowing through my chest. I stepped closer, hissing in reply. "If Ford ever finds out that they're linked to releasing that video, I promise you there will be a war."

"Dad wouldn't allow him to, Sis," Taryn added her thoughts, but she didn't know what I felt deep in my gut.

"The second Ford becomes president, he will." If he wasn't already.

"So we don't let it leave this room." Nova suggested with a shrug of her shoulder.

Taryn checked with me first, but all I did was give her a nod. "It doesn't leave this room."

Nova finally stood, concluding this. "I better go, so they'll leave the area."

Taryn pulled her friend into a hug first, and then Nova came over to me. "I have a feeling our entire world that we grew up with is about to be tossed on its head, Royce. I'm glad you and Ford stayed. I never knew why he did, but it seems like maybe it was because of you."

She pulled away, and I couldn't help but let my mind wander to the possibility of that being true. Ford had an entire plan in place for college, and to become a mechanical engineer, and then out of the blue, two months before he was set to leave, he decided to stay. I had never asked him why, nor had I cared, but now it seemed it was all I could think about.

Maybe Nova was right. Perhaps everything I knew was about to be tossed on its head.

NINETEEN
FORD

"WE CAN'T KEEP THIS CHARADE UP." JAMESON'S RASPY VOICE ECHOED through the room as he tipped back the glass of whiskey.

The late afternoon light cut through the top windows of the club, making dust motes dance in the air. As if it were simply a lazy summer day and not a tense lockdown that had our members nervous about who was patrolling our town. I checked my watch to see if Royce was done talking to Nova, and she'd confirmed so hours ago.

I was ready to head back to her when she informed me she was taking a shower and had some work to do, telling me to come find her when I was done. I never thought I'd have to balance running the club and feeling pulled to leave it simply because I didn't like being apart from her.

Johnson immediately caught my eye before checking with my dad, and Killian to see if they agreed. The club had been called in for the lockdown, but most of them were outside, keeping post while a few milled about but out of earshot.

The wolf who wanted to rip my throat out flashed an angry look at me before replying to Jameson. "You think it's time to let people know?"

Jameson tipped his glass back again, this time emptying it. "I think that I'm tired of there not being a clear and understandable line of leadership. We need to get the men used to Ford because if we're thrust into a war tomorrow, they're only going to listen to Killian. The whole point of this was so that they'd listen to you, Ford. We're too old to be fighting these young fucks who want to start shit for the fun of it."

Killian took a sip of liquor, but his angry glare slid up, landing on me. I was about done with his glares and the bullshit attitude he kept giving me. I didn't shy away from handing him the same ire in my stare. My gaze stayed directly on him while I sipped my drink, daring him to throw a punch. I hated to say it, but I was starting to see why Lance had such a problem with him. Once Killian had you on his bad side, it was all brambles and thorns, teeth and blood. The man was vicious.

"Shit, we're about to become grandparents in a few years. All of our kids are grown, I want to be that old fuck who rocks on his porch and gives his grandkids rides on the back of my motorcycle," my dad said, his voice full of emotion. He could easily be talking about Ellie, but I suspected he was talking about Royce and me. Based on the conversation we'd had in the office, how they knew why I'd stayed behind, he knew I was in love with her, and now I had her.

Killian wouldn't be able to cope with the idea of his daughter becoming my wife, or the fact that I'd be his son-in-law and his grand-kids might have my eyes and carry my last name.

"That what you want too, King?" Killian asked Jameson.

Connor's dad nodded, setting his glass down against the wood bar. "Yeah, I could see that. If I could get Nova to stop leaving so much, and she'd stick around or Connor to come back home, fuck it'd be nice to have that. See little kids running around Penny's legs while she takes them out to the pond. I wouldn't hate that."

Killian scoffed, tilting his head back. "While you pricks are all picturing this life of retirement, my daughter is about to become the target of these fuckers who are after this club. All because Ford couldn't keep his goddamn dick in his pants."

There was a roaring in my head, but you could hear a pin drop in the room. I moved, but my dad moved faster. His hands gripped

Killian's leather cut and pushed him. Killian pushed him back. "You're out of line, Kil."

"*He's* out of line. He was supposed to leave like everyone else!" Shoving against my dad's hold, Killian pointed at me. "You fucked everything up when you stayed. You were never supposed to be here, and now she's going to be targeted because of it. She's going to be tossed into this world that I never wanted her in. We drop this charade, and she starts wearing that patch telling everyone who she belongs to…and that's it. She's done."

His voice cracking made my chest ache, and I knew it affected my dad too because he loosened his hold on him.

Normally, I wouldn't give a flying fuck about his opinion, but I could empathize with the fact that he was worried about her. "I tried to stay away from her, Killian. I did. This wasn't something I wanted for her either."

Killian got that crazed look in his eye that we all knew was associated with the moniker of the wolf given to him. He was about to attack.

"You didn't stay away. Ford, you waited. You fucking chose to remain here, in Rose Ridge, after I tried so hard to get everyone out. You weren't supposed to become a Stone Rider. We didn't intend for you to be our legacy. You were supposed to leave so that when the shit came down, all of you would be safe."

My anger rose, forcing my words to come out sharp. "We are safe. We're safe because of everything I've done to ensure we are. The men might not follow me, but at least we have enough weapons, money and allies to protect us."

"By getting into bed with the fucking Mafia." Killian scoffed. "We were finally getting free of all the shit your grandfather put us through by making this club a one-percenter club."

My dad shook his head, lowering it so he stared at his boots. "You're being unfair, Kil. We all agreed to go back to that patch. You grew up with Simon, you know exactly why this club has always carried that patch. Ford did what he had to, and he did it with the blessing from the club. You're pissed about Royce, but truthfully, she couldn't have picked better. She's safe with Ford. She'll be protected here."

A vein seemed to emerge in Killian's forehead as his face contorted in anger. "But is her heart? He couldn't even admit to us why he stayed."

"Because of her!" I roared, frustrated that he was being so obstinate and in front of men that I was now leading. "I dumped my entire fucking future because of her, is that what you want to hear? When I realized she'd be staying behind, I didn't trust you or your men to keep her safe. Not the way I would. None of you would watch her like I would. None of you loved her the way I did." My heart raced as I ran my hand through my hair. "The way I still do. This club has been the outline of my life for years, Killian, but Royce has always shaped the center. She's been my constant dream. The one that made all others pale in comparison."

Killian searched my face while his chest rose and fell heavily. My dad's eyes were glassy, and Jameson's anxious gaze combed the space between us. Finally, Killian stepped closer until he was directly in front of me. "Then you owe it to her to explain who you are in this club, and what it will mean to wear your patch. More importantly, you'll need to make sure she knows why Rodney is going to pass her over for this job promotion."

"Fuck Rodney, we're going to buy the Hollow anyway," I spat.

Killian paused as he walked past me. "We'll own it for the purposes of our illegitimate business. She wanted to own it for herself. So, in a way, yes, by claiming her, you're also stealing her dream. Maybe give her the choice, Ford. She chose her dream over Connor, think she'll choose differently with you?"

Fear was a tight thread, looping through my heart. No, I had no delusions whatsoever that she'd choose me. But I wasn't like Connor; I could never just walk away from her. So, if she didn't choose me, then I'd stay until she did.

Royce was forced to miss a night of work because of the lockdown, which meant she was in her room when I went looking for her. Killian had decided to stay with his family during this security breach, so none of them were required to travel over to the clubhouse to stay. This, of course, he hadn't relayed until hours after I'd waited to hear from him. He made it seem as though they were all headed over, but hours later none of them showed. So, I had gone home, packed a bag and now, here I fucking was.

I gently rapped my knuckles against her door after sweet-talking Laura into letting me into the house. It was Taryn I had to convince to let me up the stairs, and neither of which planned to tell Killian.

"Come in!" came muffled from the other side of the door.

I pushed it open, seeing Royce sitting up in bed with a notebook in front of her and her phone playing some video of a band playing. She was in a thin pink tank with tiny straps and a pair of pink underwear.

Jesus.

"I was wondering when I was going to see you again." She smiled up at me, pushing back against the pillows.

"Sorry, I had some club business to attend to."

She folded the notebook and set it aside, same with her phone. "Did you sneak up here?"

"Nope." I shook my head and then slid out of my unlaced boots. "I brought a secret weapon with me." My coat was also half undone, which made it easy to grip the ball of fur inside.

"You brought Gus?" Royce launched off the bed and immediately pulled him from my arms. Her mouth went to his face where she kissed him and then began whispering sweet nothings. Her arms came together, making her cleavage practically spill out of her flimsy tank top. My cock throbbed behind my jeans, and the ache I'd carried for her since early this morning came roaring into focus.

"So my cat gets kisses before I do?"

She gave me a sexy smirk. "Maybe."

Well, then, fuck. While she held Gus, I pulled her by the waist and lightly tossed her onto the bed. She let out a small yelp while clutching Gus tighter. I gripped her ankles and spread them wide. "If you get to kiss *my* pussy cat before you'll kiss me, then I get to kiss *your* pussy."

"Ford," she gasped, "Did you even lock the door?"

No, I did not. "How about I press you up against the door and that way we'll know if someone tries to come in." I slid out of my jacket, and then fit my shoulders between her thighs, dragging her closer to the edge of the bed.

Pressing my nose against the fabric of her underwear, I groaned deeply. "Fucking hell, you smell good."

I wanted to stay right there for the rest of the night, but I also needed to taste her. My tongue darted out, licking along the seam. She released Gus, and sank her fingers into my hair as I teased her, biting the pink fabric and tugging it away from her slick center. "Ford." She pushed me closer to her while tilting her hips forward. I ripped the fabric to the side in a rush and swirled the tip of my tongue over her clit. She released a sharp cry that was followed by the sound of a door slamming down the hall. She froze beneath me, which was the only reason I paused.

"Shit. Hang on." Her legs closed, forcing my head away. Then she jumped up and gently placed her ear to the door while sliding the lock into place. Once she turned back to face me, she whispered.

"Take off your clothes. If you're going to sleep here, then you need to be out of your cut and jeans. I want to feel your skin against mine."

I didn't hate hearing that she wanted me here, so I did as she said. She watched with a hazy gleam in her eye as I slipped my shirt up over my head and then pushed my jeans down. I was in my socks and boxers when she finally pushed off the door. Crossing her arms, her fingers gripped the hem of her tank top before pulling it up over her head. I stared, dumbfounded, over how fucking perfect she was.

Her breasts lightly swayed as she pushed her delicate underwear down her legs. I stared at her, taking in every small detail. Every curve of her body, the way her belly button dipped, and how, when she walked backward, I saw how her pussy gleamed. She clicked the lamp, plunging the room into shadow. There was a small, glowing light from the corner of the room, but it was difficult to make out all the details that made her so perfectly defined.

I was obsessed with the bow of her lip, the freckle over her left breast, and the way she smirked when she felt challenged. Even if she never let me fuck her, I'd be obsessed with her. Even if all I ever got to do was stand there and study her. That would be enough.

"My father might kill you for being here." Her fingers slowly traced near my throat, up along my jaw. My eyes slid shut, and I tried to press the feel of her hands into my memory like a dried flower into a journal, so even when she chose her dream over me, I'd remember her. I'd remember every touch, how she smelled like roses, how her eyes looked like the ocean at first light, and how her heart was as beautiful as that meadow she loved so much.

"Let him come, Rose. He knows better than anyone that I won't be leaving your side. If he wants to waste his energy fighting me, then he can. I'll find my way back up here into your bed, next to your fucking perfect skin and this hair that smells like a flower that I hope to God someone lays across my grave when I die because that scent has marked my very soul."

I caught her chin as it wobbled the smallest bit, and without another word she rushed forward and pressed her mouth to mine. Cradling her head in my palms, I moved my tongue along her lips, making her gasp. We walked backward toward the bed, where she pressed her knees into the soft mattress. I followed her, my arms still cradling her to me while we eventually made our way down where her back was pressed into her pillows and her legs wrapped around my waist.

The truth I owed her was a heavy, incessant tap against my mind, drowning out all the filthy things I wanted to mutter against her ear. I knew I had to come clean, I had to tell her, but I also knew the second that I did, I'd lose her. And I couldn't risk losing her when I'd just barely gotten her, not after watching her every move for so many years. Not after loathing her just so I'd stop obsessing over her.

With my cock notched at her entrance, I slowly pushed inside her. My breath caught in my chest, a choked plea as her fingers ran over my scalp and her hips rose to take more of my length.

"Ford."

Her broken gasp undid me. Gripping her hip, I pulled her closer, driving my cock deeper inside her cunt. I needed more of her. Fuck. "I need all of you." Our bodies moved ardently against one another, my desperate moans sliding along her throat while I lowered my mouth to her pebbled nipples. My tongue slicked over one, while tugging the small bud into my mouth.

Her hips rose and fell in a brisk cadence while I rotated forward, pulling her closer.

"Fucking perfect. Fucking mine," I rasped.

Her breathing was labored and sharp. Her moans were growing louder, so I quickly reached up and covered her mouth. The second my hand was in place, she arched her back and released a scream behind my palm. She was so fucking tight that I came too, letting out my own moan into her neck while I continued to rock into her. Once I was spent, I slowly removed my hand from her mouth, and she gripped my wrist and pressed a kiss to my palm.

The action made my heart skip.

Once I pulled out of her, and we cleaned up, I slid back into bed. My head was down on her pillow, smelling her intoxicating scent when I pulled her against my chest.

"I could get used to this," she joked.

It wasn't funny to me, and perhaps she didn't quite understand the gravity of this. "Fuck, please do, Rose. Because unless death is trying to tear me away from you, I plan to have you next to me every foreseeable night in the future."

She turned toward me, slowly pushing her hands into my hair. A movement I was starting to love.

"Ford, what is this between us? You speak about me like—"

"Like I love you?"

Her eyes were so bright I could see how wide they'd grown even in the dimness of the room. When she didn't reply, I chuckled lowly before stroking her side and up along her back.

"Does that scare you?" The sound of Gus purring could be heard from where he'd curled up near our feet. I urged again, "The idea of me loving you, does that scare you?"

The pads of her fingers moved over my lips. "No, it thrills me, Ford. I've wanted to be inside your head the way you've been inside mine for a long time."

She still didn't get it. "Rose, you're not in my head. You're in my veins, my fucking blood. You've consumed me for far longer than I think you'll ever comprehend. When I was ten and I kissed you…"

"Then told me you wished you really hated me because it would be easier?" I saw her brow flick up, and I traced it with my finger. "It *would* have been easier. I wasn't lying about that."

Her voice was broken with awe as she asked, "You truly wanted to hate me?"

If only she knew the depths of how desperate I was to despise her. "It was either watch Connor tell everyone he'd grow up to marry you or hate you. It became easier to want distance from you."

She stroked my jaw, dragging her finger over the hair there. "Must have been so hard for you when you found out I was staying in Rose Ridge."

"Hard for me?" Connor left her here, just fucking walked away as if she was the kind of woman you'd find twice in one lifetime. Fucking idiot.

"You planned to go to college and had a full-ride scholarship. I always wondered what happened with your family that made you stay behind."

I needed to find a way to tell her all of it, but she was stroking my jaw, and it felt so fucking good. Having her in my arms, and feeling the heat from her skin, it was too much. I couldn't give this up.

"Do you want to know a secret, Rose?"

She leaned in and pressed a kiss to my chin. "Always."

I sucked in a silent breath. "That night when I went to Connor's and he said to give you that box…there was something that snapped inside of me. It was like this dam that I had tried to build with twigs and mud, it just burst. He was leaving you, letting you go, and I saw this box full of moments that didn't belong to me. Connor was just letting it all go, and I couldn't seem to fathom it. I couldn't seem to wrap my head around it. How could he release this one thing that I had envied of his all this time?"

"So you kept the box?" Royce joked. I could hear the smile in her voice, and I wanted to swallow it.

"No, baby. I stole it. The life he wanted, the girl he loved, the dream…I decided right then and there that I'd take what he was so easily willing to give up. I'd take it for myself, and I didn't care how long it was going to take, I knew that one day we'd be here. With you in my arms, and me confessing how fucking insane I am for you."

She didn't say anything, so I pressed my mouth to her forehead in a gentle kiss. Then I brushed the space under her lashes and realized she was crying.

"You weren't supposed to be sad about all that. I'm sorry, I know I'm—"

"I love you, Ford," she cut me off with a raspy confession. My chest grew tight as I froze and she continued. "It's easy to say that maybe I always have, but not like this. Not this desperate, wild thing that seems to have burrowed deep into my heart over the past month. I've known you my entire life, and yet these moments we've stolen and—I wasn't ready to hear that you'd secretly pined for me."

I smiled, regardless that she couldn't see it, I knew she'd sense it. "I'm feeling a little insecure because I think if I line it up, you fell for me after you met Gus."

Her laugh was warm against my face, but went deeper, sliding under my skin.

When her arms came around me in a tight hug, I held her to me completely and utterly terrified that if I let up even the smallest bit, this moment would fade and somehow I'd wake up to find this all a dream.

TWENTY
ROYCE

The tablet might as well have been glued to my chest for how tightly I clutched it. The band playing was one that I had been emailing for months to come visit, and the fact that they'd actually agreed was currently blowing my mind. They'd announced their stop on their social media, which had close to five hundred thousand followers, and suddenly our little venue was packed to the brim.

People were ecstatic, especially because I'd talked to Charlie and planned a specialty cocktail that was tailored to the band's name: *Dark Theory*.

A hand came down across my shoulder, startling me into a slight jump.

"Sorry, didn't mean to scare you." Nick said, pulling me into his side. I immediately stepped out of his hold.

"No worries, but don't touch me, please." He'd never given me creeper vibes before, but I didn't like any person touching me just because they thought they could.

He immediately lifted his arm. "Sorry, just wanted to congratulate you. I can't believe Rodney is still gone and missed this. If he doesn't give you the promotion after all of this, he's insane."

I noticed out of the corner of my eye and saw Ford watching Nick intently. His arms were crossed over his leather cut that had his name stitched in red. My heart seemed to do a dip at knowing he was close. While Nick wasn't dangerous, I secretly loved that my boyfriend was bothered that a man had touched me. As a little girl, I grew up watching my father act crazy possessive over my mother, not in a controlling way. She had the freedom to live her life, and do whatever she wanted, whenever she wanted but if a man stood too close, or watched her from across the room, or on the rare occasion, had the audacity to flirt with her, Dad would become *the Wolf*. I wanted that, deep down somewhere secret. I had invisible hopes and dreams stitched across my heart, and having a man look at me like Ford was looking, while seeming murderous toward the man next to me, was doing things for me.

"Thanks, I appreciate it," I muttered to Nick. While his intentions were kind, I knew he'd never say that I deserved the promotion in front of Rodney. He'd never once had my back during the few years that I had to push and pull to get ideas approved around here. Him bringing up the fact that Rodney was still gone made me reconsider my earlier idea that Nick and Rodney were talking but leaving me out. Just like me, Nick had no idea where our boss had gone.

"Have you heard when he'll be back?" I asked as the band finished another song.

Nick eyed the stage but shook his head. He was enjoying this little break. The band had their own sound guys who would handle all the tweaks and mic modifications for them. Nick was given the night off, but since he was still required to oversee any questions, he was hanging around.

"I think he's on vacation or something. Super weird though that he hasn't said anything to either of us."

Super weird indeed. I thought back to the bikers I saw him meet, and recalled that he was dealing with a rival club, which meant he was an idiot and likely into something deep. Honestly, he could be dead, and we just didn't realize it yet. I decided I'd had enough of Nick's presence and headed over to the darker part of the club where Ford stood.

Knowing he'd like it, I stopped directly in front of him with my back to his chest, my head notching directly under his chin. I felt his warm breath against my hair seconds before his hands landed on my waist, yanking me closer.

"He nearly lost that arm." His raspy voice warmed my ear, sending a shiver down my spine. He couldn't see me smiling, but I grinned from ear to ear.

His arm looped around my middle, his palm resting against my stomach as he swayed to the song. I closed my eyes and allowed myself to get lost in the beat and the way their voices melded perfectly with the moody guitars. Their music was art, and I felt so alive standing there, knowing I was the reason they were currently in Rose Ridge. There were now hundreds of tags, and tweets, and posts about being here, and how delicious the Dark Theory cocktail was. There were a few trending posts about how this tiny gem, hidden in a small town was a must-visit. This was what I had worked so hard for. I wanted the Hollow to become a place that people from all over would visit simply because they wanted to be a part of the magic. I'd check in with Annie upstairs who was running the bookstore, but I was sure her coffee shop and used bookstore were doing incredibly well tonight too.

If we had nights like these consistently, it would be a total game-changer. Not to mention the way it would boost other businesses in town.

Ford's mouth came down next to my ear again. "I can't believe you pulled all this off, Rose. This is truly incredible."

This time I couldn't help but let him see my smile. I spun around, looping one arm around his neck while still clutching the tablet, and kissed him. The tune of the song slowed, and transitioned into something sexy and dark, which had our kiss sliding from PG to PG-13 really fast. His hands roamed down to my ass where he squeezed tight, eliciting a moan from me.

"I've been fantasizing about this leather miniskirt all fucking night." His fingers trailed over the hem, which grazed my fishnet stockings. "I know you're working, but I just need a table, something I can bend you over."

Heat pooled in my belly, making all logic and sense leave my brain.

I was working, but I wouldn't need to do anything for at least another half an hour. I was just watching and enjoying the music until they finished their set. Pulling his hand, I led him to Rodney's office.

I quickly unlocked it, and once we pushed inside, the tablet went to the small side table as Ford walked me backward. His hand went to my jaw as he pulled me in for a kiss. It was heated and messy as his tongue warred with mine, but then in a quick movement he pulled away and turned me so I faced the desk.

"I know you're not wearing underwear." He grated against my ear.

Fuck, this was insane. No one had ever made me feel this alive, or made me not wear fucking underwear to work, but here I was, guilty of being bare, with just the stockings under my skirt.

"How?" I asked, heavy and raspy with need.

His laugh was low and dark as his teeth pulled my ear lightly. "Because you leaned over the bar earlier, baby. You were quick, I doubt anyone else saw, but I did. I saw your ass, and my cock has been hard ever since."

"I wouldn't have ever done this before, Ford. You make me crazy. I knew you'd come tonight, and I thought it might excite you." My confession was all choppy as I tried to breathe normally.

He pushed my chest against the desk as his hand began stroking over my ass. My skirt was flipped up, and he toyed with the flimsy netting. "So you did this in hopes that I'd fuck you at work?"

God, I was a mess, but yes. As horrible as that made me, yes, I hoped he'd lose his control and fuck me in a random corner.

"Answer me, Rose." His finger slid through the gap in the wide netting, finding my slick center. My eyes closed as I released a shuddery breath.

"Yes. I hoped you'd fuck me tonight."

"Good. Now tell me if you like this." His finger stroked up and down my pussy, making me buck my hips toward the desk.

"Ford," I begged, my chest was on fire with how good he made me feel. I had never been so turned on in my life.

"One last question, baby." His tongue traced the shell of my ear as his fingers played with the wetness of my cunt, which was only increasing the more he touched me. "These might tear a little, you okay with that? I'll do my best to fit my cock through these gaps, but I don't plan on fucking you slow or gentle."

I instantly pictured the black netting tight against my ass while he slid in and out of me, using one of the holes to fit his thick cock through. It would definitely rip. "Tear it if you must. Just fuck me, please." I sounded like I was about to die, but honestly that's how it felt. The ache between my legs was so intense, I worried I'd die from need.

Ford shifted. I assumed he was lowering his pants. He moaned happily as I felt the warm tip of his cock prod at my thigh, and then there was a ripping sound as the he met my soaked center. He stroked up and down my slit before he began pushing forward. My fingers curled around the edge of the desk, which toppled a pen holder and forced a stapler to drop to the floor.

I gasped as he gripped my hips and pushed further inside, filling me entirely. The skirt around my hips constrained me in a way that made this hotter, and his deep strokes more intense. He groaned loudly as he pulled his cock out of me, and then shoved forward, forcing the desk to slide.

"Oh, fuck," I cried. My eyes slammed shut, my fingers tightly holding on as Ford lifted my waist and began hammering into me at a brisk pace. He wasn't gentle, and he wasn't slow. No, he was so rough and fucking desperate that he had my orgasm building faster than it ever had before. I was panting, but the aggressive movement of his jolts had me scrambling for a better hold on the desk, which knocked even more things off.

"Do you have any idea how this looks, Rose? My swollen cock sliding in and out of your pretty cunt while you have these fishnet stockings on? Fuck, baby, this image will be ingrained in my memory forever." His voice was strained and his breathing was labored as he continued his rough pace.

The desk was noisily moving, which would surely have alerted anyone that we were in here if the music wasn't blaring loudly in the hall.

"Fucking mine. All mine." He rasped in a choppy, hoarse voice.

My cheek was plastered to the desk; tears had gathered from how good he felt inside of me. I was frantic in a way I hadn't felt before. I needed to rip my fingers through his clothes, tear his skin, brand him in the same way he'd branded me. I needed him to keep moving and keep going even though I was fairly certain a pen was lodged into my hip.

"Harder, Ford. Fuck me harder."

His fingers gripped my ass cheek, and he let out a grunt. "Already milking my cock so fucking tight, baby, I—" But his movements became more untethered, as another rip sounded and then somehow his cock landed so deep inside me that it set off an earth-shattering orgasm. My voice was shrill as I came undone with a scream. His dirty praises increased as his movements quickened, and he slammed home, and then a roar came from him as he froze.

I wasn't even aware of him pulling out, but I felt when he'd gently started cleaning me with tissue. "Do you need me to go find you anything?" He pressed a kiss to my forehead as he helped me up from the desk.

I shook my head. "I'm okay, thank you."

"How bad did I rip them?" He winced, which was cute and made me smile. I didn't care about the tights, or the fact that I was at work. I loved that he was here every night with me. I'd moved from being worried about his presence and how it would impact my promotion to not caring. Over the past two weeks, we'd fallen into a routine that I loved. Every night, I was in his bed, just as he'd requested.

We were in a bit of a bubble, which had him removed from the club at night, and had me not going home. I'd go see my family during the day, but by dinner, I was driving over to Ford's. Some nights I'd cook for him, other nights, we'd go out and find a spot to eat together or Ford would cook. It was the happiest two weeks of my life. I'd stopped worrying as much about Taryn, although she'd check in with me from time to time. I was gloriously unaware of any drama that existed outside of my bubble, and that's exactly how I wanted to keep it.

"Let me go to the bathroom and freshen up, and I'll be right out," I said before dipping into a crouch to pick up all the things that had fallen from Rodney's desk. Ford immediately dropped down to help.

"There is some small pleasure this brought me," Ford joked.

I smiled over at him. "Fucking me on Rodney's desk?"

He nodded before picking up the stapler that had fallen, but a piece of paper immediately floated from the bottom as he lifted it.

Furrowing my brow, I reached forward, plucking it up. "What is this?"

Ford was over my shoulder, reading.

Topher McDaniels

563-222-9468

"Why the fuck does he have the phone number for the president of the Murdoch Devil Riders?"

My face swung his way. "You know about the Murdoch Devil Riders?"

His eyes narrowed. "Of course I do. How do you know about them?"

Oh shit. All I could think of was Nova. If I said how I knew, then she'd hate me, and it would eventually lead back to the fact that they were behind the video, or at least the ones hired for it. I didn't want to get her in trouble or throw her under the bus, not when she seemed to be happy with the guy she was dating.

"Just talk," I said easily, then asked, "Could these be the bikers Rodney was meeting with that day you told me not to follow him?" I knew what Connor had told me, but I didn't want to let on that I'd been keeping things from him.

Ford's thick brows curved as confusion tugged his mouth down. "No, those were Soul Reapers."

Why had Connor said they were the Murdoch Devil Riders then? Something wasn't adding up.

"Could they be working together?"

Ford took the paper and then stood, stuffing it into his pocket. I rose as well, watching him wearily.

Before he could respond to me, he pulled his phone out and placed it next to his ear.

"I need you to come down to the Hollow. Kody and Rev need to go through every single item in Rodney's office. Check everything. Sweep for bugs too."

Once he hung up, he slid the phone into his pocket. I was tempted to pull out mine and call my dad, so I could ask why Ford was the person who just made that order. I waited as a band seemed to wrap around my chest. Why wasn't he telling me?

I refused to guess it, to make it easier on him. If we were going to be in a relationship, he had to do this. We had to be able to trust one another, and this was so far beyond club bullshit that the men liked to keep secret. This was about who Ford has been to me my entire life, and who he'd become over this past month.

He said he loved me, which meant he'd include me.

"Come on, Rose, I want you out of here." He gently touched my hip and guided me out of the room. My chest flushed pink as irritation scratched and reminded me how close I was to losing him. Worse, reminded me how I might not have ever even had him in the first place.

Ford waited for me to finish work. He'd resumed his spot near the wall, but kept his phone in his hand, except for when his guys arrived. When they came in, he'd disappeared back into the office. I didn't follow or ask about the note we'd found. I knew it was no longer my business according to Stone Rider law. However, I had my own secret with Taryn and Nova, and I felt a sense of pride over owning that. Not to mention, Connor had shared a piece of information that didn't line up with the information Ford had and I wasn't sure what to do with that.

While I was annoyed with Ford, I still straddled the back of his bike and hugged his chest on the way home. Except we didn't go home. We rode to the clubhouse, and while my stomach flipped at the implication of what this might mean, I decided not to be bothered by it. If anything, I could walk over to my house, or steal Ford's bike.

The club was packed with people. Music played, beers were sipped, and a few women milled about. I didn't think Jasmine would be in because while I didn't like her, I knew she wasn't the type to be toyed with.

Ford held my hand as we walked in through the throng of members. He was careful to keep me close, especially as a few men eyed me with hooded gazes. It made me curious when Ford planned on giving me his property patch. It would be nice to walk around the club without worrying that I would be harassed or groped by anyone. Things were different because it wasn't just my father who would kill a member if they touched me: It was also Ford.

"Need you to stay here, baby." He set me on a stool near the bar and then slid his leather cut off his shoulders and placed it around mine.

I quirked a brow at him. "Thought I was getting my own."

His smile was tight as he pulled my hair from under the leather. "It's coming, I promise."

I opened my mouth, about to challenge him on why he was waiting when I knew it didn't take that long to make them, considering my mother was the one who ordered new cuts and property patches. But Jameson suddenly burst in through the back door, yelling.

"Just fucking stop!"

"Dad, please, you're not even giving me a chance to explain!" Nova ran in behind him. My little sister was right behind her, with her chin lifted and her fists clenched at her sides. Connor walked in after her, looking exhausted and annoyed.

Ford placed his hand on my thigh before checking the room.

"You have to explain this to me, Nova, because you're not making any sense," Jameson argued. Ford took the opportunity to get up on a random table and yell at all the members.

"Give us the room, go outside. Just get the fuck out."

They started moving, but a few stayed behind as if they didn't care that it was Ford who was asking. It made me rethink what I had assumed about him being the president because no one would dare defy his order if he was. My dad suddenly threw open the office doors and walked out, yelling at the stragglers. "The fuck are you waiting for? Get out!"

The members scrambled up off their chairs and ran outside. The vast room emptied, save for Jameson in the center with his two kids and my sister. My dad glanced at where I sat with Ford's leather cut on and stopped short. We hadn't talked much since I entered my bubble with Ford. I had a feeling he was aware of when Ford stayed over at our house that night during lockdown, but he'd never said anything about it. Although the following morning, he was cranky as hell. Ford had walked downstairs with me, stared my father right in the eye as he kissed me goodbye and left through the front door.

"You aren't even giving me a chance to explain—" Nova screamed, bringing my mind back to the moment.

Jameson shoved his hand through his hair, letting out a sigh. "Nova, you fucking know better than to date someone from a rival club."

"It's not that simple, Dad!"

"Which club?" Ford suddenly interjected.

Jameson turned toward him. "Murdoch Devil Riders."

Ford's head swung back to me, but so did Nova and Taryn's.

It was Nova's shaky voice that asked, "What did you tell them, Royce?"

"Nothing," I snapped. I felt Taryn's gaze hard on Nova.

"Nov, you already know why Royce wouldn't say anything."

Ford glanced between the three of us while Connor rubbed his brow. I didn't know why he was even here. "Tell me what the fuck is going on. Now."

He directed the question to Jameson, but Nova was the one who nervously replied.

"I started dating a member of the Murdoch Devil Riders."

Ford dipped his chin. "Yeah, I got that much. Why is this club suddenly being discussed, right after Royce and I found the president's name and number taped under Rodney's goddamn stapler?"

"Rodney was working with them." Connor spoke up.

Ford's brows dipped as he argued. "No, he was working with Soul Reapers."

Taryn stared at me as if I was supposed to say something. There was the matchbook address we had found, the news Nova had given us, and now this bombshell regarding the stapler.

This was like a twisted game of clue.

Staring back at her, I tilted my head as if to knock her off the idea of saying anything, but then Ford ruined it.

"You're doing the sister thing. I know that look." His hand raised as he pointed between us.

"How do you know what our sister thing is?" Taryn asked.

Connor sighed. "Because you two are ridiculously obvious about it."

Ford scoffed. "And I've watched Royce's every move for the better part of twenty years. I know how she looks at Taryn when they're hiding something."

Well, shit. How was I supposed to stay annoyed with him when he reminded me how much he loved me all the time?

"Nova, why did you come here, needing to talk to Royce two weeks ago?" Ford directed his question with a raise of his brow.

She bit her lip nervously, which was when Jameson stepped closer to her and pulled her into a hug. "I'm sorry, honey. I shouldn't have yelled. I don't want you to feel like we're ganging up on you."

Her eyes watered which made my heart ache. How did I get her out of this?

"Ford, I found a matchbook with the address, and I didn't want to tell my dad about it because we were worried that perhaps we didn't have enough information. Then Connor told me that Rodney was working with the Devil Riders. I just didn't tell you, but I—"

"Royce," Nova interjected with a bit of a sob, "I'll tell him."

"Nova, I just did." I tried, but she stepped forward and ruined everything with the truth.

"The guy I'm dating, Matt… He told me that Murdoch Devil Riders were paid to take that video of Royce and distribute it. They were supposed to make it look like a hacker did it."

"Wait," I sat forward, now confused. "I thought a hacker sent it to them. Do they know who provided the video?"

Ford's angry gaze fastened to me, but I was too curious to worry that he'd found out I knew more than I had let on. Jameson spoke up, breaking the tension. "If you found a note with their info in Rodney's office, I'm going to go out on a limb and say it was him."

I met Ford's crazed expression straight on. He rubbed his hand over his jaw, his voice strained as he said, "You know this for sure, Nova?"

She gave him a sharp nod. "I was in their club when they started joking about it. They had it playing on the screen—"

Ford flipped the table closest to him, tossing it against the wall. "Fucking son of a bitch!"

I flinched, wishing the smallest bit that Nova hadn't shared that part about the video playing. I could only imagine what was running through his head. It made me slip off the stool and go to him. I cradled his face in my hands, speaking quietly to him.

"Ford, look at me. It's okay. I'm fine, and Nova got them to take it down. It's gone now."

He was shaking under my hands. That crazed way his eyes were searching my face told me he was two seconds from walking out. I knew he was on a razor's edge and about to go start a war. I had to find a way to stop him.

He kissed my palm, then stepped out of my hold. "Keep that leather cut on, baby. Keep it on every single time you enter this club and keep your phone on you."

"Ford, no. Please," I begged him as a cry cracked my voice. He took another step away.

Panic reached inside my chest, yanking at my heart.

"Wait, you—you can't go without your cut…your colors," I cried anxiously, "My dad, he didn't give you permission to go, you can't go."

Johnson appeared in the hall behind us. I turned as tears gathered on my lashes.

He held something leather in his hands, and for two idiotic seconds, I thought maybe it was my property patch. My dad was suddenly at my shoulder, his hand carefully cupping it. "Come on, honey. Your mother is on her way."

"Why?" I turned my head. "Tell him no. Tell him he can't go. He can't go without your permission. He's not authorized to go to war with another club, no matter what the reason is."

My dad's eyes were full of remorse, but he wasn't looking at me anymore, he was staring behind me. I turned to see that Ford was slipping the leather on that Johnson had been holding. It was an exact replica of the one currently on my shoulders, swallowing me in black. Except for one difference.

There, over the left breast, was stitched something new. Something I knew deep down and stupidly ignored.

President.

My mother suddenly entered through the back of the club, storming in on high-heeled boots. She was close enough that when my father confessed, she heard him. "I can't, Royce. Ford's word is law, and if he wants to go to war, then we go."

My mother froze mid-step.

Jameson searched the space between my mother and father, then me, before speaking up. "Ford, we're supposed to be preparing for war against the Destroyers, I think we're playing into their hands."

Ford refused to look up, but his fists clenched and shook.

Connor added his thoughts too. "Ford, think this through. You were obviously given incorrect intel from someone, which is a huge red flag. Besides, they took down the video at Nova's request. That means she holds some sway with them. Let this ride out, and then we'll still be ready—"

"No!" Ford slammed his hand on the bar, making the glass rattle. "You know if they'd done this to Penny, or Laura, or fucking anyone else, you wouldn't hesitate."

My mother was furious as she stepped closer, likely trying to play catch-up. "Am I understanding this correctly, Ford? You're the president of the club?"

"I am."

Mom's eyes blazed with fury as she glanced over at my father. "And for how long?"

"Daisy—" Dad started, but she cut him off.

"How long?!"

Ford's gaze locked on me. "Seven months."

I felt the floor nearly fall from beneath my feet. I had assumed perhaps it was recent, but seven months...that meant when I had gone and asked my father about this initially, Ford had already been leading the club for six months.

"Well, then, I'm not sure why there's even a discussion." Mom folded her arms over her chest. "Your president has made a decision."

"Mom." I whined, as tears still gathered along my lashes. My heart felt too heavy to keep in my chest.

She lifted her chin. "Come on, Royce. This is a world we don't belong in. They've made sure of that."

"Fuck, Daisy, you know—" My dad tried arguing, but she turned and stormed off, back through the exit. Meanwhile Ford just stared at me.

I stared back, confused and hurt. I slid his leather cut off, and he shook his head.

"Do not make me choose between defending what they did to you and having you. It's not in my blood to walk away from this."

I tried to gather as much resolve as I could. All the strength within me to be like my mother. She'd married into this and had been at the mercy of a man who didn't have it in his blood to walk away from any of this either. Yet, she never once backed away from the fire in her veins.

"Mom's right. If you need war, then go get it, Ford. Just know that there will be another one waiting for you when you get home."

I still clung to the leather cut because I couldn't seem to release it, but I turned and followed my mother outside, knowing Nova and Taryn wouldn't be far behind.

TWENTY-ONE
FORD

"FORD!" KILLIAN YELLED SOMEWHERE BEHIND ME. I KEPT WALKING toward the garage where all the firearms were kept. "Ford, I'm talking to you!" Fuck him for giving me no choice but to teach him a goddamn lesson. I stopped mid-step and as soon as he got close enough, I turned around and threw my fist into his face. He instantly fell to the ground and stared up at me in shock.

I pointed at the patch that now boldly proclaimed that I was the president. The members of my club were watching our interaction, my closest men stood in a circle around me, while Jameson stood off to the side. My dad would be here soon, along with everyone else that wanted to remain a patched member.

"Watch how you speak to your president, Killian. You'll always hold a place of honor here, but let me be clear about disrespect." I pressed the heel of my boot into his chest. "It won't fucking be tolerated."

Once I let up, I glanced around the dark yard, seeing a group of confused members. I took that opportunity to address them. "I'm your new president. You owe me your allegiance, and if you don't think you can give it, then you can leave. I know you might have questions, and I'll try to answer them as I can, but here's a few answers. Killian is staying in the club, as long as he can accept that I'm going to marry his daughter someday."

I glared over my shoulder, seeing Jameson help him up.

"Johnson is your new vice-president." I gestured over at my second, who had slid on his new cut that revealed his title. He stood with a grim expression toward the group.

"You know we've been on guard regarding the threat from the Destroyers all these years. We have reason to believe that a club might be working with them, if not more. We're now allies with Death Raiders and the Chaos Kings. Mayhem Riot up in New York remains a loose ally, although their allegiance may shift, as I've heard they also have a new president. The Murdoch Devil Riders are currently connected in releasing the video of Killian's daughter."

One of the men tugged his toothpick out from between his lips, "So we goin' to war?"

"No. We're not." I dipped my chin, gathering my resolve.

Killian's jaw lifted, his busted nose mostly cleaned up. I knew he assumed we were about to go to war, which was why he planned on yelling at me.

"This battle is mine because Royce is mine."

Killian made a sound like this was painful for him. I ignored it.

"I'm going to war with them, but I want Killian to stay back with all of you. It's possible that it's a trap and they want us to play into their hands."

"I'm with you, prez," Johnson said, trailed by Kody, Rev, and the others that had been with me from the beginning. Jameson and my dad would stay back, but what surprised me was Connor stepping forward.

"If you're going to war, Ford, then I'm coming."

I was already shaking my head, but he cut me off. "You're my best friend. Not a chance in hell that I'd let you walk in there without me."

Fine, if he wanted to get himself killed, then he could. I didn't stick around to hear what anyone else said. I booked it toward the garage where the armory was stocked.

Killian followed me closely, and once we were out of earshot and eyesight from the club, he pushed me up against the cement wall.

"You're being a fucking idiot. We didn't go through all of this to keep everyone safe just for you to piss it away on a hotheaded decision."

I shoved him away from me, seething. "What do you suggest I do then? I hope you didn't have to see that video, Killian, but I did. Those fuckers played it in their—"

"I know they did! That's my *daughter*, you think I'm willing to allow that to slide? I'm fucking not, Ford. But you have to be smarter than this. You have to think this through. They targeted her on purpose because she was easy to get to through Rodney. He tried to manipulate her, then humiliate her with that video, and he hoped it would push us into this. He wants you to do something stupid. My gut tells me that Max is behind this, and if that's true then it's not worth it. We'll find him another day, but right now my daughter is hurting over the fact that we lied to her. You wanted me to get on board with the idea of you being with her then prove it to me right now. Prove that you can walk away from war when love is on the line."

I released a painful breath that felt like I'd been holding it for hours. He took a step back and then another while his angry glare remained on mine. "I may not be happy about my daughter being tied to this club, but if what you say is true and you love her, then I'll trust that. I'll trust you."

I didn't even know how to respond. Worse, I had no idea how the fuck I was supposed to let this go. I felt like fire burned under my skin every time I pictured those fuckers watching Royce's body in that video. It made me curious if they'd been in the Hollow and watched her in person, or if they'd found other modeling clips of her. Had any of them dated her? Fuck, I wanted to kill someone.

"As her father," I called out to Killian's retreating form. He paused and looked over his shoulder. "How do you push the images out…the rage? How do you stay when all of you just wants to ride, and put a bullet in someone's head?"

He paused, then said, "Daisy. She grounds me, keeps my head clear."

My fists curled. "And if it were videos of Daisy playing on their screen right now?"

Killian's head lowered, but I pressed on. "The truth. What would you do if someone had leaked a video of her, and you knew they were watching it?"

His jaw tensed, and then he ground out, "I'd burn it all down, Ford. I'd kill every last one of them."

I knew it.

"But if there was a chance I'd lose her by doing it? I'd bide my time. Silas had to wait to kill someone who hurt Natty, took him years of waiting before he finally had his chance. We don't always get a clear-cut path, but we do what will keep the people we love safe."

With that he left the garage while I stood there staring after him. He was likely on his way to apologize to his wife, and somewhere in that house was Royce, hurting and upset.

And I was here, weighing the outcome of war with a rival club. What the fuck was I doing?

TWENTY-TWO
KILLIAN

Twenty-five years I'd been staring at the same view and had yet to grow tired of it. A set of blue eyes that stared so deep into my soul that I worried she'd remove it all together. Silky blond hair that slid through my fingers when she lay on top of my chest while we watched our favorite shows. She was my everything.

My boots echoed as I stopped on the top floor of our house. It was reserved for my wife and her songwriting. It was a space that we'd converted into a bit of a studio where she could record music. I'd convinced her to record ten of her songs within the past twenty-five years, but she loved writing them. She'd even offered to write for a few bigger artists, but she did so under a different name, so no one knew they were even her songs.

I was still so in love with her that when she'd get angry with me, fear would wedge somewhere inside of my sternum, making it difficult to breathe. I fucked up too many times to count, never over anything other than the stupid club. Staying too late or not communicating. Choosing danger when there were two little girls waiting at home for me, and a wife. My beautiful, patient wife.

"I'm in no mood to talk." Her sharp tone made smiling difficult, but I did it just the same, desperate to lighten the mood.

I shoved away from the door and sauntered into her space. A long seat ran the length of the large window, with a soft cushion and various throw pillows. That was her favorite place to sit when writing, but occasionally she'd head to the plush chair in the corner, or her piano.

"Wanna fuck then?" I joked.

She didn't look up from her notebook, which meant she was incredibly pissed.

"Daisy, I—"

She slammed the pad shut and threw it across the room as hard as she could. It crashed into the small table, knocking over a vase of flowers.

"How could you keep something that big from me?" Her voice rose about ten octaves, and I saw how red her eyes were, probably from crying. It made me feel like shit.

I kneeled where the flowers tipped and fixed them, trying to figure out exactly how I was going to explain myself. The truth was difficult to accept; I still hadn't grasped it even after knowing for months.

"You know that I would never lie to you. Ever," I said softly.

Her thick black lashes gathered more tears as she angrily swiped them away. "That's what I thought, Killian. Our entire marriage, you've been honest with me. You've been devoted and loyal, but you know, that for me, if there's even a hint of doubt…it can't work. I can't be worried that you're not being honest with me. Not when you're in that club."

Rushing to the space in front of her, I kneeled and placed my palms on her thighs. "How could you ever assume in any lifetime that I wouldn't be loyal to you? There is no undoing what we are, Daisy. Not ever."

Her hand came to my chest, where under my shirt was my tattoo. It was the flower I'd had stained into my skin when I wasn't even legally old enough to get it. A daisy to represent the dream of finding that one person who would get you when the whole world didn't.

Her voice was rough as she asked, "Then why keep this from me? I don't understand."

My head lowered in shame. "I've wanted to explain this for nearly a year, but every time I opened my mouth"—I shook my head back and forth—"I can't find the words."

Her fingers ran through my hair, then over my neck. "Killian, you need to tell me. I'm with you to the end, you know that. Through thick, thin, and all the fuckery in between. I've stood by your side as your woman, your old lady, your wife. Tell me."

She was right, and it wasn't like I didn't believe that. But I knew she'd panic once I explained all this, still I tipped my head back and told her. "Silas came to me about six years ago with a letter he'd received. There was no return address, and no stamp. It arrived on their front step. It was addressed to Rook, asking if he'd picked a side yet."

Laura's lip wobbled. "Max."

"A week after that another letter arrived. This time it was a warning for them to get out of Rose Ridge."

"That's why you were so insistent on getting everyone out..." she trailed off.

I nodded. "I kept expecting the shit to hit the fan, Daisy. If you remember, I tried to get you to leave with the girls...it's why I begged Connor to propose to Royce. I was desperate to get everyone out of here."

My wife nodded absently while staring across the room. "I remember. You were panicked on a level that I hadn't seen before. It scared me."

"It forced me to make some choices that I wasn't proud of. There were deals I began making that slowly pushed us away from being legitimate. Mostly we flirted with the line, but it helped me feel a little bit safer. Time passed, everyone left, and then nothing happened. I kept waiting and waiting for something to go wrong. We filled the tunnels, and increased security. Then, about a year ago, another letter arrived, but this time it arrived on *our* doorstep."

Daisy had gone pale, her fingers gripping the edge of the window seat. "He was here?"

"Someone was."

"What did the letter say?" she asked nervously.

I didn't want to tell her this part. This was the shit I'd been hiding and burying for the past year. Why I gave up the club, and why I was here, fucking up and about to defend idiot Ford if he decided to go to war.

"It was a question, asking if Royce or Taryn had picked a side or not. Two pictures were included in the envelope of both girls."

She'd stopped speaking and instead wiped at her brow with a shaky hand. I continued confessing.

"I knew then that we needed to do something different. He was still coming for us, but I didn't feel as sharp as I did back when we first got together, Daisy. I felt old, like a worn-out picture, folded in too many places. I didn't feel equipped to do what I knew needed to be done, so I went to Wes with all of it, and Ford walked in on our conversation. Because he heard that Max had left a photo of Royce, he offered on the spot to take over in secret. He wanted to do whatever it took to protect everyone. It was his idea to keep it a secret, that we needed to take Max by surprise when he showed up again. Ford's been making the decisions for the club, which has led us to new business ventures and reluctant allies."

My wife finally stood, letting out a heavy sigh. She ran her hands through her thick blond hair while pacing. "How bad is it?"

"Archer Green connected us with his brother-in-law…a man named Juan Hernandez…he's Mafia. We're working with his sons who have taken over the business since Juan retired. They're rather unconventional in their methods, but just as ruthless as their father. We do things for them, bury evidence, hide what needs to be hidden. Funnel product, all through Ford's construction business."

"Killian, this could put you in prison. If the Feds find out…"

"This is why I haven't wanted to say anything, Daisy. By trying to fix it, we've inadvertently made things worse. Ford is keeping up with what we owe the Hernandez family and ensuring they don't come to collect. I've been trying to make it look like everything is okay in the club. Meanwhile, no one knew that Ford had been acting president of the club all this time."

Laura's face twisted. "I'm confused. What good does it do to have him be the president secretly if none of the men will follow him? They'll all follow *you* into a war not him."

"Max will come for us assuming I'm the one in charge. We're going to have the advantage of a surprise. Ford will have a whole new regiment of men who are loyal to him. He's already made an ally out of Lance, and I have a fairly good idea that the Hernandez boys don't hate Ford. They're Archer Green's nephews, and the group have met on a few occasions. Which means if it came down to it, we'd have Archer's club, as well as his tie into the Mafia."

My wife rubbed at her eyebrow, still pacing.

"Honey, this is insane. I can't even believe you'd risk so much, and all because of one man…why haven't we gone on the offense with him and hunted him down?"

I shook my head, frustrated, but only with myself. "We weighed that option. Heavily considered it, but in the end, we agreed that it was too dangerous. Why run after a bear after it decided not to make you it's meal?"

"But he's been toying with us. He sent photos of our children, Killian. It's not like you to hide in your tower while someone threatens your family," Laura argued, tossing her arm out while wearing a path into the carpet.

This part was what I'd been subconsciously avoiding. I felt depleted, and empty. As if I had nothing left to give.

"I feel like a wolf with no teeth, Daisy. How was I supposed to tell you that I was scared? How was I supposed to explain that nothing had ever scared me so much in my life than during that Christmas when we were all stuck here, and Silas nearly died. We would have all died that night if Archer Green hadn't showed up. Max seems to always have the upper hand, and he wants to erase this club from existence. That fucking terrifies me."

She paused walking and sucked in a sharp breath. Then her feet moved quickly as she got to her knees in front of me. "You're allowed to get scared, my love. Growing old scares me too. Let's be scared together."

I placed my palm over hers, which was against my jaw. "Deal, Daisy."

When she lowered her mouth to mine, I smiled and let her kiss linger. Right as I slid my hands around her waist and pulled her into my lap, my phone rang.

Laura's brows dipped as she watched me fish my cell out. "Who is it?"

"It's Silas." We stared at one another as worry threaded my heart. Silas Silva wouldn't call me for any reason, ever. Unless someone's life was in danger. Natty would call Laura if anything. With a bit of hesitation, I answered.

"Silas?"

There was a pause before a gruff voice replied, "Killian, we're back."

I didn't reply because I wasn't sure what this meant, but then he added, "Do you know why there's a pink motorcycle parked in front of my house? The only person I remember seeing who had pink everything was your kid."

The world seemed to tip sideways. Getting to my feet, I began pacing frantically as I tried to process what he was saying.

"Is anyone inside your cottage?"

"No, it's empty. We've checked the perimeter. No one is here."

Laura's eyes rounded, and then she darted for the door.

"Silas, I need you to find tracks, whatever you have to do…I'm not even going to waste time contemplating. Royce is missing."

TWENTY-THREE
FORD

I'd never been in a relationship before, and the only one I had ever pictured was with Royce. How did I go to her and tell her I'd been an asshole? I had no clue what the fuck I was doing, and now I was parked in front of her house, saw that her bike was gone and she wasn't answering my texts or calls. I knew that likely meant she needed time, but how long? Would she be even more upset if I pushed her boundaries and went to track her down? I wanted to talk to her, tell her I know I fucked up and that I scared her. I saw the fear in her eyes when she begged me to stay. Then I dropped the bomb that I was the president and had lied to her.

Shit. How the hell was I supposed to get out of this? Maybe if I gave her Gus, or if I bought the Hollow for her? But Killian was right, if I bought it, then it would belong to the club, and she'd never love it the same.

I was sitting on my bike, staring at my cell when Rook's name flashed across the screen with an incoming call.

"Hey," I answered roughly. Was this tightness in the throat thing also part of being in a relationship? I felt like I was going to cry every five seconds.

Rook's voice came out rushed as he said, "Ford, my parents are back in town. Dad called me, asking if I've seen Royce."

I froze. That tension practically strangling me as fear began clouding my vision. I was too scared to ask why he was calling. He wouldn't be calling me if Royce was happily chilling in their cottage. He called me because something was wrong.

"Her bike is here, but she isn't."

I knew where she was…there was a place in the orchard she'd go as a kid. She had to be there. She was likely just clearing her head.

Swallowing thickly, I explained that to Rook. "I'll take care of it."

Once I hung up, I started my bike and set off toward the orchard. The entire way, I thought about what I would say to her and how I'd apologize. I rehearsed how I'd explain that I knew I'd gone too far and that I had fucked up by not being honest with her. I was trying to figure out how to say it all, how to demonstrate exactly what I'd do if she gave me another chance when I approached the northern side of the orchard.

When we were kids, we'd play hide-and-seek out here, and as we grew, those games would evolve into capture the flag and other various competitions. Each of us would participate and more often than not, it would be the girls against the guys. They were great memories, but Royce had a special attachment to one of the larger hickory trees outside of the orchard. She'd hide there when the rest of us were supposed to pick lemons or help Uncle Silas.

I parked toward the entrance, so as not to startle her or spook her from staying put. The idea that she might be up in a tree and I could merely climb up to her felt sort of romantic and just the sort of gesture I needed to convince her to talk to me.

The lemon trees were staggered every few feet, yellow fruit hanging among the leaves. The ground was soft earth under my boots, the sky a periwinkle blue. Fuck, nearly the entire night had passed, and I hadn't even slept yet. Which meant Royce hadn't either. Maybe she was curled up in that hickory with a blanket, snoozing. Maybe she'd let me hold her.

The sound of birds waking and cooing filled the air, and then a distant shout.

Something painful twisted inside my stomach, tightening with every step toward the tree. There on the ground was a pile of black leather. As I got closer and dipped to pick it up, I realized it was my leather cut…the one I had slid over Royce's shoulders and told her not to take off. My head swung up, searching the grove, but all I saw were trees and sky.

I scoured the dirt for any signs of where she might have gone, finding only her pink cell phone in a clump of tall grass. My hands shook as I picked it up, and then I heard another distant shout.

With my heart twisting painfully in my chest, I took off running.

TWENTY-FOUR
ROYCE

Never in my life had I ever considered for a single moment that the magical lemon orchard from my childhood would be the place that my worst fears would manifest. I wanted something familiar, something that reminded me of a happier time. Initially, I parked in front of the cottage, but then I remembered when I was there last how it felt like someone was watching me. So I cut through a secret path that only Uncle Silas and all of us kids knew about.

I was warm under Ford's leather as my arms remained fastened to my chest, my gaze on the ground. On the edge of the grove was a massive hickory tree that I used to climb and relax in. It seemed like the best place to curl up and cry, thinking over the way my heart had cracked and splintered over Ford's lies. I realized how in love with him I was, and how deeply he'd sunk into my soul, and worst of all, I realized he'd never left that space.

I'd invited him in when I was just a girl, and it seemed I'd never let anyone else fill it. Not even Connor. I needed a little time to gather up my hurt, sort it, and then begin to heal. It was right when I reached my favorite tree that I realized my stealthy exit plan wasn't so secret.

"I hate to do this to you, Royce," a man's nasally voice sounded in my ear, "But I'm out of options." I froze, immediately recognizing that voice as Rodney's and the metal at my neck was the barrel of a gun.

Panic seized me so tight, I couldn't move. I slowly reached into the leather, going for my phone when Rodney suddenly shoved me. It was such a hard jolt that my phone fell to the ground. "None of that. Let's go, I need you to leave the phone." Rodney kept the gun on me, while shoving me forward again.

"And take this off," he seethed. His fingers gripped the edges and began ripping the leather from my shoulders.

"Fine, fuck. I can do it!" I yelled as he manhandled me. I was too angry to cry, but as I faced him, seeing that stupid triangle patch of hair on his chin, I lunged for him.

The butt of the gun whipped across my face, forcing it to the side. I tried to right myself, but a sudden bout of dizziness hit, making me see double. I couldn't seem to get my feet under me as I tripped toward the tree.

"I don't have a choice, Royce. The entire point of them releasing that video was to draw Ford out and place him at the mercy of the Murdoch Devil Riders. But guess where your stupid as fuck boyfriend is right now?" His mouth was close to my ear, the barrel of the gun pushing into my back.

Rodney began pulling me in the opposite direction of the cottage. I tried to look behind me, but Rodney yanked my arm even harder, shoving me forward.

"He's on his way here, Royce. He was supposed to be headed south, but the fucking idiot is on his way here. Do you know what the Murdoch Devil Riders will do to me when they realize this didn't work? They're going to kill me. So, I thought up a plan B. I'll take you, and Ford will follow."

"Rodney, stop." I tried to fight him, but he kept twisting my arm with a bruising hold. My heart thrashed as I tried to get my feet under me. I knew self-defense; I could use a move to stop him if I could get him to stop pushing me for two seconds. Even digging my boots into the dirt to add resistance so I could pivot didn't work. He shoved my back, making me lose my balance.

"No, Ford is already on his way here. I have to get you out of here."

That meant Ford might be able to hear me. Without giving it another thought, I opened my mouth and screamed.

Rodney slammed the butt of the gun into the back of my head, making me fly forward.

"That was a warning, but if you do it again, I will be forced to knock you out. Now move."

With my head throbbing, my vision blurring, I kept shuffling forward.

I couldn't get in the car with him, or allow them to bait Ford. He wasn't thinking clearly where I was concerned. I had no idea what sort of president he was, or planned to be, but I knew from hearing things from Dad, and a few comments Mom let slip that Ford couldn't afford to rush into a trap. I was still angry with him over the lies, but I also still loved him enough to do whatever I could to prevent it.

Up ahead there was a small ditch, which would force Rodney to lose his grip while navigating the terrain below it. When we nearly approached it, I dropped my weight, which forced us both to fall, and the gun he was holding landed out of reach. I maneuvered to my feet before he did. He wouldn't actually shoot me because he wanted me alive. Which gave me the edge I needed and ran.

Without looking back, I took off toward where we'd come from. I remembered what Rodney said about Ford being close, so I let out another scream. Although uncertain if he really was on his way, I knew it could help me if he had a direction in which to go.

I kept pumping my arms, lifting my legs as I covered more ground. My mind kept going back to Ford. To seeing his hazel eyes again, that warm smile that he'd finally started sharing with me. I thought of Gus, and how Ford and I had barely started our relationship, and someone was already threatening to tear it from us. I began whispering his name as I ran, my heart pounding angrily. My pulse hammering.

There was someone ahead, I could make out their shape. I knew it was Ford. It had to be him. A smile stretched along my face, as tears slid down my cheek. Relief nearly made me falter, but I kept running. He was here. He'd come for me.

He was running toward me, when suddenly a loud shot rang out through the orchard. I worried that Rodney had seen Ford and shot him, but it was me who went down to the ground, my hands landing in the loose dirt and my face sliding against it. It was me who had blood coating my skin, and I realized that perhaps it worked to Rodney's advantage for Ford to see me die as much as it would to discover that I'd been kidnapped.

I'd fucked up, and now I was going to die because of it. My eyes were on the sky, and my pulse felt really weird, my body tingled, my extremities going numb. I wanted to hang on until Ford got there, but it wasn't easy. Darkness clung to my vision, and then I couldn't see anything at all.

TWENTY-FIVE
FORD
AGE FIFTEEN

Our entire school had gathered in the gym to watch the talent show.

Personally, I thought it was childish to still have to go to these, and now that I was in high school, I had hoped to skip it. In fact, I had told Connor I was going to leave at lunch to avoid this event. He, of course, told me he'd be front and center for Royce. He wanted to show her support.

Because, of course, he did.

Royce had many talents, but singing wasn't one of them, and the fact that someone had put it into her head that she could was a travesty. Maybe she thought because her mom could sing, she'd try it too… or maybe it was one of her dumb friends that convinced her, but either way, I knew Royce would not like the outcome of this show.

I suppose deep down I slid onto the wooden bench for the same reason that Connor had decided to show up. More than supporting her, I wanted to see her step up to the microphone and open her pretty lips. I wanted to see what outfit she wore. I wanted to see how her hair looked under the house lights. I couldn't seem to stop this small obsession that I had with her, and adding this mental image of her standing on that stage was a necessity.

I already knew Connor was sitting down on the gym floor in one of the chairs. I stuck closer to the back where Royce wouldn't catch me staring.

There were a few acts ahead of her, each of them boring and none of them pulling me away from my sketchbook long enough to watch all the way through. Then I heard Ms. Mulligan introduce the only girl I'd ever watched so carefully that I knew exactly when she planned to laugh, or cry, or hit someone. I knew every twitch of her lips, every meaning behind that left brow raising. This unfortunately meant I knew when she liked what Connor said to her. She walked onto the small stage wearing a pink dress that fell to her knees. The top was strapless, which made her insecure because she kept pulling it up every few seconds as she walked. Her golden hair was curled and bounced against her back, which meant her little sister had done it for her. Anytime Royce did her own hair, the curls didn't last, and they looked too frizzy. I, unfortunately, found it endearing and it made me like her more.

She closed her eyes as she stepped up to the microphone, then wet her lips. Before she even opened her mouth, I knew what tune I'd hear. Mostly because I knew her, but it was no secret that she had a deep obsession with music from the '90s. Sure enough, she began singing along with the guitar to the dramatic tune to "Iris" by the Goo Goo Dolls. She started off strong, but as the song transitioned, her voice couldn't quite carry the right tune, and then her voice cracked. I could see her face flushing even from where I sat, but things got worse when a group of guys started laughing.

I glared at the backs of their heads as they crowded together and joked. One of them pointed and then yelled. "Isn't her dad in jail or something? Is she singing for tips?"

"She's fuck hot, but her voice sounds like it got trapped in a garbage disposal."

I was two rows above them, but I sat my sketchbook to the side and then shifted down a row, shoving between two girls. They glared at me, but as Royce continued singing her song, her voice went shrill, making the cluster of boys laugh even harder.

From where I was now, directly behind them, I shoved my foot forward, kicking them in the back. It forced them to fall forward into the other kids. One of them stood up and tried to swing at me, but I ducked and threw my fist into his nose. Another one flew at me, trying to get my stomach. I lifted my knee and hit his nose, making blood spray smear his face.

The last kid began screaming at me, "If you want her so bad, just say so. You don't have to pretend to like her voice or attack us for calling it like it is. She sucks!" I stood up and threw my forehead into his face, and several kids gasped and that's when I realized Royce had stopped singing and the school police officer was heading toward us.

Everyone was watching me, including Royce, whose gaze held a look of hurt and confusion. The principal and the dean of students were angrily making their way up the bleachers. Royce held her elbow while everyone ignored her and watched me. Connor ran up to the stage and put his arm around her, helping her off. I stood there, staring at their retreating forms, wondering if all I'd ever be was the guy who messed up. I'd be the villain in Royce's life while Connor and every other guy in her life remained the hero.

Just one time I'd like to be the one who saved her. Just once, I'd like to be the hero in her story.

TWENTY-SIX
FORD
PRESENT

MY LUNGS BURNED AS I RAN, AND BY THE TIME I CAME SKIDDING TO A STOP I thought they might burst. Red blood stained Royce's clothing, my vision blurred, and I dropped to my knees, not even focused on where her abductor might have gone. My shaking hands gently plucked out a twig that had gotten into her flaxen hair. She was turned away from me, so I gently scooped her into my arms, realizing the blood was due to a bullet that had grazed her bicep. She bled from her temple as well, but it looked like it was from hitting a rock on her way down.

Her arm was bleeding badly as it'd ripped her skin open to a wide gash.

"I got you, baby. It's okay." I rocked her while my entire body shook.

She was still unconscious, but it didn't stop me from talking to her.

"We'll get this cleaned up, and we'll take you to the hospital, and it'll be okay." Realizing I needed to get into action, I took a deep, shuddery breath and set her back on the ground. I slipped my jacket off and propped it under her head, and then ripped the bottom part of my T-shirt until it was a thick strip. I wrapped her arm up as tightly as I could, tying it off, and then covered her with the cut I'd grabbed from the ground.

My cell. I needed to call an ambulance, but instead I dialed Killian. He'd get here faster, and he'd ensure we had the protection to get back to the hospital.

The phone rang a few times before I felt something cold and metal press against my neck.

"Hang up." I recognized the voice but couldn't quite piece together who it was.

Anger stirred in my veins as I remained kneeling next to Royce. The leather over her body had a knife tucked inside the pocket, so I carefully began pulling it out as I set the phone to the side.

"Hang it up!" he urged, pressing the gun into my skin.

I shook my head. "No can do."

"You weren't supposed to be here. You fucking idiot, now look…" he sputtered angrily, and I realized it was Rodney who was holding me at gunpoint. Fucking Rodney, of all people. "Look at what you did. You made me shoot her. I didn't want to shoot her. I wanted to take her, and you ruined that."

The folded knife was in my palm, but I'd need to slide the blade free.

"So you wanted to take my girl, from the northern part of the orchard, and have me chase you so you could lay a trap?" I knew Killian was listening, and now I'd told him where to go.

Rodney shifted his feet behind me, but the gun remained against my spine.

"They knew you stepped in as president, I don't know how. They asked about Royce during one of our meet ups, we always shoot the shit, ya know. I talked about how she wanted my job. They told me to dangle it in front of her with the ultimatum. My guess is they were using her to push you guys into a corner, but I'm telling you this because I don't want any more blood on my hands. I'm showing good-will, okay?"

"Who is we, Rodney?" The blade slid out as I gripped the handle. I needed to keep him talking, though.

"How about a little trade? You tell me where you buried money for the Hernandez family, and I'll tell you who hired the Devils to come after you."

"Was it Max?" I asked, mostly to gauge his reaction, but I was also curious if he'd tell me.

"Who the fuck is Max?"

Well shit. I had assumed this would all lead back to the fucker, but I guess not. Someone had hired them, and whoever it was knew that I had stepped in as president.

There was an echo of a motorcycle that reverberated from behind us, which I had to assume would catch Rodney off guard enough that he'd get distracted. I rotated my shoulder, while spinning around and plunged the knife as deeply as I could into whatever I could get to. Rodney shot his gun, but the bullet hit a nearby tree. He fell backward as my knife hit its mark in his stomach. Panic had his eyes widening and his breaths coming in short. I kicked the gun away as I stood over him. The pummel of the blade stuck out from his gut. If I pulled it out, he might bleed out.

Unfortunately for him, I didn't have a conscience about this sort of thing. I'd be the villain in Royce's story in every lifetime if it meant I was the one who hurt whoever hurt her. Smiling down at Royce's boss, I yanked the knife out of his stomach, ignoring his cries of pain, and then shoved it into his chest.

"You piece of shit. You scared her, you left bruises on her arms, and then you fucking shot her." I pulled the blade out again and then sank it into another part of his chest. His screaming faded as his voice became hoarse.

There were footsteps drawing closer to us, along with a motorcycle. I knew Killian had arrived, and possibly Silas. I didn't look up as I locked my gaze on Rodney's terrified expression.

"If I had more time to torture you, I'd take it." With one last tug of the knife, I sank it into his throat for the final blow.

"Jesus, Ford." Killian came to a running stop next to me. He had a gun drawn, but quickly slid it into his back waistband when he realized Rodney was the only threat.

"No one else?" Silas suddenly appeared, also holding a gun loosely pointed at the ground.

I shook my head. "He was taking her to the Murdoch Devils, it was a trap."

Wiping my brow with the back of my sleeve, I leveled Killian with a firm stare. "You were right. They wanted me to attack. It was all a big fucking elaborate plan."

I sank to my knees again, gently pulling Royce into my arms. She groaned, but turned in to my neck as I carried her out of the grove.

Killian followed close behind us, his voice breaking as he asked. "Where did he hurt her?"

"Bullet grazed her arm, she injured her head…and he manhandled her pretty rough, she's got bruises already appearing on her arms."

"Son of a bitch." Killian spat.

Silas grumbled next to us. "Now I can see why you stabbed him so many times."

Our strides were quick as we tried to get back to cottage. Killian asked, "How did you know where she was?"

"Rook called me, told me her bike was at the cottage."

Silas quirked an eyebrow at me. A bit of silver had lightened his always pitch-black hair. He had crows feet near his eyes and a few more wrinkles than I remembered, but the same pale blue eyes, and that permanently pissed off expression.

"But you didn't go to the cottage."

I shifted Royce in my arms so she was higher, and I felt her nose graze my throat. "When Royce was little, there was a hickory tree she loved going to. It was her go-to hide-and-seek spot, where she snuck off to when she went missing at six. Where she wanted us to stargaze and have meetings. I had an inkling she'd gone there. Found her phone, and my cut, and then I heard her yell."

Killian was silent, but Silas laughed. "You saved her life, Ford. And only you would have known those things about her. Guess it all worked out in the end. I made a bet when you were about seven that you'd be the one to end up with her. Thought I'd lose that bet too, but then Killian came up with that crazy plan to have Connor propose, and I knew that was the end of them."

I wasn't sure what to say to all that. I didn't care that there were people who bet on me ending up with her just as long as I did. Killian let out a small laugh. "Hey, I was desperate at the time. Ford was supposed to leave."

Silas clapped me on the back as we approached two bikes and Killian's truck.

"Well, it's a fucking good thing you decided to stay."

Yeah, now if I could just convince Royce of that.

TWENTY-SEVEN
ROYCE

I WOKE UP IN THE HOSPITAL, SURROUNDED BY PINK ROSES ALL STUFFED INTO various glass vases. My throat was dry, my arm hurt like a bitch, and I was starving. I tried sitting up but couldn't apply any pressure to my arm, so I sank back into the bed.

"Oh, good, you're up!" A nurse walked in, looking chipper.

"How long was I out for?" I asked, feeling groggy and tired.

The nurse walked over to my arm and removed the bandage, gently touching the sewn-up wound. "You slept for about five hours, honey."

"Slept? You mean the drugs knocked me out?"

Her brown hair, which was swept up into a sleek updo, looked flawless. Her mouth twitched, though, as she replied. "We didn't have to administer any drugs, just a topical anesthetic. According to your boyfriend, you hadn't slept the night prior. Your body was likely exhausted and needed the nap."

Oh. I fought the blush invading my face, but lost. "So, I could have gone home...hours ago?"

"Yes, but it's no big deal. We'd rather ensure you're nice and rested."

I gazed over at all the pink flowers, which made it seem like I had been here for days. "What about all of those, why are they here?"

The nurse smiled again, closing the bandage on my arm. "Your sister, I believe. She came in and said the room was too bleak."

Oh Taryn, my favorite human at present. "Are my parents here, or anyone else?"

Did they really all leave me here?

"They're all here. We asked them to leave the room because they couldn't agree on who would stay. I seem to recall there being a rather surly guy who said he wasn't leaving because you were 'his'…not sure what he meant by that, but he seemed very invested in you being okay. Then there was your dad who seemed really upset, and your mom sat down and refused to get up. Your sister and two other girls stopped by…I'm not entirely sure what happened, but security told them all to leave."

That sounded about right.

"Could you ask my sister to come in please?"

The nurse thinned her lips in a placating sort of way. "Honey, you're discharged. We've been waiting for you to wake up. You can go whenever you're ready."

How could they be so nonchalant about this? "I was shot…"

"You'll be fine, but I will send your sister in to help you load up all these flowers." She patted my shoulder on her way out of the room.

Unbelievable. Pushing the covers down, I realized I wasn't even in a gown. They'd ripped my sleeve so they could access my arm. Otherwise, I was still completely dressed.

"Royce, oh my gosh, are you okay?" Taryn rushed into the room. With the way her hair was styled today, she looked almost like Florence Pugh. I was so jealous of how easily she changed her hair or her makeup to test out something new or that might look different on her.

"I'm fine, just a little embarrassed."

Taryn slid onto the bed, her golden brows furrowing. "Why?"

My shoes were tucked under the nearby chair, but Taryn saw where I was looking and jumped up to grab them.

"I was only admitted because I was tired. I've been discharged for a while…but they were waiting for me to wake up."

My sister's mouth spread into a smile. I pointed my finger at her. "Don't laugh."

She bit her lip as if to hold off the sensation.

"Only you would get shot by a bullet and need to sleep it off. And only you would actually be allowed to stay and sleep."

Pushing my feet into my shoes, I stood up. My head ached, right along with my arm.

"Grazed. I was grazed. How did I get here anyway?"

My sister let out a dreamy sigh, falling back onto the bed. "Ford carried you. I guess he found you out there…and the rest I probably can't talk about here."

Right. Rodney. A swarm of raw emotion filled my chest. It was mostly anger and hurt, not any sadness at all. While I didn't remember what had happened, I knew the Stone Rider world well enough to know that Rodney wouldn't have made it out alive.

"How does Ford seem?" I asked hesitantly.

My sister grabbed my purse and leather cut that somehow made it back here.

"Protective, angry, and tired."

"Shit, he hasn't slept either." I rubbed my brow.

Taryn waved me off. "He napped in one of the chairs out there, he's fine."

"Well, is he waiting for me out there or what?"

Taryn lifted her shoulder. "I mean, I think he's taken with you, sis. Aren't you guys together now?"

Yes, but I was still upset with him. My sister would know that, though.

With a sigh, she walked with me. "You might want to hear him out…Mom forgave Dad."

"Of course she did." I laughed. Mom and Dad could never stay mad at each other for more than a few hours. But this was a big lie…It made me curious about his side of things. I was actually jealous that Mom got to hear what was going on, and I hadn't yet.

"Can you sneak me out the back or something? If they were all kicked out of here because they couldn't agree on who stayed with me, then it's going to be a mess in agreeing who will take me home. I'm still pissed at Dad and Ford."

Taryn pulled out her bike key and smiled. "You got it, sis."

We got home before anyone else. I wanted to shower, but I was too afraid to get my bandage wet, so Taryn helped me wrap it with plastic wrap.

"Do you need me to help you?" Taryn watched me attempt to pull my shirt up over my head.

With the fabric half over my mouth, I explained that I could do this.

"Just get me a fresh towel please!"

Taryn raised her hands while walking out of the bathroom. Once I was finally out of my clothes, I stepped under the hot spray. I was frustrated with myself about the encounter with Rodney. I knew I did everything I could, but I still felt angry over how I was the one in the end who got shot. Rodney nearly blew my fucking arm off, and the asshole had the audacity to try to kidnap me. My mind raced, tossing the scenario that Rodney had spewed over and over.

"Just putting this on the toilet!" Taryn yelled, but I didn't turn to look. The door clicked shut and I finally had the breakdown I'd been holding in since I discovered that my father and boyfriend had lied to me.

Lifting my face to the water, I let the scorching heat wash away my tears. It was nearly impossible to nail down all the ways I'd fucked up. I didn't see the betrayal from Rodney coming, or Ford, fuck, not even my dad. How was I so blind? Or worse, if I really wanted to dig into that ball of pain inside my chest, I'd confront that I felt stupid.

"Royce?" Someone yelled through the door.

I wanted to sink to the bottom of the shower, but I knew I had to keep my arm dry.

Turning off the water, I was about to reach for the towel left for me on the toilet seat when the door opened and Ford stepped inside.

Seeing him sent a rush of pain to my chest, but maybe that was just my arm.

"What are you doing here?"

Ford's gaze slowly traveled down my body as I wrapped the fluffy white towel around me. "I tried to see you at the hospital."

His voice was achingly soft, and with him standing in front of me in a stark, white T-shirt and clean jeans, and not a hint of his patches or colors, made my lip tremble. Like he was just Ford again. The one I grew up with. The one who kissed me when I was nine, and the one who'd stuck to my heart like an extra vein all throughout my life. I turned away from him so he wouldn't see the hurt on my face.

"I know that you might not want to see me, and I understand that. I just—I needed to see you." He stepped closer, and then I saw his expression in the mirror as the steam dissipated.

"You saw," I clipped out.

He stepped closer. "How's your arm?"

I found my toothbrush and began prepping it with toothpaste. "It's fine." Not true. It actually ached and burned like a son of a bitch. I knew I needed to go get some pain medicine and some food.

"I know you're—" Ford started, but I turned on my electric toothbrush, locking eyes with him in the mirror. He stopped talking, knowing I couldn't hear him over the loud buzzing sound.

His chin fell to his chest, making the hair that was longer on top slide forward.

After taking an extraordinarily long time to brush, I finally turned it off and rinsed.

"Royce, come on. Please talk to me."

Spinning around, I pushed past him, heading for the door. Ford's hand came above my head, keeping it against the door so I couldn't leave.

With my back against the wood, I crossed my arms over my chest.

"I need to go get dressed. I want to get medicine, and I'm hungry."

Ford's sad gaze searched my face, as if he needed to see me up close to ensure I really was okay.

"Would you let me take care of you? Please?"

I hated how badly I wanted to curl into his chest and let him hold me. I hurt physically and emotionally, and his strong arms around me would feel so good. But as I tipped my head back and met his sad stare, I remembered that exact moment when I realized he'd been lying to me.

"What happened to Rodney?" I asked.

Ford's jaw tightened as his free hand came up and gently tugged on a loose piece of hair that fell near my ear. "I killed him."

I wasn't sure why it mattered that Rodney died. Deep down, I already knew it, but part of me worried that Ford would lie to me again.

"Good. Maybe now I can have his job." I tried to joke, but my voice came out broken and pathetic. I'd known Rodney my whole life...once upon a time I thought of him like an extended member of my family. Then he'd started being a jerk about the promotion and giving me that ultimatum. It was all planned...he'd played me, and I danced so easily. Dad had lied as if it were the easiest thing in the world, and Ford... he'd just not cared enough to share that part of his life with me.

"I'll buy it for you, Rose. If that's what you want, I'll buy it and you can run it."

I shook my head as a tear fell from my lash. "No, I don't want that. It'll be tied to the club. I don't want anything tied to the Stone Riders." There was enough mirth in my tone that he knew how angry I was with him.

"That club is in your blood, Royce."

I lifted my chin defiantly. "And yet I was lied to by that very club, and the man who said he loved me."

Ford's chest heaved. "I do love you, Royce. I didn't have the freedom to tell you. There was too much on the line, and the people we're in business with...lives were at stake, including yours."

I didn't want to think that through because logic had no place among my heartache.

"Let me go to my room," I deadpanned, staring over his shoulder.

"Will you please let me take care of you at home? Come be with me and Gus."

Yes, that was all I wanted actually, but he'd lied to me. "Why do you want me there? I'm not going to fuck you."

He gave me a nasty glare which nearly made me apologize, but I held firm. "You really think that's all I want from you? After everything?"

I smiled up at him, tilting my head back. "Well, you don't want to be honest, so, yes. Fucking me is all I think you care about."

My hand went to his chest, shoving him away, and this time he let me. I escaped to my room with a set of tears in my eyes and a dull ache in my chest.

TWENTY-EIGHT
ROYCE

Every time I closed my eyes, I'd go back to the grove where Rodney pointed that gun at me. I'd go back to that moment I started running, stupidly assuming he wouldn't shoot me. I'd slip back to that tiny second of time that I worried it was my life he'd claimed instead of some stupid dream I'd had my whole life.

Someone would stop me if I tried to go to work. I heard what Rodney said about them toying with me. They were watching my every move, and since he was trying to take me to the Murdoch Devil Rider's, it meant we still weren't safe. In the grand scheme of things, me wanting to run the Hollow seemed so frivolous. It was a dumb dream.

Just like being with Ford once was.

That tender spot at the center of my chest ached. It felt as if the bullet landed there instead of grazing my arm, and the longer I held off talking to Ford, or replying to his texts, the worse it felt. So far, I had withstood five days without him.

Five whole days where he'd come in and out of the house, checking on me, trying to talk to me, but I wouldn't give him the time of day. Each night, I heard something hit my door, almost as though a head had fallen back against the wood, but I was too nervous to check if it was him. If it was, then that meant he'd been sitting outside of my bedroom door every night.

Which, if true, meant my father had changed his tune regarding Ford. I wish he would be anti-Ford again, because then I wouldn't have to endure the scent of his spicy cologne that lingered at the base of his neck. I craved burying my nose there. Every time I walked out of my room I smelled it. He felt like a ghost, and yet he'd make it a point to lay eyes on me once a day.

As if he couldn't continue with his day if he didn't.

On the sixth day, my sister made her way into my room, finding me at the window. I stared out at the spring weather, missing the fields I used to walk through. I wanted to go down there, but I also knew that nothing felt the same. Rodney hadn't really considered me for that job, it was all tied to the club, like everything in my life was. That club made up half the blood in my veins. The Hollow made up the other half.

"You're still moping?" Taryn asked, blowing out a breath that made her bangs fly up.

I kept staring outside at the fields. "What else should I do? Go to work, or maybe I should disappear every other day like you."

"Ouch. You're bitchy today." I felt the ice in my sister's tone, but I didn't care. What I said was true. She'd been gone way more than she ever was in the past, and she'd yet to talk to me about it.

Turning toward her, I tried to keep my temper in check. "I think I'm warranted some bitchy days."

Her face fell, and it made me want to dig into the secrets she was keeping, but I was exhausted and didn't have the bandwidth to care at the moment.

"You are. I'm sorry." She finally moved to sit next to me. "I came to gossip."

I never could turn down any good gossip, but I was still irritated with her. My arms were crossed tightly while I turned back to the window, but that didn't deter her.

"I was just downstairs and I overheard Dad on the phone." She hesitated, which pulled my attention to her. Taryn's brows caved as her hand came up to my shoulder. "Ford's house burned down."

I froze, unsure if I was delirious or still sleeping. "What did you just say?"

Taryn's worried expression deepened. "Ford's house…I guess it caught on fire last night, and since he was here, no one caught it in time. It's almost completely gone, Royce."

Shooting to my feet, I brushed her hold off and began pacing. My heart was already too bruised from his and my father's lies, but now this…this—he could have been hurt. I tried to swallow past the lump in my throat, but I couldn't.

"Is he okay?" *Oh God.* "Is Gus okay?"

Taryn got up and carefully gathered my hands into hers. "It's okay, calm down."

It was difficult to breathe. I couldn't seem to get any air down. I kept picturing his kitchen burning, and poor Gus trapped inside. "Where is Ford now?"

"I don't know. Dad was talking on the phone with him."

I brushed past her, realizing too late that I was in my pajamas. Turning back toward my dresser, I yanked out a pair of jeans and a T-shirt. "Where did they put my bike key when they brought it back?"

Taryn hesitated, which had me glaring at her over my shoulder.

"It's on the hook downstairs, but, Royce, maybe you should stay and—"

Once I was dressed, I ignored her and hurried downstairs.

"Royce, I don't think it's safe for you to go—" Taryn yelled from behind me as I scaled the stairs. My mom peeked out from the kitchen, catching my eye.

Her mouth opened. "Hi honey, I—" I walked past her, cutting her off. I grabbed my key then slammed the door behind me.

I was two feet from my bike when I heard my father. "Royce, honey…wait!"

Ignoring him, I slid my helmet on and started my bike.

"We don't know who ordered the hit, we know they want you… honey, please. Ford would lose his mind if he knew you left here without protection."

I lifted my head and slid my visor up and snapped, "Then protect me. You owe me at least that much."

His green gaze slid to the ground, but I caught the small nod. I didn't give him time to get his key, or anything else. I took off down the driveway, knowing he'd catch up.

The fire department was still in front of Ford's house when I pulled up. My boots landed against the asphalt as I took in the charred, smoking mess in front of me. My heart did a full dive into my stomach. All of Ford's things were inside, pictures of him with his family, and memories with me. Our first sleepover, and the first time I traced over his soft skin that held its own set of memories.

It was all gone.

Ford stepped into view, wearing a pair of sunglasses and his leather cut. My dad rolled to a stop behind me, but I didn't pay him any mind as I slid my kickstand down and dismounted.

A few of the firefighters talked here and there as I walked past, but once I got within Ford's line of sight, his eyes lifted from the cop he was talking to and landed on me. His mouth stopped moving, and he started walking toward me. I stopped just outside of his metal fence, unsure if I wanted to go any closer.

"You're here." Ford came to a stop in front of me, his wary gaze searching my face.

I ignored how he prodded at me with those eyes and how I knew he wanted me in his arms. He'd have to settle for me merely standing in front of him.

"Is Gus okay?" I asked, glancing over at the charred remains.

Ford's eyes never left my face as he nodded. "He was with my parents."

Relief sagged within me, making my lip wobble. "Was anyone hurt?" What I wanted to ask was if he was okay, but I was too angry with him to reveal that I cared. I knew he wasn't in danger of the fire, but losing your house was horrific and he had to be upset.

"No. It was fine yesterday, but as soon as I left, someone must have shown up."

A firefighter passed by us, his blue eyes trailing over my body as he went. Ford caught it and glared back at the man, his jaw tight.

"Where were you last night?" Some part of me needed to hear him confirm that he'd been at my house.

A gleam entered his eye as he smiled. "Same place I've been every night."

"The club?" I lifted a brow.

He shook his head. "Outside of your bedroom door, baby. I can't be away from you. So, if your door is as far as I can go, then that's as far as I'll go."

"If you'd been here, you might have stopped them," I said, pulling my arms across my chest. The blue-eyed firefighter was making his way back toward us when Ford slid his hand to my hip and pulled me off to the side.

"Greedy fucker," he mumbled. "I'd rather lose a thousand homes if it meant I made sure you slept safe at night."

My mind toyed with his words, trying to convince my heart that he loved me. My heart flipped my brain the bird. "I don't feel safe, Ford," I said, low and quiet, as I stepped back. "Where will you go after this?"

Ford watched me as if he were watching a piece of his anatomy wander away. "The president's apartment at the club."

I pushed past the annoyance I held over him settling for a small apartment after having an entire house to himself. "Gus will be okay there?"

"Until I find a new place, yeah…it'll be safer at the club."

I dipped my chin, knowing that was true.

His finger gently pulled my face up, his worried expression searching mine for something. "I'm placing extra bodies around the Hollow tonight…my house was a piece of shit, but I know you won't be okay if they burn your favorite place down."

No, I wouldn't be okay.

"I need to stop in there, check emails, and figure out what the owner wants to do."

Ford wet his lips in a childlike manner, almost as if he were nervous to ask what he was about to. "Could I go with you?"

Memories of him slamming into me as he fucked me on Rodney's desk slid back into my mind. Heat and anger swirled like a dangerous cocktail as I remembered how good it felt to have him behind me, holding me and whispering all of those deliciously dirty thoughts into my ear.

Slamming my eyes closed, I shook my head. "Dad will go with me."

He gave me a slight nod as I took another step back.

"Just be safe, Royce. The Murdoch crew was working for someone…we've pissed off whoever that person is, and they know you are a way of getting to me. Unfortunately, it means you're not safe."

Story of my fucking life.

I turned and walked away from him, catching my father's hard gaze as I returned to my bike.

TWENTY-NINE
ROYCE

I parked directly in front of the Hollow, uncaring that I'd always been told not to. No one heading into the bookstore was going to mind that me or my dad was in front, parking our bikes there, and if they did, then they could go fuck themselves.

I unzipped my leather jacket as I hiked the steps leading into the space, but was stopped by Heather, one of the baristas who ran the bookstore and coffee shop.

"Royce, oh my gosh!" She rushed over, panic stamped all over her round face. Her reddish-brown hair was tied into a knot on top of her head.

"Hey, Heather."

She frantically explored my face, then flicked her gaze to my father, where her eyes went huge. "Uh..." She cleared her throat, and, stepped closer, whispering, "Who is that extremely hot man behind you?"

"That's my dad, Heather." I rolled my eyes, moving to the stairs leading down to the club.

"Sorry, I was distracted." She shut her eyes, then walked close with me, talking quietly. "Rodney was found dead, Royce. I wasn't sure if you heard or not, but you were gone this week, and I assumed maybe you did. We're all freaking out over here. Bernie said he was going to reach out to you about taking things over. Nick said he couldn't get in touch with you."

That's because I had turned off my phone. I'd met the owner, Bernie Hatfield, a few times throughout the years that I had worked at the Hollow, but he typically dealt with Rodney over everything related to the club.

"Yeah, I came to check in on everything. I didn't know Bernie had tried getting in touch with me."

"He's actually downstairs right now, trying to sort out Rodney's files."

"Perfect," I said, but Heather wrapped her hand around my wrist, stopping me. "I'm so sorry about Rodney, I know you guys were close."

It took all my strength not to scoff. Instead, I let Heather hug me, and then I turned away, feeling numb as I descended the stairs.

Dad was directly behind me as we passed by a few stickers of Mom's that she'd put up on the wall. My father's fingers traced them as we walked, and my heart lurched at the familiarity of it. The lights were all on as I trailed deeper into the house until I was on the bottom floor, seeing Charlie behind the bar, organizing bottles. Nick was on the stage, fixing a few electrical wires. I waved as he lifted his head. He waved back, then froze as he watched my father follow me inside.

"They're still not big fans of our club, huh?" Dad mumbled behind me.

"No. We're not." I snapped in reply.

I moved across the floor, heading toward the office, and paused at the open door, seeing an elderly man wearing a pair of Wranglers and a snap-button, checkered shirt inside. He was seated at the desk, rubbing his brow.

Once I filled the doorway, he lifted his head, and visible relief cut across his pale face.

"Oh, Royce, thank goodness. I'm so lost on what all this means… Rodney wasn't being entirely truthful with me about our profit, or who he was dealing with."

I dropped my chin, disgusted that Rodney would steal from such a sweet man.

"Can you make any sense of this?" Bernie handed me the binder. I gently accepted it, but then I closed the plastic flaps. "I'm so sorry that Rodney wasn't being honest with you, Bernie. Sadly, I think his choices caught up with him."

Bernie watched me carefully before giving me a knowing nod. The quiet in the room was tense until Bernie let out a heavy sigh, covering his eyes with his hand. "Royce, you've been here for years...you wouldn't be interested in running this place, would you?"

I wasn't sure where the bout of bravery came from, but I straightened my spine and looked this elderly man in his face. "No, sir. I'm interested in owning it."

His garbled laugh had me glancing back at my father who stood slightly behind me, watching the space that led into the hall.

"I like your fire, girl. I've been wanting to get rid of this place for years...and the Stone Riders recently informed me they're not interested in buying anymore. I feel a little out of sorts, and at a loss of what to do."

Humiliation pricked at my sternum, making me wish my father wasn't right behind me to witness it. The Stone Riders had plans to buy? Of course they did...but did that mean Ford had called it off? "Uh...well, I don't have...I haven't talked to a bank yet, so I'm not sure if I have the funds. What would you sell it for?"

Something told me he wasn't going to sell it for anything within my range of affordability, but it didn't stop me from hoping he would. He considered me for a moment. His back had a slight hunch to it, making me consider he might be much older than I realized.

"Tell you what, Royce...Rodney earned a bonus check that, after talking to Nick, I discovered should have gone to you. How about I let you use that as a down payment, and we work out a monthly payment schedule? I'm eager to relieve myself of the stress of this place, so it's yours, kiddo. Use that bonus as a way to secure it, then we'll draw up some legal paperwork, ensuring it's yours after a few payments."

Oh my God. Was this really happening? I glanced back at my dad, unsure if I were dreaming or insane. His huge smile told me that Bernie had really just offered to sell the Hollow to me.

"I'm—" I started, then cleared the excitement from my throat. "I'm not sure I'd make enough monthly to clear the payments."

His laugh again made me freeze until his warm hand landed on my shoulder. "Darlin', you're going to be making Rodney's salary, not yours. I never agreed with how little he paid you. You'll be able to afford the monthly payments and still live comfortably off it."

I couldn't believe this was actually happening. My dream was literally about to land in my hands, and I wasn't sure what to do with it.

"Are you sure?" I asked, fighting the urge to cry. This couldn't be real.

Bernie lifted his hand and then glanced back at my dad. "I'm as proud of you as I was of your mother, Royce. You both know what this town needs, and this place. I'm honored to leave it in your hands as you've really done a lot with it. You might want to check a few of those messages, sounds like a few bands are eager to book a spot here."

His wink landed like a shooting star, making me follow his retreating form like a starry-eyed girl who had just been told all her dreams had come true. As soon as Bernie was out of the hall, my dad stepped into the room, and while I let out a hiccup, he scooped me into his arms.

"I'm so proud of you, honey. I can't believe I was able to witness that. I wish your mom was here to have seen that, but goddamn, I'm glad I was."

My arms were wrapped tightly around his neck, and I ignored how angry I was at him at the moment. I was so excited that he'd been here for such a big moment in my life.

"I knew you'd own this place someday, and I knew you'd do it on your own terms, in your own way." Dad set me down, and I stepped back, tucking my hair back.

"Dad, you swear to me you had nothing to do with this."

"I swear it, honey. I know I wasn't honest about stepping down, but that was a one-off. I swear to you that I, nor Ford, had anything to do with this."

My eyes found the floor as he searched my face. I wanted to believe him, but I was still so wounded over what he'd done.

He seemed to pick up on it because he stepped closer. "I'm so sorry, Royce. I'm sorry that even for a second you had to doubt believing me. Your mother wasn't happy with me either, and I don't blame either of you. I fucked up and all I can do is tell you that as long as it keeps you safe, I won't ever do it again."

"Dad, see..." I sighed. "That right there makes it seem like you will do it again."

"If it keeps you safe, then I won't."

My face lowered, but my dad caught it between his hands. "You, your sister, and your mother are my entire world. I live to protect you, and sometimes that protection doesn't always look like honesty. That's maybe why you didn't share with Ford or me about what Nova shared with you about the video, right?"

Dammit. I stared at him, and he jostled my shoulders jokingly. "Am I right? You were keeping Nova safe by omitting really important information to Ford, and to me."

"Fine, yes."

"Then you get it. Deep down, you do. You know that both Ford and I love you deeply. But we'll always work to keep you safe, no matter what it takes."

I hated that he made me think about this from a different perspective. He was right. If there was something that would keep them safe, or even Taryn, then I'd lie. But only to protect them.

Bumping my dad's shoulder as we exited the office, I asked, "As long as it isn't gross, how did you get Mom to forgive you?"

The last thing I needed was an image of my parents doing anything physical as a way to stop fighting. I'd seen and heard them plenty throughout my life, not that they meant to, in fact, they were always careful to guard us from ever experiencing them being in love like that, but the two of them were like a wildfire. Now that I was older, it was actually something I hoped would happen for me someday. To find someone you could be in love with for well over twenty-five years was an incredible concept.

"I told your mother the truth."

I glanced over at him, my brows dipping as I tried to make sense of that.

"The truth about what?"

"About everything, kiddo. All the scary, terrifying details." He walked ahead of me as we walked near the bar. Nick was waiting for me, so I knew I had to come back to this conversation, but first, I glanced up at Dad's solemn face and asked, "Will you tell me too?"

He considered something for a second before he dipped his face. "Yeah, honey. If you give me and Ford another shot, I'll tell you too."

That night, I waited in my room for that thud against my door, proving that Ford was there again. He hadn't come by for dinner, and when I'd turned my phone on, I saw he hadn't texted me either. He had to deal with his house burning down, so I didn't expect him to really…but I was worried about him. Or rather, I was worried he'd given up on me. Maybe he'd head to the club and stay there, that's where he lived now. I'd have to come to terms with that sooner or later.

I could simply text him or call him. But my pride was still too tender.

Finally, near midnight, I was about to give up and pull on some headphones. I slid out of bed, irritated and angry. I paced the length of my bedroom and then paused in front of the door. So what if he stopped sleeping outside of my room? It didn't matter because I wasn't ready to forgive him.

Or was I?

Dammit.

The information Dad had told me about the letters and the lies… everything was circling my brain like thick smoke, clouding all my thoughts. So badly, I froze in front of the door ready to yank it open when the knob turned and Ford stepped inside.

My mouth dropped as I stepped back, confused at his sudden

arrival. He'd never come inside before… Instead of asking why, I looked down at his arms. "You brought Gus?"

Ford made his way inside and then shut the door with his boot. "Yeah, figured he could sleep with us tonight."

A thrill shot through me that he was back to being bossy Ford. "With us?"

"Yes, Royce. With us." He set Gus on my bed and then slid out of his work boots. I hadn't even registered that he might have had to go to his real job today.

"When did you get off work?"

He stretched, taking off his leather cut, then his T-shirt. "I had to make up some work after dealing with all the insurance stuff. So, I got off about an hour ago. I went up to my folks' place, and they wanted me to stay…it was a whole thing."

"Why didn't you?" I asked, already moving to the bed in preparation for his strong arms to come around me.

Ford was slipping out of his jeans when he scoffed with a shake of his head. "If I'm staying anywhere, Royce, it's with you."

Hope had my throat swelling. I was petting Gus, not responding when I finally risked a bit of the ire I had that still weighed me down.

"Why bother, Ford?" I knew why my father lied. I understood what was on the line, but Ford loved me in a different way. One where he knew everything about me but didn't give me the chance to truly know him. He owed me an explanation similar to what my father had shared. I wanted to scrape my nails against his soul and see if I'd made a mark there. I needed to know that I had a place somewhere inside of him that was permanent.

He stood in front of me in his dark boxers, his strong thighs highlighted by the soft glow from across the room. His face was hard, the lines telling a story that could have been ours if he'd been honest with me.

"Why bother?" he asked, his voice grating along my veins like a knife.

I nodded, still stroking Gus. Ford pressed his knee into the mattress, making it dip.

"Because I still haven't seen you in a wedding dress, or how you'll smile at our baby when they laugh for the first time. Because I haven't found us the perfect home yet, and I haven't gotten to dance in our kitchen with you while you're barefoot, and it rains hard against the roof. We haven't lived yet, baby."

I tried to hold myself rigid like what he said didn't completely undo me, but I wasn't sure it mattered.

"I didn't tell you the truth about my position in the club, Royce. I didn't share—"

Shaking my head, I grappled for the resolve I had to ensure he didn't get off easy for what he did. I would not brush this under the rug. "No. You lied about it. You knew exactly what Rodney had threatened me with. You made me look like an idiot."

His hand came up to my jaw, stroking. "That's fucking impossible, Royce."

I went to push his chest but ended up letting my fingers drift down his abs. He wasn't a regret I was willing to live without for the rest of my life. I knew I'd forgive him, but I was still hurt.

"You lied," I whispered.

"I also stayed, baby." He searched my face, bringing his hands up to stroke over my shoulders and gently over my arm that was still healing. "I might not know how to tell you everything, Royce, but one thing that has never changed is that I have stayed. Even when you weren't mine. Even when you were just a dream. When it didn't make any sense, when it cost me a future. I stayed right the fuck here. I might not always know how to explain shit, baby, but I'd never leave you. I know you better than anyone else, and if you tried to run, I'd find you. Because you're mine, Royce. You're always going to be mine."

Tears gathered along my lashes, diving down my cheeks unchecked.

"Maybe you should have left, maybe it would have been easier," I softly whispered on a cracked cry.

He smiled, swiping away my tears with his thumb. "Nah, you were worth staying for, baby. I'd stay in every lifetime."

My arms went around his neck as our mouths crashed against one another. His firm hands gripped the back of my head, pulling me close as our tongues warred for this future we both desperately wanted. He gently lowered me to the bed, where he worshipped my body with kisses and promises. Vows that sewed up the gash in my heart where his lie had lived.

When he sank into me and we moved together to a rhythm of only our breaths, I closed my eyes and I pictured all the things he said. Us dancing in a kitchen that we picked out. A baby in my arms as he watched us with that protective stare. Our wedding. My hips lifted, meeting his every thrust as I mentally tried to seal that image into my mind like a vow across the heart.

I wanted it, all of it.

"I love you, Ford," I whispered into his shoulder. My climax claimed me moments later, and his lingered in a deep groan as he chanted his love for me in return. "Then move in with me Royce. Stop making me wait. Let me wake up to that smell of roses in my nose, that feel of silky skin against mine, and those blue eyes that I fell for as a kid way too fucking young to understand those butterflies in my stomach."

I laughed as my limbs became boneless and I flopped against the mattress, undone.

"I'll move in with you, you idiot. Just know that if you ever lie to me again, I'll wreck your bike or something, do you understand me?"

His mouth covered mine in a lingering kiss. "As long as you're not on it when you wreck it, then that's fine by me."

I wasn't even sure how to reply to that, so I didn't. I pulled his face back to mine, rolled over, and made him fuck me again.

THIRTY
FORD

I knew I was pressing my luck with this move, but I was tired of waiting. Royce had barely forgiven me, and I wasn't wasting any more time before sliding my name over her back.

She was still sleeping when I crawled out of bed and moved to the spot in her closet where I had secretly hung the leather cut. I doubted she'd dug through her clothes to see it, which worked out for me. Being here in her house for the past week allowed me all kinds of liberties, like napping in her bed where I could inhale that rose scent and let it brand my lungs. She had no idea that I'd invaded her space, but I was past caring. She'd invaded my entire life, so she could deal with me creeping around hers.

I hadn't really told anyone that I didn't even care that much that my house had burned down. She wasn't hurt, and all the important things that I had kept inside of it were now in her possession anyway. Gus was protected, the rest was just old flooring and ugly walls. I wanted to rebuild a life with Royce, and with this property patch I intended to do exactly that. The leather was fresh, the white stitching that identified her as the president's wife was bright and stiff. The skull patch representing the Stone Riders was in place, but I also added a small wolf howling as homage to her father. For me, there was a pink rose I had stitched into the back which was soft under my touch. It was the rest of the back that tugged my mouth into a smile.

Property of Ford Ryan

Under that, in smaller stitching, I had another few words added, and I knew they'd make Royce laugh.

Fucking finally.

Pressing a kiss to her neck, I felt Royce stir, and then eventually turn. The sheet was barely up over her tits, but her nipples pebbled and poked through the thin fabric, making my cock stir in my boxers.

"Morning." She smiled up at me with the cutest fucking sleepy expression that it made my smile drop. Fuck, I was in love with her. She might as well have tugged my heart out and sewn it inside of hers.

I leaned down and kissed her.

"Morning."

"I could get used to waking up to you." Her raspy words were kindling to the fire burning in my chest.

"Good." I brushed a piece of her hair off her brow. "I have something for you." I held the leather in my hands, suddenly feeling nervous that she might change her mind about us…about this. She sat up, pushing her palms behind her, then curling her arm around the top of the sheet to keep it over her naked chest.

"Is that—" Her eyes darted to the leather as she lightly bit her bottom lip in curiosity. I knew it was nerves too. She did that when she didn't want to get an answer wrong, or she worried that she might be embarrassed.

"Before I give this to you, I need you to know that it's not just because you're mine. It's not just because I want the whole world to know it. I meant what I said when I told you this club is in your blood. You were always meant to have this patch across your back, and I'm so fucking proud that you're wearing it with my name there too."

Her gaze became misty as it dropped to the leather in my hands. I took a deep breath and pushed on.

"This isn't a light thing for me. I've never given a patch to anyone…I've never even wanted anyone but you, Royce. If you decide you don't want this, I'll respect it."

She moved, throwing her arms around my neck. I held her to me, with the leather between us.

"I have always wanted to be yours, Ford."

I pulled back and held her jaw, cradling it tenderly while I memorized her face.

"So you'll wear this?"

She smiled. "I'll wear that, Ford, and I'll even move in with you in that apartment."

I laughed into her mouth as I pulled her in for a kiss.

Once I kissed her enough that she was breathless, she plopped back into her pillows. I stood up and tried to tug at the sheet. "I want to cuddle, come back."

She flipped over, showing her bare ass cheek, which I gripped with my palm. "We gotta go shopping for some furniture and shit, so get up."

I didn't want to leave. Cuddling sounded really fucking good actually, but I needed to get some shit for the apartment. Killian had been gracious enough not to kick me out as I sat against his daughter's door night after night. However, I knew that was because I wasn't touching his daughter. I had no doubts whatsoever he'd tell me to get the fuck out now that I'd gotten back into Royce's good graces.

"Okay, fine," Royce huffed. She rolled back over and sat up with a fresh gleam in her eye. "But we're getting one of those cat backpacks with the airholes, that way Gus can come with us."

Royce had picked out my new living room set and the bedroom set. I didn't care as long as she was happy with it. I'd helped her pack up her things from her room, but the more we packed, the more she wanted to keep at home, saying she wanted to be able to come back and visit and have a space to hang out when I was busy with the club.

So, she basically took her clothes, and a few notebooks for work, and two boxes worth of bath and hair care shit.

Taryn had been in and out enough to see the new apartment and check on Royce, only to dart off again. Now that we were near the club, and Royce was safe, I took my first public church meeting as president where we gathered upstairs in the main part of the club.

It was the original room where Killian had held all his church meetings, and my dad before him, and my grandfather when he led. It felt good to sit in the head chair, wearing the president patch.

The room filled with my men, then Killian, my dad, and Jameson… and shockingly, Silas joined. His pale blue eyes met mine as he gave me a slight nod, and then he slid into a chair off to the side, not at the table. If he were anyone else, I'd kick him out, but I knew his history with this club. I knew that my own father revered him, and not to mention, Silas was like an uncle to me. Once the table was filled, Kody shut the church doors, and we got started.

"What have you found out about the Murdoch Devil Rider's?" I asked Killian. He'd led a team down south to figure out who had hired them to dig up that video. Silas led the conversation with the leader, although I hadn't asked for details on how or which methods he used.

Killian glanced at Silas briefly, then cleared his throat. "They didn't give up a name exactly, but they told us they knew which club he was from."

I glanced at the men at the end of the table, seeing the way they shifted in their seats. The way Jameson's jaw was hard, and his eyes focused on the surface.

"Which club?"

Deep down, I already knew, though. I wasn't even sure how, or who exactly, but I knew.

"Chaos Kings." Killian's chin dropped to his chest as a silence covered the room.

Jameson spoke up, his voice rough. "Not Giles. I already confirmed it wasn't him."

"Then how the fuck did they know I had stepped into this role before anyone else in our own club did?" I yelled. Giles had been with us as long as Silas or Lance…but Giles was like another family member to us. He gave me presents growing up, he was blood-related to Jameson. There was little chance it was him, but I had no idea who else would have known.

"That's what we're going to figure out," Killian explained to the room.

I wanted more answers than what they were giving me, but I knew I had to be patient. "How exactly are we going to do that?"

The church doors opened, and Connor walked in. His face was gaunt like he'd gone through a battle of his own. He wore a leather cut, with a patch and insignia on it, but it wasn't ours. *It wasn't fucking ours.*

I stood from my chair. "I knew you were over there figuring things out, but you fucking pledged?"

Connor dipped his face. "I'm your best bet at figuring this out, Ford."

"Why?" I scoffed, feeling outraged that my own best friend had left me for so long, and now appeared in a different patch and different colors than the ones he always swore he'd wear.

Connor leveled me with a firm stare, and that's when I realized he wasn't just in any cut.

His looked nearly identical to mine, except his name was in gold instead of red, and his president patch was on the right side of his breast instead of his left.

"Fuck you, Connor." I pointed at the patch.

He pointed at mine. "Fuck you back, Ford."

"We need to stay focused here. If you're gonna fight, then go outside, but Connor is going to help us," my dad spoke up.

My jaw rotated as I processed what this meant. "You're leading the Chaos Kings now, and you're going to work with us to find the mole in your club?"

I didn't buy it, not if he was the new president. "Where is Giles? How come he isn't here?"

Connor's head dipped again, and his jaw now looked about as tense as mine.

"He was found dead in his home two nights ago. I'm trying to play catch-up as much as I am determined to figure out who leaked your shit. We're both being attacked, Ford. We're going to work together on this, or we're going to fucking die trying."

I stared up at my friend, and I realized after such a long time that it might actually be nice to have him back.

"Fine, help us but stay the fuck away from Royce. I don't care that you're friends. Don't touch her and don't try shit. She's mine."

"I want you both to be happy," Connor said honestly.

Killian tapped the table with his knuckles. "Great, so where the fuck does that leave us?"

I glanced back at my best friend who stepped closer to the table to address everyone. "I have someone who's been helping me keep tabs on men in the club. We've had a hunch for a while that there might be a mole, so I've had someone unsuspecting following a few of them around and keeping notes. We'll bring her in, and then from there we can figure out a direction to go in."

"Are the Murdoch Devil Rider's going to be a problem?" I asked Silas.

He shook his head. "I left the leader intact, and with incentive to work with us."

It still boiled my blood that I didn't have a chance to deal with him, or his men for watching that video, but I had to focus on keeping Royce safe, that was the most important thing.

Killian suddenly tilted his head and asked, "Who is it you've been working with, Connor?"

My best friend nervously tapped the surface of the table, and then his Adam's apple bobbed. I watched his expression, knowing mine was twisting with confusion. He seemed apprehensive to share, and I almost thought he wouldn't until the doors opened again, and in strutted the youngest Quinn sister.

With blond hair styled, her high-heeled boots echoed against the floor, and I think she was even chewing gum.

"That would be me." Taryn smiled at the table in front of us. Connor winced, and Killian shot to his feet.

The whole room erupted into chaos, and how fucking fitting as Connor was now the king of it.

EPILOGUE

Callie
Three Months Later

For the first time in nearly a decade, Dead Roses was closing early.

I had flicked the button on the sign to indicate that we weren't taking any more walk-in clients, and anyone on the books was called and rescheduled.

There was a tiny ball of excitement that had been building inside my stomach ever sense Ford first turned down his scholarship and chose to stay in Rose Ridge. I'd never forget how my son looked that day he informed us that he wasn't going to college. His boxes had been packed, his room nearly empty as we prepared to move him to the dorm. Wes and I had planned the route and all the stops along the way as we prepared to say goodbye to our eldest child.

We were proud, hopeful but when he'd told us that he was staying, my husband had glanced at me and I knew right then and there this was about her.

The girl who had kept my son busy sketching well into the night. The one who had come to my house more times than I could ever count to clean, or bake, or wash our cars. The reason was always obscure but not enough to veil the true intention.

Royce had grown up with a crush larger than life on my son, Ford. It was endearing and even adorable at times, until I realized how big of a mess things might have become. Connor had his heart set on Royce, and Ford was nothing if not the best kind of friend you could ask for. So, years ago when all this began, Wes and I knew that our son would end up with the broken heart. The one left behind as the girl who liked him would go shunned and ignored because of the code he lived by to not take something that his best friend desired.

So when Connor left, and Royce stayed, I wasn't surprised in the least bit that Ford had chosen to abandon his dream and remain in Rose Ridge. Because of all the dreams he had, Royce Quinn had always been the largest, and the most out of reach. Wes and I supported Ford, we never even questioned why he wanted to stay.

I knew by staying that meant he'd join the club, and I knew it meant I had to allow the tender part of my heart that might not want that for my child to bleed or heal, but regardless, he was going to be in the Stone Riders. I knew it was just a matter of time.

What I did not expect was how long it took for Ford to finally make a move toward Royce. Six years passed and with each month, I began to worry that this was all for not. That Ford would simply miss his chance at this great love, and he'd be stuck watching her from afar. I could nearly scream with how frustrated I was over his lack of action.

And then it happened, the two were thrust together that night at dinner and I saw the way Royce looked at Ford, with awe and a bit of surprise. There was plenty of animosity too, but I saw hope there too. Laura had tugged my hand after dinner and with her eyes blown wide, and no words needed we both had begun thinking the same thing: They were finally going to start this thing that had been brewing for the better part of twenty years.

Did Laura and I secretly hope our kids would one day end up together? Of course we did because Laura was my chosen sister, and my best friend but we had never done anything to try and force that or even encourage it.

Now, here we were, three months after the two started dating and they were coming in to get tattoos together. Royce had been the one to reach out and ask if they could reserve a slot together, and if I would be the one to do the tattoos. I was so honored that she'd asked me that I had shut down the whole shop for them.

The bell over the door rang as Royce entered the shop with her blond hair swept up into a sleek pony tail.

"Hi, Callie!" She called sweetly.

My son trailed her, holding her hand as he entered and locked the shop door behind him.

Things were on edge, which was partially why I had closed down the shop.

"Hi." I stood and pulled her into a hug. My eyes landed on Ford as I did and the soft way he watched us made my heart flip. My son was in love and he had finally got the girl who had taken up so much of his heart and hope throughout his life. Countless conversations with him and Wes where he'd encourage him to move on for the sake of his happiness but our boy never would.

Once we broke apart, I set Royce up first for her tattoo. She wanted hers printed along her wrist, and from what she described it would be small.

I got to work slowly drawing the numbers into her skin while he talked about the club apartment they were in and the different houses they had gone to look at. There wasn't anything yet although Ford had a house that he'd started building in secret that I knew would eventually become their home.

He was going to surprise her with it but I wasn't sure when. I just listened and continue to ink the date onto her skin. Once I was finished I sat back and wiped it. "Okay what's the significance of—"

"Mom, will you do mine before she tells you?" Ford asked. He slid out of his jacket and took Royce's spot in the chair. Royce sat in the waiting chair with a secretive smile on her face and my stomach had that ball of excitement churning inside of it. I had so many hopes and dreams for my children, and with how much Royce loved Ford, it was everything I had ever hoped for.

Ford instructed me to begin tattooing the same design into his wrist that Royce did. Once I was finished, I sat back and glanced between the two.

"Okay tell me why you both got December twelfth tattooed onto your wrists."

Ford smiled, and that's when I realized Royce tugged something out of her back pocket.

"Because it's our wedding day." She held her hand out to me, revealing a rose-colored diamond ring.

My nose burned as I swung my gaze back to my son who was smiling at Royce in a dopey, happy way that made a tear fall down my cheek. My son was getting married.

Ford was marrying the girl he'd loved since he was old enough to understand what love meant.

"Are you serious?" I asked on a sob.

Ford sat forward and pulled me into a hug.

"Yeah, Mom, we're serious."

My little boy was getting married.

Laura's little girl was getting married.

Another sob came out of my chest as Ford held me. With a sniff I pulled away. "Does your mom know?"

Royce smiled and then glanced up. Wes, Killian and Laura were all crowding the back hall, waiting until the time was right. I swiped at my face as a laugh bubbled up from my chest.

"You all were in on it?"

Wes made his way through the group and pulled me into his arms. "No, we were told to meet here. I was supposed to unlock the back for Laura and Killian."

"We had no idea." Laura cried as she made her way over to Royce. She pulled her daughter into a hug and I watched as Killian shook Ford's hand. "Congratulations."

I leaned against Wes while I watched Royce curl into Ford's chest. The two were completely enamored with one another.

Laura caught my eye as a tear slipped down her face. "Well, I guess this is official. We're family, Cal."

"We've always been family." I laughed even as a new burning sensation claimed my nose and throat. I knew what she meant but I meant it. Laura was my chosen family was my sister in every way that mattered.

"But now we're going to be grandma's together, and share holidays. I used to hope for this when they were kids."

I did too. Especially when Royce began coming over as frequently as she did, and I began learning how special of a person she was. Something happened when the kids were fifteen and sixteen though and all that hope fled when Royce began dating Connor and my poor son merely watched from the sidelines.

"Now we just need to make sure you two tell Ellie and Taryn." Laura said with another swipe under eyes.

Ellie was on her way to Europe to dance in a prestigious showcase, but she'd come back for her brother's wedding, I was sure of it.

"Taryn is still gone, but we wanted to tell you all first." Royce explained sadly.

I knew things between her and her sister were strained, but it wasn't until I glanced over at my best friend that I realized how strained. Her pained expression told me things hadn't been smooth these past few months, and were still strained.

"Well don't worry. The wedding is still several months away." I tried to sound encouraging but deep down I wasn't sure how this would all get cleared up. Taryn had made a mess, and it had created a rift not just between the Quinn sisters, but between the Chaos Kings and the Stone Riders.

With a heavy pause between everyone, it was Wes who finally spoke up and broke the awkward silence. "Dinner?"

Killian made a sound of agreement and just like that, the conversation had transitioned but the unease in my stomach remained. I hoped this would smooth out before Christmas…I mean it had to, Royce and Taryn were best friends…but would that be enough?

Want a few more POV's from this book?
Click here for bonus content or go to my website at www.ashley
munozbooks.com/bonuscontent

Are you ready to continue the series?
When You Followed
Book two in the generations of Rose Ridge series is coming this fall.

Want to know who Juan Hernandez and his sons are?
Start wtih Juan's book: King of Hearts
His son's is The Lost Kings
Both are in Kindle Unlimited

Haven't read the first generation of Stone Riders? Start with Where We
Started, keep reading for a sneak peek.

ACKNOWLEDGMENTS

This one is a little bit different...

This year has been a rough one.

While there were many things that were incredible that took place, there were also a lot of hard, painful moments to digest. Moments that have had me rethinking this career and whether or not I can even continue in it. For far too many reasons that I couldn't get into, that one day I might just say 'fuck it' and spill all the beans, but that day is not today...

I am first and foremost grateful for my team that has been supportive, encouraging, and present. Erica, Amanda, Catie, Melissa, Julia, and my agent, Savannah. Thank you so much for all your help as I balanced writing two books at once. I was stressed, and I know that had to make a few of you stressed, but I am so grateful for your dedication and your unrelenting support.

A huge thanks to Qambar designs for creating two gorgeous designs for this book while under horrific and dangerous conditions, facing your physical safety as an unprovoked war began.

Of course, my family and friends make it possible for me to write. But as grateful as I am to all of these people, I have had to do a lot of soul searching this year, and so I'm going to do something a little odd and put this gratitude into print to make it real.

I thank *myself* for getting up every day and still choosing to open my laptop when every word felt forced. I thank *myself* for still looking in the mirror and choosing to see someone worth keeping when so many people have walked away and told me that I'm not. I thank *myself* for reminding people that I'm still here, and I still have stories to tell.

I thank *myself* for tending to the very broken heart in my chest and reminding it that there is still more to do, there is more joy to be found, and more happy days ahead.

I thank *myself* for not giving up when, at one point, it felt so easy to.

Lastly, I am grateful to you, dear reader, for giving this book a chance and hopefully this whole series.

Let's check back in with each other next book… 🩶

- Ashley

ALSO BY ASHLEY MUÑOZ

Mount Macon Series

Resisting the Grump

Tempting the Neighbor

Saving the Single Dad

Stone Riders Universe

Where We Started

Where We Belong

Where We Promise

Where We Ended

A Rose Ridge Christmas

When You Stayed

Standalone

Only Once

The Rest of Me

Tennessee Truths

Rake Forge University Universe

Wild Card

King of Hearts

The Joker

The Lost Kings

My Darling Mayhem

The Broken Queen

Finding Home Series

Glimmer

Fade

<u>Anthology & Co Writes</u>

What Are the Chances

Vicious Vet

ABOUT THE AUTHOR

Ashley is an Amazon Top 50 bestselling romance author who is best known for her small-town, second-chance romances. She resides in the Pacific Northwest, where she lives with her four children and her husband. She loves coffee, reading fantasy, and writing about people who kiss and cuss.

Follow her at www.ashleymunozbooks.com